Victor Pemberton was born in Holloway, in the London Borough of Islington, in the early 1930s. His first job was as a Fleet Street postboy but after two years' National Service he went to work in the travel industry and wrote the radio play, 'The Gold Watch', which was broadcast by the BBC and has since been repeated five times. He went on to write radio and TV plays full time and in 1971 became the script editor for the BBC's 'Dr Who' series, later writing for the series himself. In recent years he has worked as a producer for Jim Henson and set up his own production company, Saffron. His first novel, OUR FAMILY ('a wonderful story' – Nerys Hughes), was based on his highly successful trilogy of radio plays of the same name and, like his second novel, OUR STREET ('never a dull moment in this charming story' *Romford Recorder*), is also available from Headline.

Our Rose

Victor Pemberton

HEADLINE

First published in 1994
by HEADLINE BOOK PUBLISHING

First published in paperback in 1995
by HEADLINE BOOK PUBLISHING

10 9 8 7 6 5 4 3 2 1

ISBN 0 7472 4765 X

Typeset by Keyboard Services, Luton, Beds

Printed and bound in Great Britain by
Cox & Wyman Ltd, Reading, Berks

HEADLINE BOOK PUBLISHING
A division of Hodder Headline PLC
338 Euston Road
London NW1 3BH

For Pauline
with love and affection

and dedicated to
all those who lived
and died in the Blitz.

Before

The sky above Bethnal Green was dark and ominous. It was a cold, wet March evening, with a persistent icy drizzle which settled on the shining grey paving slabs. A helpless moon constantly struggled to break free from the dark rain clouds. The winter had been dreary so far – rain, snow, fog, subzero temperatures, and endless heavy skies – not the kind of weather to cheer people up in the middle of a war. But at least the first three months of 1943 had been quiet. Since those horrific nights during the Blitz, the bombing had eased off and London's East Enders were beginning to hope that they would never again hear the wail of the air-raid siren.

In the busy Roman Road, which had already had more than its share of bomb damage, there was a much friendlier sound than that of the air-raid siren. A small group of people, all in their twenties, were singing 'Side by Side' as they hurried along. Any passer-by could be forgiven for assuming that the youngsters had just come out of the Bricklayers Arms pub just down the road. Although it was true, none of them was drunk, just high-spirited. After all, it was a special occasion.

There were seven in the group. Out in front, arms linked

1

together, were four girls and one boy. Each was wearing a heavy winter coat and woollen gloves, and the girls wore headscarves which protected their ears from the cold. Two of the girls, in identical clothes, were obviously twins, and their flaming red hair was the same colour as their two older sisters'.

As the song finally came to a raucous end, the high-spirited group burst into cheering and laughter.

'Which way?' called the boy up front, the shortest and youngest member of the family, with the same red-coloured hair as his sisters.

They had come to a halt at a road junction, which seemed eerily deserted for so early in the evening.

'Cross over Cambridge 'Eaff Road,' came a very masculine voice from behind. It was the boy's elder brother, in Army uniform and heavy khaki topcoat. 'The bus stop's just over there on the left.'

'I still fink yer'd be better off takin' the tube down Stepney Green.' The third male in the party, togged up in a peaked cap and heavy multi-buttoned navy-blue fireman's jacket, lit up a fag as he tagged on behind the others. 'Yer'll get so perishin' cold waitin' at that bus stop, yer nackers'll fall off!'

The fireman's comment brought another roar of laughter from the party.

'Don't be so coarse, Bill!' Even though she disapproved of such talk, the eldest sister shook her long red hair across her shoulders, and joined in the laughter.

'Well, make up yer mind!' grumbled the youngest boy, who had already half crossed the main road. 'Which way? Bus or tube?'

By the time the others had followed him to the opposite side of the road, the decision was dramatically made for them. The quiet night air was suddenly pierced by the shrill wail of the air-raid siren.

'Air raid!' yelled the twins in unison.

All eyes turned towards the dark night sky, which was already streaked with the thin white beams of Army searchlights.

Taken completely by surprise, the group just stood exactly where they were, not knowing what to do. Their first inclination was to run, but their experience during the Blitz had warned them not to panic. One thing however was certain: if anyone wanted to be heard, they had to shout above the deafening cacophony of the siren which was perched on top of the nearby police station.

'Let's get back 'ome!' yelled the eldest sister, above the wailing siren. 'Quick as we can . . . 'urry!'

By the time the group had rushed back across Cambridge Heath Road the chilling sound of the air-raid siren had given way to the menacing drone of enemy aircraft drifting in high above them from the direction of the Mile End Road and the Essex coastline beyond. It was a sound that the people of London had come to dread, as if a deadly swarm of giant wasps were moving in for the kill.

Determined not to give in to the approaching intimidation, none of the youngsters showed any panic as they hurried back along the Roman Road. As they did so, the streets were suddenly filled with people who were emerging from houses, pubs, and the nearby cinemas. What had only a few moments before been a quiet Bethnal Green evening, was now transformed into a scene of frenzied activity. Women were carrying small children, their menfolk following on behind with blankets, holdalls – anything they might need for a long night's stay in the public shelter. Simultaneously, ARP and Home Guard volunteers appeared, wearing tin helmets and carrying hand torches, their eyes turned towards the rapidly menacing sky.

The youngsters had only just reached the corner of Globe Road when the first salvo of anti-aircraft rockets streaked up into the sky.

'Keep goin'!' yelled the eldest sister. 'We can all get inter the Morrison back 'ome!'

No sooner had she spoken when a new, more terrifying sound filled the air. It was a screeching sound, like nothing anyone had ever heard before. The explosion that followed caused buildings to shake and shudder, and the ground vibrated as though the East End were experiencing its first earthquake. Somebody screamed, and as the group of young people huddled together for protection, people all around were throwing themselves to the ground.

'Christ Almighty!' called the fireman, who shielded the eldest sister tightly with his arms. 'What're they throwin' at us now?'

As soon as everyone in the street had recovered sufficiently from the ear-shattering effects of the explosion, there was a mad rush towards the public shelter in the new Bethnal Green Tube Station on the corner of Cambridge Heath and Roman Roads.

'What're we goin' ter do?' yelled the youngest boy in the group, as a double-decker bus stopped alongside and its passengers and crew joined the frightened crowds heading off towards safety. As he spoke, another salvo of rockets shot up into the sky and exploded with terrifying intensity high above the rooftops. Some of the women in the crowd shrieked with panic. From that moment, the rush towards the tube station became a race.

'It's too late to get 'ome!' called the fireman. 'Down the tube! Quick as yer can!'

Although the new Central Line tube station was not yet open for passengers, it already had the reputation for being one of the safest public shelters in the district. By the time the group of youngsters reached the narrow unfinished entrance, they found it jammed with a surging mass of frightened people, all desperate to find safety before the next wave of mysterious explosions.

When those explosions finally came, there was pandemonium. Everyone shoved and squeezed through the wooden entrance, determined to reach cover as quickly as possible. The group of youngsters was soon sucked into the crowds and separated from each other. Many different names were being called out as the crowd surged down the unfinished concrete and wooden steps, but every so often the fireman's voice could be heard above the others, shouting out, 'Rose! Where are yer, gel? Are yer all right?' There was no reply. The fireman did manage to catch a distant glimpse of heads of familiar red hair, but the few steps leading down to the booking hall were so densely jammed that it was quite impossible to reach any of them.

From the booking hall, the youngsters were swept in an orderly crush with the rest of the crowd towards the top of the staircase which led to the platforms below. As they got there, another deafening salvo of explosions rocked the entire foundations of the station. Convinced that a new type of bomb had dropped close by, the crowd just entering the station entrance behind panicked, and in a chorus of shrieks and screams surged forward, pressing as hard as they could against those who were already packed tight into the inadequate booking hall. What followed in the stifling atmosphere was a living hell.

'Mum...!' 'Georgie...!' 'Lil...!' 'Vera...!' 'Mike...!' 'Sidney...!' The cries and yells were desperate in the darkness of the staircase leading down to the platforms. Something had happened below, and people started to tumble. There were no handrails, no crush barriers. Try as they might, no one could keep upright; their feet were quite literally collapsing beneath them. 'Stop pushin' back there!' came repeated cries from the crowds on the staircase. '*For Chrissake ... stop ... pushing...!*'

After what seemed hours, but which was in reality just a few moments, there was a split second of silence. Then came sobs and tears and calls for help.

The staircase was piled high in a seething heap of bodies. Everyone was gasping for what little air there still remained in the confined space of that ghastly hellhole.

Anguished voices were calling out names again. 'Queenie...!' 'Polly...!' 'Millie...!' 'Gus...!' 'Bill...!'

There was hardly any light from the absurdly low-watt bulbs dangling above the treacherous staircase. It was impossible to see who was still alive. All anyone could do was to lie – and wait.

And so the cries and tears continued. Name after name was called: 'Georgie...!' 'Polly...!' 'Gus...!' 'Millie...!' 'Queenie...!'

'Rose...! Rose...!'

Chapter 1

'Wotcha, Peanut! 'Ow's yer belly off for spots?'

For a ten-year-old, Rose Humble had the cheek of the devil. But the barrow boys in Chapel Market were used to her mischievous humour, and looked forward to her early morning stroll amongst their stalls.

'You just watch it, old muvver carrot-top!' Although he was one of the most endearing characters in the market, Peanut, like his pals, was always ready with a pretty good quip of his own. 'Yer give me too much lip, an' yer don't get no free 'and-outs for yer birfday!'

Rose's eyes widened and her mouth dropped open. '*Peanut!* 'Ow d'yer know it's me birfday?'

'Give over, Ginger! Yer've bin tellin' everyone in the market about it for weeks!' Peanut reached down underneath the stall and came up with a piece of old newspaper bulging with unshelled peanuts. ''Ere!' he said with a sly grin. 'Fink yerself lucky ter get somefin' free out of me in this day an' age!'

This was 1931 and nobody could afford to give away anything. With two million people out of work, the year was turning out to be one of the worst economic depressions the country had ever known.

'Fanks a lot, mate!' Rose was already breaking open one of the peanuts, a pile of which were on display on the nut and bean stall for ha'pence a pound. 'I promise not ter nick any more.'

'Not 'til that lot's finished, y'mean!' grinned Peanut, as he watched Rose hurrying off through the market crowds, to shouts of "Appy birfday, Ginge!' from the barrow boys and girls.

Saturday mornings in the market were always busy, for it was here that people could pick up the best bargains and cheapest food. Although the sun was streaming through the coloured awnings above the dozens of stalls, there was already an early October nip in the air, and many of the barrow boys were wearing warm caps and chokers. Like most kids of her age, however, Rose didn't feel the cold, so she was wearing little more than one of her father's old striped shirts, cut down to fit her, and a well-worn pinafore dress, made out of some second-hand curtains given to her mum by her friend Jessie on one of the used remnants stalls.

Rose loved the market. Although she couldn't actually see the stalls from the tiny room she shared with her three sisters above the piano shop in the next street, she could hear the sounds of 'Ripe termaters! Get yer ripe termaters 'ere!' and 'Apple-a-pound, pears!' and 'Come on, my darlin's! A farvin' for two pickled onions!' But most of all it was the smells that Rose loved – the aroma of whole potatoes baking on an open-grilled fire, of strawberries and Italian water ice in the summer and roast chestnuts, saveloys and pease pudding in the winter. And stewed eels and mash at any time! Not that she ever tasted such luxuries. They were well beyond the reach of the Humble family.

Rose stopped to shell a peanut for a couple of pigeons, busily searching for any scraps in the kerbside. As she watched them fighting over her meagre offering, she wondered what the market would look like to a bird hovering above the hustle and bustle of such a place. Like fairyland, she thought.

'Many 'appy returns, ol' gel!'

Rose looked up to see a big fat man behind one of the vegetable stalls, raising his battered straw boater at her. 'Fank yer, Mr Cabbage,' she replied with the sweet smile she reserved for her favourite friends.

'An' wot great age 'ave we reached terday then?'

Rose stood up and pulled back her shoulders proudly. 'I'm ten years old – at 'alf-past one dinner time.'

'Are yer now? Well, that's special, my gel – an' no denyin' it. Reckon yer doin' very good for someone as old as that!' The old chap chuckled to himself and scratched the large goitre which was protruding unkindly from the side of his neck.

Rose wiped her nose on the back of her hand, feeling a little self-conscious. She wasn't a particularly pretty child, but she already had very sharp, rather pointed features and lovely dark eyes which were a perfect complement to the shoulder-length red hair she constantly tugged behind her ears.

'So then a special day calls for a special present – wouldn't yer say?'

Rose, still clutching her newspaper bundle of peanuts, stared in astonishment as the jolly-faced Mr Cabbage came

9

out from behind his stall and presented her with something minute wrapped in a piece of tissue paper.

'The missus chose it, so don't blame me if yer don't like it!'

Rose quickly tucked the bundle of peanuts under her arm, ripped open the tissue paper, and gasped with excitement.

'It come from Nobbie Perkins' jewellery stall next door.' As he watched Rose's reaction, Mr Cabbage brimmed with satisfaction. 'It ain't real silver, of course. But it's the thought that counts.'

Rose held up the piece of jewellery in both hands. On the end of a very fine chrome chain was a tiny brooch in the shape of a pair of scales. 'Oh, Mr Cabbage, it's – smashin'!'

'Scales for Libra! Born in October – that's yer birf sign, gel!'

Rose threw her arms around Mr Cabbage and hugged him. 'Oh fank yer, Mr Cabbage! Fank yer! Fank yer!' Although she was quite tall and slender for her age, she could only just manage to get her arms around the rotund old boy's thighs, and that in itself was quite a challenge.

Then Rose was rushing in and out of the market stalls, back to the rooms above Mr Popov's second-hand piano shop. She leapt up the narrow staircase alongside the shop two steps at a time, breathless with excitement. She couldn't wait to show her family her birthday presents. But as she reached the first-floor room, and threw open the door, it was obvious that something was wrong.

Rose's mother, Nellie Humble, was sitting at the kitchen table, her hands covering her face.

Rose, immediately anxious, stopped dead in the open doorway.

'Mum's lost 'er job at the canteen,' Rose's sister Queenie explained. She was a year younger than Rose, and easily the prettiest child in the family, with a moon-shaped face like her mother. 'They're cuttin' down on staff 'cos of money.'

'Wot?' Rose slammed the door, threw her birthday presents down on the table, and rushed to comfort her mother. 'Why, Mum? They can't get rid of *you*. Yer work 'arder than anyone!'

Nellie slowly looked up. She had a pretty, but weary-looking face, with a dimple in the middle of her chin, and a small mole set attractively on the side of her left cheek. Like her daughters, her hair was a vivacious red, and long, but she kept it tidy in a hairnet at the back of her head. Nellie's eyes were dark and friendly, but now they looked tired. 'They've got ter make cuts somewhere, Rose. London Transport say they can't afford ter keep more than one or two people on in the staff canteen.'

Rose's face had a look of thunder. 'But the bus an' tram drivers 'ave ter 'ave their cups of tea an' rock cakes, don't they?'

'You 'eard wot Mum said, di'n't yer?' snapped Queenie, who was sitting in front of the kitchen fire grate, busily re-tying a piece of ribbon around the back of her long red hair. 'They ain't got no money!'

'You shut yer mouff, Queenie!' Rose was in danger of flying into one of her regular tempers. 'Nobody asked yer opinion!'

'Don't talk ter yer sister like that,' said their mum. She

looked much older than her thirty-eight years. 'It doesn't 'elp to 'ave a go at each uvver. Specially on yer birfday.'

Rose had temporarily forgotten her birthday. Now it all seemed quite meaningless. As she watched her mum trying to compose herself, Rose felt a mixture of anger and sadness. It didn't seem right that someone so good and hard-working as Mum should be treated in such a way. It was bad enough that all the family had to be squashed up into two tiny rooms above a second-hand piano shop, but why should she have to struggle *all* the time? Why couldn't there be just one day when something nice happened? Rose looked around the tidy little room with her mum and dad's double bed crammed in one corner and the small kitchen table and stools pressed against the one free wall. And she decided right there and then that one day she would give both her parents and the family all the things they deserved to have.

Nellie suddenly brightened up. 'We've got a surprise for yer, Rose. When yer dad gets 'ome, we're all goin' ter 'ave a special birfday tea for yer. We're goin' ter toast some crumpets at the grate, and when I left the canteen they let me 'ave some Chelsea buns and marge left over from the mornin' break.'

Both Rose and Queenie whooped with delight. Suddenly Rose felt special again, and she rushed across to throw her arms around her mum, squealing out, 'Oh, Mum!'

'An' I'm goin' ter make yer some of yer favourite – black treacle toffee.'

Rose practically yelled with excitement.

'Mr Popov downstairs paid for the treacle. If yer ask me, I fink 'e's a bit partial ter toffee 'imself!'

* * *

By late afternoon, Rose had carried a jug of water up from the back yard, and washed herself more thoroughly than she had ever done before. Then she put on the plain cotton dress her nan had bought for her in a jumble sale the previous Christmas, which she was already beginning to outgrow. One of her few personal possessions was a small handbag mirror she had found one evening in the kerb after the market had closed, which she guarded jealously from her sisters. After retrieving it from its hiding-place in the family chest of drawers, wrapped up in a pair of her knickers, she went downstairs to the outside lavatory in the shop's back yard, locked herself in, propped the mirror against the wall, and put on the brooch and chain given to her by Mr Cabbage. For nearly ten minutes she sat there, admiring the brooch at her neck, and feeling like a princess.

As Rose crept up the stairs to the room she shared with Queenie and her twin sisters, Polly and Millie, she could smell the treacle toffee cooking in the oven. She knew her father was home then, for she could hear him talking to her mother, who was once again in tears. For a few moments, Rose stood listening.

'I don't know wot we're goin' ter do, Bert. I just don't know,' sobbed Nellie. ''Ow are we goin' ter feed the kids an' pay the rent wiv no money comin' in?'

'I don't know,' sighed Albert Humble, who was clearly just as anxious as his wife, but doing his best to put a brave face on things. 'Somefin'll come up in the next few days, yer'll see. I was down the Coal Yard this afternoon. Mr Jackson was sayin' 'is two 'orses are definitely goin' ter need some groomin' pretty soon, and 'e's promised ter give me the job.'

'But yer've bin on the dole for nearly six months, Bert,' said Nellie, her voice hardly audible. 'I've spent every penny I've earnt up the canteen, an' there's not a farvin' left in the box.'

'Don't worry, gel!' replied Albert, unconvincingly. 'We've always managed ter pull fru before, an' we will again – yer'll see! I promise yer – I've got plans.' Then he lowered his voice. 'But let's keep it to ourselves, gel,' he begged. 'Just for ternight.'

At six o'clock on the dot, the Humble family were seated around the small kitchen table where, despite the air of gloom, Rose was made to feel special. The table itself was laid with a bright clean tablecloth, and although the enamel family teapot was badly chipped, the few Chelsea buns, bread and fish paste, newly toasted crumpets, and a tin of black treacle toffee were arranged in such a way as to make everyone feel that it was a meal fit for a princess. Even Rose's peanuts had been piled into a white cooking basin, and were just waiting to be attacked by the youngest member of the family, George, who had fairly recently celebrated his seventh birthday. But before anyone could lay their hands on anything, there was a family ritual to be observed.

'For what we are about ter receive, may God make us truly fankful.'

Albert Humble had known from the start that Nellie Wilson believed in God. Not that she was very religious, but she was convinced there *was* someone or something she could turn to when times were difficult. Ever since she and Albert married in 1918, Nellie had insisted that the family show gratitude for anything they received.

Nellie had hardly opened her eyes and unclasped her hands when George stretched out across her to grab a handful of peanuts.

''Ang on now, George! If yer want some of them peanuts yer should ask yer sister first. It's 'er birfday, not yours!'

When Albert Humble spoke, the family always listened. He wasn't a hard father, but with six kids to keep an eye on he insisted they behave themselves, especially at the table.

'It's all right, Dad,' said Rose. 'I can't eat 'em all on me own.'

George didn't need to be told twice, and immediately grabbed a handful of nuts.

''Ope they choke yer!' snorted Queenie, who was sitting next to her young brother, reaching for half a toasted crumpet.

George kicked his elder sister under the table, but when he caught his father glaring at him, he decided to concentrate on shelling his peanuts. With his dark brown hair disciplined by a short-back-and-sides haircut, Albert Humble looked a formidable figure at the head of the small table. He never failed to turn up for meals with a clean shirt done up at the neck with a front collar stud, and trousers and braces with all the buttons done up.

As always, the twins, Polly and Millie, were the best behaved, making quite sure they were never intimidated by their younger brother, born a year after them. The two identical sisters were known in the market as 'The Toffs', mainly because they never swore or played wild games in the street like their brothers and sisters. Polly was the eldest twin by one and a half minutes, but in every way the

15

two were alike, with the same red hair as their mother, Rose, Queenie, and George, and a lisp that when used in unison endeared them to everyone.

'So wot 'appens now yer've lost yer job, Mum?'

Gus's ill-timed question was innocent enough, but it was enough to cause a moment's tension in the happy birthday atmosphere.

Nellie bit her lip anxiously as she poured tea.

'That's nuffin' for yer ter worry about, son,' his father snapped, saving Nellie from having to answer. 'Yer mum an' I know 'ow ter sort these fings out.'

Gus, at twelve years old, was the eldest of the brothers and sisters, and the only child without red hair. For a moment he seemed content to leave the question un-answered, but he was a tactless boy at the best of times. 'But if there ain't anyone bringin' any money 'ome each week, 'ow we goin' ter 'ave any food ter eat?'

Albert suddenly snapped, ''Ave yer ever gone 'ungry, Gus?'

Gus looked up from eating his bread and fish paste. 'No, Dad.'

'D'yer fink me an' yer mum would ever let yer go wivout food?'

Gus was beginning to look nervous. 'No, Dad.'

'So wot're yer askin' stupid bleedin' questions like that for? Wot yer mum an' I do is none of yer business!'

'Don't, Bert – please!' Nellie quickly put down the teapot.

'Gus di'n't mean no 'arm, Dad – honest.' As usual, it was Rose who came to her big brother's aid. ''E was only tryin' ter be 'elpful, wasn't yer, Gus?'

Gus swallowed a mouthful of bread and fish paste in one gulp. 'Yeah. Yeah, that's right. I was only tryin' ter be 'elpful.'

Nellie quickly put her arm around her husband's shoulder and kissed him on the forehead. It was enough – but only just enough – to prevent more tension. From that moment on, Albert decided to keep quiet. After retrieving the stub of a home-made fag from behind his ear, he shoved it in his mouth and lit it. It was a smell Rose hated, for the tobacco her father used was usually left over from the stubs of other people's fags, which he collected from the street outside.

For several minutes everyone sat in silence, and the only sound was of George shelling peanuts.

'Right, everyone,' said Nellie, finally. 'I fink it's about time we give Rose 'er present.'

'Yes!' came the triumphant dual response from the twins.

Rose looked genuinely bewildered as her mother got up from the table, and collected something from beneath the eiderdown on her bed.

'It ain't much, Rose,' said Nellie, apologetically. 'But I made it meself, so I know it won't fall ter pieces in five minutes. 'Ere.' She handed Rose a small parcel wrapped up in soiled brown paper, and whilst kissing her gently on the forehead, called out, 'Many 'Appy Returns ter our Rose!'

Everyone then stood up and shouted, 'Many 'Appy Returns our Rose!' Then they all sang ''Appy Birfday To You!' and whilst they did so Rose ripped open the parcel. She was completely overcome by what she found inside. It was a patchwork doll, beautifully stitched together by her

17

mother out of small remnants of material from the dresses
made over the years by Nellie for her four daughters.

'It's – oh – I don't know wot ter say!' Rose's eyes were
wide open, rather like the buttons her mother had used for
the doll's eyes. She decided immediately that she would call
it 'Baby', and that as long as she lived she would never part
with it.

During all the excitement, both Gus and George looked
bored and used the opportunity to clear what was left of
Rose's peanuts.

Albert Humble did his best to join in the merriment, but
he was clearly agonising as he watched Rose hugging and
kissing her home-made birthday present. He waited just
until he had finished the last of his fag, then got up from the
table. 'I'll see yer later, kids. 'Appy birfday, Rosie.' Then
after kissing his daughter on the forehead, he collected his
jacket and cap, put them on, and left the room. Rose's face
crumpled as she watched her dad go.

Nellie bit her lip nervously, then, as she got up from the
table, tried to give Rose a reassuring smile. 'I won't be a
minute,' she said, going to the door.

Whilst the others engaged in one of their usual table
battles, Rose got up, went to the door, and listened. She
knew that it was wrong to listen to other people's private
conversations, but it was an impulse that she had never
been able to resist. However, with all the noise going on at
the table, she couldn't hear very much, just her mum and
dad having a heated exchange and trying to keep their
voices down. After a minute or so, she heard her mother
coming back to the room, so she hurried back to her seat at
the table.

As soon as her mum returned, it was obvious to Rose that the poor woman was trying to hold back tears.

'Right!' said Nellie, gallantly. 'Who's for a nice piece of treacle toffee?'

'Yeth, pleeth!' yelled the twins in unison, arms upraised.

At that moment, Rose heard the front street door slam downstairs.

It was exactly eleven o'clock that night when Rose heard her dad returning home. She could hear the clock chiming the hour from the big church tower in nearby Upper Street.

Rose hadn't slept at all since her birthday party. It wasn't only because she had been over-excited by her presents; she knew that her mum and dad were in serious trouble. Beside her, in the large double bed she shared with her three sisters, was Queenie, who all through the evening had done her best to conceal how much she resented the special attention being paid to Rose. At the opposite end of the bed lay the lisping twins, both with identical smiles on their faces, even in sleep. Rose couldn't see any of them in the darkness despite a thin beam of light which filtered through the threadbare net curtains at the one small window. Its source was the public gaslight mounted on the wall of the corner house opposite the piano shop. Sometimes the light kept Rose awake, but when she didn't want to sleep she was just able to make out the stucco mouldings around the gas mantle in the middle of the room. Many a night she had been mesmerised by the plaster decorations with their tiny replicas of grapes and cupids. Sometimes in her mind, the figures came to life and hovered above her, and she became so frightened it sent her off to sleep. But

19

other times, her eyes flicked around the dark sloping walls of the small attic room until her eyelids became so heavy that they just closed without her knowing it.

As she lay there, Rose's mind was desperately trying to think of a way that she could help her mum and dad, of something she could do to stop them from worrying about where they were going to find the money to buy food. With a sigh, she pulled Baby closer and gently rested the small patchwork doll's face against her own. By now Rose's mind was buzzing. If there was no money coming in, how were they going to be able to pay Mr Popov the rent for the two tiny rooms the family were crowded into? Even though their landlord only charged them a few shillings a week, the poor old bloke also had to make a living, for during these hard times when most people were fighting for every penny they could find, buying a second-hand piano was not exactly everyone's priority. There *had* to be a way of making ends meet – there just had to be. For a ten-year-old, young 'carrot-top' Humble was remarkably practical, and she was determined to work out a plan that would save the family from disaster.

Rose had only just got to sleep when she was woken by a sound which she at first thought was part of her dream. Someone was banging on the front street door downstairs. Sitting up with a start and with Baby pressed firmly against her shoulder, she quietly slipped out of bed. On the landing outside the door, her two brothers were fast asleep on the floor, snoring loudly, and covered only by one double eiderdown. Rose had to stretch carefully across them to reach the top of the stairs. Then she heard voices.

Creeping quietly down the stairs, she reached the first-floor landing, where she stopped, pressed her face against the banisters, and listened.

The first thing she could hear was her mother crying. And then there were murmuring sounds, as though several people were having a row. Rose pressed closer to the banisters, hoping to catch a glimpse of who was downstairs, but as there was no light, she really couldn't see anything, only the long shadows of figures cast along the narrow front passage.

Suddenly there were shouts of protest from Rose's father. 'It's not true, I tell yer! It's bloody not true!'

Only then did Rose start to panic. Voices! She could hear other men's voices that she didn't recognise. Who were they? What did they want with her father? What *was* going on down there?

Rose could hear her mother quietly sobbing: 'No – please! I'm sure it's all a mistake. It *must* be a mistake!' It sounded as though the poor woman were pleading with whoever was down there.

'Albert . . .!'

The moment she heard her mum shout, Rose rushed back upstairs, leapt over her brothers, who solidly refused to wake up, and burst into her own bedroom where the twins were already sitting up in bed, rubbing their eyes wearily. Still clutching Baby to her shoulder, Rose quickly climbed up onto the bed, and strained to peer out of the bottom of the small window, which was set in one of the sloping attic walls.

What Rose could see in the dimly lit street outside were two burly police constables, leading her father off by the scruff of the neck to a waiting police wagon.

Chapter 2

It wasn't the first time that Albert Humble had been in trouble with the police. On at least two occasions during the past couple of months he had been found sitting in the deserted market kerbside at pub closing time, totally incapable of standing on two feet. But this was more serious. Now he was accused of stealing spare change belonging to another customer, who had inadvertently left it on the pub counter after buying a round of drinks for his mates.

'It's 'is own fault,' sniffed Gus. 'Yer know wot the old man's like. When 'e's boozed like that, 'e don't know 'alf of wot 'e's getting up to.'

'Don't yer talk about Dad like that!' Although Rose adored her elder brother, she would never hear a word said against any member of her family. 'The 'ole fing's a mistake. Anyone can see that. Dad wouldn't fieve from no one. 'E ain't no crook!'

The water from the back yard tap was cold, and as they washed their face and hands in the old stone sink together, they could feel the blood rushing through their veins.

'Mum says the bobbies accused Dad of pickin' up two tanners an' a threepenny bit from the counter.' Rose was shivering as she wiped her wet eyes on the towel. 'But when they searched 'im round the nick, 'e di'n't 'ave no money on 'im at all.'

'So wot's that supposed ter prove?'

'It proves,' snapped Rose indignantly, 'that Dad di'n't walk out the pub wiv that man's change. And don't use all the soap. Polly, Millie an' George ain't 'ad their wash yet.'

Gus quickly tired of his young sister's constant bossy manner. So after drying himself, he stormed inside through the back door.

Rose suddenly felt awful. She hated upsetting her brother. Gus was her real favourite because he was a boy, and she preferred being with boys because they were tougher than girls. Many a time she wished her mum and dad had made her a boy, too.

'' 'Ang on!' she called, as she followed her big brother up the narrow back staircase. 'Wot we gonna do about it, Gus?'

Gus carried on climbing. 'Do about *wot*?' he called over his shoulder.

'About Dad o' course! They've kept 'im in the nick all night. If we don't do somefin', 'e might get time.'

'So wot?' Gus grunted, as he reached the first-floor landing. 'It's 'is own fault for gettin' boozed.'

'Gus!'

Rose, still drying herself on the shared towel, watched Gus disappear up the stairs to the attic room. Although he was always a bit of a hero in Rose's eyes, even she was surprised by her big brother's selfish disinterest in what fate might have in store for their dad and the rest of the family.

On the landing outside her bedroom, Rose found George still fast asleep and snoring loudly. She quietly stepped over him and went into her room to comb her hair and finish dressing. Then she crept back down the front stairs. As she passed the door of her mother and father's room, she could just hear Queenie eating her breakfast, mouth full of bread and dripping, and singing to herself at the same time.

Rose hurried down the front staircase and out into the street. She paused only for a moment to peer in through the window of Mr Popov's piano shop, where Polly and Millie were taking advantage of Sunday closing to tinkle on the keyboard of one of the highly polished uprights.

The market was already in full swing, with the sound of Rose's barrow boy pals filling the air: 'Get yer luvely taters 'ere, gels!' 'Come on now, ladies! Carbolic soap for yer complexion. Two bars an 'apenny!' For Rose they were thrilling sounds, and she could spend all day just sitting on a wooden applecrate listening to them, but today she had more pressing matters on her mind.

To Rose, Highbury Police Station was an awful-looking place. It was all grey stone and windows with blinds so that you couldn't see what the bobbies were getting up to inside. And the blue lamp that hung outside with a huge word 'Police' stuck on it – well, that had been smashed to pieces plenty of times by the local kids. Of course, Rose had passed the place many times before – usually when

she went out for an evening stroll with her mum and dad
and the family, down Upper Street to Highbury Fields –
but she had never climbed those awful stone steps to peer
inside. She wouldn't have dared! But today was different.

'Rose! Wot're you doin' 'ere?'

The first person Rose saw as she pushed open the main
door was her mum. Her eyes red with tiredness, she was
sitting on a bare wooden bench placed against an ugly
green and whitewashed wall. 'Mum!' Rose rushed straight
into her arms and hugged her.

'Yer shouldn'ta come, Rose. I'm just waitin' ter see yer
dad, then I'll be 'ome ter cook dinner.'

'I wanna see Dad, too!' Rose said, raising her voice
defiantly. 'Where is 'e? I wanna see 'im!'

'Keep yer voice down, young lady.' A skinny-looking
bobby was glaring at her from the reception counter
nearby. 'By rights, you shouldn't be 'ere. Kids ain't
allowed.'

'I'm not a kid!' Rose snapped back. 'I'm ten years old,
an' I wanna see my dad!' She disliked the man on sight.
He was a bobby, and nobody in their right mind liked a
bobby.

'Go back 'ome, Rose – be a good gel.' Nellie Humble
broke loose from her daughter, straightened the child's
hair, and tried to give her a loving smile. 'There's nuffin'
yer can do. There's nuffin' anyone can do. Yer dad's got
ter spend the night 'ere.'

Rose was outraged. 'Wot? *Anuvver* night?'

Nellie sighed. 'There ain't no magistrate sittin' on a
Sunday. Yer dad can't go up before 'im 'til termorrow.'

Rose felt sick in her stomach. She hated this place and

all it stood for. The idea that her own dad had to spend two nights in a prison cell with all the smells of whitewash and stewed tea and bobbies' freshly shined boots seemed to her to be a crime in itself. 'But why're they keepin' Dad 'ere? 'E said 'e di'n't take the money, di'n't 'e?'

Nellie peered anxiously across at the desk bobbie ''E di'n't take it,' she whispered. 'But *somebody* did.'

Rose creased up her face. 'Then why are they blamin' Dad?'

''Cos 'e 'appened to be at the counter where the barmaid left the Prince's change.'

'Prince? Wot Prince?'

Nellie pulled her daughter close. 'Prince Monolulu. The racing tipster.'

Rose frowned, as she always did when she got angry. 'You mean that old black man?'

'Rose! Don't be so rude!' Suddenly Nellie's anxiety had turned to embarrassment.

Rose stood her ground stubbornly. 'But that's wot 'e is, in't 'e? 'E's the one who goes up an' down the market wavin' 'is umbrella, an' wears them funny clothes and fevvers in 'is 'air.'

Just as Nellie was about to scold the child, the bobbie called to her from the counter. 'You can come in now, Mrs 'Umble. Five minutes, that's all.' He unlocked a door at the side of the counter to let her in, adding pointedly, 'No kids allowed.'

Rose glared at him as her mother got up and quickly went to the door.

Nellie paused briefly to call back over her shoulder, 'Go 'ome, Rose. I'll see yer later.'

Rose waited just long enough to see her mother disappear through the door, and listen to her being led off to see Albert Humble in his cell.

As Rose made her way back towards the Angel along busy Upper Street, there was still a chilly autumn nip in the air although the sun was working hard to fight its way through the bullying grey clouds. There were plenty of people heading in the same direction as Rose, for the base-toned bells of nearby St Mary's were drawing people in for the popular early morning service. Most times Rose loved to watch the congregation filing through the church doors, all of them wearing their Sunday best, the gentlemen in their three-piece suits and trilby hats, the ladies in neat three-quarter length dresses and coats with pretty hats to match. But today was different, for Rose felt that all these fine people belonged to a different world from hers. Somehow she could never imagine any of them living in two small rooms above an old piano shop.

Deep in thought, Rose ambled her way along the edge of the kerb in the busy main road. Two trams passed each other and rattled off in different directions, and children squealed with delight at Mr Pirelli's barrel organ on the other side of the road, but Rose's eyes were focused on the ground as she walked. All she could think about was the face of that bobbie in the nick, and how he treated her like a kid. She wasn't a kid! Or at least she didn't feel like one. In her mind's eye, she could see her dad sitting in his cell, sad and lonely, unable to prove his innocence because no one was prepared to believe a boozer. Without realising it, Rose was grinding her young teeth so hard that she was in danger of chipping them. If only she was just ten years older – then she'd give that fat-mouthed bobbie the sharp edge of her tongue.

'Cheer up, Ginger! It may never 'appen!'

Rose turned back with a start to find Peanut, her barrow boy pal from the market, calling down to her from his cart. 'Give over, Peanut,' she growled. 'I don't feel up to it.'

Guv'nor the old carthorse was always a little nervous in the main street, so Peanut had to keep a tight hold of the reins. 'Sorry ter 'ear about yer old man. Wot's 'e bin up to this time then?'

''E ain't bin up ter nuffink!' Rose snapped back. 'They said 'e nicked the Prince's change down the pub. But 'e di'n't!'

Peanut pushed his cap to the back of his head. 'Then wot'd they lock 'im up for?'

'Why d'yer fink! 'E was on the booze again.'

Peanut shook his head and sighed. 'Whoa there, Guv'nor!' The old carthorse was obviously becoming seduced by the smells from Mr Trimble's nearby toffee-apple stall. 'Take it easy now, boy.' Peanut looked a bit older than his thirty years, for he had to work hard for his modest living, but he had a heart of gold and felt genuine concern for his young pal. 'So wot does the Prince say about all this?'

'Couldn't tell yer.' Rose was idly stroking the horse's rump. 'I s'pose the woman in the pub said Dad did it.'

'Woman in the pub?' Peanut leant down to talk to her. 'Yer don't mean old Doris behind the bar?'

Rose nodded, without looking up.

Suddenly Peanut roared with laughter. 'Old Doris! That bleedin' troublemaker? She'd shop anyone, that old bag!'

'It's not funny!' Rose snapped back. 'They've got Dad locked up in the nick. They're takin' 'im ter court termorrer mornin'.'

Peanut waited for another tram to rattle past before he answered. 'Then go an' find out wot really 'appened in the pub last night. Ask the Prince. 'E's a funny old geezer, but 'e wouldn't do anyone down.'

Rose felt her spirits rise. Peanut was like all the barrow boys in the market: when it came to a crisis, he had a clear head. 'But where *is* the Prince?' she spluttered. ''E don't live round 'ere.'

Once again Peanut roared with laughter. 'Don't be narky, Ginge! Every street in London town is where the Prince lives. Just ten minutes ago I saw 'im up at 'Ighbury Fields, givin' out racin' tips ter an 'ole lotta suckers...'

Rose didn't wait to hear any more. 'Fanks a lot, Peanut!' She raced off down Upper Street in the direction of Highbury Corner.

'I gotta horse! I gotta horse!'

This was the ecstatic shout Rose could hear as she darted in and out of the traffic at the junction of Upper Street and Holloway Road. It was a shout she had heard many times before, ringing above the weekend crowds in the market or along the busy main roads around the Angel, Islington. The man's voice always made her laugh, for it was unlike anyone else she had ever heard – high-pitched, hoarse, but laughing after every few words. But if the voice was unusual, Rose never stopped marvelling at the black man's funny clothes.

Nobody really knew where Prince Monolulu came

from, but he claimed to be an Abyssinian prince. He spent most of his days touring the streets of London waving his umbrella in the air, yelling out his famous catch phrase, '*I gotta horse!*' to passers-by, who had long got over the shock of seeing such an extravagantly dressed man with dark-coloured skin laughing his way through the crowds. Over the years, the locals had developed an affection for the Prince and his high-pitched laugh.

'I gotta horse! I gotta horse! Come on, gents. Three-thirty at Sandown tomorrow afternoon. I gotta sure winner!'

Rose pushed her way through the crowd of men surrounding the tipster, whose head, strapped with multicoloured feathers, she could see above the dozens of trilby and bowler hats, and the screen of fag smoke that was drifting up towards the patchy blue sky. By the time Rose had managed to get to the front, the Prince. who was standing on a wooden applecrate to address his audience, was launched into a very unmusical version of an obscure song called, 'Lucky Ole Me'. While he was doing so, some of the more cheeky onlookers were taking the mickey out of his multicoloured sequined waistcoat, which they reckoned made him look like a Red Indian chief. The Prince managed to get through the song, to a roar of approval from the whole crowd, but when he started preaching about racehorses again, he was completely taken aback by a tiny but penetrating voice squealing at him from the front of the crowd.

'Mr Prince! Mr Prince! I got ter speak ter yer! Please, Mr Prince!'

With a large, beaming smile the Prince leant down to

the youngest member of his audience and said, 'Sorry, lil' lady. I don't give out no tips to your age.'

This brought a chorus from the crowd of 'I gotta horse! I gotta horse!'

Above the noise, Rose yelled out the only thing she could think of. 'You got my ol' man in the nick! Why d'yer do it? Why?'

Although the chorus of crowd rabble continued unabated, the Prince lost the beaming smile on his face for the first time. Coming down from the applecrate, he asked her, 'What's that you say, lil' miss?'

'You got my dad in the nick,' snapped Rose. ''E was in the same pub as you last night – up our way near the market. The bobbies said 'e picked up yer change. They put 'im in the nick. 'E's been in the nick all night.'

Now clearly anxious, the Prince quickly took hold of Rose's hand. 'You come wiv me, lil' lady.'

'Now wos dis all about, lil' lady?' said the Prince, once he had led Rose away from the protesting crowd. 'You tell me you dad in de nick? For pickin' up my change in de pub?'

Rose stared up at the dark-skinned man with a firm determination. 'That's wot they say up the nick!'

'Dis pub. De Queen's Head, you mean? Up near de Angel?'

'Yes! An' 'e di'n't steal no money from yer – 'e di'n't! My dad in't no feif!'

The Prince said nothing, and Rose became quite mesmerised by his rolling white eyes. Then after thinking about it all, he said, 'How much dis change, you say?'

'One an' froopence. Two tanners an' a froopenny bit.'

The Prince scratched his chin with his umbrella, and frowned. 'Dat's right. One and threepence. Dat was the change I got from two bob.'

This only made Rose more angry. 'I tell yer my dad di'n't take it!'

'I bought a round of drinks—'

'My dad di'n't pick up yer rotten ol' change!' Rose yelled.

'I *know* he didn't!' replied the tipster, who refused to be forced into a shouting match with a child. '*I* picked it up.'

'*You?*'

''Course I did! I pick it up an' put it in my pocket. Then I say g'night to everyone and go home. Nobody steal nothin' from the Prince. Nobody!'

Rose found herself staring straight into the funny man's face. But he wasn't funny, and he wasn't nasty. He was one of the kindest men she had ever met. Rose felt she wanted to cry, but she was Rose Humble, Albert and Nellie Humble's eldest daughter, who *never* cried just because times got difficult. Besides, she had a lot of things to take care of if she was going to get her family out of its present troubles. No, girls don't just sit down and cry, they get on with things. For one fleeting moment, however, she felt oh so good! So much so that she quite impulsively threw her arms around the Prince's waist, and hugged him.

Rose would never know that the man with the rolling white eyes and funny coloured clothes never did pick up that one and threepence from the pub counter.

Albert Humble was released from the nick just before midday on Sunday. Waiting for him were Nellie and the kids. To his surprise, however, Rose wasn't with them, and it was not until later that he discovered why.

Turning into Chapel Market, Albert found himself cheered all the way back to the two rooms above Mr Popov's piano shop. There were pats on the back and shouts of 'Good ol' Bert!' and 'Well done, mate!' from every stall he passed. Albert was astonished by the reception, for he was the kind of person that no one ever really noticed. By the time he turned into his home street, he felt a huge lump in his throat, and when he got his first glimpse of Rose standing outside the piano shop, his eyes began to fill with tears. She seemed to be so small and frail, with arms and legs that had hardly any flesh on them at all. But he knew only too well that what his eldest daughter lacked in flesh, she made up for in determination. It was Rose who had spread the word of her dad's innocence, making sure his name was cleared in the neighbourhood. Albert Humble was not normally an emotional man, but as soon as he reached Rose he threw his arms around her and hugged her so tight that she could hardly breathe.

Over the following days Rose thought up an ingenious plan to get her mother back to work. The idea came to her quite accidentally, when, during one of her daily strolls through the market, she noticed how many of the barrow boys went through the day without eating any decent food. So, after chatting them all up, she persuaded each of them to fork up a penny, which she then put into a kitty and gave to her mother to make tea and bloater sand-wiches. Gradually, the whole family joined in, helping to cook soup from meat bones and make cheap mutton pies.

What started as a modest experiment in home catering soon made sufficient profit for the family to earn a decent living.

At the age of ten, Rose Humble was already showing that she was going to be a force to be reckoned with.

Chapter 3

In the summer of 1936 Rose got her first real job, helping to prepare the pickled onions and red cabbage on Elsie Dumper's bottled preserves stall in the market. It only paid a shilling a week, but it was enough for Rose to give her mum a regular tanner towards the family expenses, threepence towards new socks and underclothes for herself, Queenie, and the twins, and a weekly threepence for 'a rainy day', which had to be carefully hidden away from the prying eyes of young George, who would have been quite happy to find a suitable way of spending it on himself. Rose had actually left school the year before, when she was nearly fourteen, for she had never exactly been a star pupil. These days, her mum was more or less running the family's home catering for the market single-handed, so Rose spent most of her time doing odd jobs for her barrow-boy pals, which gave her the chance to earn a few valuable pennies, which she stacked carefully away in her hiding-place on top of the cistern in the back yard lavatory. Now almost fifteen, Rose was becoming quite a business tycoon! She was also the driving-force behind the family's change of fortunes.

Albert Humble had taken to referring to his children by

numbers, which depended on the order of their arrival. The eldest child, Gus, was number one, Rose was number two, Queenie number three, the twins were four and five, and last came George at a very cantankerous number six. Albert himself was now a very different man from the one who five years before had been accused of stealing Prince Monolulu's change, for he had found himself a part-time job grooming carthorses in the local coal yard. To most people, Albert's transformation was amazing, as he was now often seen laughing with his kids, and playing tag with young George up and down the market. But the reason was obvious: it needed only the most modest job to restore his pride and dignity.

Rose was growing into a lovely young girl. Each day, as her features became more and more defined, many of her barrow boy mates thought she was beginning to look like a 'ginger-'eaded dago gel'. Her most appealing features were her flashing brown eyes and devastating smile. Her greatest admirer was Mr Cabbage's young grandson, Badger, who had been given his nickname by some of his mates in the market because they reckoned he looked like an animal character they had seen in one of the comics. He fawned after Rose every time she passed the vegetable stall. Rose had grown shrewd enough to be aware of Badger's interest, and often flirted with him mercilessly, stopping to shake her waist-length red hair whenever she noticed him watching her. She knew what she was doing was cruel, but somehow it gave her a feeling of power to know someone was admiring her.

Only two problems prevented Rose from enjoying her life to the full. One of those was her sister Queenie.

Ever since they were young kids, playing together in and out of the market stalls, Queenie Humble had made it perfectly clear that she resented being a year younger than Rose. Somehow it made Queenie feel inferior, so that anything Rose ever said to her was taken to imply criticism. It was amazing that they had survived so many petty quarrels, for Queenie had a rasping temper which completely belied her beautiful angelic features. But in the hot summer of 1936, at the age of fourteen, Queenie deliberately set out to undermine her elder sister's position as the brains of the family.

The opportunity came on the afternoon of Bank Holiday Monday. As he had recently made a little extra money on various odd jobs, Albert Humble decided it was time he gave his family a treat. This meant a walk along the towpath of the majestic Islington canal, where they could watch the colourful coal-barges being tugged along by the hard-working horses, and where young George and the twins were given a penny each to buy an Italian water ice from the stall just beneath Canonbury bridge. The setting could not have been more idyllic. The canal was steaming from the rays of the hot sun, and the sheer humidity had persuaded afternoon strollers everywhere to discard their cardigans and jackets so that the towpaths on either side of the canal were dazzling with brightly coloured blouses and open-necked shirts and braces, straw boaters and summer bonnets.

'Oh, I wish this day'd never end!' sighed Nellie, as she, Albert, and Queenie shared a tiny wooden bench overlooking the canal. 'It's as though the 'ole world in't such a bad place ter live in, after all.'

Rose beamed. There was nothing she loved better than to see her mum smile, the sparkle in her eyes defying all the tribulations she had had to put up with.

'Mind you, it would've bin nice if Gus could've come, too,' said Nellie, her eyes transfixed by the reflection of the sun on the water. 'Then the 'ole family would've bin togevver.'

Albert had given up smoking the remains of other people's fag ends and was now lighting up a pipe of cheap tobacco. 'Can't expect a boy of that age ter keep 'angin' round 'is family,' he wheezed, puffing smoke out from the side of his mouth. ''E's got uvver fings ter do.'

'Wot fings, Dad?' Queenie's question sounded innocent, but it was enough to drain the smile from Rose's face.

'Number one i'n't a boy no more,' puffed Albert. ''Ow old is Gus now? Seventeen? At 'is age I was knocking around wiv mates of me own.' And with a sneaky but affectionate side grin at Nellie, he added, 'An' not only blokes!'

'Bert!' Nellie snapped out of her daydream, and chuckled.

Rose was now with young George and the twins, all of them sitting down on the edge of the grass towpath with their bare feet dangling idly in the water.

On the wooden bench behind them sat Queenie, her ginger red hair framing a sly grin, which meant she was up to no good. 'I fink Gus ought ter be 'ere, instead of goin' off wiv some of them people 'e knocks around wiv.' She paused only briefly, then flicked her eyes across to her eldest sister. 'Wot say you, Rose?'

Although she didn't want to answer, Rose finally had to.

'I don't know who Gus knocks around wiv. That's 'is business, not mine.'

Queenie, delighted that Rose was rising to her bait, persevered. 'But you know who 'is mates are, Rose,' she said innocently. 'Everyone knows where Gus spends most of 'is time.'

Albert became curious. Taking his pipe out of his mouth, he asked, 'Wot are yer talkin' about, gel?'

'Take no notice, Dad!' said Rose quickly. 'Queenie's only makin' up fings.' She turned to glare at her sister. 'As usual.'

'I ain't makin' up fings!' snapped Queenie, her smile immediately transformed into a scowl. 'Gus spends all 'is time round Cable Street.'

'Don't listen to 'er, Dad!'

'It's true!' Queenie yelled. 'Yer're always tryin' ter cover up for 'im!'

Now it was Nellie's turn to look anxious. 'Cover up – for wot?'

'Ask 'er!' growled Queenie, pointing straight at Rose. 'She knows!'

With teeth clenched, Rose stared down into the water determinedly as her dad called across to her.

'Rose? Wot's all this about Cable Street?'

Rose made the mistake of not answering her dad, for he suddenly became alarmed.

''Ere – wait a minute!' said Albert, half to himself. 'Gus i'n't mixed up wiv them Blackshirts, is 'e?'

Rose didn't have to respond straightaway, for they were distracted by the approach of a long, narrow barge, the toot-toot of its horn piercing the calm summer's day. Rose,

41

George and the twins quickly stood up and moved out of the way, as the old horse snorted past them, pulling the long towrope behind him. The twins became very excited as they watched the brightly coloured vessel glide past, its deck bulging with a freight of logs, no doubt destined for a factory somewhere up in the Midlands. They exchanged waves and shouts with the skipper and his family, and by the time both horse and barge had disappeared out of view beneath Canonbury Bridge, the vessel had left a thin trail of black smoke from its tiny chimney, which twisted up and up, floating across the clear blue sky like some exotic tropical bird in a flight of slow motion.

'Is Gus a fascist, Rose?'

Rose turned around with a start, to find her dad standing just behind her. 'Dad! 'Ow can yer say such a fing?'

'Then wot's 'e doin' 'angin' round the East End? Everyone knows Mosley and 'is gang are tryin' ter stir up trouble against the Jews there.'

Rose didn't really know how to answer. She knew exactly where Gus was, but would sooner die than tell anyone what she knew. And she despised Queenie for bringing up the subject. 'Gus i'n't no fascist, Dad,' she said finally. ''E 'ates 'em.'

''E should keep away from the East End, Rose. It's not a safe place ter 'ang around in these days.' There was a steel-like but anxious look in Albert's eyes as he looked straight at his daughter. 'Mosley's bad news. Give 'im 'alf a chance an' 'e'll get us caught up in anuvver war.'

Rose sighed deeply, took her dad's hands, and stared straight back at him. 'It's not true, Dad. Gus i'n't no fascist. 'E 'ates everythin' they stand for.'

'Politics is every man's downfall, Rose.' Albert was puffing hard on his pipe again. 'One way or anuvver, it always leads to a punch-up.'

Queenie was determined to keep up the pressure on Rose. 'Honestly, Dad,' she whined, coyly. 'Yer should just see some of 'is mates 'e knocks round wiv. Specially Micky 'Awkins . . .'

'You shut yer mouff, Queenie!' snapped Rose.

'I won't!' Queenie yelled back, getting up from the bench to confront Rose. 'You ain't my muvver!'

Rose's eyes were now blazing with anger. 'I said shut yer mouff, or I'll shut it for yer!'

'I won't! I won't!' Queenie was hopping up and down with indignation.

Young George was at last beginning to enjoy the outing. There was nothing he liked better than to see his two elder sisters having a row. But the twins, looking alarmed and frightened, kept together as their mum leapt to her feet. 'Stop it you two!' she called.

'It's not my fault, Mum!' protested Queenie, spluttering with rage. 'It's just 'cos I mentioned Micky 'Awkins.'

'I'm warnin' yer, Queenie 'Umble!' snarled Rose, whose face had turned almost the same colour as her hair. 'You just keep yer mouf shut about Micky 'Awkins!'

Queenie spat back at her like a viper. 'Yer're only sayin' that 'cos yer fancy 'im!' By this time, she was practically eyeball to eyeball with Rose. 'Well, let me tell yer somefin', *Rose* 'Umble. Micky 'Awkins wouldn't touch yer wiv a bargepole. An' d'yer know why? 'Cos 'e reckons yer more like a bloke than a gel!'

Rose didn't wait another moment. She swung her

clenched fist, and landed it straight on to her younger sister's face.

Queenie let out a piercing shriek, and fell back with a thud on to her bottom on the path.

'Rose!' yelled Nellie, as she rushed to help Queenie.

Rose moved forward as though to take another swipe at her sister, but Albert grabbed hold of her arm and twisted it behind her back.

Young George was by now thoroughly enjoying himself, but the twins looked increasingly terrified and bewildered.

Queenie was sobbing, and there was a small trickle of blood coming from her lip. 'I 'ate yer! I 'ate yer!' she yelled at Rose over and over again.

Nellie dabbed the blood from Queenie's lip, and looked up sternly at her eldest daughter. 'Oh Rose. 'Ow could yer?'

Rose couldn't meet her mother's eyes. She knew what she had done was wrong, but in that split second of anger was unable to restrain herself. Queenie was a born troublemaker, and everyone knew it. But Rose was not going to let her get away with it this time. To try and cause trouble for Gus was one thing, but to accuse Rose of being a bloke was truly hurtful. She *wasn't* a bloke, she was a girl, and despite the way she behaved and stood up for her family, she had feelings just like any girl.

'Go 'ome, Rose,' said Albert, releasing Rose's arm from behind her body.

Rose had never seen her dad look so stern, and it upset her. With the twins hugging each other on the edge of the canal, and Queenie sobbing her heart out in her mother's arms over on the bench, Rose suddenly felt guilty. So she quietly backed away and made her way off along the towpath.

'Rose!'

Rose stopped and glanced back briefly at her dad.

'Don't ever let me see yer do that ter yer sister again.'

Rose paused, lowered her eyes, and walked off.

Nellie, still comforting Queenie in her arms, looked up and watched Rose making her way over the bridge. She seemed such a small, crushed figure, who only a short while ago had been enjoying the company of the family that she cherished so much. When Rose had finally disappeared from view, Nellie told herself how ashamed she was that her eldest daughter could have behaved in such a way.

But in her heart of hearts, Nellie knew only too well who was right.

Chapter 4

Rose loved Sunday mornings in the market. Not only was it one of the busiest days of the week, but it was also a time when people gathered around in groups to chat and put the world to rights. But from the moment she got out of bed early that morning, Rose knew that 4 October 1936 was going to be no ordinary Sunday.

She sensed it, too, when she saw Mr Cabbage's grandson, Badger, deep in conversation with a group of barrow boys near the fresh fish stall.

'Wot's goin' on then?' Rose called, as she approached the group of serious-looking faces. 'Someone die or somefin'?'

As soon as he saw Rose, Badger's face lit up. 'We're just talkin' about the punch-up, Ginge. Sounds like it's goin' ter be a bit nasty down there terday.'

Rose was puzzled. 'Punch-up? Wot yer talkin' about?'

'Don't yer read no newspaper, 'Umble?' quipped Smudge, a thin and scraggy boy, who had large ears and looked as though he was now old enough to start shaving. 'It's all over the front pages, yer know.'

'I don't read no newspapers,' Rose snapped back. 'An'

yer call me 'Umble once more, an' yer'll get me fist in yer eye!'

Smudge had to be restrained by the others from having a go at Rose, but she was ready for him. She didn't mind any of the barrow boys teasing her about her surname when they did it with affection, but this little git was trying to be sarcastic.

Badger quickly put his arm around Rose. 'Yer mustn't let Smudge get at yer, Rose. 'E's just a bit simple, yer know that.'

Rose allowed herself to be led away through the crowds. 'Wot's all this about a punch-up?' she asked sulkily.

'Yer ain't 'eard about the march then?'

'March?'

'Mosley an' the Blackshirts. They're stirrin' up trouble again.'

Rose, immediately alarmed, came to a sudden halt. 'Blackshirts? Where?'

'Up the East End. Cable Street.'

Rose's mind went completely numb. For several moments she just stood there, surrounded by the hustle and bustle of the market, listening to Badger's fast-talking patter without actually hearing what he was saying. All she could think about was Gus, who had been up before anyone else in the family that morning. For some time now she had known about her elder brother's involvement in the anti-racist riots in the East End. Many a time Gus had told her how, if he ever had the chance, he would kill Oswald Mosley stone-dead. Gus was hot-headed and impetuous, yet, in her heart of hearts, Rose felt the same way as her brother. She hated the fascist gangs for the way they were carrying out violent attacks on harmless Jewish people. Just who *was* this Oswald Mosley, togged out in his menacing black uniform, cap, and armband, whose pictures she saw in bits of old newspapers on the pickle stall each day? What was it about this old git that excited boys to join him and his so-called British Union of Fascists on marches through the streets of London, screaming out hateful slogans like '*Get rid of the Yids!*'? It was frightening.

'Feel like a penn'f tram ride later, Ginge?'

Rose was suddenly snapped out of her thoughts by Badger, who was holding both her hands and staring straight into her eyes. 'Huh? Wot d'yer say?'

'After the market closes. Before it gets dark.' Badger was mooning at her like a love-struck mongrel. 'We could go down 'Olloway Road, look in some of the shop windows.'

'Don't be a nark, Badge,' Rose replied ungratefully. 'I can't go on no tram rides.'

'Why not? Don't yer like me?'

Badger's direct question and pained look immediately disturbed Rose, for although it irritated her that he fancied her so much, she would never do anything to hurt him. 'Of course I like yer!' she snapped, desperately looking for an excuse. 'I just – don't like goin' out on Sunday evenin's, that's all. I – 'ave fings ter do.' Whilst she spoke she was slowly slipping her hands out of his.

Badger's face seemed to crumple up with disappointment. It was a younger-looking face than his fifteen years, and as he stood there, with the Sunday morning market shoppers brushing past him, his tall gangling body, with its baggy trousers and creased up cap, made him look more awkward than ever. 'Oh – right,' was all he could say, rubbing his nose with the back of his hand.

But as he turned to move off, Rose suddenly grabbed his arm, and gave him a reassuring smile. 'Maybe we can go some uvver time – eh Badge?'

Badger's face lit up immediately. 'Can we, Rose?' he said eagerly. 'Yer not 'avin' me on or nuffin', are yer?'

'Course not. We're mates, ain't we?'

Badger was now beaming. 'Yeah! That's right! We're mates!' He turned to leave, but then stopped. 'An' I tell yer somefin'. I fink Rose 'Umble's a nice name. If anyone tries ter take the mickey out of it while I'm around, I'll smash their face in.' And to Rose's absolute amazement, he gave her a sudden mischievous kiss on the cheek. 'See yer later – Rose!'

Rose watched Badger in disbelief as he quickly disappeared into the market crowds. Then she wiped her cheek with the back of her hand. Badger's stolen kiss had been cold and wet, and it was a feeling she didn't like at all. Not that she didn't like Badger – she just didn't feel that way about *any* boys, that's all.

Not yet anyway.

Gus Humble got home at about half-past eight that evening. It was already dark outside, and the flickering street gas lamps were casting sinister shadows on to the large window of Mr Popov's piano shop. By late afternoon that day, everyone in the market had been talking about the news on the wireless, about the riots with the fascists in the East End of London. As soon as Rose heard Gus

stumbling up the front staircase, she knew that her brother
would have been involved.

'Gus!' Rose was waiting for him on the first-floor
landing. There was panic in her voice. 'Wot's 'appened?
Are yer 'urt?'

'Quick, Rose! Give us an 'and!' It was not her brother
calling to her but Gus's pal Mick Hawkins, who was half
carrying Gus up the narrow staircase.

Rose hurried down, and helped Mick support her
brother up to the first-floor room. 'Oh Gus! Wot yer bin up
ter? Wot's 'appened?'

Gus was now groaning in pain, and as Rose and Mick
lowered him into a chair, he slumped his head down on to
the table.

'Quick, Rose!' There was urgency in Mick's voice as he
knelt on the floor, and feverishly started untying the lace of
one of Gus's boots. 'We 'ain't got much time. They'll be
'ere any minute.' He glanced up at Rose, who was looking
bewildered. 'Don't just stand there! 'Elp me roll up 'is
trousers!'

Rose quickly knelt down beside Mick and did what she
was told. She gasped when she saw that blood was seeping
through one of the trouser legs. Gus let out a yell as the
material was rolled up, for there was a deep gash over four
inches long in the calf of his leg, and it was bleeding
profusely.

'Gus!' Although Rose wasn't scared of the sight of blood,
to see so much of it coming out of her brother horrified her.
''Ow d'yer do this?'

''E got in a scrap wiv a Blackshirt. The sod cut 'im up wiv
a bread-knife.'

51

Rose felt her stomach turn over.

Gus groaned again. His face was contorted with pain.

'We've got ter stop the bleedin'. They'll be 'ere any minute.'

''Oo will?' asked Rose, quickly taking off her apron and using it to dab Gus's wound. ''Oo're yer talkin' about?'

'The coppers, Rose! The coppers!' Mick was a dour-looking, thick-set eighteen-year-old, who never really got on with girls because he always felt as though they were laughing at him. Now he had to rely on Rose. 'We've bin up Cable Street. There was this big punch-up wiv the Black-shirts. It was like a blood-barf up there. The coppers are out lookin' fer troublemakers. Me and Gus're on their list.' He took off his flat cap and wiped the sweat from Gus's forehead. 'Where's yer mum and dad?'

'They've gone over wiv my bruvver George ter see me grandad at Walfamstow.' Rose was busily trying to wipe the blood away from the wound on Gus's leg. 'This cut needs stitchin'. We've got ter get 'im ter 'ospital.'

Gus suddenly sat up in his chair and let out a loud wail. 'No! I'm not goin' ter no 'ospital!'

Rose yelled back at him, 'Yer've got ter, Gus! Yer'll bleed ter death!'

'Stop bossin' me around, Rose!' Gus was now shouting at the top of his voice. 'Yer're always bossin' me around! I won't 'ave it. I'm not goin' ter no 'ospital – and that's final!'

The sound of the yelling match brought Polly and Millie bursting into the room. 'What's wrong?' they recited in unison.

Rose turned to them with urgency. 'Millie! Go an' put on

the kettle! I want a bowl of 'ot water, soon as yer can!' She was frantically rolling up the sleeves of her dress. 'Polly! See if yer can find me some ol' bits of clean rag. There's some in Mum's cleanin' box under the bed.'

'Wot thort of rag?' asked the bewildered Polly.

'Anyfin', Polly! Anyfin! Just 'urry up!'

The twins squirmed at the sight of so much blood, but quickly did as they were told.

'Can *I* be of help?'

Rose turned to find Queenie standing in the open doorway. There was a huge smirk on her face.

Her hands and apron now covered in Gus's blood, Rose got up from her knees, and went to her sister. 'You say one word ter anyone about this, an' I swear ter God – I'll kill yer!' With that, she slammed the door in her sister's face.

A few minutes later, Millie brought across the bowl of hot water. Rose quickly broke off a small piece of table salt, dropped it into the bowl, and stirred it around with a wooden spoon. Meanwhile, Polly tore up some strips of clean floor rags, originally part of a sheet. Polly turned out to be the more practical of the twins, for, unlike her identical sister, she was more than prepared to face the sight of blood if it meant she was able to help her big brother in a time of crisis.

Whilst Rose was waiting for the salt water to cool, she listened to the lowered voices of her brother and his companion, talking about the day's events and all they and their comrades could have done if it hadn't been for the coppers' interference. Rose kept asking herself how much longer all this madness would last. She blamed everything and everybody for all the blood that had been shed that day

53

in Cable Street, and on other days in various parts of the East End of London. Most of all she blamed the politicians, and especially the Prime Minister, Mr Baldwin. How could he and his National Government allow someone like Oswald Mosley and his disgusting BUF to excite boys of all ages with promises of 'glory for England' if they helped rid the great British Empire of the 'evil threat of Semitism'. Rose hated the pictures she saw in the newspapers of boys wearing ugly black shirts and uniforms, marching and rioting in the streets. And girls, too. She even knew one or two girls of her own age who were always going off to listen to Mosley's mesmeric style of speech-making. They seemed to be enraptured by every word he spoke, and adored him as much as other girls adored film stars like Robert Taylor.

As Rose watched her big brother and his pal in animated conversation, she felt that everything her family stood for was under threat. She didn't quite understand how or why. All she knew was that anyone who told young people to fight each other just had to be wicked.

Rose snapped out of her depression, and quickly tested the temperature of the salt water with her bare elbow. Then she took the bowl across to her brother. 'Don't blame me if this 'urts,' she said sharply. 'It's yer own fault for gettin' involved.' Then she dipped a piece of clean rag into the salt water, and squeezed it out. ''Old 'is leg out for me, Mick.'

''Ang on a minute,' said Mick, taking a packet of Woodbines and a box of matches from his pocket. ''Ere, mate. 'Ave a pull on this. It'll take yer mind off.' He took out one of the fags, put it into Gus's lips, and lit it with a match.

Rose watched her brother inhaling and exhaling smoke

with a curious fascination. She had never seen him smoke before, and he suddenly didn't look like a boy any more.

Polly and Millie turned away, holding each other, as Rose bathed the gaping cut in Gus's leg. The fag may have helped a bit, but it didn't stop the searing pain he felt, and his agonised groans, as the salt water stung his wound.

Just as Rose was tying up Gus's leg with a clean strip of rag, there was a loud banging on the street door at the bottom of the stairs. A wave of panic swept through the entire room as everyone looked up with a start as though a thunderbolt had just struck the roof.

'Coppers!' whispered Mick, springing to his feet. 'It's them! I knew they'd come!'

'Keep calm!' replied Rose, who finished what she was doing, and quietly got up from her knees. 'There's nuffin' they can do.'

'Wot d'yer mean?' snapped Mick, who was desperately looking round the room for a quick way to escape. 'If they see Gus like this, they'll know where 'e's bin!'

Rose watched Mick's agitation with disdain, only too aware that he was the one who had lured her big brother into the dangerous game of political street fights. In those few tense moments, she found it hard to believe that she had once fancied this tough bruiser who could go to pieces at the first sign of danger. 'They won't find out where 'e's bin,' she said coolly. 'Not if we just keep calm.' Then she started to move quickly, first of all taking the bowl of salted water to the sink and pouring it away. 'Polly!' she called urgently, as she hurried back from the sink. 'Bring me that quart bottle of brown ale – the one Dad brought 'ome from the off-licence last night. It's underneaf the bed. 'Urry up!'

Polly did as she was told.

Rose was now taking off her blood-marked apron. 'Millie! Go an' cut some slices of bread.'

'Slithes of bread?' asked Millie. 'What for?'

'Don't ask questions? 'Urry!'

Millie, obeying her sister without further question, hurried across to get a loaf out of the cupboard.

Just as Polly brought the bottle of brown ale, there was another, more impatient banging on the street door downstairs. Polly, looking ashen white, gasped.

'Stay calm,' said Rose reassuringly. Then she took the bottle of ale from Polly, and unscrewed the cap. 'Now go downstairs and answer the door.'

'Me?' gulped Polly nervously.

Rose gave her a smile, and kissed her young sister on the forehead. 'There's nothin' ter worry about, Polly. Yer wanna 'elp Gus, don't yer?'

Polly nodded. 'Yeth.'

'Then just go downstairs, open the door quietly, and tell 'oever's there that yer mum an' dad are out, an' that yer shouldn't let strangers in uninvited. Okay?'

'Yeth.' Polly rushed to the door.

Polly opened the door and turned.

'Take yer time,'

Polly took renewed courage from her sister's reassuring smile, and calmly left the room. As she went slowly down the stairs, there was more banging on the street door, this time more vigorous. And then a man's voice could be heard calling through the letter box: 'Open up! Police!'

'Wot am I goin' ter do? Wot am I goin' ter do?'

As Rose rushed across to her brother, she had forgotten

all about Mick Hawkins, who was pacing up and down the room like a crazed dog.

'Get yerself down to the lav in the back yard!' she ordered, nodding towards a door at the side of her mum and dad's bed. 'Use that door over there.'

Mick didn't have to be told twice. He made a dash for the door, and disappeared immediately.

'Lock yerself in 'til I tell yer!' Rose yelled in as loud a voice as she dared.

Then, to Gus's astonishment, Rose went across to him and poured some brown ale all over the front of his shirt.

'Rose! Wot the bleedin' 'ell are yer . . .?'

'Drink!' she snapped bossily.

'Wot?'

'Do as I say! Drink!'

Rose put the bottle up to his lips, and poured so much brown ale down his throat that he was practically choking.

'Stop it, Rose!' spluttered Gus, with brown liquid seeping out of his mouth, down his chin.

'As much as you can!' Rose was virtually forcing the drink down him. Then, as she heard footsteps coming up the stairs, she quickly poured more of the stuff over his shirt and jacket.

By the time the door opened, Rose had completely composed herself.

'Thith gentleman is from the polithe station,' announced Polly, at her most demure.

A burly-looking constable was standing in the doorway. He was so tall, he had to stoop to enter. With him was another man, but he was smaller and was wearing civilian clothes – a raincoat and trilby hat.

'Are you Augustus Humble?' boomed the constable, looking straight past Rose to Gus, whose head was once again slumped down across the table.

Rose immediately answered for him. 'Yes, that's Gus. I'm 'is sister Rose. Wot can I do for yer?'

Rose's cheeky response took the copper slightly aback. 'We'd like ter know 'is whereabouts from ten o'clock this mornin' ter five o'clock this evenin'.'

'Wouldn't we all!' Rose came back, quick as a flash. 'Though it's not 'ard ter guess, eh, mister?'

In the background, Millie was at the draining board, spreading marge on to endless slices of bread, whilst her twin sister was busily poking the empty fire grate.

'What's that supposed to mean, young lady?' This time it was the constable's plain-clothes companion who asked the question.

'Well – take a whiff for yerself,' replied Rose dramatically, as she stood out of the way and allowed the two men to approach Gus. 'Bin at it since dinner time.'

The two men drew close to Gus. The stench of beer was overpowering.

'Phor!' sniffed the constable, trying to fan away the sour smell of brown ale. ''Ow much 'as this one 'ad then?'

Rose shrugged her shoulders. ''E was at it soon after we'd finished the bread an' butter puddin'. 'E's always the same when Mum and Dad go out for the day. Yer know what they say – when the cat's away . . .'

The plain-clothes man did not react. Rose thought he had a sinister face, like someone who looked more dead than alive, and he never once raised his eyes to look at her.

The constable lifted Gus's head to look at his face.

Gus, who had by now realised what Rose was up to, played along with her by groaning, swivelling his eyes, and appearing to be thoroughly drunk.

'Yer know, I could charge 'im for this,' growled the constable, staring disapprovingly into Gus's face.

Rose felt her heart miss a beat. 'Charge 'im? For wot?'

Still holding Gus's chin up, the constable turned to look back at Rose. 'For drinkin' alcohol under age.'

Gus retched, as though he were about to be sick. The constable quickly dropped the boy's head back onto the table with a thud.

Rose breathed a sigh of relief, but was alarmed when she suddenly noticed Gus's blood-stained trouser leg stretched out beneath the table. 'Me an' my sisters was just about ter 'ave somefin' for our supper,' she said, quite chirpily, whilst discreetly placing herself in front of Gus to block the plain-clothes man's view. 'Is that bread an' marge ready yet, Millie?' she called, over her shoulder.

'Yeth, Rowthe,' squeaked Millie's timid voice, as she reluctantly came forward carrying a large plate of bread and margarine.

Rose helped herself to a slice, and immediately bit a huge lump out of it. With her mouth full, she took the plate from Millie and offered it to the two coppers. 'Want some?'

The constable, po-faced, and well used to this kind of cheek from street kids like Rose, shook his head. 'Just make sure your bruvver keeps away from the East End. 'Cos if 'e don't – we'll be watchin' 'im. 'Im – *and* 'is pals. Right?'

Rose swallowed what bread and marge she had left in her

mouth. 'The East End ain't our patch, mister. It's much better in the market.'

The constable exchanged a brief icy look with her, and then made his way swiftly out of the room. His plain-clothes companion let him go, but paused before following him down the stairs. Turning to throw a quick glance at Rose, his face suddenly broke into an awful death-like smile. Only then did Rose realise that the man had a tiny scar just beneath his right eye. 'How old are you, young lady?'

To Rose, the man's voice sounded posh and not a bit like anyone she'd heard in the market. 'Fifteen,' she lied confidently. 'Goin' on sixteen.'

For a brief moment the plain-clothes man just stared at her, his mouth curled up at the ends in a knowing smile. Then, without another word, he left the room.

Everyone waited in hushed silence until they heard the street door close downstairs. Then the twins let out a great yell of relief, rushed across to Rose and hugged her. 'You woth wonderful, Rowthe!' proclaimed Millie, kissing her older sister over and over again on one cheek. 'Abtholutely wonderful!' proclaimed Polly, who was planting just as many kisses on Rose's other cheek.

Whilst all this was going on, Gus, fag in mouth, eased himself up from his chair and hobbled across to join them. 'Fanks, Rose,' he said, with difficulty. 'Yer saved the day.'

Rose broke free from the twins to stare him straight in the face. 'Saved it? I di'n't save nuffink. But I'll tell yer somefin', Gus.' With the back of her hand she wiped her lips, which were still greasy from the bread and marge she had gulped down. 'One of these days they're goin' ter catch up wiv yer. An' it'll be yer own fault.' There was concern and anxiety in her voice as she spoke. ''Cos when you and yer mates get into punch-ups wiv these scummy Blackshirts, yer doin' exactly wot they want yer ter do. Don't yer understand that, Gus? Don't yer?'

Gus could do nothing but lower his eyes guiltily.

Rose sighed despondently and left the room. On the landing outside, she paused briefly before going upstairs to her bedroom. But as soon as she started to climb the stairs she remembered Queenie was up there, and it made her depressed to think about how her younger sister would be gloating over Gus's brush with the coppers. So she stopped halfway, sat down on one of the stairs, leant her head back against the banisters, and closed her eyes.

Her mind was racing. Thank God her mum and dad hadn't come home while the coppers were there. But then, she thought, even if her mum and dad had come home, would they have known how to cope with the situation? Gus was a rebel with a mind of his own. There was nothing you could say that would change his ways. You just had to be as strong-willed as he was. It wasn't a question of Rose trying to boss her big brother around. But someone had to be strong with him, to be strong with the whole family. And as much as Rose loved her mum and dad, she knew only too well that they were just not up to it. She sighed deeply, forlornly. The future. What future would there be in store for the Humble family?

As she sat there with her eyes still closed, Rose's stomach felt like jelly, and she suddenly realised that her whole body was shaking from head to foot.

In this first quiet moment she had had all day, Rose no longer felt like a fifteen-year-old. In the course of one horrifying evening, she had felt so much older.

Chapter 5

Rose adored her twin sisters, Polly and Millie. To her they
were everything young sisters should be – funny, sweet-
natured, clever, and good company. That is not to say that
the twins were saints, for they occasionally had a slanging
match with each other, usually over a boyfriend that they
had both fallen for. In fact they were always getting crushes
on boys, and now that they had reached sixteen the rivalry
was becoming intense.

Rose was very proud of the fact that they were the
brightest members of the Humble family, who had not only
won scholarships at school but had since got very good jobs
in the Islington Public Library. Polly, the more confident
twin, had quickly become familiar with every book in the
classic literature department, and Millie, who had a
tendency to be slightly shy, relished her work getting to
know all about art and music. In Rose's eyes, her two
young sisters were the classy ones in the family. To their
scruffy younger brother, George, however, they were 'too
clever by half'.

Apart from Rose and their mother, the twins' greatest
friend was undoubtedly the owner of the piano shop, Mr
Popov.

Oleg Popov, now in his late seventies, was an émigré
from the Russian Revolution. Born in the Ukraine, he
and his wife, Ludmilla, had, in 1917, fled from the
violence their country had been plunged into. They were
aristocrats and would have faced certain death if they
had remained behind. Unfortunately, Ludmilla was too
stressed and weak to survive the long journey across
Europe, and had died of heart failure soon after the
couple had reached Paris. Thoroughly dispirited, Mr
Popov arrived in England and spent the money he had
smuggled out of Russia on the old piano shop in a street
close to Chapel Market. Once the Humble family had
moved in as lodgers, he felt confident enough to buy a
little flat for himself in the Holloway Road. For the last
two years thanks to Polly and Millie Humble, his life had
taken on a new meaning.

Each evening, after Mr Popov had gone home, the twins
had taken to sneaking downstairs to the shop, and, sitting
side by side on the piano stool, gradually taught themselves
to play basic popular songs. Although she strongly disapproved of the liberty they were taking, Rose often went
down to listen to her young sisters, and was utterly
entranced by their dual rendering of piano pieces such as
'Chopsticks' and 'God Save the King'. But one evening,
when the upright piano was echoing to the sound of two
pairs of hands playing 'The Blue Danube', Rose and the
twins were suddenly horrified to hear Mr Popov's fractured
English calling to them through the shop window, 'Vot is
zat terrible noise you are making!'

Convinced that Mr Popov would now evict the family for
the liberty the twins had taken, Rose was all ready to plead

forgiveness. But to her surprise, there was a broad grin on the old man's face as he entered the shop.

'Play zat again!' demanded Mr Popov, taking off his brown velvet trilby hat to reveal a mass of white hair.

Whilst the twins performed their double act, too terrified to let their small fingers hit a wrong note, Mr Popov sat on one of the other piano stools, twisted the ends of his white bushy moustache between his fingers, and listened. When it was over, he told the twins that he would only forgive them for what they had done if they promised to come down to his shop every Saturday afternoon from that moment on, and repeat their party piece for his customers. And before he went home he told Rose that if her young sisters would really like to play the piano, he himself would pay for them to have lessons.

And so for two years, Polly and Millie attended piano lessons once a week with Mrs Wheeler, who taught them in the sitting-room of her terraced house in Brooksby Street.

By 1939, the twins had exceeded even Mrs Wheeler's expectations. They had quickly learnt how to read music, to do scales and arpeggios, and in no time at all to play melodies, including parts of some of Chopin's preludes. For Mr Popov it was a wonderful return for his generosity. The twins not only played to him frequently, but their company and eager chatter brought him friendship after years of loneliness.

During the summer of that year, Rose found herself a job as a part-time waitress in a workman's café out at Bethnal Green Road in the East End. It meant taking a tram for some of the way, and then changing onto a bus, but R didn't mind travelling, for it gave her the chance to see other parts of London and the time to ponder over everything that was happening in her life. From the top deck of the bus she loved to watch the shops being opened in the morning, the horse-drawn beer wagons making their deliveries to the pubs, and flocks of pigeons fluttering around the feet of an old lady who regularly stopped to feed them in the small graveyard of a local church. One thing that she didn't like, however, were the newspaper bill-boards, which daily announced in bold letters some new crisis in Europe concerning Adolf Hitler. Every time Rose saw that man's name, a chill gripped her.

At the age of eighteen, Rose had become a truly striking young woman. Her hair seemed to be more scarlet-coloured than ever, and although she tied it back with a piece of ribbon for work, she continued to let it grow. She had also developed a well-rounded figure. If the fact that she was an eye-opener hadn't occurred to her before, it certainly did once she started her job at the café, where her customers were mainly red-blooded young men who worked at a local railway goods yard. After a while, Rose began to enjoy the attention she was getting, but she drew the line when she was occasionally touched up by a customer who was trying to show off to his mates. Our Rose was more than capable of hitting back with 'a good fourpenny one'.

By the end of the summer, Rose was not only taking more notice of boys, but she was becoming more conscious of the way she herself looked.

'Not much good lookin' at yerself if yer don't 'ave a feller do it for.'

In the Humble sisters' bedroom, Queenie was quick to notice her eldest sister studying herself in a full-length mirror behind the door.

Rose immediately moved away from the mirror. 'Don't talk such rubbish, Queen!' she said self-consciously. 'I was just lookin' ter see if I 'ad a ladder in me stockin's.'

Queenie grinned. 'I know a feller who can get some *real* silk stockin's. 'E nicked 'em off this lorry up the West End. If yer want, I could ask 'im ter get yer some.'

Rose immediately snapped back. 'Forget it, Queen! I don't want nuffin' that's bin nicked. An' if yer got any sense, neiver do you!'

'Fellers like ter see gels in a good pair of stockin's. It gives 'em ideas.'

'Shut up, Queen.' Rose sat on the edge of the bed and started to pull on the same pair of shoddy flat-soled shoes that she had worn practically every day for over two years. 'Yer don't know nuffin' about boys. Wiv you it's just wind, that's all.'

Queenie sniffed indignantly. But she was still grinning. 'That's wot *you* fink!'

For the past year or so, Rose's relationship with Queenie had more or less stabilised. It was a kind of truce where neither of them talked to each other more than was absolutely necessary, for if they did, it invariably ended in a row. But of late, Queenie had tried to be less cold and antagonistic towards her elder sister, and had even shown a willingness to have friendly chats with her. On her part, Rose had responded by helping Queenie get a job as a machine-setter in a local Small Arms factory.

'As a matter of fact I know someone 'oo fancies yer like mad.'

Rose hesitated briefly without looking at her sister. 'Now wot yer goin' on about?'

Queenie knew instinctively that Rose was interested, so she sat cross-legged on the bed at the side of her. 'I'm not kiddin'. 'E told my pal Josie Thomas 'e finks yer the sexiest fing 'e's ever seen. 'Is name's Michael.' Queenie leant forward, practically whispering into Rose's ear. 'Works up the City. Ever so posh.'

Rose quickly finished putting on her shoes and stood up. 'Cut it out, Queen! You ain't funny.'

'It's true – honest it is, Rose!' Queenie followed her sister to the door. ''E told Josie 'e's seen you gettin' off the bus on yer way 'ome from work. 'E nearly 'ad an 'eart attack when she told 'im she knew yer sister.'

Rose refused to listen and quickly opened the door. 'Look, Queen, why don't yer stop makin' up stories an' get on wiv yer own boyfriends? I ain't got time ter listen ter all this rubbish.'

Queenie took hold of Rose's arm and held on to it. 'Wot makes yer fink I'm makin' up stories? Yer're a real good-lookin' gel, Rose – everyone knows that. So why shouldn't a feller fancy yer if 'e wants ter?'

In the brief moment that followed, Rose asked herself that same question. Yes, she was a good-looking girl and she was getting noticed more and more by boys. Every time she walked through the market she got quite a few wolf whistles, and young Badger never stopped drooling every time he caught even a glimpse of her. And in that moment, Rose felt a surge of blood through her veins. It wasn't a feeling that she had experienced before, but she was certainly excited by the thought that a boy whom she didn't know actually fancied her.

'Would yer like ter meet 'im, Rose?'

Rose emerged from her moment of deep thought to find Queenie still holding on to her arm.

'I could get Josie ter fix it up. Yer'd 'ave the time of yer life.'

Rose suddenly brought Queenie back into focus. 'Oh Queen! Pack it up!'

She broke loose, and left the room.

On Sunday morning, the first Sunday in September, Rose slept in late. It was unusual for her; she was always up long before the rest of the family, with the exception of her mum who every day seemed to be up and about doing odd jobs no matter what time it was. But as she sat up in bed and rubbed her eyes, Rose knew that something was wrong because the large double bed was empty and she was totally alone – no twins or Queenie. The mystery intensified when she went to the window, opened it, and couldn't hear any Sunday morning sounds coming from Chapel Market. She quickly dressed and opened the door on to the landing. This only confirmed her worries, for both her brothers had already abandoned their mattress. At that moment she heard voices coming from her mum and dad's room on the floor below, so she immediately rushed downstairs to find out what was going on.

The whole family were huddled around the room with glum expressions on their faces, listening to the posh voices that were drifting out of the chunky walnut cabinet wireless set that their mum so proudly polished each day.

The moment Rose entered the room, she guessed what all the gloom was about. ''As it started then? Are we at war?'

Nellie's face crumpled with anxiety. She looked as though she were about to burst into tears.

'Chamberlain's comin' on at eleven,' said Albert, who was sending out great puffs of sour tobacco smoke from his pipe. 'Don't look good.'

Rose glanced at the small wooden clock on the mantelpiece over the oven grate. It showed two minutes to eleven. She crouched down on the floor between the twins and put her arms around their shoulders. They responded by leaning their heads on her shoulders, their mood reflecting the intense anxiety that was being projected by their mum and dad.

The next two minutes seemed to be the longest Rose had ever known. As she leant her head back against the pantry door beside the grate, her mind quickly blocked out the sombre posh voices that were mumbling inside the walnut cabinet. She closed her eyes, still seeing in her head her family's anxious faces. Mum and Dad had gone through one war already and knew what another would do to their family. These past few weeks had been a great strain on everyone, for the talk of war had dominated the streets, the pubs, the shops, and especially the newsreels at the Blue Hall Cinema in Upper Street, where there were endless pictures of Nazi soldiers jack-booting their way across Europe. Already all kinds of things like food, clothes and petrol were being rationed, and lights everywhere had to be blacked out by half-past seven in the evening. Even in the market the barrow boys could talk of nothing but war, and

how this Adolf Hitler bloke should be ''ung, drawn, an'
quartered'. Rose couldn't understand how grown men
could talk like this when they themselves would be the ones
who would have to go out to foreign countries and fight and
perhaps be killed, and it was this thought that chilled her.
In her mind's eye she could see her elder brother, Gus,
standing before her in a soldier's uniform, a gun strapped
across his shoulder ready to leap in and out of a muddy
trench like his dad had done in the last horrible war. Each
day Rose had shuddered as she passed newspaper billboards
with headlines such as: 'GENERAL MOBILISATION!'
and '*CONSCRIPTION FOR ALL MEN OF 20*'.

The sound of Big Ben booming out the hour from the
walnut cabinet suddenly brought Rose back to earth with a
bump. As her eyes sprang open, the first thing she saw was
Gus, sitting on the edge of his mum and dad's bed in the
back part of the room, listening intently to the wireless.
The sombre voice of the BBC Announcer said: 'We go now
to Number Ten Downing Street, for a personal message
from the Prime Minister, the Right Honourable Neville
Chamberlain, CH, MP.'

By the time the broadcast had ended, the Humble family
and millions like them had been told that they were now at
war with Germany.

When the Prime Minister had stopped speaking, Gus got
up from the bed, and turned off the wireless.

'An' about time too!' he barked. 'If this country 'ad
armed itself a few years ago, we could've stopped 'Itler,
Mosley, an' all the rest of 'em fascist sods! Give me a rifle
an' bayonet an' I'll tell yer wot I'll do wiv 'em!'

'Don't Gus!' Rose held the twins firmly in her arms. Her

71

eyes were blazing with anger. 'Killin' people always involves more killin', then it goes on an' on. There's never any end ter it!'

Albert held Nellie close to him. 'Don't worry, gel,' he said gently. 'Mark my words, it'll all be over in a fortnight. 'Itler an' 'is lot ain't got a chance against the likes of us.'

By now the room was thick with tobacco smoke, Albert puffing hard on his pipe, Gus on his fourth Player that morning.

'Can I go down 'Ighbury Fields, Dad?' yawned young George, who had become very bored by the morning's drama.

'No!' Nellie, immediately alarmed, quickly broke loose from Albert. 'There's a war on, Georgie! It's dangerous ter go too far.'

Nellie's panicked response endeared her to all the family. To her surprise, everyone started laughing at her. 'Wot are yer all laughin' at?' she asked, nervously. 'Di'n't yer 'ear wot Chamberlain said? The war's started!'

This only made Queenie laugh even more. 'Don't be daft, Mum!' she spluttered. 'There ain't no Germans 'ere yet.'

'No, an' there won't be any eiver!' Albert smiled affectionately at his wife, and put a reassuring arm around her waist. 'They'll be lucky if they get any furver than Soufend Pier!'

The family laughter was in some way a relief of tension as much as anything else, but it stopped abruptly when a deafening wailing sound began echoing across the rooftops.

'Blimey!' said Albert, staring at the ceiling as though it was about to cave in on them.

'That's the air-raid siren,' said Rose, remembering the practice run of the dreaded sound just a few weeks before. 'It's comin' from the police station in Upper Street.'

'The Germans!' proclaimed George excitedly. 'They're comin' over ter bomb us!'

Nellie shrieked, which is exactly what George hoped she would do. 'Wot're we goin' ter do?' she yelled above the din.

'Everyone take cover!' Albert's quick thinking was a throwback to his Army training during the last war. 'Under the table! Quick as yer can!'

Absolutely terrified, the twins immediately obeyed.

'We can't all get under the table.' Needless to say, Queenie was the first to complain.

'Do as yer're told, Queen!' ordered her father. 'You too, Nell!'

Albert virtually pushed his wife and Queenie under the table, where they and the twins were quickly joined by Rose. It was a tight squeeze, with not an inch to spare.

'Come on, Georgie!' yelled Nellie. 'There's plenty of room.'

George tried to crawl under the table, but try as he may, the only parts of his body he was able to protect were his arms. 'I can't get under 'ere!' he grumbled. 'There ain't no room!'

'Over 'ere, son! Quick!'

Albert and Gus grabbed hold of George's feet and dragged him out from under the table.

'In the cupboard, boy! Come on now!'

Albert opened the door of one of the two cupboards on either side of the oven grate. The bottom half was full of cleaning cloths, polish, a bucket, brooms and mops. In just a few seconds, Albert and Gus had cleared everything out that they could.

'I'm not goin' in there!' scowled George, who tried to get away.

'In!'

Gus grabbed his brother around the waist, practically threw him into the cupboard, and slammed the door.

'Let me out!' yelled George angrily. 'I can't breeve!'

'Under the bed, Gus!'

Albert led the way, as he and his eldest son fell to the floor on their stomachs, and inched their way under the narrow opening on opposite sides of the large double bed.

''Urry!' squealed the terrified Nellie at the top of her voice. 'They're on their way over. I'm sure I can 'ear planes!'

Then there was an eerie silence, only broken when a dreadful thought suddenly occurred to twin Millie. 'We haven't got our gas masks.'

Nellie gasped. All the family had been issued with gas masks which they had been fitted for at the Town Hall at least four weeks ago. But, like most other people, after a great deal of fun scaring each other by parading around the place in them, they had put the awful smelly masks back into their square cardboard boxes, and tucked them away into the loft above the landing.

'Don't worry,' Rose said in a low reassuring voice. 'There won't be any gas. 'Cept from Dad's pipe!'

All three giggled nervously, and then there was silence again.

The following few minutes seemed like hours. Poor Nellie was convinced she could hear German warplanes flying overhead. But when, after only a very short time, the air-raid siren wailed its one-tone all clear sound, nobody could believe that they had taken so much trouble to take cover for what had turned out to be a false alarm.

The following day started, as far as Rose was concerned, just like any other. She took her usual tram and bus to work in Bethnal Green Road, and watched all her regular favourite sights on the route. It was only when she got to the café that she was really conscious that this was the first day of war.

On working days the café was usually full during the morning as casual customers from the nearby railway goods yard popped in to have a quick cup of tea and a sugared rock cake. But today was different. The place was practically deserted but for old Duggie, who sold newspapers on the corner of the road.

'Fings're goin' ter be different from now on,' said the scruffy old codger, the perpetual dewdrop at the end of his nose in danger of dropping into his cup of tea. 'Looks like yer'll 'ave ter get used ter us old 'uns, eh, Rosie gel?'

Rose wiped his table with a damp cloth. 'Wot d'yer mean, Dug?'

Even though he had no sugar in his cup, the old newsvendor kept stirring his tea. 'They take the young 'uns first. Then there's nuffin' left 'cept the dregs – like me.' He looked up, and as he grinned, Rose could see that there wasn't a tooth left in his mouth. 'That's war for yer, eh, gel?'

Rose liked old Duggie, and tried to smile – the old slump had only said what she already knew – but all she could think about were the blokes of her own age who were such a part of her life – like Gus, and Badger and all her other young mates in the market. She had listened to them so many times, bragging and boasting about what they would do to Hitler and his lot when they were called up for the Army. Rose's stomach churned as she considered the thought that some of them, including her own brother Gus, might never return. War! How she hated the very sound of the word.

'Reckon it'll be up ter you now, gel,' spluttered old Duggie, as the dewdrop finally dropped into his tea. 'You gels're goin' ter 'ave ter take over some of the jobs yer've never done before. Gord 'elp yer!'

Wiping his nose on the back of his hand, he pulled a few coppers out of his raincoat pocket, dropped them on the table, and left the café.

Rose watched him go, then picked up the coppers from the table, thinking about what the old man had said. It was probably true. If the war went on for any length of time, girls and older people would have to take on the jobs left behind by the boys. Someone would have to make the ammunition for the guns and all the other weapons that were going to be needed to fight the war. And what about all the jobs at home – tram and bus conductors, porters on the railways, the police, fire brigade, ambulance drivers – the list was endless?

At lunch time, there were only four customers in the café

and most of those were elderly or middle-aged men from the rail yard. Even Mr Ridley, the café proprietor, looked anxious. 'If this is 'ow it's goin' ter be, Rosie, I don't 'old out much 'ope for this place.'

Rose left the café at her usual time soon after a midday meal. On the way home she subconsciously scanned the streets below to see how many young fellers were around. There seemed to be fewer than usual, and although she realised that they wouldn't just be plucked off the streets overnight and thrown into the Army, she did have a nagging feeling inside of how awful it would be to go through life without having any boys of her own age to talk to.

When she got off the tram in Upper Street, Rose ambled slowly back towards Chapel Market. She stopped briefly at the sweet shop near the corner of Liverpool Road to buy her mum two penn'orth of her favourite fruit pastilles. While she was sorting through the loose change in her purse, she was startled to hear someone talk to her from behind.

'Hallo, Rose.'

Rose turned. The boy talking to her was no more than her own age, with devastating good looks. At least, that's what Rose thought. And although it was quite a warm afternoon, he was dressed in a fine three-piece suit and a trilby hat, which he took off the moment she looked at him.

'I'm sorry,' Rose replied. Her eyes were wide, and she had the most peculiar feeling inside. 'Don't fink I know yer, do I?'

When the young man smiled at her with the largest blue

eyes she had even seen, Rose thought her legs would give way beneath her.

'You don't know me, but I certainly know you.'

Rose was almost mesmerised by the soft, cultured voice. She eagerly shook the hand that the young man was offering to her.

'I believe your sister knows Josie. She's a mutual friend. I think she might have told you about me.'

By now, Rose's heart was beating so fast, she thought it might explode.

'My name's Michael. Michael Devereaux. But I hope you'll call me Mike.'

Chapter 6

For the next two hectic weeks, Rose was convinced that she was in love. Although she had only met Michael Devereaux for a drink in the Angel pub one Saturday lunch time, he had treated her like no other boy had ever done before. It wasn't just that his manners were impeccable, but that he had a way of looking at her that made her feel she was someone special. Rose had never felt so good in all her life, and she could hardly believe that it was Queenie who had made it all possible. Life had suddenly taken on a completely new meaning for Rose, and when Michael asked her out for their first date on the third Sunday in September, she practically counted the days, hours, and minutes to the time when they were due to meet.

As Rose made her way home after work one evening, she noticed that little seemed to have changed since Mr Chamberlain's sombre broadcast about the start of the war with Germany. Everyone was going about their business in exactly the same way, and although some food and clothing was not as plentiful as it used to be before the war, the shops were open as usual. Of course, there were signs that more and more young men were being conscripted. Some

of Rose's friends from the market seemed to have disappeared overnight. Luckily Badger was still too young to
be one of them.

'Wotcha, Ginge! Where yer bin all me life?'

As she passed the vegetable stall in the market, she
could easily recognise Badger's cheeky voice above the
shouts of the other traders offering bargains to potential
customers.

''Allo, Badge.' There was a bit of condescension in
Rose's smile. 'Busy are yer?'

'Never too busy for you, darlin'.' Badger wiped his hands
on his baggy trousers, and left his grandfather, Mr Cabbage,
to carry on serving their customers queuing at the stall.
'Don't see yer much down the market these days. I've
missed yer.'

Rose shrugged her shoulders. 'I 'ave ter work, yer know.
Takes me a time ter get back an' forth ter Befnal Green.'

'Got somefin' ter ask yer,' Badger said, taking hold of
one of her hands. 'It's important, so yer can't say no.'

Rose had a sinking feeling inside her stomach. She could
see that puppy-love look in Badger's eyes again, and didn't
know how to react. But she had long ago decided that
whatever she did, she would never hurt him, so she merely
smiled back at him weakly.

'It's me birfday next Sunday. I'm eighteen. Gran and
grandad are givin' me a party. Some of the gang round 'ere
are comin'.' He drew closer, and squeezed her hand. 'Yer
will come, won't yer Ginge? It wouldn't be the same if you
weren't there.'

Rose felt her stomach turn to ice. Badger's eighteenth
birthday – and on the same day that Michael was taking her

out on their first date. And even if she wasn't going out that day, she wouldn't want to go to Badger's party, because people would think that she was his girlfriend. Oh hell, she thought! What could she do? What could she say that wouldn't hurt Badger's feelings? Luckily, before she had the chance to reply, Mr Cabbage called out from behind the vegetable stall.

'Come on, son! We got customers, yer know!'

Badger turned and yelled back, 'Comin', Grandad!' Then he quickly returned to Rose. 'So – 'ow 'bout it, Ginge? Yer won't let me down, will yer?'

'I – I . . .' All Rose could do was to splutter.

This was enough for Badger, who decided that Rose's hesitation meant that she would come to his birthday party. After giving her a quick hug, he rushed back behind the stall, calling, 'See yer on Sunday at six. Don't yer be late – or else!'

For a moment, Rose just stood there, too disturbed to move. Then she took a deep breath, and rushed off into the crowds.

When Rose got home, George was having a tooth pulled out. It was not a sight that any of the family relished, but George always made such a fuss when he went to see Mr Toynbee, the dentist in Essex Road, that his terrified shouts usually scared away all the other patients in the waiting room. Besides, as Albert always said, it was a lot cheaper to do it at home.

'Why do I 'ave ter 'ave me toof out?' George complained bitterly. 'It don't 'urt.'

'That's not wot yer've bin sayin' all week.' His dad was busily tying a piece of string to the landing door knob.

'D'yer 'ave to, Dad?' Rose shuddered at the thought of her young brother's ordeal. She could almost feel her own tooth aching in sympathy. 'Surely it's loose enough ter come out on its own by now?'

'Yeah!' groaned George. 'Look!' Mouth wide open, he searched for the offending tooth in the middle of the lower set, and wriggled it with two fingers.

'Come 'ere!'

Albert had no mercy. Grabbing his son firmly by the shoulder, he swung him round and attached the other end of the piece of string to the wobbly tooth.

'No, Dad! Wait!' The squeal came from Polly, who had been sitting on her mum and dad's bed, trying to deafen the sounds of George's extraction by covering her head with a pillow. But the tension was too much for her. 'Let me get out first!'

Polly leapt up from the bed, and rushed straight out of the room. If it hadn't been for Rose, she would have slammed the door and pulled George's tooth out before the instrument of torture was properly in place.

Luckily, Rose was not at all squeamish. 'It's all right, Georgie,' she said, standing behind the boy and putting her arms around him. 'Just close yer eyes. It'll be over before yer've 'ad time ter fink about it.'

'But I *am* finkin' about it!' George was now trying to talk with the piece of string pulled taut on his wobbly tooth. 'Don't do it, Dad! Please . . .!'

The sound of Albert slamming the door hard competed with George's deafening yell.

'Ow . . .!'

Rose was convinced that the murderous sounds he was

making would be heard at least as far as the Nag's Head in Holloway, nearly four miles away.

The wobbly tooth had gone flying into the air at the end of the piece of string. George immediately broke loose from his sister's grasp and in a state of high anguish rushed around the room clutching his mouth, which was now firmly shut.

Rose took a cup, put a pinch of salt into it, then pushed the cup into George's hand. 'Take this down to the yard an' get yerself some water, Georgie. Then wash yer mouf out 'til all the blood's gone. It'll soon feel better.'

Groaning profusely behind the hand that was covering his bleeding gums, George tore out of the rear door.

'Yer can tell 'e's an 'Umble, all right. Just look at that!' Albert was proudly holding up George's tooth, which was still connected to the piece of string.

Rose didn't look at all happy. 'Yer know, Dad, I don't fink we oughta pull teef on our own. We should leave it ter the dentist.'

'Get orf!' Albert took George's tooth to the empty rubbish pail, and dropped it in with a clang. 'Yer grandad always pulled my teef. Never did me no 'arm.'

Rose knew there was no point in arguing with her dad. Love him as she did, she knew that he was very set in his ways. 'Wot time's Mum comin' 'ome?'

For some reason, Albert pretended he hadn't heard. He just rolled down his shirt sleeves and buttoned them up.

Rose persisted. 'Dad? Wot time does Mum get 'ome from work?'

'She's goin' ter be a bit late. I fink yer'd better make the sandwiches ternight.'

Rose was suddenly puzzled. For the past few months, her mum had given up cooking snacks for the stalltraders in the market, and had got a job working as an assistant cook in the kitchens at the Royal Northern Hospital in the Holloway Road. But she was always home in time to get the family's tea. 'Is anyfin' wrong, Dad?'

Albert looked up. 'Wrong? Nah. Course not – why?' Then he sighed, and scratched the back of his head, always a sign that he was worried about something. 'Well, ter tell yer the truth – Gus 'as gone ter meet 'er. 'E's got somefin' ter tell 'er on 'is own, wivout us lot makin' fings worse.'

Now Rose was really concerned. 'Makin' fings worse? Dad? Wot yer talkin' about?'

Albert was never a man of many words, so he used the business of filling his pipe with tobacco to help him say what he had to. 'Yer bruvver – 'e's got 'is callin'-up papers.'

Rose clutched her hand to her chest. 'Wot?'

''E 'ad a letter this mornin'. 'E come 'ome early from work an' told me. 'Ad the medical already. A-one. Course 'e is. Fit as a fiddle, just like all the 'Umbles.'

Rose was so shattered, she had to sit down at the table. 'But – 'e's only just 'ad 'is twentief birfday. They can't take 'im already.'

'Oh they can, Rosie. Callin'-up age's twenty. They've gotta move fast. 'Itler's marchin' inter France. If we don't stop 'im, 'e'll be in Buckin'am Palace before Christmas.'

Rose leant her elbows on the table and rested her chin on them. 'I can't bear it, Dad. Gus in the Army. It's 'orrible! If anyfin' should 'appen ter 'im, I don't know wot I'd do.'

Albert sat opposite her, put his pipe down into the top of an empty Zubes tin, and took hold of her hands. 'Listen, gel. Gus'll be all right. 'E's got a good 'ead on 'im – knows 'ow ter take care of 'imself.' He sighed. 'The one I'm worried about is yer mum.'

As her father lowered his eyes, Rose noticed for the first time that he was no longer the young man who used to carry her piggyback on his shoulders when she was a little girl. There were lines around the edges of his mouth, and small puffed-up bags were beginning to form under his eyes.

'She knew this was comin', Rosie. Bin dreadin' it ever since the war started. That's why Gus wanted ter tell 'er on 'is own.' Albert looked up at Rose again. 'She's goin' ter take it 'ard – real 'ard.' He leant back in his chair and aimlessly stroked the day's stubble on his chin. 'She'll feel like a part of 'er own body's bin taken away from 'er.'

Rose had been feeling sorry for herself, but now she realised that, despite feeling proud of having a son who was going to fight in the war just as he had once had to, Dad was going to feel as much pain as everyone else in the family, parting with Gus. 'Don't worry, Dad.' She got up from her chair, and went to him. 'We'll keep an eye on Mum – you *and* me.'

In his heart of hearts, Albert had always known that Rose was so much stronger than he, stronger probably than all the family put together. He didn't know where she got it from, only that whatever happened during this war, his eldest daughter was the one he could always rely upon. 'I can't bear it when yer mum gets upset,' he said, almost like a child. 'She's bin so good ter me since we got married, never argued or lost 'er temper, stood by me all the time I've bin out of work. I don't know wot I'd 'ave done wivout 'er all these years, Rosie – honest I don't.'

Rose couldn't bear to see her dad like this. He was such a strong-looking man, but inside he was as soft as a marshmallow, and had always found it difficult to face up to a crisis. Rose knew how much he loved her mum. The two of them were so well matched, and they had such a wonderful unspoken understanding of each other. As she watched his face crumple up with anxiety, she stroked the back of his head, and smoothed down the prematurely greying hairs that looked as though they needed a comb through them. 'Some'ow we'll get through this war, Dad,' she said, almost in a whisper. 'It ain't goin' ter be easy, but we'll get fru it – you'll see.'

The two of them didn't say another word to each other. They didn't need to.

Half an hour later, Rose decided to wash her hair. As there was no tap in either of the family's two rooms, she had first of all to boil up a kettle of water, wash her hair in an enamel bowl of warm water in the girls' bedroom, then rinse it under the cold water tap in the back yard. Luckily the September weather was still quite mild, so there was no great hardship in doing all this in the open air. And her hair felt really good when she dried it with a towel, for on her way home from work she had stopped at Mrs Jangler's toiletries stall in the market, and lashed out on a twopenny shampoo, a luxury she hadn't treated herself to in a long time. For a few minutes she sat down on one of Mr Popov's old broken piano stools, and turned her face up to the day's last thin shaft of sunshine which was just filtering through a gap in the tall houses bordering the tiny back yard. Many a time Rose had come out into the yard to ponder over her problems. For her it was a kind of refuge, the only place where she could grab a few minutes of peace and quiet away from the family. When the war had started a fortnight ago, Mr Popov had wondered whether the family wanted to have an Anderson shelter fitted in the yard, but they all declined the offer, saying that not only was there not enough room for such a horrible thing, but that if there were any air raids they would probably be just as safe inside their own two rooms.

As Rose ran her hand through her long red hair, her attention was suddenly drawn to a small brown sparrow perched on top of an empty milk bottle, chirping at her tetchily for something – anything to eat.

'Sorry, mate. Don't yer know there's a war on?' Rose said.

The sparrow seemed to understand, took flight, and searched for better luck in another back yard. For a few important minutes, Rose had managed to forget the aching feeling she felt inside her stomach, the feeling that her big brother was the first member of the family to leave home, and might never return.

When she got back to her bedroom, Rose found Queenie there, stripped down to bra and knickers, and cooling off after a hot day in the small arms factory where she worked.

'Guess 'oo I just saw.' Queenie, sitting in her usual cross-legged position on the bed, was taking large bites out of a rather hard apple. 'Your boyfriend, Michael.'

Rose looked up with a start. 'Where?'

''E was on the same tram as me. On 'is way 'ome from work. Did 'e tell yer about 'is job? Stocks and shares or somefin' – up in the City. Don't understand it all meself.

Got 'is own place in Canonbury Square. I tell yer, Rose, yer're on ter a good bet there!'

'Give over, Queen.' Rose carried on drying her hair with her towel. ''E ain't my boyfriend. We've only ever met once.'

Queenie was grinning mischievously, her mouth full of apple. 'That's not wot 'e finks. 'E never stopped talkin' about yer date wiv 'im this comin' Sunday. Says if the wevver's fine, 'e's goin' ter take yer out for a spin on 'is motorbike.'

Rose stopped drying her hair and swung round. 'Motorbike?'

Queenie shrugged her shoulders innocently. 'Don't ask me. That's wot 'e said. Sounds like yer in for a good ride!'

'Queen!' Rose turned away in embarrassment as her sister roared with laughter at her own dirty joke.

'No, but seriously, Rose, Michael does like yer. 'E likes yer an awful lot. 'E's a nice feller. Bit different from some of the one-tracked dregs round 'ere.' Queenie waited a moment or so. While taking tiny bites out of the apple she was eating, she was watching her sister closely as she combed her waist-length hair at the mirror behind the landing door. 'There's only one fing, though,' she said, uncurling her crossed legs and getting off the bed, 'one fing Michael says he don't like about yer.'

Rose flicked her eyes up to watch Queenie's reflection in the mirror behind her. 'Don't like? Wot yer talkin' about?'

'This, Rose.' Queenie took a handful of Rose's damp hair in her hand.

''E don't like me 'air?'

''E don't like *long* 'air. Specially as long as yours. 'E says it don't suit yer. Reckons yer 'aven't got the right shaped face ter wear 'air this long.' Queenie, who was shorter in height than her sister, peered around from behind Rose's shoulders. 'Nuffin' ter do wiv me, of course. Wot d'yer fink, Rose?'

Rose stood there for a moment, just staring at herself in the mirror. She had never considered that her hair was such an important part of her, that it had anything to do with the shape of her face or anything else. All she had done was to let it grow over the years, and to tie it up in a bow whenever it got in the way. But the longer she stood there, the more she could understand what Michael was implying. Yes, she *did* have the wrong shape face for such long hair. And the more she thought about it, the more she disliked the way she looked. 'Maybe I could sweep it up be'ind me 'ead or somefin',' she said, and to demonstrate what she meant, she used both her hands to pile it high.

Queenie pulled a face and shook her head. 'Makes yer look like a schoolteacher.'

Rose immediately let her hair fall again. 'So wot do I do?'

Queenie hunched her shoulders. 'It's up ter you, Rose. I know wot I'd do if a feller like Michael fancied me.' She moved away from Rose, and sat on the edge of the bed.

Rose felt herself go cold. 'Cut it?' she asked, her voice barely audible. 'D'yer fink – I should cut it all off?'

'Short 'air's in fashion, Rose. Got somefin' ter do wiv the war I suppose. I reckon I'll do the same meself sooner or later.'

Rose swallowed hard, then turned to look back at herself in the mirror, trying hard to imagine herself with short hair. 'Yer really fink it – it would suit me?'

Queenie smiled just slightly. 'I tell yer, Rose, long 'air don't do nuffin' ter 'elp yer good looks.'

Rose lowered her eyes, and for several moments she didn't utter a word. When she did speak again, she had made up her mind. 'Will yer do it for me, Queen? Will yer – *please*.'

A few minutes later, Rose was sitting on a hard wooden chair. A towel had been placed around her shoulders, and Queenie was using a large pair of kitchen scissors to cut Rose's long hair. As she heard the scissors clicking away behind her, Rose felt her heart beating faster and faster.

Every chunk of hair that Queenie was cutting from Rose's head fell on to the bare floorboards, and soon, the chairlegs were engulfed by a heap of silky, scarlet tresses, which glistened beneath the dim glow of the electric light.

While it was happening, Rose kept her eyes closed. She felt as though a large part of her life was also being cut away from her.

Chapter 7

Most of the Humble family did not take to Rose's short hair. Polly thought it made Rose's neck look too long, like a giraffe, and Millie criticised the way Queenie had hacked at it. Young George said it made her look more bossy than ever, just like the hated maths teacher he used to have at school. Gus thought it was a good idea for Rose to have a hairstyle that made her look different from any of her sisters, but Albert Humble wasn't so sure. He cherished memories of Rose's long hair.

The only person who had no real comment to make on Rose's new look, was her mum. As expected, Nellie Humble had been devastated by the news of Gus's conscription into the Army. When he had come to meet her as she left work at the hospital, she knew immediately that her worst fears had been realised. As she lay awake, snuggled up in Albert's arms, she watched the first light of the day filtering through a chink in the new blackout curtains. All night long she lay there, turning over in her mind what it would mean to her and the rest of her family if anything should happen to Gus. Her eyes only closed when she heard the usual two pigeons billing and cooing on the windowsill outside. But by then, of course, it was time to get up.

As Rose was to discover, there was clearly a lot more on her mum's mind. On Saturday afternoon, they stopped to rest on a wooden bench in Islington Green after one of their regular window-shopping strolls down Upper Street.

'Rosie, there's somefin' I've bin meanin' ter talk ter yer about. Somefin' I want yer ter do for me.'

Rose dug deep into the bag of broken sweet biscuits she had just bought in the market. When she found a piece of digestive biscuit, she gave it to her mum.

Nellie took the biscuit piece. 'Wiv this war goin' on, I've got ter be prepared.'

Until this moment, Rose had not listened to her mum too carefully. But when she heard the way she was talking, she gave her an immediate scolding look. 'Now, Mum, I know yer upset about Gus bein' called up . . .'

'No. It's got nuffin' ter do wiv Gus. It's about yer dad, an' you, an' all the family.'

Rose sighed. Over her mum's shoulders, she could see Collins' Music Hall overlooking the Green, with its large posters advertising some forthcoming visit by Randolph ('On Mother Kelly's Doorstep') Sutton. 'Wot's wrong, Mum?'

Nellie hesitated. Although she was holding the piece of biscuit to her mouth, she wasn't actually eating it. 'If anyfin' should happen ter me—' she started.

'No, Mum!' Rose was suddenly irritated. 'I won't listen ter this!'

'Yer 'ave ter listen to it, Rosie!' Nellie responded firmly. 'We live in dangerous times. If they start bombin' us—'

Rose threw the bag of broken biscuits back into her shopping bag. ''Ow many times do I 'ave ter tell yer – there ain't goin' ter be no bombs! Look at the sky up there. D'yer see any Germans?'

'Not now. Not yet. But maybe.'

'Maybe! Maybe!' After she had huffed and snorted for a moment, Rose realised that she was being a little too insensitive. 'Look, Mum. Even if there was any bombin', we can take care of ourselves. The 'Umbles ain't useless, yer know. The council's buildin' a public shelter down Liverpool Road, an' we can always take cover down the tube.'

Nellie ignored everything Rose was saying. 'I've left a note,' she said calmly. 'It's in that tin box where I keep me bits an' pieces. Yer'll find it under the bed by the back wall. It'll tell yer everyfin' I want yer ter do if I go first.'

Rose, exasperated, leant back on the bench and glared at the grey sky, which was threatening rain.

'Don't be obstinate, Rosie.' Without realising it, Nellie had crumbled the biscuit piece in her hand. 'Yer've always bin obstinate – just like yer dad. It's no good. Sometimes we just 'ave ter face up ter facts. I've bin fru a war, remember. I know wot it's like. So does yer dad. It ain't pleasant, Rosie. From day ter day yer never know wot's goin' ter turn up.

'When Gus goes,' Nellie continued, half talking to herself, 'yer'll be the oldest one of the kids left. If anyfin' should 'appen ter me, Rosie, I'd want yer ter take care of the family . . .'

Rose snorted and tried to get up from the bench, but her mum grabbed her arm, and eased her down again.

'I know it's a lot ter ask of yer, Rosie, 'cos one of these days yer goin' ter find a nice young bloke of yer own, an' get married, an' 'ave yer own kids.' Then she sighed again. 'But the fact is, yer dad wouldn't know 'ow ter cope. 'E can't even boil an egg for 'imself. It scares me, Rosie. It scares me ter fink wot 'e'd do if I went first.'

Rose could bear no more. 'Mum! Yer far too young ter be talkin' like this.'

'In wartime, Rosie, bein' young's got nuffin' ter do wiv it. If yer don't make arrangements, yer could leave yer family in a terrible mess.' She threw her crumbs down on to the ground in front of her. 'Well, I won't 'ave it, Rosie. I'm determined ter be prepared.'

A fat sparrow immediately fluttered across to the biscuit crumbs.

'Now listen ter me, Rosie.' Nellie took hold of her daughter's hand. 'Please listen.'

Rose found herself staring straight into her mum's eyes. How ridiculous, she thought, that this woman should be talking about death when, despite her weariness after years of struggling to care for her family, she still looked so young.

'I've left instructions. It's all there in the note. Mind you, yer may not be able ter read it too well – yer know wot my writin's like!'

Rose tried to smile at Nellie's attempt to make light of what she was saying, but inside she felt only despair.

'Just do wot it says, Rosie, 'cos it's important ter me. Yer a good girl – always 'ave bin. So strong an' clear about wot yer doin'. Look after the family, Rosie. Look after 'em for me.'

Rose lowered her eyes. For a brief moment, she didn't know what to say. Finally she looked up. 'Mum, yer goin' ter be around for quite a time yet. There ain't goin' ter be no bombs round our way – believe me.'

Nellie smiled back at her gently. 'Yer won't let me down – will yer, Rosie?'

At their feet, the fat sparrow's head was bobbing up and down as he devoured the last few crumbs from Nellie's broken digestive biscuit.

On the wireless that evening, there was a report that two enemy aircraft had been sighted over the east coast of England. They had been quickly chased off by the RAF, and described by the Air Ministry as having posed no threat at all to any of the civilian population.

After Sunday dinner, Rose met up with Michael Devereaux outside the Angel pub in Upper Street. As it was three o'clock in the afternoon, the pub was just closing. Some of the people coming out worked in the market, so there were various calls of 'Wotcha, Rose gel!' and ''Ow are yer, Ginge?' A couple of Badger's mates also came out, so, remembering that she was not going to be able to get to Badger's birthday party that evening, Rose kept well out of sight.

Michael wasn't actually in the pub, but turned up on his Triumph motorbike, wearing a thick pullover, grey flannel trousers, and a face-free bike helmet.

'So where would you like to go, Rose?' he said, after lifting the heavy-looking machine on to its stand.

'I di'n't know yer 'ad a bike.' Rose wished she hadn't said that because it sounded really coy.

Michael smiled broadly, revealing a perfect set of white

teeth that were straight out of an advert in *Picture Post*. 'I've got quite a lot of interesting things that you don't know about.'

Rose didn't quite know how to take that remark, so she passed it off with a casual chuckle.

'I thought we'd go out into the country,' Michael said, his way of speaking softer and gentler than anything she had ever heard in the market. 'I know a nice little café just outside London. We could have some tea there, wander around a bit, then find a pub to have a drink when they open again. How about it?'

To Rose it sounded wonderful, but she didn't want to look too keen. 'Okay by me.'

A few minutes later they were speeding off down Upper Street, then into Holloway Road, passing under the Archway Bridge, and off towards Finchley, Barnet, and the open countryside of Hertfordshire. Being a pillion passenger on Michael's huge motorbike was the most exhilarating feeling Rose had ever experienced. With the wind battering against her face and whistling through her newly shorn hair, she clasped her arms tightly around Michael's waist as though her whole life depended on it. Soon she realised that her choice of cotton dress and cardigan had been unwise, for her legs and thighs were practically blue with the cold.

By the time they had left the populated streets of North London, Rose was seeing a world that she hardly knew existed. Since she had never ventured much further than Islington or Bethnal Green, the sight of green fields, hedges, and endless trees was little short of a revelation: wide open spaces with farm girls on tractors, and fields now cleared of crops. Even the grass seemed to be so much greener than the few blades she had seen popping up between the broken flagstones in the back yard of the piano shop. All this made Highbury Fields look like a small back garden!

They seemed to travel for miles out into the countryside, and there were long stretches where Rose couldn't detect a single person. All the signposts had been taken away in case they were of help to the enemy, so Rose had no idea where they were. Michael was a good rider, but the speed he travelled at set Rose's heart beating faster and faster, and it was only when they had to stop at a railway crossing that she felt the blood in her veins cooling. Once they were on their way again, that tingling sensation returned, for she could feel the warmth of his body as she snuggled up tight, with her face resting on one side on the back of his shoulders.

They eventually arrived at a small café called The Singing Kettle, away from the main road. When they got off the bike, they found the place shut and boarded up. On the front door someone had pinned a huge poster which showed a man and woman each with a shovel, and in thick lettering above:

FIGHT HITLER
DIG FOR VICTORY!

'Must be the war,' said Michael, taking off his helmet. 'Why do people have to be so stupid? This place would still be open if it wasn't for fools like Chamberlain.'

Rose looked puzzled.

'We should have been prepared, Rose. Now we're in it up to our eyebrows.' Realising he was becoming too serious, he smiled apologetically. 'Sorry about this.'

With eyes like that looking at her, thought Rose, she could forgive him anything. She smiled back. 'It's okay.'

Michael took out a packet of cigarettes from the saddlebag of his bike, and offered Rose one. 'Cigarette?'

Rose was about to shake her head. She hated cigarettes. She even hated the smell of other people smoking. But all the other girls of her age smoked these days, and smoking was fashionable. Just recently she had even caught sight of Queenie doing it when her mum and dad weren't around, so if Queenie could, why shouldn't she? 'Fanks,' she said, pulling a cigarette out of the packet.

Michael did likewise, took a lighter from the back pocket of his trousers, and lit both their cigarettes. As he did so, their eyes met, and Rose could feel him looking right inside her. But when he had lit her cigarette, and the sharp taste of nicotine started tearing at her throat, she practically choked. Oh God, she thought, if Dad could see me now, 'e'd kill me!

'Pubs'll be open in an hour or so,' Michael said, ignoring Rose's problem with the cigarette. 'Feel like a stroll?'

After exhaling a mouthful of smoke faster than she had puffed it in, Rose smiled and nodded. To her surprise, Michael put his arm around her waist, and they moved off down a winding lane. Whilst they were walking, Rose waited for the right opportunity, then dropped the partially smoked cigarette on to the path behind her. 'My sister Queenie tells me you work up in the City,' she said, trying to make polite conversation.

The last thing on Michael's mind was his work, but he duly answered, 'Yup. My father has a small business in Lloyd's.'

'Lloyd's? Wot's that?'

Michael turned to look at her. He grinned wryly, something he was constantly doing. 'Never heard of Lloyds of London, Rose? Tut-tut!'

Rose felt her stomach tense. Oh, why had she made such a fool of herself? Why didn't she just say, 'Yes, of course I know about Lloyds. I know *all* about Lloyds'? That's how Queenie would have answered.

'Don't go up that way much meself,' was all she could reply. When Michael suddenly leant across and kissed her gently on the neck, without thinking she added, 'Does that mean yer won't 'ave ter go in the Army then?'

To Rose's astonishment, Michael suddenly broke loose from her, his eyes flashing a moment of anger. 'What do you mean by that? Are you calling me a conscientious objector?'

Rose was stunned by his reaction. 'No, Michael!' she said quickly. 'Course I ain't. I just fought – well, 'avin' an important job like that—'

'As a matter of fact I've already applied for a commission in the Royal Engineers. But as I'm not twenty 'til the New Year, I can hardly be blamed for that, can I?'

Rose was so upset, she just didn't know what to say.

Michael threw his cigarette end to the ground, and stamped his foot on it. 'You shouldn't say things like that, Rose. I'm not a conchy! I'm not a coward! I hate bloody conchies!'

'That's not wot I meant, Michael – honest it ain't!'

99

When Michael saw the distress on Rose's face, he broke into a broad grin. Then he started to roar with laughter. 'Of course you don't mean it, Rose! Of course you don't!'

For a moment, Rose just stood there, watching him convulsed with laughter. 'Then wot yer laughin' at?'

'I've only just noticed. Your hair!'

Rose's hand immediately reached up to touch her hair. 'Wot's wrong wiv it?'

'You've had it cut!' Then, doubled up with laughter, he yelled, 'You look just like a chap I used to play rugby with!'

Rose was too horrified to speak. She slowly backed away from him, then suddenly turned, and ran off into the adjacent woods.

Michael stopped laughing immediately. 'Rose! Come back! I didn't mean it!'

Rose ran as fast as she could. She wanted to cry, but she felt far too hurt to do even that. The woods were thick, and she had no idea in which direction she was heading. But as she ran, Michael was not far behind her, calling amongst the tall pine and elm trees.

'Rose! Come back! It was only a joke!'

Rose ran as fast as she could, but the ground beneath her was rough with hidden weeds and broken tree stumps. She only stopped when she reached the edge of a large natural pond, covered in a profusion of tiny yellow-coloured wild water lilies.

Michael soon caught up with her. 'Rose,' he said, out of breath, 'why d'you have to take me so seriously? It was only a joke.'

Rose turned her back to him, and stared out at the pond.

'Look,' he said, moving up close behind her, 'I think your hair looks wonderful.'

'You told my sister you hated my long hair.'

'I think you look wonderful, Rose,' he said, putting his arms around her waist. 'As a matter of fact, I think you look – quite something.'

For a moment, the two of them said nothing, and just stared out at the pond, where a thin shaft of sunlight had filtered through the tops of the tall trees, and was now reflected on to a small patch of water on the pond. There, the waterlilies seemed to respond to the modest ray of light, for their petals were open wide and they spread a yellow glow throughout the dim shadows of the surrounding woods. Rose became conscious of the clean country air she was breathing, and the dozens or maybe hundreds of birds that were singing and calling to each other from the trees. Chapel Market seemed so far away!

After a while, Michael turned Rose around to face him. Then he put his hand under her chin and raised her face. As Rose stared into his eyes, she forgot everything that had happened a few minutes before, for her heart was racing again. Michael pulled her close to him, and she was watching his lips move slowly towards her own. The sensation she felt as he kissed her was electrifying. This was what she had longed for during all the restless nights she had had to share a bed with her three sisters. This was the first time a man had pressed his warm body, his warm lips against her own. She could feel the excitement running through her veins. Was this what everyone meant by love? Surely this must be love because this man was showing that he really cared for her? This was what she had been waiting for all her life, someone who was warm and gentle and who treated her as someone special. This surely had to be the kind of man she wanted to spend the rest of her life with, the man who would treat her as his equal.

When their lips finally parted, Michael was staring straight into Rose's eyes again. 'I want you, Rose,' he whispered. His hands were sliding down her back, and coming to rest on her rear cheeks.

There was now so much going through Rose's mind that she just couldn't say anything. She felt she ought to tell him to keep his hands to himself – but why? This was what she had wanted. This is what she had craved for. And when his lips started to kiss her neck, her ears, and then each of her breasts, she was breathing so hard that her face was burning with the rush of blood to her cheeks.

But when Michael's hands started to explore further, she pulled away in panic. 'No, Michael! No more. We've gone far enough.'

Michael looked surprised, almost hurt. 'Come on now, Rose,' he said impatiently. 'I'm ready for you.'

'It's too risky,' she replied, trying to pull away.

But Michael held her arms firmly, and pulled her back to him so that their lips were almost touching again. 'There's no risk. I've got something. There's no risk – I promise.' Then he kissed Rose so hard, that this time she could hardly breathe. When their lips parted he whispered into her ear, 'I love you, Rose.'

Rose was panting hard after that last aggressive kiss. 'Yer mean it? Yer really *do* mean it?' And she looked into his eyes to see if she could trust him. 'Yer love me?'

Michael smiled back earnestly. 'Of course I do. Can't you tell?'

For the next half-hour, they made love. For Rose, sharing her body for the first time with a man was bewildering and exciting. It was also not what she had expected, for until then, Michael had seemed to be so careful and gentle, the epitome of consideration. But when he made love, Rose was terrified. Michael's whole physical approach was like an animal, hardly stopping to realise that he might be hurting her. And hurt her he did, for her arms were sore and red from his grip, and her legs and thighs were throbbing with rough handling.

When it was all over, and they were lying on the ground flat on their backs, staring up at the little patch of sky above the trees, Rose decided that if this was how making love with a man had to be, then so be it. She had given herself to Michael, and he loved her. That's all that mattered to Rose, and it raised her confidence as a desirable woman more than she had ever dared hope.

A few minutes later, it came on to rain. Just as well, for whilst they were getting dressed, the peace of the woods was suddenly shattered by a heavy rumbling. It turned out to be an Army tank approaching along a path on the other side of the pond, out on manoeuvres.

The war clearly had many more secrets to unfold.

Chapter 8

During the last week in September, Gus Humble had received notice that he was to report for military service at a training camp in the South of England. To his dad's delight, he had been accepted in the Royal Artillery, which was the same outfit Albert himself had fought with during the 1914–18 war.

On the night before his departure, Gus invited the family to have a farewell drink with him at the Angel pub. As usual, the place was jammed to capacity, the air thick with fag smoke and the smell of draught beer, and Alf Layton, who ran a cockles and whelks stall in the market, was busy thumping out 'Daisy, Daisy' on the upright, which badly needed tuning. Most of the family had managed to squeeze around one small oval table, but George was very disgruntled because he and the twins were underage to drink alcohol, so they had to be content with a ginger beer each and a packet of crisps. Although Queenie was allowed a port and lemon, her mum was anxious that the landlord, Jim Ramsden, didn't ask to see the girl's Identity Card, for she was not yet eighteen years old. Rose and her mum stuck to a glass of draught Guinness each, but Gus and his dad, standing with their backs to the bar, were already on their third pint of dark brown. What the family did not know was that Gus had a second reason for inviting them out to the pub that evening.

'Mum and Dad, I want yer ter meet someone.'

Gus had left the family group for a moment, picking his way back through the crowd of customers, with him a young blonde-haired girl.

'Listen everyone,' he yelled proudly over the deafening piano sing-song, 'this is my friend, Sylvie Parsons.'

The family looked up with a start, taken aback.

'Sylve,' he started, indicating each of the family as he called their name. 'This is me mum, me dad, sisters – Rose, Queenie, Polly and Millie. And this is trouble,' he continued, looking straight at George, 'really big trouble. Me bruvver, Georgie.'

George, busy unravelling a blue sachet of salt inside his packet of crisps, merely flicked his eyes up.

'Pleased ter meet yer,' said Gus's blonde, who had a far more pleasant voice than her rather brassy appearance suggested.

'Up yer get, George,' Albert said immediately. 'Let Sylvie sit down.'

'Oh, I don't mind standin',' Sylvie assured him, feeling a bit uneasy.

'Don't be silly, dear,' said Nellie, offering Gus's friend her hand. 'There's plenty of room. Come an' sit next ter me.'

Rose had to stand up to let the new arrival take her seat between Mum and herself. She tried to smile at the girl, but didn't somehow feel comfortable doing so.

'Wot can I get yer, young lady?' asked Albert. 'Guinness? Stout? Or would yer like a short?'

Gus replied for her. 'Sylve don't drink. Not booze anyway.'

'I wouldn't mind one of those.' Sylvie was nodding her head towards George's glass of ginger beer.

George took the hint and quickly gulped down as much ginger beer as he could.

Albert turned to the bar, but there was a crowd in front of him waiting to be served.

In the few moments before old Alf Layton started up the next sing-song, Rose attempted a polite conversation with her brother's blonde friend. 'So 'ow long 'ave you an' Gus known each uvver then?'

'Ooh – Gawd knows. Must be a couple of months now, eh, Gus?'

'Somefin' like that.'

Gus had been a bit nervous about the way the family might react to Sylvie. Most of the girls he had introduced to them in the past had been brassy, blonde, full-bosomed, with nothing between the ears. If they had brains, well, that was a bonus. On first sight, Sylvie seemed to be no exception. Gus was particularly concerned about the way Rose would treat his new blonde friend. In the past, she had been sour about every girl he took home, and had made very little effort to be nice to them. The trouble was that Rose was possessive about him, as she was about all the family. But he was determined the family should like Sylvie, because *this* girl was different.

'D'yer live round this way, dear?' enquired Nellie, giving Sylvie a warm smile.

'Oh no. I live up near Mare Street, 'Ackney. Real Cockney.'

'That's funny,' Rose interrupted. 'I always fought a Cockney 'ad ter be born wivin the sound of Bow bells.'

Sylvie's reply came back like a flash of lightning. 'Depends if yer've got cloff in yer ear'oles!'

Rose's back stiffened. She had got more than she bargained for and she didn't like it. From that moment on she avoided too much conversation with her brother's new girlfriend. All she knew was that she hated her on sight, and was sure it wouldn't be too long before Gus got rid of her, just like all the other dumb blondes.

Luckily, the tension was relieved when Alf started thumping on the old 'joanna' again. And he really did thump – not only with his fingers vamping on the keyboard, but with one foot on the pedal and the other stamping on the floor. This time it was a rousing version of 'Show Me the Way to Go Home', and the pub roof practically came down with the chorus of half-boozed customers singing their heads off. The family joined in too, and with the exception of Rose they were all amazed to hear what a good voice Sylvie had.

During the 'joanna' thumping, Albert had managed to fight his way back through the boisterous singing customers, but by the time he had put Sylvie's glass of ginger beer on to the table, quite a lot of it had been spilt by the constant pushing and shoving.

'Live at 'ome wiv yer family, Sylvie?' asked Albert, who had to shout above the laughing and joking going on over by the dartboard.

'Ain't got no family,' replied Sylvie, sipping what was left of her ginger beer.

'Sylve's a Barnardo girl,' explained Gus. 'She was brought up in an 'ome over near Bow Green.'

'Could 'ear the church bells all day,' said Sylvie wryly, only too aware that Rose was watching her reflection in the large gilded mirror close by.

'Wot does that mean – Barnardo?' asked Nellie.

'They're orphanth, Mum,' lisped Millie. 'There woth a boy wunth in our thcool. 'E woth brought up in a Barnardo'th 'Ome – 'til they found 'im a new mum and dad.'

Nellie was horrified. 'Yer mean yer didn't 'ave no mum and dad?'

Sylvie leant her head back and laughed. 'They found me wrapped up in a blanket in some telephone box. Lucky it was in the summer!'

Even Albert was shocked. 'Bloody 'ell! Yer poor little cow.'

'It ain't made much difference,' Sylvie assured them all. 'People 'ave bin very nice ter me. As soon as I was old enough ter get a job, I managed ter stand on me own two feet.'

Rose, still slyly watching Sylvie's reflection in the mirror, was becoming more and more curious.

'No mum an' dad. 'Ow terrible!'

'Why di'n't no one adopt yer?' was Queenie's first and only contribution all evening.

''Cos I was too much of a tearaway. I run away from the 'ome four times. Took a long time for me ter calm down. I'm okay now though.'

Nellie was distressed. 'I'm so sorry for yer, dear. 'Ow could yer mum an' dad do such a fing to a little baby? It don't seem right – 'avin' no one ter love yer.'

'Yeah, well that's all changed now.' As all the family turned to look at Gus, there was a great roar of jeering from the dart players, as one of them scored a final victory. 'Got someone ter love yer now, ain't yer, Sylve?'

The family were astonished to see him lean down and give Sylvie a long lingering kiss on her lips.

The twins giggled, Albert felt a bit embarrassed and exchanged a surprised look with Nellie, Queenie looked furious, and George was just bored. Rose, however, tried not to react. She merely picked up her glass of Guinness and sipped it.

Gus stood behind Sylvie with his arms round her shoulders. 'From now on, we're goin' ter spend quite a lot of time tergevver – eh, Sylve?'

For the first time, Sylvie looked a little embarrassed, and a flush came to her cheeks.

'Fine thing ter say when yer just goin' off in the Army,' said Nellie, who suddenly dreaded the pain she would be feeling when Gus left home the following morning.

There was a desolate look in Sylvie's eyes, too. 'I know 'ow yer feel, Mrs 'Umble. I feel the same way. 'Ow I 'ate this war!' Then, to Nellie's surprise, Sylvie put her arm round her shoulder. 'Never mind. We'll just 'ave ter keep the 'ome fires burnin' for 'im, won't we?'

Nellie, puzzled, smiled at Sylvie, then exchanged a fleeting bewildered look with Albert.

'Don't look so worried, Mum,' said Gus, a wide grin on his face. 'I've asked Sylve ter marry me. We're engaged.'

There was a gasp from everyone round the table.

'Engaged?' Nellie's eyes were wide open with surprise.

'Go on, Sylve. Show Mum yer ring.'

Sylvie held out her left hand to display a modest cut-glass ring on her fourth finger.

'Oh, Sylvie!' Nellie stared in awe at the ring, then threw her arms around her future daughter-in-law. 'It's wonderful, Sylvie! Really wonderful! I'm so 'appy for yer both. Now yer've really got a Mum an' Dad of yer own!'

Sylvie was practically in tears as her future mum-in-law repeatedly hugged her.

'Where d'yer get that from?' asked George, glaring sourly at Sylvie's engagement ring. 'Woolworf's?'

''Ow d'yer guess?' laughed Sylvie.

Everyone laughed with her. Everyone – except Rose.

The following morning Gus had to leave early to catch his train from King's Cross Station. Nellie didn't sleep a wink that night, for there was so much on her mind. Happy though she was that her eldest son had found the girl of his choice, she lay awake listening to the alarm clock ticking noisily on the floor at the side of her bed. As every minute passed, it told her that soon her boy would be leaving home for the first time in his life. She dreaded the moment when she would hear her two pigeon friends billing and cooing on the windowsill.

Rose also slept very little that night. Her thoughts were muddled and confused. Gus going away to fight in a war was a fact of life that she and the Humble family should face up to, and she resented the fact that this new girl was going to be the one he wanted to see when he got home.

Things were made worse when, after eating his final breakfast his mum had cooked for him, Gus had to go through the ordeal of saying farewell to the family. It was a difficult and tearful parting. Nellie did her best to be strong and not upset her son, but poor Albert found himself breaking down, and when the family went to the street door to see Gus on his way, Albert stayed upstairs, and watched his son's departure from the first-floor landing window.

The really difficult moment came when Gus told Rose that he did not want her to come and see him off at the station. It was even worse when Rose heard that Sylvie was meeting her brother at King's Cross, and that they were having a cup of tea in the cafeteria before he left.

At that last moment, when Gus kissed Rose on the cheek and made off down the street, Rose couldn't move from the spot where she was standing, hugging her mother, and waving with the rest of the family, but once Gus had disappeared around the corner, Rose hurried after him.

'Gus!'

Gus, raincoat over one shoulder, suitcase in hand, came to a halt and turned.

Rose rushed straight into his arms. 'Be careful, Gus,' she said. 'If anyfin' should 'appen ter yer, we'd all fall ter pieces.'

Gus stared back at her. He had still not forgiven his sister for the indifferent way she had treated Sylvie in the pub the previous evening. 'Take care of 'em all, Rose,' he said, without emotion. 'You, too.' Then he leant forward, gave her an unaffectionate peck on the forehead, and moved off.

Gradually, Gus merged into the market crowds. One or two of the barrow boys called out to him as he went: 'Watch it, Gus!' and 'See yer in France, mate!' But on the whole, no one took much notice of Gus Humble with his raincoat over one shoulder and a shabby suitcase in one hand. But as he passed all the familiar stalls, and made his way towards Upper Street and the Angel Tube Station, he knew only too well how much he was going to miss all those appetising market smells that had followed him from the day he was born: the eels and winkles and fresh crabs, the roasting chestnuts in winter and the strawberries in summer, the seductive smell of saveloys and pease pudding, and fish and chips, and the unsold rotting vegetables at the end of a busy day. Not once did Gus look back. He just couldn't.

Rose watched her big brother go. She found it hard to imagine that she would ever see him again.

A few days later, Rose saw Badger and did her best to put it right with him about not turning up at his birthday party. As usual, Badger bore Rose no ill-feeling, but let her off with a warning that if she didn't turn up for his next birthday party, he'd go out and search for her! Good old Badger, thought Rose, never a one to bear a grudge, always a loyal mate, always reliable and understanding, always full of fun and laughter. So why couldn't she fancy him in the same way that she fancied Michael Devereaux? Ever since that Sunday afternoon in the Hertfordshire woods, she couldn't help thinking about those piercing blue eyes and smooth words of love. She *had* to see Michael again, she just had to! When he dropped her back at the

Angel on his way home, he had arranged for them to meet in a small pub just off the Pentonville Road, where he assured her he drank most evenings. But Rose had gone to the pub several times, and, despite waiting for as long as she dared on her own, Michael had never turned up. As she had no idea where he lived, her only alternative was to meet him as he came out of the place where he worked – Lloyds of London.

The opportunity came one afternoon after Rose had finished work early at the café in Bethnal Green. After enquiring where the Lloyds office was, she took a bus to Leadenhall Street and stood outside the main entrance to the huge stone-faced Royal Exchange building where the Lloyds' underwriters conducted their business. She had no idea how long she would have to wait, but imagined that City gents didn't have to work too long a day, for they were all so rich and prosperous.

Whilst she was standing there, with traffic trundling past, and City people in their striped suits, bowler hats, and umbrellas rushing from one building to another, Rose was made only too aware that there was indeed a war on. As a precaution against possible bomb blasts, all the windows of the red double-decker buses were crisscrossed with sticky tape, there were notice boards directing people to the nearest air-raid shelters, and sandbags were piled up outside the entrances to some of the official-looking buildings, such as the Royal Exchange itself. The narrow winding City lanes had a wary look about them, for the Belisha beacons were no longer allowed to flash, and the traffic lights themselves were half covered to prevent any possible pin-point bombing by enemy pilots. As Rose looked around, she thought it all so pointless, for even if German planes did manage to cross the English coast, they would never reach as far as London. And yet, the newspaper billboards were proclaiming ominous signs such as: *'WARSAW FALL NEAR!'* and *'BLACKOUT TO-NIGHT 7.00 P.M.'*

Rose quickly dismissed all the gloom from her mind. All she could really think of was how Michael would greet her when they met. Would he be as daring as she expected and kiss her right here in the street in front of all these bowler hats and striped three-piece suits? As every minute ticked by, Rose's heart was beating faster and faster.

At four o'clock the first wave of bowler hats appeared. Rose was quickly engulfed by the surge of men streaming down the steps of the massively ornate building, rushing to join the endless bus queues or reach the distant Bank Underground Station. She turned this way, then that, desperate to see if one of those rushing figures was Michael. But it was hopeless trying to pick anyone out, and when the main part of the mass exodus had evaporated, Rose was convinced that Michael had by now found himself a seat on a bus home. Just then, the great clock above the nearby Mansion House sounded the half-hour, and Rose decided it was best she made her way back to Islington.

Just as she was about to head off in the direction of Cornhill, she heard a familiar laugh that she recognised at once.

Michael was just coming down the steps of the Royal Exchange, two young men of about the same age on either side of him.

'Michael!'

At first, Michael didn't hear her – or at least, appeared not to.

'Michael!' Rose, running back to the steps, was shouting at the top of her voice.

Finally, Michael and his two friends stopped and turned. 'Rose?' he asked, thoroughly taken aback. 'What are you doing here?'

It wasn't quite the greeting Rose had anticipated, for Michael made no attempt to embrace her.

'I went inter the pub every night. Yer said yer'd be there.' The three suited figures were staring at her, and in their black trilby hats, Rose thought they looked a bit menacing. 'I ain't 'eard from yer. I got worried.'

For a brief moment no one said anything. Then: 'So what's all this, Mike, old chap?' The tallest of the trio was speaking. He had what can only be described as a smirk on his face.

'Been up to your larks again, have you?' said the second, shorter man, twitching his pencil-thin moustache. 'Naughty, naughty, Michael!'

With this, all three roared with laughter.

'You're stupid, Rose,' Michael spluttered through his laughter. 'Fancy coming all the way up here to the City. This is not your part of town, you know.'

Rose stared at him in puzzlement and disbelief. 'W-wot d'yer mean?'

'I mean, that just because I take a girl out once, I don't expect to be followed all over the place.'

Michael's two friends concealed a chuckle, and exchanged a wry grin with each other.

Rose felt as though all the blood was draining from her body. 'Follow yer? Wot d'yer mean – follow yer? In case yer've forgotten, yer told me ter meet yer in that pub. Yer told me yer was in love wiv me.'

Michael's two friends let out a loud cheer, and patted him on the back.

Rose hated this, and with eyes blazing, turned on them. 'Why don't you two shut yer mouvs! Yer're like a bleedin' Punch and Judy!'

The tall man took exception to this, and moved a step towards Rose. 'You just watch it, young ginger-head! Nobody talks to *me* like that!'

'Oh no?' snapped Rose, more than ready to take him on. 'One more peep out of you, mate, an' yer'll get me fist in yer teef.'

Michael quickly had to restrain her. 'Please chaps!' he said hurriedly to his pals, 'leave this to me. I'll catch up with you at the bus stop.'

Michael waited until they were at a safe distance from Rose's fists, then spoke to her. 'You had no right to come here,' he said very forcefully.

'No right!' Rose couldn't believe Michael was talking to her in such a way. 'Are yer forgettin' wot 'appened the uvver Sunday? For Chrissake, it's only a coupla weeks ago!'

'Who *cares* how long ago? Michael snapped back. To Rose he suddenly looked so different from the boy she fell so madly in love with during that magical afternoon in the Hertfordshire woods. 'A lot of things can happen in two weeks.'

'Such as?'

'There are plenty of other girls in the world besides you, you know!'

Rose felt the walls of her stomach collapsing. 'Yer told me sister yer fancied me. Yer told 'er, yer *really* fancied me. Yer told 'er yer preferred me 'air short . . .'

'I couldn't care less whether your hair is long or short, Rose. It was a joke. Do you understand that? It was all a joke.'

Rose, her face quite expressionless, stared back at him. 'A joke? *My* sister an' you set *me* up – as a joke?'

'Look, Rose.' Michael tried to take her hand, but she pulled away from him. 'We had a good time, didn't we? I know a lot of girls. We get together for some fun – that's all there is to it. We had a good time, Rose. Why can't you just take it at that?'

Michael's ingratiating smile prompted Rose to spit straight into his face.

She said no more, she merely turned, and walked off.

Wiping Rose's spit from his face, Michael yelled at her angrily, 'Bloody tart! You wouldn't know how to be a good lay if you tried!'

Rose ignored him, and walked off. Not once did she turn to look back. She just walked on and on and on. All she wanted to do was to get away – as far away as possible. As she crossed the road, she walked straight into the path of a pedal cyclist, who yelled after her as she rushed to jump on to the first bus she saw. She had no idea where the bus was heading, and didn't care.

On the top deck she had a choice of sitting next to a middle-aged man or a young woman smoking a cigarette.

Despite the thick curls of smoke that were blowing straight at her, Rose chose the young woman.

As she peered out between the crisscross of sticky paper on the bus windows, Rose looked out at the people walking along the pavement below. She hated every man she could see down there. Hated them because one of them had made her feel dirty.

Without realising it, Rose felt tears trickling down her cheeks. She had never cried before, and vowed never ever to do so again.

Not for her sister Queenie. Nor for any man in the whole wide world.

Chapter 9

For the next few months, the 'phoney war' continued. From time to time the air-raid siren sounded from the top of Upper Street police station, but it was either a test run or just another false alarm. Nonetheless, when Albert Humble picked up his copy of the *Daily Herald* each morning, the news told of a worsening situation. In October there came the first great tragedy of the war with the sinking by a Nazi U-boat of the British battleship *Royal Oak*, with the loss of 800 officers and men. Then, in the same month, the first bombs fell on Britain when enemy aeroplanes launched an attack on the Forth Bridge. By Christmas, Londoners were either erecting corrugated-iron Anderson shelters in their back yards or making quite sure they knew the location of their nearest public shelter. Despite all this, George Humble stubbornly refused to be evacuated with a whole lot of other kids to the safety of the countryside. For once, his mum agreed with him. Always the pessimist, she told her family that 'if one goes, we might as well all go tergevver'. Rose thought that was quite a selfish way to look at things, but knew that once her mum had made up her mind about something there was nothing anyone could do about it.

The winter of 1939–40 turned out to be the coldest for forty-five years, so Rose persuaded Mr Fitch to let her buy a cheap blanket at half-price from his bedclothes stall in the market. As the Humble sisters had no form of heating in their bedroom, the extra blanket came as a godsend. With Gus now away in the army, George slept alone on the upper floor landing, but it was so cold there that eventually he was allowed to bring his mattress down to his mum and dad's room, where he took up position in front of the oven grate, which kept warm for most of the night. Although a thick curtain was hung across the room to keep his mum and dad's privacy, he soon got fed up with Albert, who had a weak bladder and had to get up two or three times a night to use the white china po under his bed.

On the Home Front the war was beginning to take its toll, for more and more young men were being conscripted into military service. As a direct result of this, towards the end of May, the café where Rose worked in the Bethnal Green Road had to close. She really hated losing her job there, for over the months she had got to know so many people who worked in the railway goods yard. As she took her final bus and tram journey back from Bethnal Green, Rose had no idea what to do next.

One evening at the end of May, Rose and her mum and dad were listening to *Into Battle*, a short programme of daily war reports from the Front, that followed the nine o'clock news. Grim-faced, they heard how the British Expeditionary Force was fighting its way down a narrow corridor towards Dunkirk, and that their retreat to England would be highly dramatic and dangerous. Although the BBC war correspondent was trying to be upbeat and patriotic, Rose, Nellie and Albert were only too aware how serious the situation was becoming. It was now quite obvious that France was about to collapse to the invading German forces at any moment, and that if Gus was amongst those troops on the retreat, his life would be in great danger. Of course, none of the three said as much, but their stony silence spoke for them.

It was only when she was lying awake in bed later that evening that Rose remembered something that the new Prime Minister, Mr Churchill, had said in his broadcast to the nation a few days before. Something about how the effort of women was going to be as vital as men when the war was brought home to the villages and streets of this country. Before she went to sleep, Rose had made up her mind what her effort was going to be.

The following morning she went to her nearest labour exchange in Parkfield Street and registered as a trainee ambulance driver with the Civil Defence. By the time news was coming through that British forces were engaged in a great evacuation from the beaches of Dunkirk, Rose had already started her training with the St John Ambulance Brigade. As the war was rapidly entering a serious phase, she had to tackle her crash training course in less than a month, but by the end of that time she had a good working knowledge of first aid, how to deal with air-raid casualties in an emergency, and, most of all, how to drive a motor ambulance. During that eventful time, Italy had declared war on Britain and France, the Nazis were carrying out massed air raids all down the coastline from Scotland to the south-east of England, and France had signed an armistice with Hitler's Third Reich.

At the end of June, Rose was assigned to a St John Ambulance division based in Whitechapel Road, although she was still of the opinion that Hitler's bombers would all be shot down before they ever got the chance to reach London.

'We have to be prepared, my dear. That's the trouble with this country. We always leave things too late, and then all we can do is to make the best of a bad job.'

Rose was getting used to this kind of lecture from the posh woman who had been assigned as her co-driver during her first weeks of duty. Amanda Harrington was middle-aged, and spoke with a rather loud voice through teeth that looked huge and gleaming white. She wore quite a lot of makeup, including face powder that constantly fell on to her tunic collar as she spoke, and false eyelashes that curled up at the tips. Rose found it hard to believe that she was sharing her duties with such a person, someone who actually came from upper-class Kensington. But Amanda was patriotic to the core. She was determined that, if her officer husband had to go out and fight in the war, the least she could do was to join the war effort at home.

'I dread to think what will happen if Jerry tries to invade us.' Amanda was busily chain-smoking a Craven A fag, which was dangling from the side of her lips. 'All we've got are a few rusty tanks and a bunch of old men who are going to be asked to defend us with wooden mallets and farm pitchforks. It's pathetic!'

Rose was trying hard not to be nervous of Amanda driving the ambulance as though it were a sports car. 'Me dad's joined up in the LDV. 'Is old Regiment told 'im 'e was too old when 'e tried ter enlist.'

'The Local Defence Volunteers may be good in theory, but God help us if they come face to face with a bunch of armed German paratroops.'

Rose was only too glad that they were on a practice run, for she was being thrown from side to side every time the ambulance turned a corner. 'Nah, seriously. D'yer really fink there'll be an invasion? Surely the Yanks'd come in on our side first?'

'The Yanks!' In her indignation, Amanda nearly crashed into the side of a bus. 'The Yanks won't join this war until they see the entire German fleet sailing into Manhattan Harbor!'

Rose had always imagined the upper class to be incapable of doing a hard day's work if they tried. But Amanda was someone who didn't mind getting her hands dirty. And on her part, Amanda was sensitive enough to know that although she could afford to take on a full-time voluntary job, the small pay on offer was hardly enough for a young girl like Rose to live on. However, at least the tunic-style navy-blue uniforms came free, and Rose looked very good in hers. Her hair was beginning to grow long again and she had to tuck it up in a thick hairnet beneath her peaked cap.

Just as they were turning into Commercial Road, a policeman on traffic duty asked them to make their way urgently to an accident near Aldgate East Underground Station. When they got there they found a small boy had been knocked down by a motorcar and badly injured. After putting their first-aid training to the test, Rose and Amanda wrapped the child in a blanket, got him on to a stretcher and into the ambulance. Their warning bell echoing around the streets as they went, they soon reached the London Hospital in Whitechapel Road. Through their efforts the small patient had survived, but owing to the severity of his injuries, he might never walk again.

On her way home that evening, Rose felt sick in her stomach. Her first contact with a life-and-death situation had deeply distressed her, and although she never went to church, before she got into bed that night she prayed that she wouldn't have to go through such a harrowing ordeal again.

A little over two months later, Nazi bombers penetrated the defence system around the outskirts of London.

The Battle of Britain had begun.

Oleg Popov loved to walk. It always gave him the opportunity to take in so many wonderful sights, like the people passing by in their different coloured clothes, and the great selection of chimneypots perched high above the grey-tiled rooftops. He also loved to peer through the window of any hardware shop he came across, for ever since he was a child back in the Ukraine, he had been fascinated by household utensils, and the great variety of tools that could be used to build and repair things. His favourite season was winter, because when snow covered the tram tracks along the Holloway Road, that too reminded him of those early days in the great city of Kiev, when the trams cut through the snow and left long trail marks behind them. Those were good days for Mr Popov and his family, long before the hated Bolsheviks took over and drove him and his wife out of the country.

But it was now September, and as he left the piano shop and made his way back towards his flat in Holloway Road,

Mr Popov hoped the oncoming winter would be as severe as the last, when the River Thames froze over for nearly eight miles.

Once he had passed Highbury Corner he reached the Islington Central Library, which brought a gentle smile to his face, for it made him think of his two young friends who worked there, the Humble twins, Polly and Millie. In his mind's eye, he could see and hear them, making beautiful music on one of his own pianos. Every time he heard their heavenly sound, he felt good to be alive.

''Evenin', guv! What'll it be ternight? *Star*, *News*, or *Standard*?'

Over the years, Mr Popov had made it a rule never to buy his evening paper from any news vendor except Popeye, who had been sitting on a wooden box outside the library for so many years that most people thought he must have been born there.

'Please – *Evening News*.' Mr Popov handed over his penny, and took the newspaper.

'Fanks, guv,' Popeye said, biting on the end of his clay pipe. 'Wouldn't 'ang 'round too much ternight if I was you. The way fings've bin goin' lately, looks like we're in for a packet or two. They say it was pretty 'ot in the City last night.'

Mr Popov already knew about the bombs that had fallen in the City on the previous night. In fact, it had been impossible not to know, for he and his neighbours had distinctly heard the sound of a screaming bomb falling in the distance. There had also been a lot of anti-aircraft fire, searchlights crisscrossing the sky, and low clouds over the City had been glowing with flames. 'We British must not be intimidated, Popeye,' he said, firmly. 'Never! Never!'

'Right, guv!' replied the old news vendor, taking off his flat cap and waving it in agreement. 'Mind 'ow yer go now.'

Mr Popov rolled up his *Evening News* and made off down Holloway Road. Whilst walking, he decided to have a quick glance at the headlines, but before he had the chance to get out his metal-rimmed spectacles, the evening calm was suddenly drenched by the now familiar wail of the air-raid siren. Mr Popov clutched his ears in pain, for the sickening wail played havoc with his ancient eardrums. For a moment or so he just stood there, not quite knowing what to do. Should he turn back to the safety of Highbury Tube Station, or should he go on? There had been so many false alarms since the war started that he was of a mind just to carry on walking as though he had heard nothing at all. But remembering that London had now been subjected to several nights of short but severe air raids he decided to hole up for a while.

The streets cleared rapidly, and Mr Popov found refuge in the doorway of a shop whose window was displaying a whole pile of suitcases. Not that he could see them too well, for it was now approaching blackout time, and there was no street or shop lighting anywhere.

After the final pedestrian had fled to either the nearest public shelter or the safety of nearby Highbury or Holloway Road tube stations, all seemed eerily quiet except for a passing tram that rattled its way past after narrowly missing the fury of a deadly aerial attack back down the track.

It was nearly ten minutes before Mr Popov finally

decided that it was safe for him to continue his journey. As he moved on, the streets remained perfectly quiet with only an occasional car or van passing by. By the time he reached the corner of Drayton Park, he was convinced that yet again the air-raid siren was a false alarm. However, when he stopped to cross the road something suddenly made him feel very uneasy. Standing quite still, he raised his head to look up at the sky. And then he heard it – the faint, distant sound of aeroplanes droning in from the east. He couldn't tell how many planes there were, but there were certainly plenty of them, a menacing buzz, like a swarm of wasps. Without warning, the buildings around began to vibrate with the pounding of anti-aircraft guns, which were firing shells into the sky high above him. These exploded into little white puffs that eventually dispersed and drifted off into strange elongated shapes. The whole sky was now covered by a great web of tangled searchlight beams, casting a flickering white glow along the entire length of Holloway Road. And in the stark glare of those beams, stately-looking silver barrage balloons were bobbing up and down at the end of their sturdy umbilical cords.

'Take cover!'

Mr Popov had no time to discover where the man's yell came from, for, at the precise moment he heard it, someone threw himself on to the Ukrainian's back and rugby-tackled him to the ground. Then the deafening approach of a German fighter-plane, flying low over the rooftops, was followed by the rat-a-tat of machine-gun fire, sending bullets ricocheting right down the centre of the deserted Holloway Road. The moment the plane had swerved off and climbed back into the sky, its droning sound was replaced by the clanging of fire engine bells from nearby Upper Street on the other side of Highbury Corner.

Mr Popov lay face down on the pavement, covering his ears. When he felt that it was safe enough to sit up again, he turned around and found himself looking into the face of the assailant who had saved his life.

'That's one yer owe me, guv'nor!'

It was old Popeye.

A few miles away in the East End of London, Rose, at the wheel of her ambulance, was heading out at speed to her first major incident in a small street off Commercial Road. The air raid had already lasted for nearly an hour, and as the ambulance raced along the wide main road, alarm bell ringing as it went, the flames from two fires were easily visible, one immediately to their left, and another dead ahead of them.

'I knew the bastards wouldn't stick to military targets.' Amanda, in the co-driver's seat alongside Rose, was doing her best to read a survey map of the area by the light of a large, clumsy torch. 'What the hell do they think they're doing, dropping bombs on a populated back street?'

'Must be makin' for the Docks!' Rose yelled, above the noise of fire engines racing past them in the opposite direction. 'Let's 'ope they 'aven't 'it any of the boats.'

'To hell with the boats! It's the people in those poor little houses I'm worried about.' Amanda turned off the torch, and looked out through the front window to try to see the name of the street they were just approaching. 'Turn left here!'

Both women held on to their tin helmets as Rose negotiated the turning.

As they made their way to the end of the street, the women could see the first signs of the emergency services gathered around a small cluster of terraced shops. The whole area was lit up like a huge fireworks party, with flames leaping out of upper-floor windows and floodlights bathing everything and everyone in a white candescent glow. There were three fire engines at the scene, and small groups of firemen were frantically aiming their hose pipes at the blazing three-storey buildings.

'Which way, mate?' called Rose, as she leapt out of the driver's seat the moment she had brought the ambulance to a halt.

A harassed senior fire officer called back as he passed, 'Toy shop on the corner! There're some people trapped there!'

Rose's heart missed a beat. She was filled with apprehension.

'The stretcher, Rose!' Amanda was already opening the rear doors of the ambulance.

Rose quickly helped her collect their first-aid satchels. Then between them they unclipped one of the two stretchers from its wall mounting, and slid it out. Whilst they were doing so, two London Ambulance Service vehicles arrived to join the army of helpers.

When they reached the toy shop with their stretcher, Rose and Amanda were horrified by the chaos. A small group of people were huddled together, trapped on the roof of the blazing toy shop. Everyone in the street was shouting out to them – neighbours urging them to stay where they were, firemen trying to find a suitable wall to lean their ladders against, and police with Alsatian tracker dogs trying to keep onlookers from getting too close to the falling debris and intense heat.

'Incendiary bombs! 'Ole cluster of 'em. Enough to burn up the 'ole bleedin' street!'

Rose turned to see who was talking to her. It was a middle-aged woman with curlers in her hair, and still wearing her tatty old dressing gown. 'D'yer know the people up there?' Rose asked, nodding towards the toy shop roof where a man and what looked like several children were waiting to be rescued.

'Know 'em? Course I know 'em. That's Fred Bentley an' 'is kids. 'Im an' Vera 'ave bin in that shop for over ten years. Worked 'ard all their lives, they 'ave. Now look at 'em – poor little sods!' She turned to Rose. The flames from the toy shop fire were reflected in her eyes. 'If I 'ad 'Itler 'ere now, I'd 'ave 'is bleedin' guts for garters!'

As the woman spoke, the man on the shop roof yelled out to the fireman who was hurriedly climbing the step ladder that was propped up against the only safe outer wall of the building. 'For Chrissake 'urry! We're roastin' up 'ere!'

Rose felt so helpless as she and Amanda watched the fireman's slow progress to the rooftop. She kept imagining how she would feel if it were her own mum and dad and brother and sisters up there. She prayed she would never have to go through such an ordeal.

The fireman finally managed to reach the sloping tiled roof and started the slow, painstaking job of carrying each of the kids across his shoulder and down the ladder.

Meanwhile, flames started to crackle out of a window very close to the ladder itself, and the fireman had to hurry down the last few steps. But, despite calls from the crowds below, the children's father hesitated to make his own escape down the ladder.

'Vera!' The man was yelling as loud as he could above the commotion. 'Where are yer . . . Ve-ra . . . ?'

Then everyone started shouting up to him to get the hell down the ladder, for the first slivers of flames were beginning to dart across the rooftop towards him. But the man refused to budge.

'Ve-ra . . . ! Where . . . are . . . yer . . . ?'

Rose couldn't bear to watch. 'Get down!' she yelled at the top of her voice. 'Somebody's got ter do somefin'!'

'No, Rose!' Amanda had to stop her from rushing across to the ladder. 'There's nothing we can do.'

'Wot're yer talkin' about?' Rose yelled. 'We've got ter get 'im down. 'E'll get burnt ter def!'

'Leave it to us, mate!' called the driver of one of the AFS engines. 'We'll get 'im down!'

Amid all the confusion, another fireman leapt on to the ladder and started to climb up to the roof of the toy shop. But he got no further than the second or third step when he was distracted by a piercing scream from a woman who suddenly appeared at a top-floor window.

'Fred! I'm here, Fred! Help me . . . !'

Her husband peered over the edge of the rooftop and discovered where she was calling from. 'Hold on, Vera! I'm coming down!'

'Mum! Dad . . . !' Their four kids, now safely down on the ground, were yelling their heads off. The smallest child, a boy, was, like his elder sister, in deep distress and crying his eyes out.

Rose immediately ran forward and picked the little boy up in her arms. 'It's all right, darlin'. Nuffin' ter worry about. They'll be down in a minute.' For one fleeting moment, she thought the poor little mite looked a bit like Georgie when he was that age. When the eldest girl joined them, Rose hugged her and kissed her gently on the forehead.

The other two kids, who were straining to watch what their dad was doing on the rooftop, were both collected by Amanda. The lady in curlers joined them, and as all the kids were still in the pyjamas and nighties they had been wearing when the fire bombs had rained down on them, they were instantly wrapped up in red hospital blankets.

On the rooftop their dad had managed to reach out and grab his wife's hand. With the crowd below looking on tensely he gradually pulled her up from the windowsill on which she had been balancing precariously. With the two of them now standing safely on the tiled roof, a great roar of relief echoed up from the crowd in the street below. But just as the fireman was only a few steps away from rescuing them, there was a sinister rumbling sound, and whilst the helpless emergency service workers looked on, the entire roof of the toy shop caved in, taking the kids' parents with it.

'Mum!'

'Dad . . . !'

The four kids were distraught. Now, all of them were shrieking and crying. Rose and Amanda hugged them as tight as they possibly could, doing their best to shield their eyes from the horror of the inferno behind them. The two women looked at each other in silence. There was nothing they could say.

A few minutes later, Amanda drove the ambulance along the small back street, and headed out as quickly as possible towards the London Hospital in Whitechapel Road. Rose sat in the back of the ambulance with the kids. Their faces were smeared with ash from the fire, and their eyes were red with crying.

'I want my mum,' the small boy sobbed.

Rose looked at him, and smoothed the young locks of hair out of his eyes. He couldn't have been more than four or five years old, and now he and his brother and sisters had to live out the rest of their lives knowing that they would never see their mum and dad again. She wondered how much of this terrible night they would all remember in years to come. Would it all just seem like a nightmare, or would their minds be scarred for ever?

'Wot's yer name?' she asked the boy.

'Don't know,' said the boy, sobbing and trying to hide his face against Rose's body.

'Don't know was made ter know,' Rose replied softly. 'Bet yer name's – Mick?'

'No, it ain't!' said the boy, sitting up, glaring at her indignantly. 'It's Jimmy.'

Rose smiled at him. 'Jimmy! Yes, of course it's Jimmy. I knew all the time.'

'No, yer di'n't!'

'Bet I did!'

'Di'n't!'

'Did!'

'Di'n't!'

135

Rose let the boy have the last word. It did the trick. Within seconds he had leant his head against her chest, and closed his eyes.

Rose took a quick look out through one of the two small rear windows. Flames could still be seen distantly leaping up from the site of the toy shop, and thousands of tiny sparks from the burning embers were exploding up into the dark evening sky, dancing across the face of the late summer moon as though flirting with the Man who was supposed to live there.

Rose looked at the small boy in her arms. Oh yes, he was a Jimmy all right, no doubt about it. And Jimmy was now fast asleep. So were his older brother and sisters, who were all cuddled up together on one stretcher, worn out by the shattering events of one horrific late summer evening. And Rose's thoughts were carried away to her own kid brother and sisters.

She didn't know why, but she just couldn't get them out of her mind.

Chapter 10

George couldn't wait for his mum to get home from work. He had a surprise for her, not a particularly pleasant one, but a surprise that would undoubtedly scare the life out of her and give him a lot of laughs.

On Rose's advice, Nellie had given up her job helping out in the kitchens at the Royal Northern Hospital. It was quite a journey by tram or bus from the Angel to Manor Gardens in Holloway, and with the old 'moaning Minnie' siren now wailing out practically every day, Rose was concerned that her mum might get caught up in a severe air raid. So Nellie had accepted the offer of a job from Charlie Spindle, who ran a fruit and vegetable stall right alongside the vegetable stall run by Mr Cabbage and Badger. The two traders were old mates, so there had never been any rivalry, and as Charlie's son had been called up, like so many other young men in the market, Nellie was only too willing to help out. She was only a few minutes' walk from home, which gave her ample time to get the family's tea before the inevitable trip to the Angel tube station, where people without shelters were able to take cover during the remorseless nightly air raids.

When Nellie got home at about five o'clock, Rose was just getting ready to go on duty. With the nightly aerial bombardment of London now in full swing, Rose spent most of her days sleeping off the rigours of each previous night's air-raid duties. But she rarely got much sleep after four thirty in the afternoon, mainly because Polly and Millie were in and out all the time, getting themselves ready for the next date with their spotty-faced boy friends, who happened to be twin brothers. The Humble twins, however, were not yet home from the library, so Rose knew that the piercing scream coming from her mum was likely to do with George.

'Mum!' Rose gasped, as she rushed into the first-floor room. 'Wot the 'ell's goin' on?'

As she entered the room, her mum was standing on the bed rubbing her hand as though she had just been scalded by boiling water. And dancing around the room in a frenzy of excited laughter was George.

'Tell 'im ter take it away – please, Rose! Tell 'im!' Poor Nellie was shaking with terror.

'Take wot away?' Rose glared straight at George. 'Wot yer bin up ter, yer little tike!'

His big sister's scolding only made George roar with laughter even more.

'In 'is 'ands, Rose!' Poor Nellie was still cowering on her bed. ''E's got it in 'is 'ands! I found it in the box of matches when I went ter light the gas ring!'

Only then did Rose notice that George had cupped something inside both his hands. 'Wot yer got there?'

'Leave it alone!' George yelled at her, backing away. 'It's nuffin' ter do wiv yer!'

Rose grabbed hold of her mischievous young brother, prised open his hands to reveal a large spider nestled there. Without another thought, she gave George a good whack to the back of his head with the flat of her hand.

'Ow...' George cried out more in indignation than pain.

'Pig!' Rose was yelling so loud at him she could have been heard in the market around the corner. 'Yer always scarin' the daylights out of Mum! Yer know she 'ates spiders! Yer know it! Why d'yer do these stupid fings, Georgie! Wot's up wiv yer?' Rose could have murdered the boy right there and then. Every time Mum came home, she was terrorised by her youngest son. George knew how scared Nellie was of all kinds of insects, especially spiders. He knew how timid and sensitive and vulnerable his mum was. And yet he still had to keep playing these terrible practical jokes on her.

Rose found herself glaring in anger at Georgie, asking herself why boys had to behave in such a way. So typical of the male sex – always making fun of other people, only thinking of how clever and funny they are. At that moment, she had to quickly pull herself together, for she suddenly realised that her hand was raised and ready to strike another blow at the small, cowering boy before her

'Get rid of it, Georgie!' she said in a restrained voice.

'Mind yer own business!' George backed away from her.

'I'm warnin' yer!' Her voice was raised again. 'Don't lark around wiv me!'

'You ain't me mum! You ain't me dad!'

Rose could take no more. With one swipe, she knocked

the spider out of George's hand, and let it fall to the floor, where it quickly scuttled off in the direction of the bed on which poor Nellie was still standing.

George immediately fell to his knees, and crawled after the spider to retrieve it. But Rose was there first and, to the boy's horror, she stamped her foot down hard on the spider and squashed it.

George let out a cry of anguish. 'Yer cow! Look wot yer did! I 'ate yer! I 'ate yer!' He leapt to his feet, tears of anger swelling in his eyes. ''E was only a spider. 'E di'n't do yer no 'arm!'

He rushed to the door, then turned back and yelled at her: 'Yer killed it, Rose! Yer know wot that means, don't yer? Yer're in for bad luck! An' it serves yer right!' George rushed out, slamming the door behind him and shouting as he raced down the stairs, 'Bad luck! Bad luck!'

Rose hesitated for a moment, then turned to look at her mum who was still standing on the bed. So she went across and helped her down. Nellie, solemn-faced, said nothing to her, but went to make another attempt to light the gas ring.

Rose looked at the squashed remains of the spider on the floor. She couldn't understand why she had done it.

Just then, she realised that someone had been standing by the room's back door, watching the ugly scene that Rose had just had with her young brother.

It was Queenie.

An hour later, the family had tea together, but after what had happened with George, Rose didn't eat very much. George himself was still in a deep sulk about Rose killing his spider, so he didn't speak a single word throughout, but Millie was delighted that Rose had very little appetite, for she was able to have an extra portion of the black market Spam her mum had managed to get from one of the barrow boys. Ever since food ration books had been introduced in January, Albert, George, and Millie had not stopped grumbling about the four ounces of butter, one shilling's worth of meat, and two eggs they were each allowed per week. And as for sweets, well, if it wasn't for the boys in the market, they wouldn't have even seen a penny bar of chocolate.

But as the Humble family sat around the table that evening, there was a more alarming matter hanging over them all, something even more serious than the constant nightly air raids.

'They've bin sayin' up the post, we could get an invasion any time from now on.'

As Albert crunched a piece of celery, he became aware that the entire family were looking at him.

'Yeah, I know. Don't sound good, do it? But we've got ter face up to it. If Jerry gets over 'ere, it's every man, woman, and kid for 'imself.'

'Wot will 'appen if the Germanth do get here?' said Millie, her childhood lisp returning with her nervousness. 'Will we all be killed?'

'Of course we won't!' Nellie added immediately, glaring at Albert for scaring the family. 'If the Germans get 'ere, we'll just ignore 'em. Then they'll get so fed up they'll just go 'ome.'

Even though Rose was not feeling at her best, she had to smile.

Polly was busy blowing at a piece of hot boiled potato on the end of her fork. 'Our music teacher, Mrs Wheeler, says that if the Germans try to land by parachute, our soldiers will shoot them all down out of the sky.'

'Yer music teacher shouldn't talk to yer about such fings,' said Nellie sternly. 'The Germans won't ever get 'ere.'

'If they do, don't yer worry – *we'll* be waitin' for 'em.'

The twins groaned as their dad spoke. Albert had never got over being turned down for enlistment in his old regiment, and ever since he had signed on with the Local Defence Volunteers he had never stopped boasting about how, if Jerry ever tried to invade the British Isles he'd have him and his pals to deal with. And now the Prime Minister, Winston Churchill, had referred to the many squads of veterans as 'the Home Guard', Albert was already claiming that their training was as good as that given to any regular soldier.

'I wonder wot really would 'appen if the Germans got 'ere?' Queenie had already finished her meal and was idly making patterns with her fork on the tablecloth. 'It'd be funny ter see foreign soldiers marchin' down Upper Street, chattin' up all the local talent. I mean, do they eat and drink the same fings as us – like cups of tea, an' sausage an' mash? D'yer fink we'd all 'ave ter speak German or somefin'?'

Nellie slammed down her knife and fork. 'Stop it, Queenie! 'Ow many times do I 'ave ter tell yer, the Germans ain't goin' ter get anywhere near London.'

Queenie, only too aware that she was being provocative, flicked her eyes up to see her family's reaction. ''Itler reckons 'e'll be sittin' in Buckin'ham Palace by Christmas.'

'Bloody rubbish!' growled Albert. 'Every man, woman and kid in this country would sooner die than let that 'appen!'

'Well, *I* wouldn't!' snapped Queenie haughtily. 'I say let the King and Queen take care of 'emselves. It's all right for them shut up wiv their two ruddy princesses, all snug an' safe inside their grand palace. Wot about us an' all the people down the East End who 'ave ter take everythin' that gets frown at us?'

Millie was outraged by her sister's remark. 'How can you thay thuch a thing, Queenie?' she lisped indignantly. 'Buckin'ham Palace got bombed only a few weeks ago. The King an' Queen 'ave never run away from the air raids. They're in jutht as much danger ath everyone else.'

'Ha! If yer believe that, yer believe everyfin'!'

'Why don't yer shut yer 'ole, Queen?' Albert slammed down his knife and fork on his plate and got up from the table. 'Yer don't know nuffin' about this war. We're up against a bunch of bloody killers 'oo don't care if yer a duke or a bleedin' dustman! This is war, Queenie! If the day ever comes we see 'Itler and Goering and Goebbels marchin' down White'all, Gawd bless yer, yer'd wish yer were never born! Wot say you, Rosie?'

Until this moment, Rose had deliberately not entered the conversation. Ever since Queenie had used Michael Devereaux to play such a cruel joke on her, Rose had treated her younger sister as though she wasn't even part of the same family. She had deliberately never talked about the incident, nor the traumatic effect it had had on her. As far as Rose was concerned, Queenie was a mischievous, spiteful girl who got her kicks out of life by being

143

provocative. Not that she meant to, perhaps. It was just that she couldn't help herself.

'When I see wot 'Itler's done ter ordinary people,' she began quietly, her eyes focused on the half-empty plate in front of her, 'I'd do anyfin' in me power ter stop 'im.'

'That's war for yer,' replied Queenie, with a shrug of the shoulders.

To Queenie's intense irritation, Rose did not look up at her as she replied, without emotion, 'Try tellin' that ter some of the kids I pull out the wreckage every night.'

For a moment or so, nobody said anything.

'I'll be off then.' Rose got up, collected her tunic that was hanging up behind the landing door, and put it on.

Whilst Rose was doing up the tunic buttons, her mum went to collect something in the back part of the room. She returned with a sandwich wrapped in newspaper. 'A bit of cheese an' pickle, Rosie.'

'No, Mum!' Rose tried not to take the package. 'I'm not takin' yer rations again.'

'Yer've got ter eat, Rosie. Yer just 'ave ter. It's a long night.' She pleaded with her eyes. 'Please, dear.'

Rose relented, and took the package. Then she put on her cap, collected her tin helmet and threw her first-aid satchel and gas mask over her shoulders. 'Get down the tube as soon as yer can, Mum,' she said quietly, hugging her and kissing her gently on the cheek. 'Don't take any chances.'

The family watched Rose as she went to the door, and opened it. 'See yer in the mornin' then!' she called back. And after she went out on to the landing, she peered around the door again and smiled. 'Gawd bless!'

'Gawd bless, gel!'

By the time Albert had called to his eldest daughter, she had gone.

Both he and Nellie waited motionless and solemn-faced as they listened to Rose's footsteps treading down the stairs.

Then the street door opened and closed.

'Moaning Minnie' wailed out soon after blackout time, but luckily Rose had already reached the ambulance station in the Whitechapel Road before there was any sign of activity. When she got there, Rose found Amanda playing gin rummy with a few of the other female drivers, so after checking the roster she decided to use the spare time still available by going up to the ARP look-out post on the roof of the building.

'Reckon we'll be in for another packet tonight, miss.' Old Mr McKay's binoculars were already trained on the London skyline. In the far distance he had picked out the first sign of ack-ack shells exploding in the sky, and the now familiar crisscross of light beams searching the sky for the approach of enemy aircraft.

'Aren't yer scared bein' up 'ere all on yer own?' asked Rose.

'Och, no, miss.' Despite living most of his life in the East End of London, Mr McKay still carried the twang of his Scottish roots. 'As a matter of fact I get one of the best views of the whole show up here. The other night it looked as though the whole of London was on fire. I felt a wee bit like Nero fiddlin' whilst Rome burnt.'

Rose didn't really follow what he was saying, but when she looked out at the dark sky ahead of her, she had a pretty good idea. Apart from the sound of ack-ack fire out in the Essex countryside beyond, for one brief moment London seemed to be at peace. The great city was in total darkness – so different to the hundreds of twinkling lights that danced across its skyline in the heady, carefree days before the war. It was an eerie feeling for Rose, standing up there on the roof of the building, staring into the pitch dark of an early autumn night. Thanks to the countless home-made blackout curtains, and glass roof windows that had been painted black, not one single light could be seen, not in the streets, nor in any of the hundreds of offices, shops, and cosy terraced houses that lined those streets. Even the autumn moon was obliterated by thick palls of black night clouds, so if there were any barrage balloons lurking amongst them, the enemy raiders were in for a nasty surprise.

'We musn't let them do it, y'know.' Mr McKay was half talking to himself.

All Rose could see was the outline of his figure looking out into the darkness. ''Ow d'yer mean?'

'We mustn't let them take this away from us. This city. The country. It's worth fightin' for.'

There was silence for a moment, then Rose heard him take a deep breath of the chilly autumn night air.

'You canna buy freedom, young lady. Och no. Freedom's something you have to fight for. I just hope I live long enough to see those lights come on again down there. Not just for me, but for all ma grandchildren. Of course, they may not appreciate what we had to go through to get them on again, but they'll feel the benefit of it all right.'

Rose thought about what he had said. And it also made her despise Queenie even more for the way she kept knocking the Royal Family, who were always visiting ordinary working-class people who had just been bombed out, always trying to cheer up homeless families by lifting their morale. Yes, Rose agreed with Mr McKay, freedom was worth fighting for. London was worth fighting for. And so were the Humble family – they were all worth fighting for, too. There would always be people who would try to tell you what they meant by their idea of freedom, people like Hitler, who saw the world as if it were a football which could be kicked around whenever he wanted. No, thought Rose, as she stood there in the dark, unable actually to see the great sprawling city laid out before her, but knowing only too well that it was there. This was *her* London, the Humbles' London, the London she was born and brought up in. Better it should burn to the ground than be left to the mercy of a crazed dictator.

The air suddenly cracked with the sound of ack-ack fire, coming from Victoria Park, just a couple of miles away in Hackney. Then, immediately behind it, the droning of German bombers.

Rose didn't wait for the alarm bell to ring. Within a couple of minutes she and Amanda were in the ambulance and racing off for their first call of the night, at the London Docks.

When they got there they found a huge riverside warehouse burning fiercely. It turned out to be a main storage depot for unloaded sugar, but the sugar itself had been heated so much by the intensity of the fire that it had turned to syrup and was oozing out on to the dockside like a great brown-coloured river.

'Can't go any closer, gels! There's a UXB stuck in the ground floor.'

Rose didn't have the foggiest idea what the young AFS fireman was talking about. 'Wot the 'ell's a UXB?'

The fireman looked at her, briefly took off his tin helmet and wiped the sweat from his forehead with the back of his hand. 'Where've yer bin 'idin' out, missus?'

Despite the fact that the fireman was under intense pressure, Rose wanted to lash out at him. She was only stopped from doing so when she was distracted by a raw burn mark on his face, which was already a deep red colour from the fierce heat of the fire.

'It's an unexploded bomb, Rose,' said Amanda. 'We have to wait 'til the BDU gets here. God knows how they're going to defuse it inside all *that*!'

They got their answer the moment they turned to look at the rapidly spreading warehouse fire, for there was one hell of an explosion which blew apart the entire facing wall of the building.

Although Rose and Amanda were some distance from the warehouse, the force of the explosion quite literally blew them off their feet, landing them flat on their stomachs on the dockside path.

'UXB. Know wot I mean?'

Lying alongside Rose was her cheeky fireman friend, who had a broad grin on his face. Rose was furious to be laughed at by this brainless nark, who, with or without the burn mark on his face, wasn't even good-looking!

A little later Rose had to tend to one of the dockers who

had had his left arm blown off. She was only thankful that she wasn't squeamish for it gave her the courage temporarily to stop the bleeding by applying a tourniquet to the stump of the man's arm. Luckily the poor bloke remained unconscious until after Rose and Amanda had got him to hospital. However, his pal, with whom he had been working when the bomb exploded, had not been so lucky, for he died in the ambulance on the way to hospital.

When Rose and Amanda reached the London Hospital, the place was, as usual, coping with a steady stream of air-raid casualties.

Once they were satisfied that their survivor was in safe hands, Rose and Amanda decided to have a ten-minute break after a hectic couple of hours down at the docks. Tired and exhausted, they sat on the floor in a corner of the Casualty Unit, took off their tin helmets, leant their heads back against the white painted wall behind them, and closed their eyes. All around them there was intense activity – doctors and nurses rushing past with serious stretcher cases, more and more injured people being led in from the succession of ambulances arriving at the emergency entrance, and from the streets outside the constant barrage of ack-ack fire, which seemed to shake the foundations of the hospital.

Strangely enough, the Casualty area itself was absolutely still and quiet. Although most patients who were waiting for treatment were tired and anxious, they remained quite calm, and kept their voices down to a whisper when they spoke to each other. Rose smiled to herself every time she heard the occasional sound of laughter, for she had become used to hearing people relieving their tension by recounting some of the funnier moments of the horrific times they were living through.

'Are you religious, Rose?'

Amanda's sudden question took Rose by surprise. 'Not really,' she replied, her eyes still closed. 'Why?'

'Well, you know what they say. We always turn to God when we're in trouble. I know I do: "Please God, help me to do this or that." Or "Oh God, don't let this happen to me." Funny, isn't it? We only ever turn to God when we want something from Him.'

Rose's response was uncompromising. 'I only believe in fings I can see.'

Amanda opened her eyes. 'Yes. I know what you mean. It would certainly help if He let us see Him from time to time. So good for the confidence.' She rolled her head to one side in order to look at Rose. 'You know you're a very practical young thing, Rose. The man who gets you for a wife is going to be very lucky indeed.'

Rose was grateful that she didn't have to respond to that, for the whole place shook when a high explosive bomb fell rather too close for comfort. There was no panic, but everyone automatically stooped their heads down into their laps and protected them with their hands.

''Allo, Rose.'

Rose looked up with a start to see who was talking to her. It was her brother Gus's fiancée, Sylvie Parsons. She was wearing her nurse's uniform.

'Oh – 'allo, Sylvie.' Rose's response was formal. Although she knew Sylvie was a nurse and worked at the London Hospital, this was the first time she had actually come into contact with her there.

''Aven't seen yer up 'ere before. Yer look all in.'

Rose immediately felt challenged. 'I'm fine,' she said, sitting up straight.

'Feel like a cuppa? I've got a quick break before me next shift.'

Rose shook her head. 'No, fanks. Got ter get back.'

'Go ahead, Rose,' said Amanda, taking out her packet of Craven A from her satchel. 'We've got time.'

Sylvie smiled sweetly at Amanda. 'Yer welcome ter come, too.'

'No, thanks all the same. I'll hang around here for a bit.' Amanda got up from the floor. 'See you back at the ambulance, Rose. Take your time!'

Rose followed Sylvie through a maze of bleak-looking hospital corridors until they reached the nurses' canteen in the basement. The place was full of cigarette smoke, for nearly every nurse seemed to have a cigarette between her fingers.

'So 'ow's Mum?' Sylvie asked, as she brought two chipped white cups of tea across to the table Rose had chosen in the corner.

'She's okay. They're all down the tube ternight.'

'Don't blame 'em. Much safer.' Sylvie paused a moment whilst she stirred some dried milk and saccharin tablets into her tea. 'I'm sorry I never get the chance ter see yer when I call on Mum an' Dad. Yer always seem ter be out.'

As she tried to cool her tea, Rose did her best not to look guilty. 'Yeah. I 'ave a lot of fings ter do when I'm not on duty.' Rose was perfectly aware that she was lying, for every time she had been told by her mum that Sylvie was

151

coming to visit, she had always made quite sure she was out.

Sylvie leant her elbows on the table and used both hands to hold her cup. 'Yer know, Rose,' she said, without raising her eyes, 'I wish you an' me could be friends. Gus'd like it so much.' She finally raised her eyes to look at Rose over the top of her cup. 'So would I.'

Rose sipped her tea and shrugged her shoulders. 'We ain't enemies, are we?'

'I 'ope not. 'E's very fond of yer, yer know – yer bruvver. I know 'e probably don't say so ter yer – but 'e is. 'E reckons yer're the strongest one in the family, much stronger than 'im an' Dad. That's why 'e 'asn't worried about yer all while 'e's bin away.'

Rose was looking embarrassed. 'Stupid nark! I'll give 'im a fourpenny one when I see 'im!' She put her cup down on the table and wiped her wet lips with one finger. 'I still can't understand why the army 'asn't given 'im any leave. Most of the blokes 'oo got away from Dunkirk had time at 'ome soon after. I don't know wot they fink they're playin' at.'

'Rose. I've seen Gus.'

Rose looked up with a start.

'He wrote an' asked me ter meet 'im. We spent a coupla days tergevver in this boardin' 'ouse up near Cambridge. 'E 'ad a weekend pass.'

Rose looked confused. 'But – 'e ain't bin 'ome? We ain't seen 'im for monffs.'

'I know, Rose.' Sylvie felt guilty, and found it difficult to look directly at her. 'Yer're right. 'E could 'ave got 'ome after Dunkirk. But the fact is – 'e di'n't want ter.'

'Di'n't – want?'

''E's changed, Rose. 'E looks at least ten years older than when we last saw 'im. Somefin' 'appened out there, somefin' 'e won't talk about. But whatever it is, 'e can't face up ter the family – not yet, not *just* yet.' Sylvie stretched her hand across the table, and placed it on Rose's. 'Yer won't tell Mum an' Dad, will yer Rose? They wouldn't understand.'

A few miles away, Nellie, Polly, Millie, Queenie, and George were trying to get some sleep stretched out beneath a couple of blankets on the cold cement floor of the Angel tube station. Albert wasn't with them, for tonight he was on Home Guard duties, fire-watching around the Islington Town Hall.

Nellie hated having to sleep rough in such a place, especially crowded together with a whole lot of strange people. The authorities had initially taken a dim view of so many people taking shelter on the platforms of tube stations, mainly because they were concerned about the possible spread of any infectious diseases, but as the air raids increased in intensity and the public demanded the right to adequate protection, they relented. Each night, though, was an ordeal for everyone who was forced to endure it.

It was already daybreak when 'Moaning Minnie' finally sounded the all clear. Nobody on the tube platform could actually hear the dreadful wailing sound, but when news of it was relayed to the sleeping crowds, everyone collected together their blankets and pillows and sandwich boxes and vacuum flasks, and filed their orderly way up the stairs to the exits.

Although there was a sharp nip in the air, Nellie was

relieved to feel the first rays of the early morning sun across her face. After the long night underground, she didn't mind one bit having to squint in the bright daylight.

The five weary figures made their way home along Upper Street. They had no idea if, in fact, they still *had* a home to go back to, for during the night rumours had constantly spread along the platform, telling of streets and buildings that had been bombed. As they made slow progress towards Chapel Market, the air was echoing to the now familiar sound of burglar alarms that had been set off by the vibrations caused by nearby bomb-blasts.

The look of despair on Nellie's face told all when she caught sight of first one gaping hole where a familiar shop had been, and then another, still smouldering from the previous night's carnage. There were people everywhere – firemen hosing down the last remnants of burning embers, police and Civil Defence workers trying to make sure that no one was trapped beneath the debris, and distraught families who had returned to find themselves homeless. The road itself was flooded by water from fractured mains, and electricity power lines were dangling dangerously from streetlamps and damaged rooftops. It was a scene of devastating chaos.

In the market, some of the traders' stalls had been covered with glass from nearby shop windows that had been shattered by the blast from a bomb in Pentonville Road, but the barrow boys were already there, cleaning up the mess and preparing to put up their 'BUSINESS AS USUAL' signs.

Eventually, the Humbles reached the corner of their own street. For a moment or so they held their breath, hardly daring to look at what might have happened to the piano shop. But, as they turned the corner and Georgie let out a triumphant yell of 'It's still there!' all the weariness of the previous night's ordeal seemed to evaporate.

Mr Popov's front window had been blown in, but at least the shop and rooms above were otherwise intact.

Unfortunately not everyone in London that night had been quite so lucky.

Chapter 11

By the end of September, London had already been under nightly aerial bombardment, not only from wave after wave of German Heinkel, Dornier, and Junkers bombers, but also from heavy long-distance guns positioned on the Channel coast of France, which was now under enemy occupation. Old 'Moaning Minnie' had become a regular feature of London life, for on most evenings she wailed out her warning at dusk and her all clear at dawn. Every night, thousands of Londoners had been killed, injured, and made homeless, and the devastation was also obliterating some of the city's most treasured ancient buildings. But the German onslaught did not go without loss to themselves, for Winston Churchill told the House of Commons that 175 enemy aircraft had been shot down in one day, and as rumours grew that the invasion of the British Isles was imminent, the RAF and the Navy shelled and bombed the vast fleet of enemy invasion barges that were massing in ports from the North of Germany all the way down to the French coast along the Bay of Biscay.

During one night in October, Rose and Amanda's ambulance was called out to a busy main road in Shoreditch, where high explosive bombs had just been dropped on to an old Victorian church, destroying the altar. It was a strange feeling for Rose, for it was the first time she had been inside a church since she was a small child. She remembered the occasion only too well for it had been at the funeral of one of her uncles, and the church in Liverpool Road had been so quiet and solemn that whilst the pallbearers were carrying the heavy coffin to the altar, Rose could hear the sound of their shoes shuffling along the stone floor of the aisle. But what she was seeing now was very different, for there was smoke and dust everywhere and the floor of this once-beautiful old church was criss-crossed with a maze of firemen's water hoses.

'Don't make sense, do it?'

Rose, trying to read what was left of an inscription on an old, badly damaged stone floor tablet, looked up with a start to see one of the firemen talking to her.

'This is wot 'appens when people start fightin' each uvver. Nuffin's sacred.'

Rose watched as he and a colleague wrestled with one of the slack hosepipes that had got tangled up amongst the rows of wooden pews.

'See that gallery up there?' the fireman asked Rose, without looking up from what he was doing. 'When I was a kid, I used ter go up there an' drop dried peas on the people down 'ere. They was usually too busy singin' their 'eads off ter notice. Sad when yer look at it now, i'n't it?'

The roof of the church was now nothing more than a wide open space bordered on each side by dangling pieces of wreckage. Even though she had never thought herself religious, Rose felt deeply despondent inside. As she looked up at the stars in the dark sky, with flames still leaping up from the old timber carvings, she couldn't help feeling that what she really believed in were not only those dedicated souls who had been inspired by their faith in God to build such a place, but also those who were at this very moment trying to save it. 'Even a church,' she said, not really expecting an answer.

The fireman who had spoken to her looked up briefly. He thought he recognised her from somewhere, but didn't have time to hang around for a chat. With the water hose draped across one shoulder, he and his mate moved off.

Rose watched them go. Until then she hadn't realised that she was standing in several inches of water, gushing out from the dozens of hosepipes snaked across the church floor.

Back in the ambulance, heading off towards the London Hospital with two casualties, Rose suddenly remembered the young fireman who had spoken to her. It was that same cheeky bloke she had been with when she and Amanda were blown off their feet during the sugar warehouse blaze down at the Docks.

Rose was still thinking about that young fireman when the ambulance reached the hospital.

Queenie Humble had never made any secret of the fact that she absolutely loathed her war-time job at the small arms factory in Stepney. To her it seemed menial, monotonous work, with nothing to show but a few rifles and bullets and a whole lot of machines that clattered and rattled all day. She also hated the smell of oil that stifled the air in the workshop, and the fact that, despite wearing white gloves all day, her hands and face never seemed to be clean. Queenie was very proud that most people considered her to be the best looking member of her family. In a way it was true, for with her butter-milk complexion and long red hair she gave an impression of beauty, even though that beauty was more often than not, only exterior.

She was very popular with her female workmates, for she spent a lot of time making fun of the few remaining men working there, who had been turned down for call-up on medical grounds. One of her favourite games was to pick on someone, then challenge his virility. In other words, if the young bloke in question hadn't asked any of the girl workers out on a date, there was obviously something 'suspect' about him. Queenie was not to know, however, that this man-baiting would one day rebound on her.

Although the small arms factory was tucked away in a quiet back street in the East End, for obvious reasons it was officially designated as 'Top Security'. The place was heavily fortified, with sandbags at every entrance and armed soldiers on constant patrol around the building. Queenie hated being shut up in a cage, especially as on the nights when she was not on late shift she had to sleep rough with her mum and the family down on the tube platform. It was on a late October morning after such a night that she came into the factory workshop tired and spiky, and just looking for trouble. Her target was a particularly shy and nervous young bloke called Harry Stoker.

''Eard about yer the uvver night, 'Arry.' Queenie was at her machine, punching screw-holes into the butt of a .303 rifle. 'Tut-tut! Naughty boy. Fancy yer doin' a fing like that ter Mavis. Wot would the guv'nor say?'

Harry, at his workbench, looked up with a start. 'Wot yer talkin' about?'

'Don't give me that one, luvver boy!' Queenie was determined to be heard above the grinding clatter of machinery all around her. 'Yer touched 'er up, di'n't yer?'

'Wot?' Harry felt the blood drain from his face. He had always felt awkward being the only young bloke left amongst so many girls after being exempt from call-up on medical grounds.

'Don't give me none of that, 'Arry Stoker. We know wot yer was after – yer randy sod!'

The machine shop echoed to the sound of girls' laughter.

'I don't know wot yer mean,' Harry stuttered, trying not to rise to her bait. 'I ain't done nuffin' ter Mavis nor anyone else.'

'That's not wot I 'eard.' Queenie shook her long red hair, which, contrary to repeated warnings from her supervisor, she had once again refused to tuck up under her regulation issue turban. 'Mavis says yer touched 'er up in the air-raid shelter the uvver night – when yer was standing be'ind 'er at the tea urn.'

'Cheap frill, eh, 'Arry?' yelled one of the girls nearby.

'Yer be careful wot yer do wiv yer plonker, 'Arry,' yelled another girl. 'It might break off!'

'Don't be daft!' Queenie replied. 'Bandy-legged men don't 'ave no plonker!'

Harry coloured up immediately as the roar of machines was almost drowned by gales of laughter from all the girls at their workbenches. He found Queenie's remark particularly hurtful because she had never stopped telling her pals that he had been turned down for the Army because he was bandy-legged. Harry had never had the courage to tell them the real reason, that he had a small dark patch on his lung.

'Is it true yer a virgin, Queenie?'

Harry's sudden question struck like a thunderbolt. Everyone around stopped what they were doing.

For the first time, Queenie was stunned into silence. All she could do was to stare in disbelief at Harry.

'Come on then. Tell us. We all want ter know. Are yer – or aren't yer a virgin?'

Queenie just couldn't believe what she was hearing. This was the bloke whom she had teased mercilessly ever since she started working in the factory, the bloke who shied away from her every time she passed by, whom nobody could ever hear because he spoke so quietly. And here he was, accusing her of something really personal, and in a voice that was as sure and firm as her own.

'Yer cheeky bloody sod!' Queenie suddenly exploded. ''Oo d'yer fink yer talkin' ter?'

'I'm just int'rested, that's all,' Harry said defiantly. 'I mean, let's face it, Queen, yer always goin' on about *my* sex life. Wot about yours? 'Ow many blokes 'ave *you* laid in yer time?'

'Plenty! Loads!' Queenie was now yelling, her eyes blazing with anger. 'I've 'ad more plonkers than you've 'ad 'ot dinners, mate!'

'Oh yeah?' This was probably the first time in his life that Harry had fought back. 'In yer dreams?' he said, staring her out.

Queenie was so stunned, she wiped her face with the back of her hand, leaving it smeared with oil. In that second, she realised she was unable to bluff any more. All her young life she had done just that, pretending to her pals that she was the bird every feller wanted to pull. How could she ever tell them that it just wasn't true, that her challenging ways had consistently scared off every bloke she had ever met? She was a fake, a bag of wind. No wonder the girls around were sniggering at her this time, and not at Harry Stoker.

'Bloody conchy!' she yelled, which was the only spiteful form of defence she could muster. 'Yer should be in the Army wiv all the rest of 'em – firin' these rifles, not makin' 'em! Call yerself a man? Ha!'

Harry lowered his eyes, and without looking at her replied calmly, 'Well, one thing's for sure, Queen. *You* wouldn't know a man – even if yer was in bed wiv 'im.'

This immediately provoked an uproar from everyone watching, and they laughed, jeered, and applauded.

Queenie couldn't take it, and she suddenly grabbed hold of one of the rifle butts on her bench and swung it straight at Harry's face.

Harry just managed to duck in time, but as he did so, Queenie lost her balance and fell backwards.

There was a gasp from some of the girls at the next bench as they rushed forward to help her, but Queenie's long hair had already become caught up in a large machine press behind her.

'Oh Christ!' she screamed. ''Elp me!'

Harry was the first to reach the machine.

'Turn it off! Turn it off!' Queenie, her hair gradually being sucked down into the machine, was half yelling, half screaming.

'I can't!' yelled Harry, as he wrestled with the all-consuming machine. 'It's jammed!'

Rose was fast asleep in bed when she felt someone shaking her.

'Rose! Wake up! 'Urry, gel! 'Urry!'

Rose opened her eyes to find her mum standing over her. 'Mum!' She sat up with a start. 'Wot's up? Wot time is it?'

Nellie was ashen-faced. 'Queenie's 'ad an accident at work. We've got ter get over there.'

'Accident!' Rose was out of bed in a flash, and starting to dress.

'The factory called the coppers round the corner. She got caught up in a machine or somefin'.' Nellie was close to tears. 'They took 'er ter the London 'Ospital up Whitechapel. Charlie Spindle's goin' ter give us a lift in 'is van. Yer dad's waitin' downstairs.'

At ten past two in the afternoon, Rose, with her mum and dad, was hurrying down the familiar stone corridor of the London Hospital in Whitechapel Road. But this time was different. The casualty was her own sister.

The first person to greet them was Gus's fiancée, Sylvie Parsons.

'Queenie's out of danger, Mum. But she's 'ad a very bad time.'

'Wot 'appened, Sylve?' asked Albert, who looked absolutely shattered.

'She got inter some kind of scrap wiv someone. Caught 'er 'air in one of the machines. It was touch an' go. She 'ad a lucky escape.'

Nellie clutched her chest anxiously. 'I want ter see 'er. Where is she?'

'She don't look too good, Mum. D'yer fink yer should?'

'I want ter see 'er, Sylvie,' said Nellie adamantly, looking at all the nearest ward doors.

Sylvie exchanged an anxious glance with Rose, then took hold of Nellie's arm. 'Doctor won't let yer 'ave more than five minutes, Mum. We 'ave ter be sensible.'

Rose sat down on a bench. 'I'll wait for yer 'ere, Mum. Better for you and Dad to be on yer own.'

Sylvie indicated that she agreed, and led Nellie and Albert into an adjacent ward.

Whilst she was sitting there, watching patients, doctors and nurses scuttling back and forth, Rose was suddenly consumed with a feeling of guilt. Ever since Queenie had used Michael Devereaux to play that cruel joke on her, she had had nothing but contempt for her younger sister. Time and time again she had asked herself how it was possible for two girls like herself and Queenie to come from the same mum and dad. Why *was* Queenie so destructive? Why *did* she want to be so different all the time? After all, she got just as much love from their mum and dad as the other kids. Maybe it was because Rose was the eldest daughter. Even when they were small kids together, Queenie had always thrown a tantrum whenever she thought that she was not the centre of her mum and dad's attention. But for some unknown reason, which Rose couldn't explain even to herself, she felt guilty for what had happened to her sister. Could she, Rose, have prevented it?

'Cheer up, Rose. There ain't nuffin' more any of us can do.'

Sylvie had just come out of the ward. 'Wot exactly 'appened, Sylvie?' Rose asked. 'Did she tell yer?'

'She 'ad a bust-up wiv some bloke,' said Sylvie, sitting at the side of Rose on the bench. 'At least, that's wot 'er supervisor told the doctor. She apparently 'ad a go at 'im, an' fell against this machine. 'Er 'air got caught up in it, an', well – it pulled her down.'

'Why didn't someone stop the machine?'

'They tried but it got jammed. The only way they could get 'er out was ter cut off 'er 'air.'

'Wot?' Rose was horrified. '*All* of it?'

Sylvie lowered her voice as a ward nurse passed by pushing a patient along in a wheelchair. 'Rose, yer might as well know. They cut it off right down ter the scalp. Only just made it in time, uvverwise—' She shook her head and sighed. 'It's made a terrible mess. Trouble is she panicked, tried ter pull loose. Ripped all the skin off. She 'ad ter 'ave over forty stitches.'

'Oh God, Sylvie. Will the 'air – I mean, will it ever grow again?'

Sylvie shrugged her shoulders. ''Ard ter tell.'

Rose hesitated for a moment, then quite impetuously slapped the palms of both hands on to her lap. 'Stupid little cow! I knew somefin' like this'd 'appen to 'er one day!'

Sylvie turned to look at her. 'You two don't get on wiv each uvver, do yer?'

'Wot makes yer fink that?' she replied indignantly.

'Gus told me. 'E also told me that Queenie—' Sylvie paused for a moment, then continued. ''E told me that Queenie can be quite difficult.'

'That's the understatement of the year!' said Rose, sitting back on the bench and crossing her arms.

For a while, the two girls said nothing. Then Sylvie swivelled around on the bench to talk directly at Rose. 'Yer know, Rose, fings are goin' ter be different for Queenie now. She's goin' ter need 'elp – a lot of 'elp. Let's face it, it's not only the injuries she's got ter cope wiv.'

Rose sat upright again. 'Wot d'yer mean?'

'Pride. Self-respect. A woman's vanity. Call it wot yer like. But Queenie's got an awful lot of catchin' up ter do.' As she spoke, Sylvie slipped her hands into her uniform pockets, staring aimlessly down at her white stockinged legs. 'Yer know, Rose, I reckon somefin' 'appened ter Queenie terday, somefin' she found out about 'erself that she'd never admitted before. I only say that, because – well, I fink the same fing must've 'appened ter me – at some time or uvver.'

They both lowered their eyes as two hospital mortuary attendants passed by, pushing a stretcher trolley which contained a corpse covered by a white sheet. Once it had gone, Sylvie continued.

'Yer see, when I was a kid down Barnardo's, I reckoned I was just about the King of the Castle. Real bruiser I was – do anyone up if they crossed me. Trouble was, nobody told me what I was doin' was wrong. They just let me get away wiv it. Well – one day, this geezer 'alf my age, 'e give me a fourpenny one right on my mouff. Knocked one of me front teef out – see – 'ere.'

Sylvie showed Rose a gap in the bottom row of her teeth.

'I wouldn't've minded so much, 'cept no one took no notice of me. No one cared wot they saw, an' I felt lousy

167

about it – humiliated. I badly wanted someone ter talk ter – anyone! But there wasn't nobody. The only person I 'ad ter talk ter was meself. I 'ad ter ask *why*? Why was I so upset just because some snotty-nosed geezer made me look such a berk in front of all the uvver kids?' Sylvie leant her head back against the wall behind her. 'I never did find out. It's a pity. If only someone coulda' told me.'

They both got up as Nellie and Albert came out of the ward. Nellie, clearly very upset, was crying.

'Go on in, Rosie,' said Albert, his arm tucked around Nellie's shoulders. 'She wants ter see yer.'

Rose shook her head.

Sylvie took hold of her hands. 'Listen, mate. If yer goin' ter be me sister-in-law, yer goin' ter 'ave ter show wot I *know* yer made of.' She leant forward, and whispered in Rose's ear: 'Go in there, Rose. She needs yer.'

Rose entered the ward. At first she couldn't find Queenie's bed, for there were so many screens that had been put up to shield the patients who had been critically injured during air raids. And the place smelt to high Heaven of ether. It sickened Rose, reminding her of the people she had seen pulled out of the debris of their homes, and who were in so much pain they had to be sedated with ether until they reached hospital.

'You must be Rose.'

Rose was met by a nurse even younger than Sylvie. Her metal-rimmed spectacles had slipped halfway down her nose, and she was wearing a protective mask over her mouth which muffled her voice.

'She's been waiting for you. You must be very fond of each other.'

Rose followed the nurse along the ward to a bed tucked away in the far corner. Close by were French windows, one half of which was open to allow in some of the fresh late October air. There were no screens around Queenie's bed, so as Rose drew near she could see her young sister. It was a distressing sight, for Queenie was almost totally covered by a blanket and sheet, with only her face visible. Her head was swathed in white bandages, through which blood was still seeping. The nurse beckoned to Rose to sit in an upright chair on the left-hand side of the bed, then left her.

Queenie's eyes were closed, and for a moment or so, Rose sat there in absolute silence. Once or twice she caught a glimpse of a fat lady in the next bed watching her, but before Rose had the chance to smile at her, the woman quickly turned away as though guilty at having been caught staring.

'So wot d'yer fink, Rose?'

Rose swung her look back to Queenie, who had just spoken, but without opening her eyes. ''Ow're yer feelin?' she asked tentatively.

'Marvellous! I feel like doin' a tango down the Angel!'

Rose tried to smile, but she couldn't. Seeing her sister like this was an ordeal far worse than anything she had so far experienced on ambulance duty. 'Yer're goin' ter be all right, Queen,' she said, without believing a word of what she was saying. 'The doctor says so. It's just a question of time.'

There was a long pause. Rose looked out through the window at the side of Queenie's bed. She could just see two cats, one of them black with a white tip on his tail, the other a tabby. They were locked in mental battle, face to face, yowling and growling at each other, their hackles raised, and neither willing to yield an inch of ground.

'I wonder wot it's like ter fall in love.'

Rose was taken by surprise. 'Wot d'yer say, Queen?' she said, voice lowered, leaning closer.

'I said, I wonder wot it's like ter fall in love. It's never 'appened ter me, yer know.'

Rose suddenly felt compelled to take hold of her sister's hand. Queenie's red fingernail paint was peeling off, and Rose was surprised that she had never before noticed how long those fingernails actually were. 'Yer'll fall in love, Queen – one of these days. It's just a matter of time.'

Queenie's eyes suddenly sprang open. 'Yer don't 'ave ter pretend ter me, Rose. I've never loved anyone, so why should anyone want ter love *me*. Scabby-head 'Umble – that's me.'

'Don't talk like that, Queen. Yer'll get yer 'air back. Just yer see.'

'It's not me 'air I want, Rose. Wot I really want is all the life I've wasted. I want ter start it all over again. Everyfing'd be so different. I'd be able ter talk ter yer. Yer'd be able ter talk ter me.'

Queenie closed her eyes again. Her face crumpled up as she felt a searing pain right across her scalp.

''Ere – Queen. I want ter tell yer somefin'.' Rose drew her chair closer to the bedside, and with the fingers of one hand, gently stroked her young sister's cheek. 'D'yer remember that time we 'ad our picture took wiv Grandad in 'is back yard up at 'Oxton? D'yer remember when 'is deckchair collapsed; an' we all laughed our 'eads off an' 'e

170

got up straight away an' said, "Yer can't keep a good 'Umble down!" D'yer remember, Queen?'

As Queenie's pain gradually subsided, she did her best to nod her head.

'Well, 'e was right, yer know. Yer can't keep a good 'Umble down.' Rose's face was now no more than an inch or so from Queenie's. 'Yer know our trouble, don't yer, Queen? You and me. We bottle fings up. We should be more like Grandad. Speak our minds. If we don't like somefin' – say so! It's better than buildin' fings up inside yer, fings that just ain't true, all bitter an' twisted. Know what I mean, Queen? Do yer?'

Queenie's eyes remained closed as she spoke again. 'I'm sorry about everyfin', Rose. I want yer ter forgive me. Will yer – will yer try an' forgive me?'

'Come off it, yer 'nana! There ain't nuffin' ter forgive! We've just got ter make up for lost time, that's all. Okay, Queen?'

Queenie didn't reply. She couldn't. All she could do was to squeeze her big sister's hand as tight as she possibly could.

When Rose got up and kissed Queenie gently on her forehead, there were tears just beginning to trickle down her sister's cheeks. It was the first time Rose had ever seen Queenie cry.

After Rose had gone, the two cats on the grass patch outside had settled their dispute. It was a decisive victory for blackie with the white tip.

Chapter 12

Since joining the St John Ambulance Brigade, the only time Rose had the chance to see any of her friends in Chapel Market was when she came home early in the morning after late shift air-raid duties. But for one night at the beginning of November, bad weather caused a lull in the endless attacks on London, and this gave her a chance to wander around the market stalls.

Tuesday mornings were traditionally the slackest time of the week in the market, but today it was even more so, for dull November drizzle had kept shoppers at home and every one of the stalls was covered with tarpaulins. But no one complained, for the bad weather was also keeping Jerry back home where he belonged.

Rose felt glad to be in her own clothes again. For the past few months she had seemed practically to live in her ambulance cap and uniform. Her raincoat was not nearly as warm as her uniform greatcoat, and as she wandered through the market, there seemed to be no protection from the cold November air. But it warmed her heart to see some of the old faces peering out from beneath the stall covers: Stan and his cut-glass jewellery, Elsie Dumper and her bottled preserves, Slasher Mullins with his used cut-throat razors, Ada and Gert with Yeast-vite, shampoos, Zubes, DDT, 'an' just about everyfin' yer need for 'ouse an' 'ome!' But some of the more familiar faces were not there, mainly amongst the younger genera-tion. Peanut had been one of the first to be called up, and Rose was sad to see his green and gold-painted stall now abandoned.

The drizzle was now becoming more intense. The sky was thick with great puffs of sulky grey clouds, and it reminded Rose of the last time she had stood here and looked up at the sky. It was in the gradually fading days of summer, in early September, when the sky was a cloudless azure blue and streaked with the squiggly white vapour trails from the frantic dogfights that were being fought high above the rooftops of St Paul's and the City of London. Leaning against Peanut's old stall, the drizzle glistening on her face, Rose remembered that eventful day when she and the barrow boys and their customers were standing in exactly the same place, staring up at the great battle that was taking place above them, a battle for the very survival of Britain.

''Allo, stranger!'

Rose didn't need to look round to know that it was Badger who was talking to her.

''Allo, Badge.'

'So – 'ow's life in the ol' St John? Grandad told me yer've bin 'avin' a rough time up in Whitechapel.'

'Oh, it's not that bad, not for me anyway. It's the people who get bombed out I feel sorry for.'

Badger looked at her admiringly. 'I tip my 'at ter yer, Rose. It takes guts ter do a job like yer doin' – pickin' up

174

people wiv broken arms an' legs, an' blood pourin' all out of 'em.'

Rose shrugged her shoulders. 'Someone 'as ter do it, Badge. Them Jerry pilots don't see what they do ter people when they let their bombs go.'

Rain was beginning to drip from the peak of Badger's cloth cap, and down on to his yellow rubber bicycle cape. 'Did yer 'ear about that one that copped it down the Cally last week? Some Jerry pilot bailed out, an' 'is parachute di'n't open. Landed on top of the fish an' chip shop, all tangled up on the chimneypot. Right mess, they reckon!'

Rose shivered. ''Ow terrible.'

'No one asked 'im ter bomb us, Rose.'

Rose wiped the rain that was running down her face. 'I'm gettin' a bit soaked, Badge. Fink I'll get 'ome.'

Badger quickly stepped in front of her. 'Any chance of seein' yer for a drink this evenin', Rose?'

Rose tensed. There was no denying that she had a great fondness for Badger, but since her painful experience with Michael Devereaux, she deeply distrusted any male who wanted to take her out. 'It's a bit difficult, Badge,' she said, trying hard to smile with rain drizzling down her cheeks. 'If it's busy up the City ternight they could call me in any time.'

'In wevver like this? Yer got ter be jokin'! Jerry wouldn't be able ter see an 'and in front of 'im if 'e tried ter get fru *them* clouds.'

'The wevver could change ever so quick, Badge.' Rose was now panicking. 'If it cleared, Jerry'd be over in a flash.'

Badger took hold of her hands. '*Please*, Rose. Just one evenin'. We could take the tram down to the Nag's 'Ead in

'Olloway. I know this geezer 'oo serves behind the bar there. 'E'd give us a free pint ...'

'I can't, Badge,' said Rose desperately, trying to move away. 'I really can't.'

'But this may be me last chance. I've got me papers. I'm goin' off the day after termorrer.'

Suddenly Rose noticed how he had changed over these past months. He was no longer the cheeky puppy, but a fresh-faced teenager who looked as though he was hopelessly in love. 'Papers?' she asked timidly.

'I've joined up, Rose.' A broad grin suddenly beamed across his face. 'I'm goin' in the Navy.'

Rose gasped. 'Oh for Chrissake, Badge! Yer can't! Yer mustn't! There's a war on. It's too dangerous. An' yer much too young.'

'I'm nineteen. I'm not a kid any more, Rose. Let's face it, yer're doin' yer bit, it's time I did mine. I'd be called up next year wevver I like it or not.'

In his bright, eager face, Rose saw there every other young hot-head of his age who craved for excitement no matter what the consequence. 'Yer should wait anuvver year, Badge. It may all be over by then.'

'Blimey, I 'ope not!' replied Badger, quick as a flash. 'I want ter see a bit of action first.'

'Action!' Rose spluttered in disbelief. 'You could get killed!'

'Yeah. I fought about that. But I'd rarver go down on a boat than be mowed down on a battlefield.'

Rose was horrified. 'Badge! Don't say such fings! If anyfin' 'appened ter yer, we'd all be 'eart-broken – yer mum an' dad, yer grandad, all yer friends ...'

'An wot about you, Rose? Would you be 'eart-broken, too?'

Rose looked up, and found that she was staring straight into Badger's eyes. 'Of course I would, Badge,' she said tentatively. 'Yer know I would.'

Badger stepped even closer to her. 'Then come out wiv me ternight. Just this once. *Please*.'

Rose bit her lip so hard it bled a little. Over Badger's shoulder she could just see her mum at Charlie Spindle's fruit and veg stall, deep in conversation with Badger's grandad on his vegetable stall. She wondered what the two of them were talking about, for although they were both pretending not to be watching Rose and Badger together, there was no doubt that that was precisely what they were doing.

Then she looked back at Badger's bright and eager face again. There was such hope there, such desire. In those few seconds before she replied, she asked herself whether there was any way at all that she could break down this barrier she had built with every male she had met since that nightmare encounter with Michael Devereaux. Suppose if she did decide to go out with Badger, and he tried to touch her, even kiss her. What would she do? How would she react? Suppose she hurt him? Suppose she allowed him to go off into the Navy remembering her as someone who had hurt him deeply? What would happen if he went to his grave at the bottom of the sea, and she never saw him again? Oh God! It would never work. She couldn't go out with this boy, she just couldn't. Every instinct she had ever had was telling her to say no, no, no!

Her only hope was that the rain would stop, and the

miserable thick clouds would roll back once and for all.
Then she could say no, and prevent what would inevitably
be a disaster for Badger – and herself. Suddenly her mind
was made up.

'I'd love ter come wiv yer, Badge,' she said. 'See yer
ternight.'

As Rose walked off through the relentless drizzle, she
could hear the whoops of joy and ecstatic cheers of one very
happy barrow boy.

That evening, the Nag's Head pub on the corner of
Holloway and Seven Sisters Road was doing good business
as usual. Its regular customers had always refused to be
intimidated by the nightly dusk-to-dawn air raids. If the
going got rough, they would usually withdraw to a public
street shelter nearby, not forgetting to take their glasses of
draught with them! It was also Badger's favourite pub, for
not only could he get the odd free pint from his mate Jack
Burns, who served behind the bar, but the Public Bar was a
friendly meeting place for a game of darts and a chat with
the pub's pet parrot.

It was drizzling when Rose and Badger arrived, but the
Public Bar was warm, with a fire burning in the grate, and
the air thick with fag smoke.

After he had introduced Rose to Jack behind the bar,
Badger managed to find a seat at a table by the fire. There
wasn't much room for they had to share the table with a
rather large lady whose hair was in curlers and a hairnet,
and her equally large husband who wore a flat cap far too
big for him and whose mouth was sagging through lack of
teeth. Rose found her shoulder almost touching the large

bird cage, where the parrot was clinging to the bars with his claws and beak, watching Rose's every move.

'Got somefin' ter tell yer,' Badger said, after he had returned from the bar with a shandy for Rose and a pint of light for himself. 'It's really a sort of – confession.'

Rose looked curious as he squeezed on to the worn leather bench at the side of her.

Badger snuggled up close, in an attempt to talk privately to her. 'Remember that time last year, when I asked yer ter me birfday party?'

Rose felt her heart sink. 'I know, Badge,' she replied guiltily. 'I really am sorry for that.'

'Yer don't 'ave ter apologise, Rose. Not ter me. All I wanted ter say was, I *knew* why yer di'n't come, but I di'n't take umbridge.'

Rose's heart missed a beat. 'Yer – *knew*?'

Badger smiled reassuringly. 'It's okay – honest it is. I knew all about that la-di-da bloke yer went out wiv. But *you* liked 'im, so yer 'ad the right ter do wot yer wanted.'

Rose sighed. She couldn't believe Badger's generosity. He was so unlike Michael Devereaux, so unlike any boy she had ever known. 'Badge, I don't know wot ter say . . .'

'Mine's a pint! Mine's a pint!' Rose was saved by the intervention of the parrot, who must have memorised his set piece for just such occasions.

Simultaneously, a very angry white mongrel dog sprang out from beneath the table and leapt up at the cage, sending the parrot fluttering and squawking into a rage.

'No, Mussolini!' the large lady yelled angrily at the small creature, who had a black patch over one eye and looked as though someone had given him a fourpenny one. ''Ow many times do I 'ave ter tell yer! Leave that bleedin' parrot alone!'

At the mercy of such ferocity, Mussolini disappeared under the table again.

'Sorry about that, dear,' said the large lady to Rose. 'Yer can see why we call 'im Mussolini. Never stops yappin', little sod!'

Her husband nodded in agreement, then lit a fag, and sucked on it with his gumless mouth.

Rose smiled back, weakly, then turned away.

'The fing is, Rose,' Badger continued, 'I always knew yer'd never stick to a ponce like that. That's why I di'n't worry when Queenie told me 'oo yer'd gone out wiv. Honest, Rose, yer're too good for 'is sort.'

'Yer're a good bloke, Badge,' said Rose. 'One of these days yer're goin' ter find a gel just as nice as you are.'

'Get orf wiv yer,' said Badger, quickly lighting up a Woodbine to cover his embarrassment. 'Anyway, I've found *my* perfect gel. I found 'er a long time ago.'

Rose lowered her eyes uneasily.

'D'yer know when I first knew I was in love wiv yer, Rose?'

Rose smiled feebly and shook her head.

'When I saw yer come down the market wiv yer mum. I was about six, an' yer stopped at my grandad's stall an' looked at me an' said, "Wot's yer name, ugly face?"' He chuckled to himself. 'I can see yer now as though it was only yesterday. Yer mum shook yer, an' told yer ter say sorry. But I said—'

'Yer said, "Yer don't 'ave ter say sorry, 'cos I am ugly."'

Badger's mouth dropped open.

Rose smiled. 'Yes, Badge, I remember. An' it wasn't true. Yer was never ugly.'

'Rose! Yer remember!' Badger was so overjoyed, he wanted to take her in his arms and kiss her right there and then. But he was distracted by the large lady, who was now dipping crisps into her pint of stout, whilst her husband was making sucking sounds as he pulled on his fag.

In the background, a boisterous game of darts had begun and one of the well-oiled players suddenly launched into a shaky rendering of 'All the Nice Girls Love a Sailor!' Before he reached the second line, everyone in the bar, including Rose and Badger, and the large lady and her husband, were all joining in.

It took a moment for Rose to realise that Badger was reaching for her hand beneath the table. Their eyes met. He had lost that puppy look now: this was Badger all grown up. As the song continued, they sang the words, without attaching any meaning to them. Rose found that for the first time she was not avoiding Badger's gaze. Their eyes were locked in contact, trying to say something to each other without speaking. Rose felt totally mixed up and hated herself for it.

The song came to an end with a rousing cheer from everyone.

'Mine's a pint! Mine's a pint!'

This was more than Mussolini could take from the trouble-making parrot, so he sprang out from beneath the table and leapt up at the cage. The parrot was waiting for him, and gave him a quick peck on the nose. The small mongrel let out a howl of pain, and rushed back under the table.

Rose and Badger decided it was definitely time to leave.

For the next hour or so, Rose and Badger strolled in whichever direction they felt like. It was a very dark night, and although it had finally stopped drizzling, the clouds were still hanging low in the sky, hiding the barrage balloons waiting for any likely intruder.

By this time, Badger felt brave enough to put his arm around Rose's waist. They stopped briefly to look in the windows of the North London Drapery Stores, but, even with the help of Rose's torch-beam, they couldn't see much of the furniture and curtain materials there because the glass was so heavily protected against bomb blast with strips of sticky paper. They decided to turn back once they had reached the Gas Light and Coke Company on the other side of Hornsey Road.

Badger told Rose practically the entire story of his life – about his mum and dad and the other baby they had had, a little girl, who had died when she was born. He had always much preferred his grandad's company to his own mum and dad's, and as soon as he was able, he wanted to get married and move into a place of his own.

Rose listened in silence. He was so eager to talk that she felt it would be cruel to interrupt him. But she just couldn't help feeling anxious. Badger was in love with her, there was no doubt about that. But she didn't love him, or at least she had never thought so until this evening. Now she wasn't sure. He was kind and considerate, and that was something she had never known before – at least not from a man. But was kindness enough? Shouldn't she be feeling something inside, like she never wanted to be parted from him? The further they strolled, the more confused she became, so much so that after a while she couldn't actually concentrate on what he was saying.

They paused to peer into the window of a pet shop inside the Holloway Arcade. By the light of Rose's torch, they could see goldfish swimming around a dimly lit glass tank, and tiny kittens huddled up together on the straw inside a cage.

'Badge, why d'yer 'ave ter go an' join up?'

'I 'ad ter, Rose,' he said, keeping his voice low as though someone might be listening. 'I 'ave ter get away.'

'Wot d'yer mean?'

'They want me ter stay there, Rose. Mum, Dad, Grandad – all of 'em. They want me ter stay there in the market. I can't do it, Rose, I just can't. I don't want ter spend the rest of me life servin' vegetables be'ind a stall. I want ter see fings, go places. I want ter use me mind. *You* understand that, don't yer, Rose?'

For a moment Rose said nothing, and just studied his face in the glare of the torch-beam. 'Yes, Badge,' she replied. 'I understand. But it's not a good enough reason for joinin' up. Yer should talk ter yer mum an' dad. Tell 'em 'ow yer feel. Yer shouldn't 'ave ter put yer life in danger just ter get away from 'ome.'

'They won't listen, Rose. They've never listened. They just don't want ter let go.' He lowered his eyes, and for the first time all evening, his infectious smile faded. 'Trouble is, I love me mum an' dad an' grandad too much ter let 'em 'ave their own way.'

Rose felt an intense admiration for Badger.

Suddenly, he stretched out his hand and turned off the torch. Apart from the dim light from the fish tank, they were now standing in total darkness. 'Rose,' he said, his voice only a whisper, 'would yer be upset if I kissed yer?'

For an instant, Rose panicked. Although she knew this moment was bound to happen sooner or later, she was completely unprepared for it. Yet she didn't want to say no. Not because she was afraid of hurting him just as he was about to go away, but because something inside her was attracted to him. 'No, Badge,' she said softly, 'I wouldn't be upset.'

Badger drew closer in the dark, put his arms around her, and kissed her gently on the lips. At first it was just a peck, but then he kissed her again, and this time it was much more prolonged.

Rose felt the warmth of his body against her own. There was immense passion in Badger's kiss, and she loved the taste of his moist lips on her own. And yet, in that kiss, something was missing. She had no idea what it was, but the blood in her veins was running just as cold as the night air.

When he pulled away, Badger whispered into her ear, 'Will yer be my gel, Rose? Will yer wait for me?'

Over Badger's shoulder, Rose could just see the goldfish swimming gracefully around their tank. Like her, they seemed to have no sense of direction.

Chapter 13

After the all-too-brief lull, once again 'Moaning Minnie' began to wail out remorselessly night after night, and the Luftwaffe resumed their efforts to bomb the heart out of the East End and the rest of London. During the middle of November, the Germans also attacked the city of Coventry, and on one night alone over 400 tons of high explosives were dropped, badly destroying the city centre and almost completely wrecking the much-loved cathedral.

Meanwhile, the Humble family did their best to cope with the hardships of war, though the strain was beginning to tell on Nellie. Every morning when she emerged from yet another sleepless night with Queenie and the twins on the tube platform, at least one of the nearby streets seemed to have had a direct hit, and she never knew what to expect when she got home.

To make things worse, young George no longer spent his nights with the family down the tube. To Nellie's horror, he had enrolled as a cyclist messenger in the AFS, and despite the fact that he was only sixteen years old, each night he found himself delivering messages from one fire station to another in some of the worst bombed streets in the City. Although Albert was furious with the boy for not seeking his permission to take on such a hazardous occupation, he never stopped boasting to his Home Guard cronies that 'my boy George 'as got the guts of a true 'Umble!'

The first few days of December turned out to be really cold, and flakes of snow fluttered down in Chapel Market. As always, the snow was at first greeted as a novelty, for everything looked so beautiful, like a Victorian scene on a Christmas card, but when the snow became frozen solid and had to be chipped off every morning before start of business, the novelty soon wore off. The kids who hadn't been evacuated enjoyed it; snowballing the traders was a game that came free, and was much more fun than most of the austere war-time toys.

The December air raids were more ferocious, the damage more widespread, and the number of civilian casualties increasing every night. Rose had even heard rumours that the House of Commons had been badly damaged during a heavy air raid on the West End, and despite Hitler's so-called decision to defer the Nazi invasion of Britain until the spring, Rose was convinced that the intensity of the raids was a softening up for a full-scale onslaught on the British Isles by his ruthless army.

On a particularly cold night in the middle of December, Rose and Amanda were called out to a major incident at an old 'bug-hutch' cinema in Shoreditch. The journey there proved to be pretty hair-raising, for enemy aircraft were still overhead, blanket bombing the entire area and devastating every street. On two occasions Rose had to stop the ambulance, for nearby bomb blasts practically lifted the vehicle off its wheels. As they sat there, with the ignition turned off, and waiting for the hostile aircraft to pass over, they could see the whole sky looking like a pinball table in an amusement arcade. Apart from the usual crisscross of searchlights, which occasionally picked out the clumsy silver barrage balloons, the sky was also shimmering to the pom-pom of tracer bullets being fired from the surrounding streets by a mobile naval anti-aircraft gun. It was an extraordinary sight, for every so often two or three enemy planes were caught in the searchlights, like flies trapped in a spider's web, with smoke suddenly billowing out of them as one of the deadly pom-pom bullets reached its target.

By the time Rose and Amanda arrived at the cinema, the building was burning fiercely, with one fire engine trying to take on a job that clearly needed more. The combination of bombs whistling through the air and exploding close by, and the thundering non-stop barrage of ack-ack guns, made the whole operation even more perilous.

As Rose jumped down from the driver's seat, a very harassed AFS superintendent was already rushing across to meet her.

'You'll have to work fast! We've lost two men in there. The whole circle caved in on them.'

Laid out on the pavement near the gates of an adjoining block of council flats were the bodies of two firemen, only partially covered by blankets. All around, the snow was melting from the intense heat of the blazing cinema.

'It's been one hell of a catastrophe!' said the superintendent, out of breath, his face a deep red colour from the heat. 'It took us over a quarter of an hour to get any water out of the hydrant. The bloody thing was frozen solid!'

Rose and Amanda got a stretcher out of the ambulance. With the fire raging more fiercely every moment, Rose had doubts that anyone had managed to survive.

'Is there anyone left inside?' she asked.

'No. Except for the manager and his wife, the place was empty. They were trapped in their flat at the back of the building. We just got them out in time— Watch out!'

He was interrupted by the sound of a bomb whistling through the air, and landing to a loud explosion in a nearby street. As Rose and Amanda covered their ears and sank to a crouching position, all they could hear was the shattering of glass and tinkling of shrapnel as it rained down on to snow-covered rooftops and pavements all around.

'Get the stretcher ready, girls!' The superintendent was already on his feet again. 'They're bringing one of our blokes out! Follow me!'

Rose and Amanda picked up the stretcher and followed the superintendent across the road to where two firemen were heavily supporting a third as they emerged from the blazing cinema. 'Is he badly hurt?' yelled Amanda, above the noise of water being hosed on to the building.

''E needs some oxygen, fast!' one of the two supporting men called back.

'Get him on the stretcher, boys!'

Rose and Amanda stood back whilst the two firemen carefully laid their injured mate down on the stretcher. Rose supported the man's shoulders, whilst Amanda removed his tin helmet.

'Try and undo his collar, dear!' called Amanda.

Just as Rose was getting to grips with the top button of

the injured man's tunic, there was an explosion from inside the blazing cinema itself. Everyone threw themselves to the ground, including the men tackling the blaze, but Rose instinctively threw herself across the injured fireman lying on the stretcher, and didn't get up again until the flying debris had settled.

'Sorry, mate!' she said to the injured man, who was now having great difficulty in breathing. 'Take it easy. We'll get yer right in no time!'

Amanda and Rose had to struggle to lift the stretcher on their own, for the firemen had rushed off to continue their efforts to control the blaze.

The journey back to the ambulance was a perilous one, avoiding the fire engine pumps that were working at full pelt, and negotiating the hosepipes that were connected up to the thawed-out street hydrant.

The moment they had got the stretcher fixed into position inside the ambulance, Rose and Amanda went to work on the injured fireman.

'Let's get his tunic off, Rose!' Amanda supported him under his arms whilst Rose struggled to pull off his tunic.

The young fireman's face was red raw with burn marks, and part of the skin on his forehead was peeling off.

'Oxygen!' Rose said urgently. ' 'Is lungs're full of smoke!'

She ripped open the top of his shirt, took the rubber oxygen mask Amanda was handing to her, and shoved it over the injured man's mouth. By this time, he was wheezing and spluttering. 'On, Amanda! Turn it on – quick!'

There was an immediate hissing sound as oxygen started

filtering through into the mask from the emergency cylinder.

'Easy does it now, mate,' said Rose, kneeling beside the fireman, and holding the mask firmly in place over his nose and mouth. 'Yer goin' ter be all right ... breeve in ... breeve ... that's it, that's the way ... luvely ... yer doin' fine, mate, fine!'

The young fireman, in considerable pain, was groaning and trying to breathe in the oxygen at the same time.

Meanwhile, Amanda was pouring some calamine lotion on to a white surgical cloth. 'Here, Rose. Take this!'

Rose took the cloth, and very gently dabbed it on the burns on the injured man's forehead. The fireman let out a strangulated groan as the cool lotion touched the burnt layer of skin.

'It's all right, mate!' Rose said, wrestling to keep the oxygen mask in place and the calamine-soaked cloth on the man's forehead. 'Let's get 'im out of 'ere. 'E needs the doctor,' she told Amanda.

As she spoke, there was an almighty explosion from the other side of the road, which practically rolled the ambulance over on its side. Rose and Amanda yelled out in unison, but kept their nerve and held the injured man down until the ambulance righted itself.

'Rose!'

As Amanda called out, a blinding light flickered through the window on her side of the ambulance. 'Incendiary!'

Rose didn't even stop to think. She grabbed a blanket from the empty second stretcher, and rushed out of the ambulance. 'Keep an eye on 'im!'

Amanda yelled out to her: 'No, Rose! It might explode!'

But Rose was already out of the ambulance, leaving Amanda to look after their injured patient.

The incendiary bomb was blazing just a few feet away from the side of the ambulance, but the fire crew were far too busy with the cinema blaze to do anything about it. Holding the blanket up to shield her face, Rose rushed straight at the fiercely burning firebomb, which looked like a paraffin blowlamp that had just been pumped up. In one swift, perilous action, she threw the blanket over the bomb, then leapt into the driver's seat of the ambulance, turned the key in the ignition, and drove off at high speed.

A few miles away, Albert Humble was also having his share of the night's drama. On Home Guard duty with Charlie Spindle from the market, he was searching the trees and bushes around Highbury Fields after reports that a German airman had been seen parachuting out of his blazing aeroplane. During the previous twenty-four hours, an inch of snow had fallen over North London, and although it had stopped and the skies were now clear, the ground had frozen, making it difficult for Albert and Charlie to move around without making loud crunching sounds with their feet. They could also hardly disguise their presence, since the brilliant white beams from their torches were bouncing in every direction.

'Wot 'appens if we find 'im?' asked Charlie tentatively, as they made their way across the Fields in the direction of Highbury Crescent.

'I know wot I'll do,' replied Albert, voice low. Like Charlie, he had his rifle poised ready. 'A couple of 'ot bullets up 'is 'ooter. Then 'e'd know wot it's all about!'

Charlie was shocked. 'Yer don't mean yer'd shoot 'im down? Before we 'ad a chance ter 'and 'im over ter the police?'

'Every Jerry's a bleedin' murderer, Charlie. The only good one's a dead one.'

'They're only doin' wot they're told, Bert. Most of 'em are kids. They've bin brain-washed by 'Itler an' 'is gang.'

Albert came to a halt. 'Listen to that din out there!' he said grittily, above the barrage of anti-aircraft gunfire coming from Victoria Park in neighbouring Hackney. 'An' look at that sky. Can yer imagine wot they're goin' fru down the East End?'

Against the rooftops of the boys' school in Highbury Grove, the whole sky seemed to be on fire.

'I'm tellin' yer, Charlie – it's murder, 'olesale bleedin' murder. Yer di'n't 'ave ter go up front in the last war. I know wot Jerry's like. Take it from me – 'e don't need ter be told wot ter do!'

Whilst they were speaking, another wave of enemy bombers came droning overhead. For a brief moment Albert and Charlie just stood there, staring up at them, caught in the beams of dozens of searchlights, puffs of white shellfire bursting all over the night sky.

'Wot's that?' Charlie said suddenly, in a loud whisper.

'Wot?'

'Di'n't yer 'ear it? Somefin' in those bushes over there.'

Albert turned to look. 'Turn off yer light! Quick!'

As both men turned off their torches, the air was pierced by the now familiar sound of a cluster of bombs whistling down from the enemy planes above. The two men threw themselves flat on to their stomachs in the snow, allowing the blast waves from the exploding bombs in nearby St Paul's Road to pass right over their heads.

Within seconds of the explosion, there was the inevitable distant sound of fire engines, police cars, and ambulances. Albert and Charlie waited for the drone of enemy aeroplanes to pass over, then sat up and tried to brush the snow off their khaki greatcoats.

'Bloody 'ell!' sniffed Charlie, adjusting his tin helmet. 'That was a close one.'

Albert picked himself up, and in doing so found that he had been sitting on something. 'Wot's this? Charlie! Shine yer light!'

Charlie switched on his torch and both men stared in disbelief. Stretched out across the snow where they had just taken cover was a parachute.

'Christ!' yelped Charlie, hardly daring to raise his voice. 'It's Jerry's parachute! 'E's 'ere somewhere!'

Albert immediately picked up his rifle, switched on his torch, and started to look around. Even as he did so, a man's voice called out to them.

'*Bitte! Ich bin hier.*'

Albert and Charlie's torch beams picked out a young German pilot, wearing a fur-collared flying jacket and helmet, and with both his hands on his head to indicate that he was offering himself in surrender.

Charlie looked as though he was seeing a ghost. 'Bloody 'ell!' was all he could splutter.

Albert immediately raised his rifle as if to fire a shot. ''*Alt!*' he yelled, using one of the few words in German he could remember from his Home Guard training.

The pilot at once came to a halt.

Albert and Charlie moved slowly, cautiously, towards their prisoner. As they got closer, they could see that he could not have been older than his early twenties.

'*Wie heissen Sie?*' Albert's fractured German sounded a little ill at ease in the middle of Highbury Fields.

'*Ich bin Deutscher.*'

'Wot'd 'e say, Bert?' asked Charlie, the rifle shaking in his hands.

Albert ignored his mate, and snapped back at the prisoner: 'I know yer a bloody Jerry! I asked yer name, yer name! *Wie heissen Sie*, yer 'Itler git?'

'*Bitte,*' replied the airman, timidly. 'I speak a little English. I am *ein Deutscher* – German – I am German. *Mein Fleuzeug* – *mein* airplane – shot down.' He looked frightened and confused.

'Good job too!' was Charlie's only contribution, but it was all the courage he was prepared to show.

'I know yer a bleedin' German,' Albert said harshly. 'I asked yer wot yer name is. Where d'yer come from?'

'*Bitte . . .*' The young airman took a step forward, not understanding.

'Stay where yer are!' Albert took aim with his rifle.

'*Halt!*' said Charlie, in his best Chapel Market German.

'*Bitte!*' pleaded the young airman, keeping absolutely motionless, with his hands pressed firmly down on to the top of his head.

Albert took aim, set the cock of his rifle, and covered the trigger with his finger. 'I'm askin' yer one last time, Jerry boy! Where d'yer come from?'

'No, Bert! 'E's right. Yer 'eard wot the sergeant said. If

we take a prisoner-of-war, the only information 'e 'as ter give us is 'is name, rank, an' number. It says so in the Geneva Convention.'

'Sod the bleedin' Geneva Convention!' Albert was still peering through the sight of his rifle. 'Come 'ere, you!'

The German flier took a few tentative steps towards Albert. The reflection from Charlie's torch was dazzling his eyes.

'*Halt!*'

For a few brief moments, Albert was enjoying the feeling of power. It was something he had not felt since his time in the Army during the last war – the knowledge that by simply pulling the trigger of his rifle, he could stop one more Jerry from killing his own people. 'D'yer 'ave any idea 'ow many people yer've killed round 'ere ternight?' he asked quietly, threateningly.

The airman, convinced that he would now be shot, closed his eyes, and took a deep, quivering breath. 'I hope zat I vill never know,' was all he could say. His face was like stone, and racked with anguish.

Albert's forefinger was throbbing against the trigger of his rifle. A fraction more pressure, and the young prisoner facing him would be dead. But could he do it? Could he really take the life of the young bloke he was staring at through his gun-sight? He had seen so many faces like this before, lying flat on their backs on the battlefields of France during the last war, Bosch and Tommies alike, their lifeless eyes wide open, staring up in bewilderment to the sky above, to the God who had created them. Most of them were just like this boy – dragged from their homes to fight a war in which they were promised so much, but nothing more than a name, rank, and number – tiny, disposable specks of dust on a polished table. For one second, Albert felt pity for this figure in his gun-sight, but then he thought of what this boy could have done to his own family – to his Nellie and the kids. They could all have been wiped out by just one bomb dropped by this killer. Yes! That's what he was. This wasn't a boy, a man – this was a killer!

'Turn round!'

Albert's order took Charlie by surprise. 'Wot yer goin' ter do, Bert?'

The young airman hesitated.

'I said, turn round! An' keep yer 'ands on yer 'ead!'

Eyes still tightly shut, hands on head, and now firmly resigned to his fate, the boy turned round.

Albert pointed the nozzle of his rifle towards his prisoner's back.

Charlie lunged forward to try to grab Albert's rifle. 'No, Bert! Don't do it! For Chrissake . . . !'

Albert pushed him away. The barrel of his rifle was now dug right between the airman's shoulder blades. 'Walk!' he commanded.

And as Albert's rifle dug deeper into his back, the boy was marched off slowly across the snow-covered fields of Highbury.

At that moment, the moon appeared for the first time through the night clouds. It was an odd sight – three eerie silhouettes, their shadows gradually stretching longer and longer across the white ground.

The thin line between life and death had never been finer.

It was still dark when Rose drove the ambulance into the courtyard of the London Hospital. She and Amanda had no help to get the injured fireman on to a stretcher trolley, for the hospital porters, nurses, and doctors were working at full capacity after the night's particularly ferocious and widespread air raid.

Rose felt pure anguish as she watched another ambulance crew taking away the covered bodies of the two firemen who had died in the cinema blaze.

Amanda was also upset. 'These boys,' she said, grim-faced. 'We owe them so much. Oh God! When will it ever end?'

Rose knew exactly what her mate meant. As she and Amanda lifted their patient's stretcher on to the trolley, she could only think of the enormous sacrifice these men were making every day of this horrific war against civilians. And not only men: women, too, were risking their lives in the Auxiliary Fire Service, providing badly needed refreshments to the fire-fighters and the bombed-out victims.

Whilst Rose wheeled the stretcher trolley down a hospital corridor, Amanda kept the oxygen mask firmly in place over the patient's mouth. By the time they got him to the Emergency Burns Unit he was breathing more naturally, but still in pain from the peeling skin on his scorched face.

With help from two nurses, Rose and Amanda carefully lifted the fireman on to the observation couch. Then, whilst they waited for the doctor to arrive, Amanda went off with one of the nurses to file her report, leaving Rose to help the other nurse make the fireman more comfortable.

The nurse moved to another patient and Rose was left alone with the fireman. Around her there were groans from other air-raid victims who were suffering from terrible firebomb burns. She leant closer to the fireman, and spoke to him in a low, gentle voice. 'Look after yerself, mate. Don't worry, yer on the up an' up.' She turned to leave, but to her surprise, the fireman's hand suddenly took hold of her own. With the other hand, he pulled away the oxygen mask. 'Hey!' she said. 'Wot yer up to?'

Only now, with her first real glimpse of his face, did Rose realise that her patient was the same cheeky bloke she had first encountered during the sugar warehouse blaze down by the river, and again in the old bombed-out Victorian church in Shoreditch.

'Oh, it's you, is it?' she found herself saying perkily. 'Bin up ter yer old tricks again, 'ave yer?'

Although breathless, his face burnt red raw, the young fireman did his best to smile back at her.

'Can't get rid of me as easy as that, Ginge,' he said, barely audible. 'I'm 'ere ter stay.'

Chapter 14

Somewhere in England
14 Dec. 1940

Dear Rose,

Here I am agin, still out on the old sqware bashin and fed up to the teeth with it! Still, my P.O. reckons Im doin O.K. and wen I've finished me trainin (though God knows wen that'll be!), I hope to get on a ship. I'd like to be a radio op. but I don't know whether I've got the savvy for all that. Anyway, it don't matter, cos as long as I get the chance to have a go at jerry, who cares?

Rose had had a tough night, and she didn't have the energy to read right through another of Badger's letters. This was the fourth one he'd written since he joined the Navy just over a month ago, and she hadn't yet got over the shock of knowing that he could write at all! She also couldn't get out of her mind what he had said to her on that night in the Holloway Arcade before he went away: *Will yer be my gel, Rose? Will yer wait fer me?* Those words still haunted her.

Stifling a huge yawn, she folded up Badger's letter, put it back in the envelope, and stuffed it into her tunic pocket. In the background her dad was fast asleep in the big double bed, and snoring so loud he sounded as though he was one of Goering's new secret bomber planes. But then Rose knew that he had been out all night with Charlie Spindle on Home Guard night patrol, and that no doubt the two of them had had one of their typically boozy sessions together.

George was curled up in his usual place in front of the oven grate, his face still filthy dirty after a night on his bicycle carrying messages between fire stations in the thick of the air raid. Just like George, Rose thought to herself. Never wash unless you absolutely have to! As it was now well past seven in the morning, Rose knew that her mum was already out helping set up Charlie's vegetable stall in the market. And, knowing that Queenie and the twins would be up at any moment, she decided to get to bed right away.

She was half asleep when she reached the top-floor landing, but the shock that was waiting for her there woke her up. Someone was hunched up in a blanket and eiderdown just outside the bedroom door.

Rose's yell of delight would have made any of her barrow boy friends really proud of her.

'Gus!'

It was unlikely that anyone was still asleep in the place after that.

Rose was too excited to sleep that morning. Gus was only home on a forty-eight-hour pass, and as she hadn't seen him for months, she wanted to make the most of being with him.

Most of the morning was spent listening to their dad's Home Guard adventures on Highbury Fields the night before, and how he and Charlie had been congratulated by their Section Commander for searching out the German pilot, and then handing him over so swiftly to the police. Rose and Gus were suitably impressed, but after an hour and a half of listening to the same story over and over again, they had to remind their dad that Mum was waiting outside in the market to show Gus off.

Gus's stroll through the market became more like a royal visit. From every stall came a cry of ''Ere 'e comes! Gawd bless yer, son!' or ''Ave a pint on me, Gus!' Hands stretched out to shake his wherever he went, and as soon as Elsie Dumper on her bottled preserves stall saw him, she burst into tears. This prompted her husband to call her a 'sentimental old bag', and Gus left them both having a right old barney. By the time he reached Charlie Spindle's vegetable stall, with its huge words written large above, 'BUSINESS AS USUAL', Nellie was so bursting with excitement and pride, she could hardly contain herself.

'Wot d'yer fink I've bin given for our tea ternight, Gus?' Nellie had to lean across the stall and lower her voice, just in case anyone could overhear. 'Scrag of mutton – two pounds of it! Keep yer mouff shut, son. It's all black market.'

After most of the traders had had the chance to pat him on the back, Gus began to feel uneasy. Telling everyone that he was dying for a pint, he and Rose left their mum, and eased their way out of the market, with the traders' cheers still ringing in their ears.

A few minutes later they found themselves crossing the Caledonian Road on the old bridge over the canal. On the way, Gus spoke hardly at all, and he walked so fast Rose had difficulty keeping up with him. It was only when they reached the towpath alongside the canal itself that Gus started to unwind, and their walk gradually slowed down to a stroll.

'It's no good, Rosie,' Gus said suddenly. 'I can't take none of all that. They don't understand – none of 'em. The boys in the market – they've got it all wrong. They treat me like an 'ero. I'm not.' He looked up briefly at Rose, hands in his trouser pockets as he strolled. 'D'yer understand wot I'm sayin', Rosie? I'm no 'ero. I'm no different to any uvver bloke in the Army. It's a job. That's all it is – a job.'

Rose pulled up the collar of her winter coat, then dug her hands into her pockets to keep warm. 'They don't mean no 'arm, Gus. They're just proud of yer, that's all.'

Gus stopped walking, and turned to look at her. 'Proud? Wot of?'

Rose shrugged her shoulders. 'Yer in the Army. Yer was at Dunkirk.'

'I'm not proud of bein' at Dunkirk! Dunkirk was a bloody mess, and you know it!'

Gus strolled on, and once again Rose had to quicken her pace to keep up. As they progressed along the towpath, a motorised barge slowly eased its way along the canal towards them. Although its cargo was covered by a huge tarpaulin piled with a layer of frozen snow, there was no doubt that it was transporting some kind of munitions. Gus and Rose stopped to watch it pass, but their minds were not on what they were seeing, for they did not return the friendly waves coming from the barge-master.

'I di'n't want ter come 'ome,' Gus said, staring out at the barge. 'Yer know that, don't yer? I could've come 'ome munffs ago, but I di'n't want ter.' He turned to Rose. 'I couldn't face it.'

Rose hesitated a moment before replying, 'I know, Gus.' Then she turned to look at him. 'Wot 'appened at Dunkirk?'

'I don't want ter talk about Dunkirk – right? I want ter forget all about it!'

'Yer'll never forget it, Gus – if yer *don't* talk about it.'

Once the barge had passed, they moved on again. As they strolled, Gus idly brushed his hand along a brick wall with several inches of frozen snow settled on it. Once he had gathered a handful, he aimlessly started to mould it into a snowball.

'When I go back termorrer night, I ain't comin' 'ome no more. Not ter live anyway.'

Rose felt a numbness inside. She had realised the best way she could help her brother was merely to listen, so she remained silent, and as they strolled casually, she kept her eyes glued aimlessly down at the frozen towpath.

'Next pass I get, I'm goin' ter move in wiv Sylvie. Won't be for some time, of course. Next year, I reckon. Won't be 'ome for Christmas. Just as well, really.'

They had come to a halt again. They could hear the background sound of the noon-time traffic hurrying across the Cally bridge. Nearer, birds were singing. Gus couldn't see any of them, but he could hear them all right.

'Funny fing. When we was on that beach, we di'n't 'ear no birds. Di'n't see none, neivver.' He looked at Rose. 'Yer'd fink there'd be seagulls or somefin', wouldn't yer? I mean, after all, we was by the sea.' Briefly, he glanced up at the sky. 'No, not wiv all that row goin' on. Birds don't like guns.' He chuckled to himself. 'They ain't the only ones!'

Rose watched him carefully, caringly. His eyes, much older eyes than when she had last seen him, were now taut and deep-set. This was no big brother who had come home to his family. This was a fully grown-up man.

'When I saw all them boats comin',' continued Gus, 'fousands of 'em, some of 'em not much bigger than rowin' boats – when I saw 'em, I fought: right, Gus, it's all over now. In a few hours' time you and yer mates'll be back in Blighty wiv yer feet up, a fag in yer mouff, a pint in yer 'and, an' everyone wavin' flags and sayin' "Well done, boys!"' He took a quick glance at Rose. 'But it wasn't like that, Rose. Yer see, when we started ter get inter the boats, Jerry come down on us from nowhere – from the air an' from be'ind the sand dunes – everywhere! We all started jumpin' back inter the sea – but they still come down on us. It was dead easy. Sittin' ducks we were. Most of me mates swam back to the beach. 'Ardly none of 'em got there. Picked off like flies – as far as the eye could see. Di'n't 'ave a chance. Let's face it, wot could anyone do? We was on our own really.'

He smiled at Rose. 'Good fing I could swim. Remember me doin' the 'undred yards at Cally Road Barfs? I did the same fing swimmin' out ter this boat. Amazin' wot yer can do when yer try.'

Rose paused a moment before speaking. 'Gus,' she said almost casually, 'I fink yer Sylvie's ever so nice. We've become really good mates. Yer a lucky sod ter get someone like 'er.'

Gus looked at her, at first quizzically, but gradually, he broke into a huge smile. Then, quite impetuously, he turned outwards towards the canal again and, pulling back his jacket sleeves, he threw the frozen snowball as far as he possibly could.

It landed with a plop in the icy water, only yards from that passing barge. Only yards from a beach that he would never forget.

Before she went on duty that evening, Rose decided to pay a quick visit to her fireman patient in the Burns Unit at the London Hospital. She couldn't understand why she was doing such a thing, for on the first two occasions she had been in contact with him, he had been too clever by half. But when she had left him in the early hours of the morning, he had been in a pretty groggy state, and she felt that the least she could do was to go and cheer him up. Of course, it never occurred to her to remember that he had asked her to come and visit him.

Even as Rose entered the ward, old 'Moaning Minnie' was wailing out again. But all the doctors and nurses carried on with their duties as normal.

'Fanks for comin', Ginge.'

The patient was propped up in bed with three pillows,

and despite the fact that half his face was swathed in bandages, he was clearly in good spirits.

'Yer've got a cheek, you 'ave,' said Rose brightly. 'Only my best friends call me that.'

'Well, ain't *I* one of yer best friends?'

Rose pulled up a chair alongside the bed, and sat down. 'I've brought yer some oranges from our market.' Then, watching him as he slowly raised both his bandaged hands, she grinned wryly, put the bag of oranges down on his bedside cabinet, and said, 'Oh well, p'raps I'll get the nurse ter peel 'em for yer!'

The fireman lowered his hands back on to the bed. 'So – if yer name's not Ginge, wot is it?'

'Rose.'

'Well, Rose, reckon I've got a lot ter fank yer for.'

'Fank *me*? Wot yer talkin' about?'

'Yer saved me life, di'n't yer?'

Rose gave a dismissive snort. 'Don't be a nark! There was two of us on duty last night. An' anyway, it was yer own mates 'oo got yer out of that picture 'ouse.'

The fireman was peering at her through his one un-bandaged eye. 'Wot about the incendiary bomb? You and that blanket.'

Rose groaned. 'Now I know yer're takin' the piss.'

'Yer wrong,' the fireman said, trying to lever himself up in bed. 'The blanket wouldn't 'ave done much good, but yer quick thinking did.'

Rose tried to help him get more comfortable.

'I lost two of my mates in that cinema.' For a brief moment, his voice became serious.

'Yes, I know,' said Rose. 'I'm very sorry.'

'An' wot's it all for, I ask meself? We could've prevented this war if only we'd used a bit of common sense.'

'We didn't start it, yer know. Blame 'Itler for that.'

The patient sighed despairingly. 'Yeah, I know. But we should've tried ter persuade 'im, tried ter make 'im understand that peace is better than war. Remember wot 'appened in the last one – all those lives wasted? An' wot did it achieve? Nuffin!'

Rose thought this was curious talk from someone who fought on a dangerous battlefield every night of his life. But then she remembered that he was probably pumped full of drugs.

At that point a nurse approached, and made sure that the blackout curtain was secure at the window beside the fireman's bed. Gunfire could be heard in the distance.

'They're early tonight,' said the nurse, checking the watch pinned to her uniform. Then she scuttled off to the next window.

'I 'ave ter be goin',' Rose said. 'I'm on duty in 'alf an' 'our.'

The fireman tried to ease himself forward. 'Don't yer want ter know me name?' he asked, cheekily.

Rose matched him for cheek. 'Not particularly.'

'Me name's Bill.'

'Bill wot?'

'Just Bill. For the time bein', anyway.'

Rose grinned, and gently touched one of his bandaged hands. 'Pleased ter meet yer, Bill. Be'ave yerself now.'

'Are yer comin' ter see me again?'

Until now, Rose had considered her visit to be quite light-hearted. Suddenly, she tensed. 'I don't fink so.'

'Why not? Don't yer like me?'

Rose was panicking. In front of her was this injured fireman, but in her mind all she could *see* was Michael Devereaux, and the image made her shrivel up inside. 'I don't get much time ter meself. There *is* a war on, yer know.'

Outside the hospital entrance, the air felt fresher. Rose stood on the step, staring up into the clear night sky. In the distance, she could already hear the first approach of the night's intruders, droning in for the kill. Then came the inevitable ack-ack fire, and in no time at all night seemed to be turning into day, as the whole sky was illuminated by a sparkling fusion of light and sound.

Me name's Bill. For some inexplicable reason, Rose could hear that fireman's voice whispering into her ear. *Just Bill. For the time bein', anyway.*

This was ridiculous! It was a stupid voice. Why couldn't she get it out of her mind?

Whilst waiting for the first wave of bombers to pass over, Rose dug her hands deep into her tunic pockets, and was surprised to find something inside one of them. She suddenly remembered Badger's letter.

With nothing else to do, she backed into a small, dark alcove near the hospital steps, took the letter out of the envelope, and tried to read it by the dim light of a slotted overhead bulb. But the light was not enough to read all three pages, so she turned to the end and just managed to pick out the last few lines.

. . . Oh, by the way, Rose, I may not be able to write to you for a bit. For obvious reasons, can't tell you why. Mum's the werd and all that! But I hope to see you won of these days – with a bit of luck!

Wait for me, Rose.

You know I love you. At least, I hope you do!

Badge

Chapter 15

Kensington was a place Rose had heard of, but never actually seen. All she knew was that it was in another part of London where the la-di-da people lived in big, posh houses, and where they spent a lot of money taking their dogs to beauty parlours. If anyone had told her that one day she herself would be a guest in one of those big, posh houses, she'd have called them bananas. But Amanda Harrington lived in Kensington, and when one day the invitation came for Rose to 'come over for tea', she leapt at the chance.

She chose to do the journey by bus for she didn't really fancy the idea of travelling all that way underground on the Circle Line.

The journey turned out to be a revelation for her. Not only did it give her the rare chance to have an hour or two's relaxation, but it was also the first time that she had ever seen the West End of London: Euston Road with its fine grand buildings, then Tottenham Court Road with a huge picture house called the Dominion, where they were showing a double bill *and* a stage show for one and ninepence – an absolute fortune, Rose thought. In Oxford Street, many of the fashionable shops had 'BUSINESS AS

USUAL' signs in their windows, which pleased Rose immensely, for it showed that the shopkeepers, just like the traders in Chapel Market, had refused to be intimidated by the bomb damage they had suffered. There was only a week to go before Christmas, so there were lots of people shopping, and, despite the austerity of war, all the windows were so beautifully decorated with home-made paper-chains and lots of cotton wool stuck on the glass in between the crisscross of bomb-blast strips.

When a seat became vacant in the front row of the bus, Rose hurried to it. From there she had a perfect view of the Marble Arch and the posh hotels in Park Lane. But the real excitement came when they stopped outside a great Victorian circular-shaped building that turned out to be the Royal Albert Hall. Rose couldn't believe that she was seeing the actual place where the Service of Remembrance was held each November, and which she and her mum always listened to on the wireless. On the opposite side of the road, there was the famous Hyde Park she'd heard so much about, the place where before the war they grew so many different varieties of flowers in beautifully kept flowerbeds, but which was now being used for growing vegetables in response to the Government's call to 'DIG FOR VICTORY!'

Rose finally got off the bus in Kensington High Street. It was very clean and tidy, but, unlike Oxford Street, most of the shops had very few Christmas decorations in their windows, including the huge Barkers Department Store. Rose was astonished to find that the High Street seemed to have more jewellers' shops than in the whole of Islington!

Amanda's house turned out to be completely different to
what Rose had imagined. It was tucked away in a quiet tiny
mews just off the High Street. But once she got a glimpse of
some of the expensive-looking cars parked there, Rose
guessed the people who lived there were not short of a bob
or two.

'There you are, dear!' Amanda was waiting at the door
the moment Rose pulled the bell. It was the first time Rose
had seen her co-driver in clothes other than her St John
uniform, and even though she was only wearing a warm
navy-blue woollen dress with one piece of jewellery pinned
to her shoulder, she looked so classy. 'You must have smelt
the scones burning!'

Indeed the scones were burning. The moment Rose entered the house Amanda started using a newspaper to fan
away the smoke that was filtering through from the kitchen.

Rose found the house deceptive. It was larger than she
had thought when she was approaching from the outside,
and the lounge, which was L-shaped, was bright and
spacious. It was also very elegant, with the most beautiful
highly polished antique furniture, and plush velvet curtains
held back with tasselled cords.

There were bronze statuettes and pieces of porcelain
scattered around on little polished tables, and when Rose
saw the massive grand piano dominating one corner of the
room by the French window, she immediately thought of
the twins. How their eyes would pop out if they saw that!
Despite the fact that her officer husband was away in the
Army, Amanda had decorated a small Christmas tree,
which was set proudly on top of the piano. But if there was
one thing that over-awed Rose more than anything else, it

was the wall-to-wall carpet, thick and deep, and a rich luxurious red colour.

Amanda brought in her home-made scones – burnt but just about edible. 'Rose, I am proud to tell you that I am the worst – no, the *very* worst cook in the whole wide world.'

Rose laughed out loud. 'I don't believe yer,' she said.

'Oh, it's true, I assure you.' Amanda picked up one of her scones, sniffed at it disapprovingly, then dropped it with a thump on to the plate again. 'Ask the Major – my husband. The last time I cooked him roast beef, the Yorkshire pudding refused to set so we had to use it as a white sauce over the cauliflower!'

Rose laughed even louder. She really loved the way Amanda ridiculed herself.

'Never mind,' Amanda said, making her way back to the kitchen. 'Bad cooks sometimes have other talents!'

Rose watched her friend disappear into the kitchen, and wondered what she was now up to.

Amanda reappeared, holding a bottle of champagne. '*Voilà!*' she exclaimed triumphantly.

'Amanda!' Rose's face was a picture, grinning all over, but shocked. 'That's not afternoon tea!'

'It is to me,' replied Amanda, unpeeling the foil from the top of the champagne bottle. 'I've been saving this until you came over. It's Christmas, for God's sake! We deserve a celebration.'

Rose was shaking her head again. 'We can't drink that. 'Ow d'yer fink we're goin' ter drive that ambulance ternight?'

'With difficulty,' Amanda admitted. 'but for once, we'll be very happy!'

And so for the next hour or so, they sat and drank champagne, and munched on rock-hard burnt scones. Rose had not felt so happy for ages. In just a short time she had managed to put all her worries to the back of her mind, and as she sank herself down on to the most comfortable sofa she had ever sat on in her life, she felt as though the blood in her body was flowing more freely than it had ever done before.

'Now I've got you all on your own, there's something I've been meaning to ask you.' Amanda's cheeks were already beginning to look decidedly more cherry-coloured than when Rose arrived. 'That name of yours, Humble, where did that come from?'

To disguise her awkwardness, Rose quickly gulped down some champagne. 'Oh, I know. It's a stupid name, i'n't it? I'm always gettin' ribbed about it down the market.'

'On the contrary!' said Amanda, defiantly. 'I think it's a wonderful name. Straight out of Dickens.' In a theatrical pose, she hunched her shoulders and squinted her eyes. ''Umble by name, my dear. An' 'umble by nature.'

Rose, puzzled, scratched her head. 'Wot's all that?'

'Oh for goodness sake, Rose! Surely you've read *something* by our greatest novelist? Charles Dickens?'

Rose shrugged her shoulders. Her head was just a little fuzzy.

'No? Oh well, why should you?' Amanda quickly refilled their glasses. 'Anyway, I like your name. It's far better than mine.' She flopped down on the sofa at the side of Rose. 'Amanda's all right, I suppose – different. But *Harrington* – I ask you! Ugh!'

'Wot's wrong wiv it?' asked Rose. 'Sounds all right ter me.'

'Don't be silly, dear. It's much too grand. Still, there's nothing I can do about it. It's my husband's name. The Major. Major-General Harcourt Harrington. I call him "H". He's grand, too, of course. But he's an absolute dear. I do miss him so, the silly old fool.'

For one moment, Amanda lost her gaiety and stared down into her glass. But she quickly brightened up again. 'You know what? I'd like to be called something like . . . Snitch.'

'Snitch?'

'Yes. Amanda – no, Ethel Snitch. Sounds fun, don't you think?' And with that she swallowed a quick gulp of champagne. 'I bet H would like the name. Just imagine it, Major-General Sir Harcourt and Lady Snitch.'

Amanda roared with laughter at her own joke. Rose joined in, until something suddenly dawned on her. 'Lady? Yer mean – a real Lady?'

'I'm not quite sure what you mean by that, Rose 'Umble!' Then she giggled. 'Yes. I'm *Lady* Amanda Harrington. But it doesn't mean a thing, dear, except it looks good on my headed notepaper, and I can afford to buy silk undies. Oh yes! Which reminds me!' She quickly sat up, put her glass down on the coffee table in front of them, then did likewise with Rose's glass. 'I've got a Christmas present for you.'

'Wot?' Rose's mouth was wide open with astonishment.

'Follow me!' Amanda grabbed hold of Rose's hand and led her up the winding staircase to her bedroom.

Rose stared around the room as though it was Aladdin's cave. It was every girl's dream bedroom, with a huge four-poster bed draped with pink chiffon curtains, and a vast eiderdown to match. In front of the small cottage-type window was a dressing table bulging with face powder and creams, lipstick and all other types of cosmetics. There were also bits and pieces of jewellery lying idly there, and as Rose leant close to peer into the central mirror, her face was reflected in each one on either side.

'It's fantastic, Amanda!' was all Rose could say. She found it hard to reconcile the Amanda who lived in such luxury to her co-driver pal in the ambulance, who helped her to do some of the most unsavoury and harrowing jobs each night.

Amanda wasn't really taking in Rose's reaction, for she was busy sorting through a huge chest of drawers. 'Oh, where is it, damn it?' In her impatience, she was pulling out all kinds of underclothes and throwing them on to the floor. 'I know I put them here somewhere . . .'

Rose picked up a silver-framed photograph from Amanda's dressing table. It was clearly of a middle-aged man wearing an Army officer's uniform.

'Is this 'im, Amanda?' Rose asked. 'Is this yer 'ubbie?'

Amanda turned to look, then came across to join Rose. 'Yes, that's him, the old reprobate. He was the one who taught me how to drink, you know. I was as pure as driven snow until I met *him*.'

Rose put the photograph back on to the dressing table. What was it she admired so much about this woman, she wondered. Amanda came from a different class, a different world to her own, yet Rose felt she had so much in common with her. Night after night, Rose had seen Amanda down on her hands and knees scrubbing out the floor of the ambulance just like herself, just like all the rest of the girls in the Civil Defence services. Amanda wasn't afraid to get

217

her hands dirty. She wasn't afraid to care for an injured patient who was dying from the most terrible wounds. Amanda was always the first one in there, swabbing, bandaging, lifting stretchers, whispering tender words to those who needed them – and that often included Rose herself. The Major-General was a lucky man. He had a wife who was so much more than just any old 'lady'.

'Yer've got so many beautiful fings, Amanda,' Rose said, her eyes scanning the dressing table. 'I've never seen so many pairs of earrings in all me life.'

'Yes, I know,' sighed Amanda. 'I seem to buy a new pair every time I go out shopping! Tell you what, why don't you take a pair?'

'No, Amanda!' Rose was shocked and backed away. 'Wot d'yer take me for? I'm not on the cadge.'

'I know you're not, you stupid girl! But I want you to have them. Come on – choose a pair.' She quickly started sorting through her jewellery on the dressing table. 'They're all clip-ons, I'm afraid. I've never had the courage to have my ears pierced.'

'No, Amanda! I don't want 'em. I won't . . . !'

'Stop being so silly and try these on.' Amanda was holding up a pair of mother-of-pearl drop-earrings. 'They'll look far better on you than me!'

Rose reluctantly took the earrings, clipped them on, and looked at herself in the dressing table mirror.

'Lovely, dear! Absolutely lovely!' Amanda was standing behind Rose, also looking at her friend's reflection in the mirror. 'You should wear them on duty tonight. That'll set the tongues wagging!'

They both roared with laughter.

'There they are!' Amanda suddenly stopped laughing, and retrieved a brown paperbag from her stool tucked under the dressing table. 'Here,' she said, holding out the bag to Rose. 'Your Christmas present. I bought them for myself before the war, so don't accuse me of getting them on the black market!'

'Wot yer talkin' about, Amanda! Yer can't go around givin' me presents.'

'Who said I can't?' Amanda spluttered indignantly. 'You're my friend, aren't you? If I want to give you a Christmas present I shall!'

Rose, overwhelmed, shook her head. Then she reached into the paperbag and pulled out the contents. She held them up, blushing. 'Amanda!' It was a pair of fashionable silk camiknickers.

Amanda roared with laughter again, and applauded. 'Silk, my dear! Nothing like it in the whole wide world! I bought them at Marshall and Snelgrove's two days before the war started. Haven't worn them though – not once! They've just been lying in my chest of drawers.'

Rose was utterly flustered. 'But – I couldn't wear somefin' – like this? Wot would people say?'

Amanda grinned wryly. 'I don't know, dear. Depends who sees them on you!' She nudged her mischievously, and they both laughed again. 'Listen, Rose, we all deserve at least one luxury at some time in our lives. This is yours.' Then she smiled again, and lowered her voice. 'I can tell you from experience, the boys will go wild when they see them on you.'

Rose's smile faded, and she suddenly became rather withdrawn. 'I don't fink it's likely any boys're goin' ter see me in these, Amanda.' She tucked the knickers into the bag, and offered them back to her.

Amanda shook her head, refusing to take the bag. 'You'll fall in love one day, my dear.'

Rose smiled gratefully, and lowered her eyes. 'Not an 'ope. Men don't mean a fing ter me. They're only out for wot they can get. The way I see it, I don't expect ter get fixed up wiv *anyone*.'

'I wouldn't bank on it, my dear. Love has a funny way of finding you when you least expect it.'

After exchanging a shy look with her, Rose kept the bag.

'Come on!' said Amanda, suddenly hurrying out of the room. 'Let's finish the champagne before we go out into the streets to save the people of London!'

Rose, still wearing her earrings, followed her out of the room.

'D'you know what I'm going to put in my will for when I die, Rose?' Amanda called, as Rose followed her down the stairs. 'I'm going to insist that all the girls wear their brightest clothes and silk knickers.'

'Oh yes?' replied Rose. 'And wotcha fink the boys'll wear?'

Amanda stopped on the stairs, and looked up at her. 'How should I know, my dear? You'll have to ask them!'

They both yelled with laughter, and returned to the almost empty bottle of champagne.

It was about five o'clock in the evening when Queenie Humble reached the Angel tube station. The rush hour was already starting, so she had to queue to buy her day return ticket to King's Cross. In the over-crowded lift going down to the platform, nearly every man seemed to be reading a newspaper, either the *Evening News*, the *Star*, or the *Evening Standard*. She didn't mind them reading, but she did object to their using her back and shoulders as a resting place for their elbows. Occasionally she managed to get a glimpse of what they were all absorbed with, but most of the headlines were quite boring, like 'Anthony Eden made Foreign Secretary', and 'Rations increased for Christmas'.

Luckily, the Northern Line train came in very promptly, and it saved Queenie having to linger too long on the platform where, in a few hours' time, she would be spending the night with her mum and the twins.

For the time of day, the rear carriage was surprisingly uncrowded, and Queenie managed to get a seat immediately. Although it was only one station to King's Cross, she sat there feeling totally self-conscious. She had not worked since her accident, and because her head had been left badly scarred, and only small tufts of red hair were growing again, her confidence was pretty low. These days she found it difficult to travel on buses, trams, or tube trains, because she was convinced that people were trying to guess what her hair looked like beneath the headscarf she was wearing.

The escalator at King's Cross seemed to take forever, and Queenie was beginning to wish that she had walked the short journey from home.

It was pitch dark as she left the station, crossed over the busy Euston Road, and made her way up one of the streets opposite. The closer she got to her final destination, the more apprehensive she became. She badly needed the job, and if not this one, then anything that might be totally different from what she had been doing before. As she walked, her rubber ankle boots were becoming covered in slush, for during the last few days the snow had thawed rapidly, which meant that there might not be a white Christmas after all.

On the corner of Jarman Square, she stopped to light a Capstan, and get her bearings. Rose had told her how to find the place. It had been Rose who had seen the advert card in the window of old Lil' Walker's newsagent shop. It wasn't exactly the kind of job Queenie was looking for, but Rose had talked her into it, saying it might give her the chance to meet all kinds of posh people. Nonetheless, Queenie was still worried that the card in that window had given her no clue as to the type of employer she was about to see.

> YOUNG WOOMAN REQUIRED
> LOOK AFTER YOUNG CHILLDREN
> DAYTIME ONLY. GOOD WAJES
> PHONE NORTH 5208 (9 am–5 pm)
> OR APPLY IN PERSON AFTER
> 5 pm TO: FLAT 7,
> 23, SEDGWICK STREET
> W.C.1.

Since she had telephoned North 5208 at least a dozen times and found it engaged non-stop, Queenie had decided to 'Apply in Person'. But when she finally located Sedgwick Street, her heart sank, for there was certainly nothing posh about this neighbourhood.

Number 23 was a rather seedy block of Victorian council

flats, and to reach Flat 7, Queenie had to climb up two flights of open stone steps. This was not easy, for it was now blackout time, and she had to use her torch to find the way. As she climbed, she was able to pick out the various slogans that had been daubed on the walls in black paint, like: 'GOOD OLD WINNIE!' and 'UP YOU ADOLF!'

The flat she was looking for was about halfway along an open balcony. There were grubby-looking blackout curtains up at the glass front door, and odd smells of foreign cooking were seeping through an open kitchen window alongside.

Queenie quickly stubbed out her fag and knocked on the front door. She could hear a woman shouting and yelling in a foreign language at what sounded like some pretty boisterous young kids.

The door was suddenly opened.

'Yes?'

Standing there was a Chinese woman, wearing a turban, tatty-looking dress and cardigan, probably aged no more than about thirty, and looking very harassed indeed.

'I've come about the advert.'

'Adlert? What adlert?'

'In the paper shop. Up the Cally. You want someone ter look after some kids.'

The Chinese woman stopped looking baffled. 'Oh – adlert!' She wiped her hands on her cardigan, and pulled back the door to let Queenie in. 'Come in, please. Me, Mrs Wu.'

''Ow d'yer do?' said Queenie, looking around apprehensively.

Mrs Wu showed her into what was probably some kind of a sitting-room, but it was difficult to tell for it was so piled high with toys, piles of old Chinese language newspapers, and children's clothes drying on a ceiling rack.

'You like chillen?' asked Mrs Wu, whose huge grin revealed a perfect set of white teeth.

'Oh yes,' replied Queenie, regretting what she was saying even as she spoke. 'Luv 'em. Got bruvvers and sisters of me own.'

'Oh – luvelee! How many?'

'Er – five. 'Ow many 'ave you got?'

'Seven.'

'Seven!' Queenie nearly dropped into a dead faint.

'You wanna see?'

'Er – well, ter tell yer the truth . . .' For once in her life, Queenie was flummoxed. 'Did yer say – seven?'

Mrs Wu ignored her, left the room for a moment, and opened the kitchen door outside in the passage. The moment she did so, all hell broke loose. A whole posse of kids aged anywhere between two and fourteen years old stampeded into the room, engulfing Queenie and practically lifting her off her feet.

Mrs Wu yelled at her kids in the most raucous Chinese imaginable. Then when they had calmed down enough for her to be heard, she turned to Queenie and said, 'Chillen.'

Queenie took a deep breath. Eight pairs of Chinese eyes – including Mrs Wu's – were staring at her. 'Wot's all yer names?' she asked, and immediately wished she hadn't as every one of them launched into a recital of their individual Chinese names.

Queenie decided that there was no way in the world that she was going to be able to cope with this lot. It was bad enough being brought up with five brothers and sisters of her own, but at least she had no trouble in pronouncing, let alone remembering, their names.

'Start toomollow – yes?' said Mrs Wu, nodding her head eagerly.

'No!' Queenie spluttered back immediately, and shaking her head frantically. 'No start termollow – I mean termorrer.' By this time the smell of Chinese cooking coming from the kitchen was just about killing her.

'Two pounds week. Okay?' Mrs Wu was still grinning away, seemingly quite unaware that two of her kids were jumping on the sofa, whilst two of the smaller ones were systematically ripping up as many old newspapers as they could find.

'I'm sorry,' Queenie said, backing towards the door, 'I don't fink I'm the person yer're lookin' for.'

Mrs Wu's grin disappeared abruptly. 'No look after chillen?' she said, with a long face.

'I'm sorry. I couldn't. I just couldn't.'

'Two pound ten shillin'?'

'No, no. It's got nuffin' ter do wiv the money. It's just that – that—' Queenie was floundering again. She felt hemmed in, with kids crawling in and out of every corner of the room, the smell of God knows what coming from the kitchen, and the feeling that if this crazy woman couldn't look after her own kids, she shouldn't have had so many. 'Where's yer 'usband?' she asked desperately. 'Can't 'e look after 'em?'

Mrs Wu looked puzzled again.

'Their dad?' Queenie yelled, as though the poor woman was deaf. 'Where's their dad?'

'Oh!' At last Mrs Wu understood, and she stretched her

hand right out to point at something on the mantelpiece over the fire-grate. 'Hlusband!'

Queenie turned to look. Amongst a welter of framed photographs of the family there was a large one of what was presumably Mrs Wu's husband, wearing an able seaman's navy uniform. 'Your 'ubbie? Mr Wu?'

'Mr Wu! Yes! Yes!' Mrs Wu's wide grin had returned, and her head was nodding up and down vigorously.

'So where is 'e?'

Mrs Wu shrugged her shoulders, and without losing her grin, she said, 'Dead. Ship. War.' The thumbs of both her hands were pointing downwards.

Queenie felt awful, and didn't know how to react. A woman left on her own to look after seven kids – it was terrible! But as she looked round at the children pulling and tugging at her, standing on their heads on the sofa, and ripping up newspapers, her pity still did not extend to taking on such a bundle of trouble.

'I'm sorry about yer 'ubbie, Mrs Wu. I really am sorry. But – I can't look after this lot – no way! Yer see, I lied to yer. I don't know nuffin' about kids, nuffin' at all. I wouldn't know where ter start.' Once again, she started to back towards the door. 'I'm really, really sorry . . .'

Before Queenie could make her exit, she was stopped in the doorway by one of the youngest kids, a dumpy little boy, who had jet-black hair with a fringe, eyes that were so slanting that she could hardly see his pupils, and a grin almost as wide as his mum's.

'Two pound, ten shillin',' said the kid. 'Okay?'

A few minutes later, despite the blackout, Queenie was

virtually running all the way back to King's Cross Station. She had no idea where she was, for the bulb in her torch had finally given up, and it was so dark, twice she bumped into people who thought she was a tart on the game. All the way, she was cursing Rose for ever seeing that bleeding awful advert card in Lil' Walker's shop window. She was so angry that when 'Moaning Minnie' started to wail out her repetitive old tune again, she yelled out at the top of her voice, 'Oh shut up!'

Queenie finally reached the safety of the tube station platform. Whilst waiting for the train she made up her mind once and for all: not in a million, trillion years would she ever even consider tying herself down to a whole lot of Chinese kids. Seven of them! Seven yelling, screaming kids who would kill her off in the first five minutes. No! Never! She would sooner go back to the small arms factory and take her chances with the killer machine.

By the time she was going up in the lift at the Angel tube station, she had already changed her mind.

A few minutes later, she was on the tube again and making her way back to King's Cross. After all, two pounds and ten shillings a week wasn't such a bad 'waje'.

Chapter 16

Christmas 1940 brought an undeclared truce in the aerial onslaught on the British Isles. For two or three joyous days, Londoners were able to look up at the sky without fear of being bombed, and get on with the traditional celebrations.

Christmas Day in the rooms above the second-hand piano shop turned out to be quite an occasion. Not only was the place decorated with paperchains and Christmas cards, draped from string, but Mr Popov's gift to the Humble family had again been a huge chicken, which this year he obtained by mysterious means from one of his former customers. As usual, Nellie and Albert had naturally insisted that he be the Humbles' guest for the Christmas midday meal, which he always looked forward to more than anything else throughout the year. All the family were there, with the exception of Gus, who had recently been posted to an unknown destination. But Sylvie was there, and just about managed to squeeze in at the side of Rose around a very crowded kitchen table.

As he was the principal guest, Mr Popov was given the honour of carving the chicken, and he relished all the attention he was being given. During the meal, everyone drank either brown or light ale, port wine, or Tizer and ginger beer. Mr Popov stuck to stout, despite the fact that thick froth on the top of his glass transferred immediately to his white, bushy moustache. One of the traders in the market had given Nellie a box of Christmas crackers as a present, so they were duly pulled, and amidst unwrapping novelties and reading out terrible jokes everyone wore different coloured paper hats.

The great treat that followed for 'afters' was, as always, Nellie's home-made Christmas pudding. But it wasn't easy getting the ingredients, for she had had to save her ration coupons over several weeks to get the sugar, let alone the flour, fruit and dried eggs. But the rationing did not deter her from putting in the most popular of all the ingredients – the tiny threepenny bits. Either by chance or through Nellie's cunning design, everyone managed to get at least one, so the meal ended in howls of delight, and a chorus of 'Three cheers for Mum!' which practically lifted the roof off. This was followed by a combined call of 'Speech! Speech!' from the twins.

As neither Nellie nor Albert would ever dream of doing such a thing, it was, as usual, left to Rose to do the honours, and she got a rousing reception of cheers, jeers, applause, and table-thumping as she got to her feet.

'Mr Popov, Mum an' Dad, an' all yer 'Umble rat-bags!' Everyone laughed, except George, who put two fingers into his mouth and let out a piercing whistle. 'This 'as bin a really smashin' Christmas dinner – the best I can remember for a long time!'

''Ear! 'Ear!' agreed Albert.

'Yer know somefin', Mum?' Rose continued, looking

straight at Nellie. 'Yer shouldn't be cookin' for the likes of us. Yer ought ter be earnin' a fortune at some posh 'otel!'

Everyone laughed, but none as loud as Mr Popov, whose complexion was now a blood-red colour.

'No – honest ter God, Mum, that chicken was done a real treat. An' as for yer Christmas pud . . .!'

Whoops and cheers for that, too – except from George, who got a sharp dig in the ribs from Polly for looking so bored.

'But the person we really want ter fank is you, Mr Popov. I don't know where yer got that chicken from – an' I don't intend ter ask . . .'

Mischievous jeers and giggles from around the table.

'But I tell yer this much, yer couldn't've given us a better present.'

This time, everyone said either, 'Too true!' or 'Fanks a lot!' or 'Good old Mr Popov!'

The old man sitting between Queenie on one side and Polly on the other, looked down shyly into his glass of stout.

'The fing is,' said Rose, talking directly to him, 'yer've always bin such a friend to this family. Always there when we're rock-bottom low, 'elpin' us out wiv a bob or two whenever we need it. We'll never forget 'ow yer've let us live in this place all these years, takin' far less money than yer should do. An' we'll never forget yer payin' for Poll an' Mill ter 'ave piano lessons – somefin' that *we* could never 'ave done in a million years. The way I look at it is that me an' Gus an' Queen an' Polly an' Mill an' George – well, we've always fought of yer like yer was our uncle. In a way, yer as much a part of the 'Umble family as every one of us round this table. Yer've bin so good ter us, Mr Popov. There ain't many people like you around – people that give so much wivout wantin' anyfin' in return. One of these days, when this ruddy war's over, we're goin' ter pay yer back – yer'll see.' Rose picked up her glass of shandy. 'Wot I'm tryin' ter tell yer is that the 'Umble family are never goin' ter forget wot yer've done for us. Never!'

Everyone called out ''Ear! 'Ear!' and thumped the table.

Poor Mr Popov was so moved he didn't know where to look, so Queenie put her arms around one shoulder and Polly leant her head against the other.

'So,' Rose proclaimed, raising her glass, ''ere's ter you – *Uncle* Popov!'

Everyone raised their glasses. '*Uncle* Popov!'

Whilst this was going on, the old man suddenly struggled to get up from his chair. 'Please! *I* would like a toast to make.' He picked up his glass from the table, and held it out towards Nellie and Albert. 'Dear friends. How can I zank you. Every Christmas have you allowed me at you table, to share you food, you wondairful cooking, and you great hospitality.' For the moment, he held the glass with both hands in front of his very full stomach. 'Every time I sit here wiz you, I sink to myself "Oleg. You are lucky man." Lucky, because you Humbles are first people I meet when I come to England. Lucky, because you become family I never had. Lucky, because you help foolish old man to live again. When I look at all of you now, I wonder for what I deserve you kindness.' He briefly put his glass back down on to the table, but kept one hand clasped to it. 'You know, sometime I hear it said that English people – zey are cold and wiz no heart. But each year at zis table I know is not true, for I hear you heart – each and every heart – I hear it beat so loud and clear. Yes, my friends. You are my dear, dear family. You will always be here . . .' He thumped his chest to indicate his heart. 'Always!' Then he lifted his glass, and offered it as if in a toast to everyone around the table. 'To Humbles – past, present, and future.'

There was a moment of silence, in which everyone seemed lulled into deep thought. The only sound was from Sylvie, who had had several glasses of port wine, and was now wiping away tears with her fingers from her heavily made-up eyes.

To everyone's surprise, Mr Popov had not yet finished. 'But now, my friends, I have one more Christmas present to give you.'

'Come off it, Mr Popov!' said Albert. 'Yer've given us loads already.'

'Ah! But zis is real present – ze *special* one!'

Nellie exchanged an embarrassed glance with Rose, who shrugged her shoulders to show that she had no idea what Mr Popov was up to.

'I wish to tell you zat from when I die, Popov's shop, Popov's house – all zis will belong to my dear friends Humble.' And, with a shy glance at Polly and Millie, he added, 'Including pianos all!'

There was a gasp around the table.

'Mr Popov!' Rose said, in astonishment. 'Yer can't do a fing like that! We ain't got no right ter this place.'

'I have said what I have said!' the old man boomed, wagging his finger at Rose stubbornly. 'Zis place is for family, *my* family! Is good idea – why not?'

Rose looked across at her mum and dad. They were in deep shock.

'Wot's it mean, Mum?' George asked, tactlessly as usual. 'Don't we 'ave to pay no rent no more?'

'George!' Albert snapped. 'Shut yer 'ole!'

'Is true, Georgie boy!' said the old man reassuringly. 'Is settled in my will. My solicitor – he write down everything!'

'Yer a good, kind man,' said Queenie. And to show her gratitude she leant across and kissed him gently on his rather flabby cheek. 'Fank yer, dear Uncle Popov.'

The old man practically purred with happiness.

It took quite some time for 'Uncle' Popov's news to sink in. But by the time they had got up from the table, he had assured Nellie and Albert that after he was gone, they and the family would never have to worry about leaving the home they had lived in for so many years. Nellie was completely overcome by the old man's kindness, and expressed the hope that it would be a very long time before they were able to accept his wonderful present.

After everyone, including Uncle Popov, had helped to wash up and dry the dishes, Polly, Millie, and George went downstairs to the shop for the highlight of the Christmas Day festivities, which was, as always, the Humbles' own concert party. This usually consisted of an hour's entertainment in which each member of the family was expected to do a party piece. Some years the evening had ended in disaster, mainly because George had thrown a tantrum after trying to exceed his fair share of items. But on the whole, it was an event that the whole family always looked forward to with immense excitement.

It was about six o'clock in the evening when Nellie,

Albert, Queenie, Sylvie, and Mr Popov went down to the shop to find the place converted into the Humbles' Music Hall. The second-hand pianos had been wheeled to one side, and kitchen chairs brought from upstairs to seat the audience. One of Nellie's bedsheets was strung across one end of the shop to serve as a stage curtain, behind which the principal 'artistes' prepared for their performance. Once everyone had topped up their glasses, the show began.

First to appear from behind Nellie's bedsheet was the compere, 'Herr Schikelgrubber', otherwise known as 'Adolf 'Itler', and impersonated (complete with false moustache and Nazi salute) by 'our very own Georgie 'Umble'. To gales of applause and laughter, the *Führer* introduced himself, Polly, and Millie, miming to one of Gus's gramophone records of the three Andrews Sisters singing 'Don't Fence Me In', which sounded just a little scratchy on Mr Popov's rather cumbersome radiogram. After that came Albert doing his Harry Champion act – 'Boiled Beef an' Carrots!', Rose and Sylvie doing a hastily made up Gert and Daisy comedy act, George miming to his hero, George Formby, and his ukelele, 'When I'm Cleaning Windows', Polly wearing her mum's hat and a chicken-feather scarf to do an hilarious impersonation of the wireless comedienne, Suzette Tarri, and Nellie and Albert singing their much-loved duet, 'If You Were the Only Girl in the World'.

Queenie had her own reasons for not participating, and watched the show from a secluded corner of the shop, laughing as much as all the others, but always unconsciously tucking her few wafts of hair under her headscarf. During the entertainment, Uncle Popov rocked with laughter, and, even though he didn't know any of the words, he attempted to join in with every song. His greatest treat came when Polly and Millie gave a demonstration of how much they had learnt during their piano lessons with Mrs Wheeler. First of all they played solo pieces, reading effortlessly from their sheet music. Then they played together, but on separate pianos, and by the time they had launched into Uncle Popov's favourite 'Blue Danube', the old man was in tears. It was during this part of the show that Rose followed her mum back upstairs to make some tea and Spam sandwiches.

'I fink Mr Popov's one of the kindest men that ever lived,' said Nellie, cutting uneven slices of bread. 'We've never given 'im enough rent money, an' yet 'e goes an' does a fing like this!'

Rose was struggling to open the tin of Spam with its key-shaped opener. 'Yeah. It's a wonderful fing ter do all right. But let's face it, we wouldn't want ter stay in a place like this forever, would we?'

Nellie stopped cutting bread, and looked up with a start. 'Not stay 'ere? Wot're yer talkin' about?'

Rose looked across at her. 'Well, it's obvious, i'n't it, Mum? The family's all grown up now. When the war's over, we'll be earnin' enough money ter move inter somewhere bigger.'

Nellie was shocked and indignant. 'I don't want somewhere bigger. This is our 'ome. It's done us perfectly well all these years.'

'Yes, I know, Mum, but—'

'We're workin'-class people, Rose. We're not like that lot that live in Canonbury Square an' places. *We* 'ave ter live wivin our means.'

'Don't be silly, Mum.' As usual, Rose was finding it difficult to get through to her. 'It's got nuffin' ter do wiv bein' workin'-class or anyfin' else. You an' Dad 'ave always made a good 'ome for us 'ere, we all know that. But the fact is, it ain't comfortable no more.'

Nellie slammed down the carving knife. 'Well, fanks a lot! I never fought the day'd come when I'd 'ear a daughter of mine talk like that!'

'Mum!' Rose was trying not to raise her voice, but it wasn't easy. 'Yer've got ter be realistic. It's not right that me, Queenie, Poll and Mill should all be sharin' one bed tergevver at our age. It's not – well, it's not nice.'

Nellie looked at her daughter as though she were mad. 'Wot's wrong sleepin' wiv 'em?' she snapped back haughtily. 'They're yer own sisters, ain't they?'

Rose sighed deeply. She knew that, in matters like this, talking to her mum was like talking to a brick wall.

It didn't help that from downstairs they could hear the sound of applause, followed by Sylvie launching into a strong rendering of 'You'll Never Know.'

Rose levered the Spam out of its tin on to a plate. 'It's not only us, yer know,' she said, taking the plate across to her mum, who had resumed cutting bread. 'There's Georgie curled up like a moggie on the rug in front of the fire.'

''E don't complain.' It was obvious that Nellie had now really taken umbrage.

'An' wot about you an' Dad? At yer time of life yer should be 'avin' a bit of privacy.'

Nellie suddenly turned on her. 'If it's privacy yer want, yer'll 'ave ter wait 'til yer get married. Then you an' yer 'usband can 'ave all the privacy yer want.'

Rose didn't like her mum talking like this. It was uncaring, and so unlike her. Suddenly Rose noticed that she had slightly cut her thumb on the sharp edge of the Spam tin. She cleaned the cut, wrapped it in her hanky, then turned around and, for a moment, watched her mum spreading marge on to bread. Nellie was now clearly so uptight, she wasn't really concentrating on what she was doing.

'I don't want ter leave 'ere, Mum,' Rose said, creeping up behind Nellie and gently kissing the back of her neck. Rose put her arms around Nellie's waist, and leant her head on her mum's shoulder. 'I love this place. I've always loved it, an' always will.' She hugged her mum tight. 'Tell yer wot,' she said, taking hold of Nellie's arm, and pulling her round to face her. 'As soon as the war's over, wot say we buy some paint an' do the place up. 'Ow's about it, Mum, eh?'

Nellie stared at Rose, smiled weakly, and nodded her head. This was a clear indication that she had forgiven her. It also meant that she hadn't believed a word Rose had just said.

Downstairs, the Humbles' Concert Party came to a rowdy end with the loudest sing-song of old favourites ranging from 'Lily of Laguna' to 'Ten Green Bottles'. For the grand finale, Uncle Popov led everyone in a rousing chorus of 'Land of Hope and Glory'. The words he sang in his fractured English may not have been easy to under-stand, but the sound of his rich baritone voice made a stirring climax to a memorable evening.

When it was over, everyone agreed that despite the rationing, it had been one of the best Christmas days they had ever spent. And when Nellie turned in that night, and felt the peace and relaxation of her own bed instead of the harsh cold platform down the Angel tube, she expressed the hope that perhaps 'Itler had a heart after all, and that after stopping his air raids on Britain over Christmas, he would try and make peace – not war.

Two nights later, the skies of London once again echoed to the sound of old 'Moaning Minnie'.

Rose was back in her ambulance, rushing to an incident in which the air-raid shelter of an old people's home in Bethnal Green had just had a direct hit. Twenty-four victims had been killed outright, and another fourteen were still unaccounted for beneath the wreckage.

It took all night for the rescue services to locate them.

Chapter 17

On the Sunday after Christmas, Rose and Amanda were back in their ambulance, preparing for what looked like another long night. Despite the fact that there were some signs of evening fog drifting around, 'Moaning Minnie' had gone off before everyone had even had the chance to draw the blackout curtains. It was typical late December weather – dank, dark, and miserable – and the pavements had remained stubbornly wet ever since the early morning fog, which only cleared just before noon.

Rose hated the fog, for it always made her feel she was breathing in fumes from coal fires all over London, but when it floated low over the rooftops like a huge magic carpet, at least there was insufficient visibility for the Luftwaffe to continue their aerial bombardment. Unfortunately, this was not to be such a night.

Soon after dark, the first waves of enemy aircraft came droning in from the south-east of the capital, and headed straight for the City. Within minutes, incendiary and explosive bombs were raining down on the ancient streets sending great balls of flame up through the fog patches, and lighting up the silver barrage balloons, which immediately became a sitting target for the enemy raiders.

'Where the 'ell's the ack-ack ternight?' yelled Rose, who was at the driving-wheel of the ambulance, doing her best to manoeuvre through the narrow City streets.

'I don't understand it!' Amanda, in the passenger seat, was holding on to her tin helmet as Rose took a corner at high speed. 'It looks as though Jerry's got the show to himself.' She tried to peer up at the sky through the front windscreen. 'There's absolutely no sign of any gunfire.'

In between the tall business buildings they could just see the dome of St Paul's Cathedral in the distance, huge and majestic, now completely surrounded by fires. Once or twice Rose had to give way to fire engines, racing along with bells clanging. This meant that she had to drive her own vehicle up on to the pavement, leaving the ambulance stranded amongst a cavalcade of other emergency services, all clearly stretched to capacity. At first Rose and Amanda had resented the call out to the City from their own base in Whitechapel, but they soon changed their minds when they saw what the night was turning into.

'D'yer fink this is the start of it?' Rose asked, as she tried to get the ambulance off the pavement and back on to the narrow street again. 'Is this a warm-up for the invasion?'

Amanda was still peering up through the windscreen. 'By the look of that sky, I wouldn't be surprised. My God, I've never seen so many planes. There must be hundreds of them ... Watch out!'

A bomb came whistling down and exploded far too close for comfort. Rose immediately brought the ambulance to a stop, and they both leapt out and crawled under the vehicle for protection.

As they lay there, with the plethora of bombs exploding all around them, they could hear the familiar after effects of shrapnel tinkling down on to rooftops and pavements.

'This is the worst I've known for ages,' said Rose, lying flat on her stomach, hardly daring to speak. 'So much for Christmas and the season of goodwill!'

'There's no goodwill tonight, Rose!' Amanda had to shout to be heard. 'Whatever Jerry's up to, it looks as though he's determined to burn down the whole City!'

Rose put her hands on top of her tin helmet, and rested her elbows on the ground. As she and Amanda lay there, their faces lit up by the flickering flames that were leaping out of old buildings all around them, Rose asked herself if this might really be the beginning of the end for everyone in the dear old British Isles. She thought about her mum and the family, taking shelter on the platform down the tube, and what future there would be for them under a Nazi occupation. Looking out, she could see the glow of fires burning in countless ancient buildings, and hear the clanging of fire engine and police car bells, people shouting out for help, panic and confusion, sheer pandemonium. And all the time, the relentless drone of enemy planes swarming overhead, dropping their deadly loads wherever and whenever they pleased. How could people survive this living nightmare? How could they stand up to this mindless onslaught? This wasn't war. It was wholesale murder!

'Come on, dear! Drink up!'

Rose suddenly realised Amanda was dangling a small silver brandy flask under her nose.

'Go on – take it! It's the only way to get through an air raid!'

Rose took the flask, and sniffed it. 'Blimey, Amanda!' she yelled above the din. 'This is enough ter blow yer bleedin' 'ead off!'

Even though she rarely drank spirits, Rose took a swig. It burnt her throat and sent her into a fit of coughing. 'We shouldn't be doin' this on duty, Amanda!' she spluttered. 'If the super finds out about this, she'll 'ave our guts fer garters!'

'Nonsense, dear!' said Amanda emphatically. 'If we're going to be blown to bits, we might as well go out in style. You know what they say: here today, gone tomorrow!'

As Amanda spoke another bomb came screeching down through the air.

A few miles away, both platforms of the Angel tube station were chock-a-block with people sheltering from the raid. Nellie and the twins were amongst them, all huddled up together beneath the eiderdown taken from Nellie and Albert's bed, and although it was only half-past nine in the evening, they were cold, tired, and very frightened. At least they had managed to find some space on the platform itself; many people had had to make up beds between the rail lines, where the power had been turned off since the start of the air raid. Tonight, there was fear everywhere. The word had gone through the crowds that something was going on 'up top', and that this was going to be a really hectic night for everyone involved in the emergency defence and rescue services.

Further along the platform a small group of people were doing their best to relieve the tension by starting up a sing-song, among them, Mr Cabbage and his missus from the market, who, together with some of the other traders, were leading a frisky chorus of 'Run, Rabbit, Run!' And by the time they had reached, 'She'll be Comin' Round the Mountains', the whole tube station population, including those overflowing on to the cold stone steps leading up to the lifts, were clapping hands, stamping feet, and yelling their heads off, as though in sheer defiance of all the horror that was being perpetuated at ground level above them. One man had even managed to get a xylophone down on to the platform, and the music that he and the crowds were making seemed to glide around the curved walls and ceilings to create a sound that was really quite beautiful.

Nellie was very relieved when she suddenly caught sight of Queenie picking her way across the sea of arms and legs along the platform, for she hadn't seen her since she left home to look after Mrs Wu's kids early that morning.

When she did finally reach the patch which her mum and twin sisters had claimed earlier in the evening, it was clear that Queenie was in a terrible state.

'It's awful, Mum,' she said, her face pale and drawn. 'I left Mrs Wu an' the kids over an hour ago. It's taken me all this time ter get 'ere. I had ter walk all the way.'

'What's 'appenin' up there, Queen?' asked Nellie, pouring her daughter a cup of tea from a vacuum flask.

Queenie was shivering with nerves. 'Everywhere yer

look there are fires burnin' all over the place. They must be takin' an 'ell of a bashin' up the City. The whole sky is lit up as far as yer can see.'

'Did you see a lot of dead bodies lying around, Queenie?' Millie asked ghoulishly.

'Mill!' her mum snapped crossly.

'D'you have to ask questions like that?' growled Polly. 'That's gruesome!'

Millie leant back against the curved wall again. 'I only asked!' she sighed indignantly.

'I 'ad ter keep takin' shelter in shop doorways. There're bombs goin' off all over the place. An' the shrapnel! I don't know 'ow I got through it, honest I don't!'

'It's all right, Queenie,' Nellie said, trying to calm the girl down. 'Just get yer breff back and 'ave some tea.'

Queenie took the vacuum top, but just held it in both hands. She was shaking from head to foot. 'There's loads of places ain't there no more. One minute there's an 'ouse or a shop, an' then – they're gone.' She was fighting back tears as she spoke, her eyes transfixed on the tea in the vacuum top she was holding. 'I came past old Lil' Walker's place. Yer know 'oo I mean, don't yer? That newsagent – on the corner, down Bixby Street. It ain't there no more. Nuffin' left. Just a pile of rubble. Looks like 'alf the street's gone.' She looked briefly up at her mum. 'That's 'ow I found my job, yer know. Rose saw a card in Lil's window. I only met 'er a couple of times. She was ever such a nice woman . . .'

As Queenie spoke, the walls suddenly vibrated to a series of explosions on the surface above. She dropped her tea, and both she and the twins threw themselves into their mum's arms. No one panicked, but Nellie and her girls could feel the tension all along the platform.

In the eerie silence that followed, Polly, pressed hard up against Nellie's chest, tried to speak. 'Mum, are we safe down here? Are we?'

For a moment, Nellie seemed as though she hadn't heard Polly's question, for she was agonising in her mind about what was happening to Rose in her ambulance, and Albert on Home Guard watch, and young George on his bicycle in the thick of it, carrying messages from one fire station to another – all of them risking their lives in streets that were paved with death. 'Course we're safe,' Nellie said, leaning back against the wall and holding on to her three daughters with grim determination. 'They can't touch us down 'ere. They can't touch us 'Umbles. We're too good for 'em!' Then she leant her face on the top of Polly's head. 'Don't worry at all, gels,' she said strongly. 'We're safe all right – yer'll see!'

But Queenie looked up and asked, 'Then wot's 'appened ter the guns, Mum? Why 'ave they stopped all the guns up there?'

At that precise moment, the whole place was suddenly rocked to its foundations by a loud explosion coming from what seemed to be a next-door room. This was immediately followed by a few seconds of sheer horror, as a violent rush of air gushed along the tunnel at an alarming speed, sounding like a hurricane. With it came a pall of thick black dust which festooned the platforms and settled on everyone and everything trying to shelter there. Some of the women screamed, but Nellie stayed calm, quick to cover herself and her girls with the eiderdown. In the chaos that followed, most people did their best not to panic, and whilst they waited for the dust to subside, they held on to each other and desperately tried to protect themselves from any falling debris.

It took several minutes for the atmosphere to quieten. There followed an eerie silence, broken only by the quiet sobbing of small bewildered children and people coughing and spluttering in the stifling dark cloud that had engulfed them.

Nellie, Queenie, Polly, and Millie gradually emerged from beneath their eiderdown to find themselves trying to focus through a black pea-souper fog. Everywhere they looked, dust was piled high on people and their belongings. It was a scene of total bewilderment, as though an artist had decided to paint his entire canvas black. But at least they were alive!

'Are we down 'earted?' yelled some bright spark at the other end of the platform.

'No!' came a thunderous yell from the crowd. The sound was so loud that the poor souls who had shacked up between the rail lines failed to notice the terrified mice that were scuttling beneath the edge of the wall beside them.

Nellie pulled back the eiderdown, and looking at her three girls said with a smile, 'Wot'd I tell yer? We *are* safe down 'ere – right?'

After sheltering underneath their ambulance for the best part of ten minutes, Rose and Amanda finally managed to continue their journey to their call-out destination in the heart of the City.

When they reached what had once been Paternoster

Row, a little street running from Cheapside to Ave Maria Lane, they found their way barred not only by a myriad of vehicles from the defence and rescue services, but by fallen debris, piled high along the complete length of the street. Masonry from the ancient buildings had come down everywhere, and the whole area had been devastated by incendiary bombs and high explosives. The men and women of the London Fire Brigade and the AFS were there in force, but despite the countless hosepipes directed on to the tall blazing buildings, they were engaged in a life or death struggle to get the situation under control. Dozens of female volunteers from the London Ambulance Brigade were waiting around in groups, eager to go in for survivors once it was permitted to do so. Together with others from the WVS, many had already risked hazardous conditions to collect the injured as they were pulled out of the debris. As they did so, explosions inside the buildings were taking place all the time, as gas mains fractured and electric junction boxes blew out. From above, and seemingly unchallenged, came the constant drone of enemy aeroplanes, raining down a monsoon of incendiary firebombs and high explosives.

'Where the bleedin' 'ell are our ack-ack?' yelled Rose, between the explosions. 'It's crazy! Jerry's got the skies ter 'imself. We don't stand a chance!'

'There's got to be a reason for it,' Amanda called back, holding on to her helmet with both hands, 'but I don't understand it.' She took a quick, daring look up at the sky. 'They seem to be getting around the balloons. For God's sake, where are our RAF boys?'

Both ducked as another high explosive bomb landed

just a few streets away, sending a giant flame shooting high above the skeleton of buildings that were already devastated.

'You girls!'

Rose and Amanda turned to find a St John superintendent from another division, hurrying towards them. She was covered in masonry dust after helping to search for survivors in the wreckage of a printing works, which had just come down in the adjoining Paternoster Square.

'They need you down the lane opposite. There are some people trapped in a shelter. You'll have to go on foot. There's no way you can get an ambulance anywhere near!'

Before Rose and Amanda even had a chance to respond, the woman was off again, climbing over a pile of still smouldering debris to return to her own harrowing search for survivors. As she watched her go, Rose reckoned the tough old bag was sixty-five years old if she was a day.

The whole area was now burning more fiercely than ever, and Rose and Amanda had plenty of light as they struggled their way along the remains of the tiny street, scrabbling over piles of fallen masonry, clutching a folded stretcher between them. Rose was overawed by the sight of St Paul's Cathedral, with its vast dome towering high above them, a powerful silhouette ringed with flame and smoke, its shining gold cross, dome, and towers standing firm against the inferno that had so far failed to engulf it. It was an image of defiance, and Rose couldn't help feeling that it was a symbol of the people themselves, refusing to give in.

Once they reached Ave Maria Lane, the full extent of

the devastation hit them. Firemen were tackling fires everywhere, dragging hoses from one building to another, shouting out commands. Others were balanced precariously at the top of fully extended ladders, struggling to lash their branches – their hosepipes – as they pumped as much water as they could into flames billowing out of the windows of blazing office rooms.

Rose could hardly believe the carnage all around her. She was scrambling across a battlefield right here in Ave Maria Lane, in Paternoster Row, and other tiny streets at the heart of the City.

'Wot's all these books?' Rose yelled to Amanda, who was leading the way over the street rubble.

Trying to avoid the pools of water from the hoses, Amanda stopped to look at the charred fragments of hundreds of books which were still smouldering. 'All these buildings used to be book publishing firms,' she called, and with her foot, kicked at the remains of a large, leather-bound book that was written in ancient script. When she looked closer, she saw that it was an illustrated copy of the Bible. 'Good old Goering!' she said cynically. 'I suppose this is his idea of a military objective!'

'Move it, gels!' Rose and Amanda were moving out of the way fast to give two firemen room to drag their hosepipes over the wreckage towards a new blaze in the back area of an old-fashioned office block, when the whole area was rocked by two explosions, in an adjoining street. Both women dropped the stretcher and fell flat on their faces on top of the rubble as masonry dust and debris rained down on top of them.

'You know something?' Amanda called to Rose, through

the mayhem. 'If I had a daughter, I'd want her to be just like you. You're just as big a coward as me!'

They both roared with laughter.

'Get those bloody stretchers up 'ere!' someone yelled from the end of the street.

Rose and Amanda picked up their stretcher and made as quick a dash as possible to a floodlit area about fifty yards away.

As they approached they saw three Alsatian police dogs on leads, sniffing over a huge pile of rubble that had been the roof of a warehouse. Rose felt quite sick as she heard someone calling out from beneath the debris, 'Bit more ter yer right! No! Yer're too far over! For Chrissake 'urry!' Someone else was calling, 'I can't move! For God's sake – 'elp me!' Others were whistling, hooting, and making any sound they could that would point the rescuers in their direction.

'Get yer stretcher ready!' The voice that called to Rose and Amanda had no time for formalities. He was an ARP warden, so covered in dust and muck that he looked as though he himself had just been rescued from the rubble.

'Doctor's just takin' off some woman's leg over there. We can't get 'er out 'til he's finished.'

Amanda took hold of Rose's arm and squeezed it. There was no need for them to look at each other.

'Yer'll 'ave ter get 'er some blood as soon as yer can,' called the elderly ARP man as he returned to help with the rescuc operation. 'She ain't goin' ter make it uvverwise!'

Rose wanted to go with him to help, but she knew her part would come when the injured woman was retrieved.

While she and Amanda waited, she looked up at the shell of the building above them, the high outer wall quivering back and forth precariously. Beneath it, men and women of all ages were tearing at every piece of rubble they could lay their hands on, desperately trying to reach those who were trapped in the company's basement shelter.

'If I live to be a hundred, I'll never forget this night,' said Amanda. The air around her was pierced by the nightmarish sounds of people yelling, groaning, begging, shouting commands, and cursing the wave after wave of alien pilots responsible for the ruthless massacre. 'I feel so bloody, bloody helpless!'

This was the first time Rose had heard her companion swear, and, coming from such a cultured voice, it sounded very strange. 'I don't know 'ow much more of this we can take,' Rose said grimly. 'This is the worst it's bin. If it goes on like this much longer, we've 'ad it.'

'No, Rose!' Amanda turned round to look at her. 'This is exactly what Hitler wants. He wants us to crack up. He wants us to feel so crushed that by the time his brain-washed young thugs come leaping out of the sky, we'll be waiting with open arms for them!'

While Amanda was talking, Rose had her eyes trans-fixed on the gruesome scene taking place on top of the rubble, where two Red Cross nurses were helping a white-coated female doctor to amputate the leg of the trapped woman.

'It mustn't happen, Rose,' Amanda continued fiercely. 'Because if it does, we're finished – as a nation, and as human beings. The future belongs to you, Rose – you and all those who follow you. If you had to bring kids into a world run by a bunch of murderous thugs, life wouldn't be worth living. No, Rose, we must never give in to all this. That would be the greatest crime of all.'

'Stretcher! Over 'ere! At the double!'

As soon as Rose and Amanda heard the call, they picked up the stretcher, and started clambering across the debris. As they climbed down the rubble to where the injured woman was being pulled out of the wreckage, more explosions in the next street sent shock waves throughout the entire area. But Rose and Amanda paused only briefly before pushing on.

Frenzied yells suddenly pierced the air: 'Down everyone!' 'Take cover!' 'Head down!'

A bomb came whistling down from the sky and by the sound of its approach, it was about to fall dangerously close. Rose and Amanda were still on their feet. For what seemed like a split second before the bomb actually landed, there was silence – no fires crackling, no people yelling, just an eerie, heart-stopping void.

Then Rose was blinded by a dazzling blue flash, and felt an enormous pressure against her eardrums, as though someone were pushing their fingers into them. Her whole body seemed to be no part of her. Her head, arms, and legs were dangling awkwardly, and she was floating in space as if in slow motion or drowning, with her entire life flashing through her mind. There was her mum and dad, dancing together to 'Let the Rest of the World Go By' at one of the family's Christmas Day parties; there were Polly and Millie playing their pianos and arguing about their boyfriends; Queenie fixing her scarf around her hairless head and putting on as much make-up as she could find; George teasing his poor mum with a spider so large that it practically filled the first-floor room above the old piano shop. Floating, floating . . .

Rose felt her body drop with a thump, and when the dazzling blue light had cleared, she could see someone's face peering down at her, calling gently, 'It's all right, young lady. Just keep still . . . quite still . . .'

Despite the plea from one of the firemen, Rose tried to sit up. As she did so, she felt a sharp pain in her back. 'Amanda?' she asked, immediately. 'Where's Amanda?'

There were now two other people at her side, both of them helpers from the WVS. 'Lie still, dear,' said the older one. 'We'll have you out of here in no time at all.'

'Amanda!' Rose insisted, trying hard to lever herself up on the pile of rubble. 'Where is she?'

The rescue workers were unable to stop her, as, with great pain, she managed to position herself on her hands and knees. She could feel something warm and wet trickling down the back of her neck. When she felt it she saw that her fingers were covered with blood.

'Amanda!'

Rose was now yelling at the top of her voice, and despite the efforts of the WVS women and the fireman, she was slowly crawling down the huge new pile of debris.

A few yards away, a group of rescue workers were desperately trying to remove rubble from a woman who was trapped beneath it. Rose knew who it was.

'Amanda!' she yelled. 'No!'

The rescue workers tried to restrain Rose from approaching, but she pushed them aside and crawled alongside her companion, her knees now badly cut and bruised.

'Oh Christ, Amanda,' she said, trying to focus, trying to pull the last pieces of rubble from Amanda's face. 'Don't die on me, yer silly cow! Don't bloody die!'

A young ARP worker leant down to take Rose's arm, but she pulled it away angrily. 'For Chrissake, get 'er away from 'ere! Can't yer see she needs 'elp?' She took hold of Amanda's shoulders and tried to shake life back into her. 'Don't die, yer silly cow! Don't die!' Rose was now half delirious, not really aware of what she was doing. 'Remember what yer said? Do yer? Yer said we must never give in! Yer said . . . yer said . . .'

One of the WVS workers crouched down alongside Rose, said quietly, 'I'm sorry, my dear. She's gone.'

Rose turned her gaze from the WVS worker to her companion's lifeless form. Blood was trickling out of Amanda's nose, and her eyes were fixed wide open. Rose leant closer and lightly touched Amanda's lips with the tip of her fingers.

'Don't do this ter me, mate,' she said, with Amanda's face already beginning to blur in her mind. 'We're a team, ain't we? Well – ain't we?' She shook and shook Amanda, but when she realised that there was no life there, she moved back to allow the WVS worker to close Amanda's eyes.

Rose let out the most piercing, agonising yell, which reverberated around the skeletal ancient buildings, and finally mixed into the all clear wail of 'Moaning Minnie'.

The following days the newspapers were full of front-page pictures of St Paul's Cathedral standing unharmed in the midst of the burning City of London. There were lots of theories on why the home defence ack-ack guns had gone silent so early during the massive Sunday night onslaught on the capital. One official explanation was that because there were so many fires burning throughout the City, to continue firing would have disclosed the position of the guns. But whatever the reasons, everyone was agreed that the night of 29 December 1940 was when Adolf Hitler was determined to start the second Great Fire of London.

He did not succeed, of course, but the events of that terrible night had left an indelible scar on the life of at least one young London girl.

Chapter 18

Somewhere at sea
11 Feb. 1941

Dear Ginge,

I was really upsett wen grandad rote and told me about your gettin hurt in that bomb up the city. What a rotten thing to happen, specialy loosin your best pal and all that. I get ever so scared wen I think about you drivin round in that ruddy ambelance night after night and with bombs droppin and things. I dont sleep to well thinkin how you are. I wish you would rite some times and tell me that your safe.

Rose felt ashamed that she had always found it difficult to concentrate on Badger's letters. He was so lively and full of news, and it seemed churlish not to at least try to enjoy them. But the harsh reality was that, despite Badger's long and loving efforts to keep in touch, his letters meant very little to her. Since he joined up, Rose had heard from him at least once a fortnight, although prior to this latest one there had been a gap of about five weeks. This was also the first letter that arrived in the form of an aerogram, which meant it was somehow shrunk down in size, censored, and photographed. There were quite a few censored lines, for Badger was a bit of a gossip, and was more than likely to give away the secret location of his ship and where it was heading! Even so, Rose still had a certain fondness for Badger. At least he was one male that she felt she could always trust.

Once she had skipped to the end of his aerogram, with its usual, 'You know I love you, don't you, Ginge?', Rose folded up the miniature letter, and tucked it away into her handbag in the bedroom cupboard. Then she lay back on the bed again, and did what she'd been doing an awful lot over the past few weeks – just lying there and staring aimlessly up at the ceiling. She didn't really feel comfortable in this position, for although the cut on the back of her head had healed, her body still felt as though it had been used as a football. It was her mind that was the main problem, however. Ever since that night of horror just before New Year's Eve, her thoughts were totally obsessed by 'if onlys'. If only the ack-ack had been doing their job; if only the RAF hadn't been so occupied bombing Hitler's invasion bases in France; if only the local fire-watchers could have tackled the small fires earlier to stop them from spreading; if only there'd been bad weather; if only Amanda ... could have held on until they got her to hospital; if only Amanda ... could have lived! No matter how hard she tried, Rose could not get her best pal out of her mind. Night after night, as she lay awake, her three sisters snoring alongside her, Rose could hear Amanda talking in that arty-farty plummy voice of hers. And she could *see* her, leaning back in the front seat of the ambulance, with the brandy flask in one hand, and a Craven A stuck between her lips, as bold and as daring as anyone could be, not caring bloody hell about anyone in authority. And although she was from a world that Rose couldn't even begin to understand, during the short time they had known each other, there had developed a bond and a sense of fun between them that had overcome class and prejudice.

Although it was not yet four o'clock in the afternoon, the room was already plunged into that dreary February darkness that seems so relentless. It was bitterly cold, with icicles hanging down from the window ledges like a snow monster's fingers.

Suddenly aware that she was becoming gloomy again, Rose sat up and rubbed her dry, weary eyes. In an hour or so her mum would be home from her job in the market, and as this was a Friday, she'd be bringing home fish and chips for the family. Rose decided to go and meet her. With luck, the cold fresh air would inject some life back into her.

A few minutes later Rose was in the market. There was an end-of-the-day feeling about the place, and most of the traders were starting to pack up. Every time Rose walked between the rows of stalls, she admired how everyone had overcome the nightly air raids. Every morning the barrow boys had turned up to find their pitches littered with glass, blown out of the surrounding shop windows, and every morning there had to be a clean-up before the first vegetable or the first pair of second-hand shoes could be sold. But, despite all that, not one of the stalls had ever failed to open up. As Rose wandered amongst all her old pals, 'BUSINESS AS USUAL' was on prominent display on every trader's stall.

''Ow's it goin' then, Rosie, gel?'

Rose always stopped to have a bit of a chat with Ned Morris on his 'Genuine China' stall. Ned usually made Rose laugh without ever having to say anything, because in any kind of weather his nose was always a blood red, with a dewdrop at the end just waiting to be wiped on his tattered jacket cuff.

'Not bad, Ned,' Rose said, pulling up her coat collar. 'Can't bear the 'eatwave, mate, can you?'

'Goin' off ter 'ave a sun-bave up 'Ighbury Fields!' he replied, dealing with that elusive dewdrop. 'Back on yer feet proper now, are yer? Feel more like yer old self?'

'I'm okay, Ned,' Rose replied, trying her best to give him a smile. 'Goin' back ter work on Monday.'

Ned came from behind the stall. 'You watch yerself this time, Rosie me gel,' he said, showing concern. 'We can't afford ter lose good mates like you.'

Rose nodded her thanks, then moved on.

As she passed, plenty of other traders called out to her. 'Wotcha, Rosie!' barked Sid Levitt from his gaudily painted 'Pets' Emporium' stall. ''Ow's about a nice mongrel puppy ter keep yer company?'

'No, fanks, Sid!' came Rose's immediate response, and to gales of laughter from all round added, 'Don't need one. We've already got our Georgie!'

At the end of the market, Rose stopped briefly at an empty stall space which, until the month before, had been occupied by Alf and Maisie Fisher, two costermongers who had travelled in every day from Hackney to trade in knitted socks and gloves. Both of them had been killed in a direct hit on their little terraced house, and it had been a unanimous decision amongst the traders in the market that their pitch should remain vacant until the war was over.

After a quick wave to her mum, who was just packing up at Charlie Spindle's fruit and veg stall, Rose strolled off towards Upper Street. She passed the Wigley brothers' fish and chip shop. As it was Friday, there was the usual long queue outside, everyone clutching their own old newspapers for wrapping up the freshly cooked fish because of the paper shortage.

When she got to Upper Street, Rose stopped outside the Angel Cinema to have a look at the posters advertising the week's film programme. Although she hadn't been to the pictures for a couple of years or so, a bob's worth of Charlie Chaplin as Hitler in *The Great Dictator*, looked as though it might help to cheer her up. But as she stood there, someone quite different from Charlie Chaplin caught her eye. A good-looking young man in an Army officer's uniform was picking his way through the passers-by, and making straight for her. For a moment, Rose was curious and thought she knew him from somewhere. Then she recognised him.

'Hallo, Rose. Good to see you again.'

It was Michael Devereaux.

''Allo, Michael,' Rose replied without expression.

'I saw you from the other side of the road. Knew it was you right away!'

Rose didn't reply. She could tell he was ill-at-ease because his eyes kept flickering nervously.

'Last I heard, you were working at that café in Bethnal Green. Still there, are you?'

Rose put her hands in her coat pockets to keep warm. 'Somefin' like that,' she said. She made a move as if to walk off.

Michael gently blocked her way. 'I'm home on forty-eight hours' compassionate leave. My father died. He had a stroke. I've just come from the funeral.'

Rose then noticed the black armband he was wearing. 'I'm sorry.'

'Oh, you don't have to be. We never got on very well. In fact, he hated my guts. Anyway, my mother's had a boyfriend for ages.'

'I 'ave ter go.'

Michael suddenly took hold of her arm. 'Come and have a cup of tea with me, Rose.' His eyes were pleading. 'Please.'

Rose looked right through him. 'Why?'

'I'd like to talk to you. I'd like to try and put things right.'

For one brief moment, Rose thought he looked more like a small boy than a grown man, but when he looked at her with those big piercing blue eyes, that same stupid feeling came over her that she'd had the first time she met him.

'I've never forgiven myself for ... well, for what happened ... when you came up to meet me outside the office. I didn't mean to hurt you, Rose. It was only meant to be a bit of fun, that's all.'

Rose lowered her eyes, and didn't reply.

'I tried to make contact with you. I didn't know where you live. I still don't know.'

Rose raised her eyes again. 'Let's 'ave a cuppa tea,' she said.

Since the war started, there weren't many places in Upper Street where you could get a decent cup of tea, especially just before blackout time. But Murphy's cake shop next to the tobacconist's was open until half-past five, and they had always had a couple of tables set aside for a quick cuppa in the back part of the shop. As it was nearly closing time, Rose and Michael had the place to themselves.

For five minutes, Rose listened to Michael babbling on about how he got a commission in the Royal Engineers, how he was singled out by his CO for exemplary leadership, and how much he enjoyed army life and would probably remain in the service after the war. But although Rose found his charm as appealing as ever, she hardly heard a word he said. All the while he was talking to her, she stared down at the cup of tea in front of her, into which she had stirred two saccharin tablets at least twenty times. Nonetheless, she didn't interrupt until he had lit a cigarette and taken his first sip of tea.

'I want ter ask yer just one question, Michael,' she said directly. 'When we was in those woods tergevver, yer said yer loved me. Why?'

Rose's question did not take Michael off guard. He had prepared for it. 'But I *do* love you, Rose. Surely you can tell?'

'Yer've got a funny way of showin' it.' She flicked her eyes up quickly, then focused them on her cup of tea again.

Michael leant closer and lowered his voice. 'When I kissed you, I meant it. I've never kissed anyone with more beautiful lips in the whole of my life.'

He tried to cover her hand on the table with his own, but she quickly withdrew it. 'Kissin's not love, Michael,' she said sharply. 'Love is about carin' for someone, about never wantin' ter be parted from 'em for a single minute. I fought yer cared for me, Michael. I fought yer wanted ter be me feller. I fought yer wanted me ter be yer gel.'

'I do want you to be my girl, Rose.'

'Oh yeah?' Rose asked acidly. 'For 'ow long? One night – or two?'

Michael sighed, sat back in his chair, and took a deep puff of his cigarette. 'You know, I don't think you're being fair. I told you, when I saw you with my friends that time, what I said was only a tease, a bit of fun.'

'For you an' my sister Queenie? For you an' yer mates? Ha bleedin' ha!'

Michael suddenly leant forward again. 'Look at me, Rose!' He was staring straight at her. 'Go on! Take a good, long look!'

Rose had to force herself to look at him.

'What do you see? A crook? A liar? Someone you can't trust?' The look on his face seemed totally sincere. 'Let me tell you something. I'm not a crook, I'm not a liar, and you *can* trust me. Believe me, Rose, if I tell a girl I fancy her, I mean it.'

When Michael looked at her like that, Rose felt a cold shiver go down her spine. During the next few seconds, so much churned over in her mind. Had she been wrong about him? Had she over-reacted up in the City, when he tried to show off about her in front of his pals? Suddenly, she felt guilt, even shame. After all, she had wanted him to make love to her that day in the Hertfordshire woods. She had wanted him to help her prove to herself that she was as desirable as any other girl. She had been completely infatuated with him, and yet, for all these months she had blamed *him* for all her own inadequacies.

Behind them, a middle-aged shop assistant was starting to pull down the blackout blinds.

'Wot do yer want me to do, Michael?' Rose asked, without raising her eyes.

'Spend the evening with me.'

Rose shook her head.

'For Chrissake, Rose!' he snapped, stubbing out his half-finished cigarette in the ashtray. 'There's a war on. In case you hadn't noticed, London's being bombed day after day. We could all be killed at any minute!'

'I'm sorry ter rush yer, dears.' The shop assistant was calling across to them from the window. 'It's 'alf-past. We want ter get 'ome before old 'Moanin' Minnie.'

'Sorry, missus,' Rose said, taking out her purse to pay the bill. ''Ow much?'

'Tuppence, please dear.'

Michael leant forward, and stopped Rose digging into her purse. 'Don't be silly, Rose. This is my treat.' He dug down into his trousers pocket, sorted out two pennies and two ha'pennies from his change, and left them on the table as they left.

'Fank yer, dear. 'Night!'

Outside, the traffic was already trying to muddle its way

around in the dark using dim slatted headlights. There was a touch of freezing fog around, so Rose quickly turned up her coat collar and put her hands into her pockets. Michael did likewise.

'So?' Michael asked rather pessimistically. 'Any chance my asking again?'

Rose thought for a moment, then looked up at him. 'What d'yer want ter do?'

'Meet up for a drink. We could go up West. I know a nice little club. We could have a dance. D'you like dancing?'

'I'm sorry, Michael,' Rose said, the condensation darting from her mouth as she spoke. 'I need time ter fink.'

Michael shook his head. 'I don't have any more time, Rose,' he said. 'I have to report first thing in the morning. I'm being posted to somewhere hush-hush. I have a feeling it might be North Africa.'

Just nearby, a fruity-voiced old cockney woman yelled a few choice words at a passing motorist as he splashed her all over with rain-water from a kerbside puddle. 'Tyke!' ''Ope yer get the clap!'

Rose didn't notice any of this. She was too busy trying to make a quick decision. She saw Michael for the first time as someone who was just as vulnerable as anyone else. If she turned him down now, she might regret it for the rest of her life.

'Okay,' she said, with a resigned sigh. 'I'm on.'

Michael's face lit up. 'Meet you outside the Gladstone pub in City Road at seven. Okay?'

Rose nodded.

'With the weather like this tonight, I don't think we'll

hear too much from Jerry. If we do, you won't be too scared being out on the streets in an air raid, will you?'

Rose smiled. 'I'll try not to be.'

Michael, beaming all over his face, straightened his shoulders. 'See you then. Bye.'

'Bye, Michael.'

He turned, and walked off, but after just a few yards, he stopped, came back to Rose, took hold of her, and kissed her.

Although Rose kept her eyes open, she felt as though her knees were turning to jelly.

When they parted, it was to go in different directions. Neither of them looked back.

When Rose got home, Nellie was just dishing out the fish and chips – three nice pieces of cod, two pieces of haddock, one of rock salmon, cod's roe for Albert, and a bob's worth of chips. As always, it went down a treat, even though George smothered his rock salmon with too much vinegar and gave himself a coughing fit.

Despite the culinary delight that awaited her, Rose was only too aware that most of the family were in a bad mood. It sometimes happened like that, not for any particular reason, but because they were either tired, or frustrated by the prospect of having to pack up immediately after tea and head off for either their air-raid duties, or a night down the tube.

The twins were unusually grumpy, and this turned out to be because Polly had discovered (rather late in the day) that she was more in love with the twin boyfriend that Millie had a crush on, than his brother, whom she was stuck with. Over the tea table neither Polly nor Millie would talk to each other, unless it was to ask for the salt or pepper. Then Queenie had apparently just had a row with Mrs Wu, who had come home from work to find that one of the smallest kids had found a pair of scissors and had used them to cut holes in her velour-covered sofa. And if that wasn't bad enough, Nellie was showing irritation with Albert for lighting his pipe whilst the rest of the family were still eating. Oh well, everything normal, thought Rose.

As soon as tea was over, Albert and the kids washed up, leaving Nellie to get the eiderdown, cushions, and tea flasks ready for yet another night on the tube platform.

It was now half-past six, and Rose was getting anxious that she would not be on time for her date with Michael. So she hurried upstairs, got out her best dress, the one with the cupid's bow motifs all over, and used the mirror behind the door to comb her hair, and put on some powder and lipstick. She had only just managed to get dressed, when the door burst open and in came Polly, utterly distraught, and in tears.

'Help me, Rose!' Polly sobbed, throwing herself on to the sisters' huge double bed. Although she was now seventeen, both she and her twin sister Millie acted younger than they actually were. 'Please, please help me! What can I do?'

'Wot is it, Poll? Tell me, gel, tell me!'

Polly sprang up, threw her arms around Rose's neck, and let out a great cry of anguish. 'I'm going to 'ave a baby!'

'Wot?' As Polly dissolved into tears, Rose pulled her

kid sister away, held her at arm's length, and growled, 'Say that again!'

'It's true, Rose! It's true!' Tears were running down the poor girl's nose, and her freckles were looking more prominent by the second.

''Oo did it, Poll?' Rose yelled, angrily shaking her young sister's shoulders. 'Tell me!'

'It was Timmy,' Polly sobbed.

'Timmy O'Hare? That little git! The one wiv the twin bruvver?'

'He's not a git!' Polly snapped back indignantly. 'He's luvely!'

Rose was now completely confused. 'Just a minute. I'n't Timmy O'Hare s'posed ter be Millie's boyfriend?'

This immediately sent Polly into sobs of despair. 'It's me he loves, not her!'

'So it's yer fault then?' snapped Rose, shaking Polly again. 'Yer *let* 'im do it? Yer stupid little cow – yer *let* 'im!'

'Yes! Yes! Yes!' wailed Polly. 'I told him not to. I told him lots of times not to kiss me like that.'

Rose did a double take. 'Yer told 'im – *wot*?'

Polly wiped her eyes and her nose on her dress sleeve. 'I told him not to kiss me – like . . . like – *you* know.'

'No, I don't know.'

'It was disgustin', Rose. I hated it! I thought it was just a kiss, an ordinary kiss. But when he stuck his tongue in my mouth . . . awgh! It was horrible!'

Rose sat back from her and tried to collect her thoughts. 'Now listen ter me, Poll. Is that *all* Timmy did? 'E kissed yer?'

'Yes. But I did warn him, Rose – honest I did. I told him if he kissed me like that, he'd give me a baby.'

For a moment, Rose sat there, hardly daring to move. Then she suddenly started to chuckle, and pretty soon she was roaring with laughter. Oh God, it felt so good to laugh again!

'What are you laughing at?' Polly asked indignantly. 'Rose! It's not funny! Tell me!'

Rose suddenly realised that she was being unkind, so she quickly composed herself, took hold of Polly's hands, and said, 'Listen, Poll. Yer don't 'ave babies . . . just fru kissin'.'

Polly stared at her big sister. Her eyes were wide, and blood-red with crying. 'You don't?'

'Of course yer don't. Honestly, Poll! 'Ow old are yer now – nearly eighteen? And yer still don't know that babies go in the same way they come out!'

This made Polly quite uppity. 'Oh, I know about *that* way!' she said haughtily. 'I've done it *that* way lots of times. But when I told Millie, she said yer could definitely get a bun in the oven by kissin' like that.'

Rose couldn't help it. She burst out laughing again. Luckily, she was saved by the sound of 'Moaning Minnie', right on time again.

'Polly!' Nellie was yelling up the stairs. 'Get down 'ere! We're just off! Rose! Don't forget ter lock up!'

'Right, Mum!' Rose called back.

A few minutes later, all the Humble family had left to resume their own individual nightly rituals.

There was the rumble of ack-ack anti-aircraft gunfire in the distance as Rose made her way along Upper Street.

She wasn't at all nervous, for the weather forecast just before the six o'clock news had said that there would be plenty of low cloud, even some fog, during the evening, so the possibility that enemy aircraft could get through to London would be remote. Even so, she kept as close as she could to the shop doorways, to protect herself when the ack-ack really opened up and shrapnel started to rain down from the sky.

As she headed off at a brisk pace towards the Gladstone pub, which was on the other side of the Angel in City Road, Rose kept thinking about Michael Devereaux, and how stupid and unfair she had been about him these past few months. Every so often the beam from her torch picked out the flaming green eyes of an alley cat, doing its best to prise the lid off one of the many pigswill bins that were placed beneath lampposts up and down the back streets. When she had passed through the now deserted Chapel Market, she had even caught a black moggie at it red-handed, but she didn't give it the boot, because she was convinced that just seeing it meant that this was going to be her lucky night.

The moment she turned into City Road, Rose caught a distant sight of Michael, silhouetted outside the entrance of the pub. She knew it had to be he, for he was constantly looking at his wristwatch, and taking off his cap and nervously putting it on again. This made her quicken her step, for she was excited. There was now no doubt in her mind that she had forgiven Michael, and she couldn't wait to have his arms around her again.

Yet as she drew closer and closer to the pub, she found her legs slowing. She didn't know why, but her feet felt like concrete, and the more she tried to move them, the heavier they became.

Now with no more than fifty yards to go, she decided to cross to the opposite side of City Road, and when she reached a position in which she could see the front of the pub quite clearly, she stepped back into the darkness of a shop doorway.

There she stood, watching the man she had come to meet, pacing up and down anxiously, watching for every customer that approached the pub. In the distance, the ack-ack was having a field day. The sky was lit up with great balls of fire over the East End, where, starting the following week, Rose would once again be picking up the threads of her anguished young life as an ambulance driver.

Why was she doing this? Rose asked herself. Wasn't this what she wanted – a man who loved her – or said he loved her – a man who knew how to sweep a girl off her feet by just looking at her? Or did she want something more? Whatever her reasons, it was cruel of her to keep him waiting in the cold like that. It was unlike her.

Rose stepped out of the shadows, walked back the way she had come, and crossed back over the road. But although she kept on walking, she found herself heading off in a different direction. A few minutes later, she had turned the corner back into Upper Street, crossed over, and stopped outside the Angel Cinema. She turned off her torch and made for the box office.

Despite the air raid, the show went on, as it always did for those customers who were prepared to remain. Rose loved the picture. She thought Michael would have found

Charlie Chaplin far more than 'just a bit of fun'. In fact he was an absolute riot.

Lieutenant Michael Devereaux waited outside the Gladstone pub in the City Road for over an hour. Then he caught a cab, and asked to be taken to a club he knew, somewhere up town, in Soho.

Chapter 19

During the first months of 1941, the good old British weather made life for the Luftwaffe very difficult. But in the middle of March, Hitler started his 'Spring Offensive', which meant an increase in the number of attacks on London and all the big provincial cities.

By then, Rose was back at work, driving her ambulance through the relentless aerial bombardment in London's East End. During the short time she had been away, several of her fellow drivers in the various London ambulance services had been killed or badly wounded, leaving a shortage of volunteers in all areas of the Civil Defence. This inevitably meant that, with Amanda gone, Rose was now on her own.

On a bitterly cold night towards the end of the month, Rose was called out to a major incident at St Katharine's Dock, which was once again outside her own duty area. When she got there, she found she was amongst an armada of ambulances, fire engines, police, and dozens of civilian volunteers, who were all fighting to prevent the fiercely burning warehouse fires from spreading to the rest of the vitally important London Docks nearby. The whole area was an inferno, and already several firemen had been severely injured trying to tackle the blaze from the tops of turntable ladders. The moment she got there, Rose got stuck in, joining up with some of the hardy AFS girls to shift countless lengths of fire hoses and water-pumps from one location to another. It was a tiring job, for the whole operation had to be carried out in the midst of choking black smoke billowing out of every window in at least three of the large warehouses, and the over-powering smell of burnt rubber from one of them meant that those who were working close to the blaze were forced to wear their respirators. On top of all that, the fire fighters themselves were under constant attack from low-flying enemy planes, who were swooping down every few minutes to machine-gun them, and the sound of frantic voices yelling for everyone to 'Take cover!' was heard over and over again.

After an hour or so of some of the most strenuous work she had ever been put to, Rose was told by one of her St John Ambulance superintendents to go and get herself something to eat. Rose always found it strange to eat and drink in the middle of the night, but the stress and strain used up everyone's energy, and a quickly taken meal break was not only a relief, but an order.

As usual, the Salvation Army had set up a mobile canteen, this time in one of the tiny residential dockland backstreets. Because of the scale of the incident, several other voluntary organisations had also sent their canteen vans, including those run by the courageous women of the AFS, and they were all working at full pitch. When Rose got there, she couldn't get over the fact that, despite the great drama being played out just a short distance away, orderly queues had formed in front of every one of the canteen van counters. It even brought a smile to her face, for somehow it seemed so very British.

'Tea, dear?' Rose was asked by an elderly Salvation Army lady behind the counter.

'Please,' Rose answered, smearing her face even more as she tried to wipe away the smoke and grime.

''Fraid there's no sugar, dear, only saccharin.' Milk was already mixed into the tea in the huge metal teapot the little lady was using. ''Elp yerself to a fish paste sandwich, dear. They're fresh-made.'

'Nah, fanks,' Rose answered, taking her chipped mug of tea from the counter. 'Don't feel 'ungry.'

'Yer should eat up, dear,' replied the Salvation Army lady, retying the ribbon under her neat little bonnet. 'Yer know what they say: fill yer tummy wiv God's food, and no 'arm'll come ter yer. I bet yer mum would tell yer the same fing.'

Rose thought the old dear was bonkers. 'I wouldn't bank on it,' she said, sipping her hot tea tentatively. 'My mum ain't 'ere – fank Gawd!'

'Oh, yes she is,' replied the Salvation Army lady, with a twinkle in her eye. 'All mums are 'ere ternight. Yer may not be able ter see 'em, but I bet yer they're 'ere all right.'

Rose smiled, and took a sandwich. Maybe the old dear wasn't so bonkers after all.

'The lady's right, yer know, Rose.'

Rose turned with a start to see who was talking to her.

'Yer can't work on an empty stomach.'

'Blimey!' Rose did a double take. In the dim battery light coming from behind the mobile counter, she could just make out Bill, the AFS fireman she and Amanda had rescued during the old picture house blaze down in Shoreditch. 'Yer're a glutton for punishment, ain't yer?'

'I'm not the only one.' He smiled sympathetically at her. 'Sorry ter 'ear about yer mate from the ambulance. That was a lousy fing ter 'appen.'

Yeah.' Rose avoided his look, sipped her tea, and moved away from the counter.

Bill went with her. 'This war's takin' all the good 'uns,' he said, sweat still streaming down his face from the intense heat of the fire. 'We've lost five mates from our station in the last month alone. It's such a waste of life.'

'It's terrible!' said Rose, shaking her head sadly. 'If it wasn't for you blokes there'd be nuffin' left of poor ol' London. If yer was in the Army, they'd pin a row of medals on yer.'

Bill didn't answer. He sipped his tea and looked out towards the Thames, which was bathed in a fluorescent blue light reflected from a full wintry moon in a clear black sky. Just a little further along the river, Tower Bridge stood proud and erect, the bridge itself lowered, and army searchlights constantly scanning the sky above, and in the grounds of the ancient Tower of London, naval pom-pom guns were firing a stream of tracer shells at the procession of enemy aircraft, silhouetted like flies as they passed across the face of the man in the moon.

'Yer know, this 'as always bin a favourite view of mine,' Bill said, after waiting for another burst of pom-pom fire to subside. 'The old bridge up there, St Paul's, the 'Ouses of Parliament up the uvver end . . . When I was a kid, I used ter fink that nuffin' could ever change all this.'

Rose sneaked a brief look at him. She was amazed how the burns on his face had healed so quickly, leaving only a few slight pink patches on his forehead.

'I was wrong, of course,' Bill continued. 'It's people that change fings.'

Rose's eyes were also scanning the ice-cold waters of the Thames. At intervals all along the banks on either side, the glow of fires was drowning the ornate old buildings in flickering shades of red. 'Yer know wot *I* like about the river? I like it 'cos it reminds me of the sea. I've only ever seen it once. A day's outin' ter Soufend from school. Cost Mum an' Dad one an' six – nearly broke 'em. But I loved it. The sun was out, and the sea was all shinin' – like jewels. Some of us went paddlin'. I cut my big toe on a stone, but I didn't mind. The water was the clearest I've ever seen. Yer could see fish swimmin' around.'

'Take cover!'

The succession of yells heralded another burst of deadly machine-gun fire from a solitary enemy plane, which was strafing the wharf area along the docks. Like everyone else, Rose and Bill immediately ducked down and crouched behind a police box, already riddled with bullet holes. When they got up again, there wasn't much left in their tea mugs.

A few minutes later, Rose and Bill were making their way back again to their duties with several AFS girls and a couple of London Fire Brigade regulars. One of them, an old-timer, was having a bit of fun teasing the girls as he walked behind them.

'Come on, gels! Wot yer doin' out on a night like this?

Yer ought ter be 'ome, lookin' after yer old man!' Some of
the firemen encouraged him by laughing out loud.

One of the girls gave a quick retort. 'If I 'ad an old man
like you, I wouldn't bovver ter come 'ome at night!'

This time, the girls laughed.

The old-timer didn't like being ribbed, and when he
answered, he sounded a bit rattled: 'Men are the only ones
'oo can wear the trousers, mate. A woman's place is in the
'ome!'

This remark provoked calls of ''Ear! 'Ear!' from the
men, and jeers from the girls.

'Don't yer believe it, Tom!' called Bill, as he followed
up behind. 'Gels ain't the weaker sex, yer know. Not
this lot. They've proved ter us they can do anyfin' *we*
can!'

Bill's remark took Rose by surprise. In fact, everything
about Bill had surprised her during their few minutes
alone. Somehow he seemed more thoughtful than when
they had first met, more mellow, and not trying to show off
all the time.

'Take cover!'

This time, the calls heralded a bomb whistling down from
one of the droning enemy planes, and everyone only just
had time to fall flat on their stomachs. As they did so, there
was one hell of an explosion in the tiny residential street
they had just come from. In the pandemonium that
followed, people were screaming, yelling, running all over
the place. Civil Defence workers were rushing into the
street to help cope with the carnage of two small terraced
houses that had been completely demolished by the high
explosive bomb. At the same time incendiary bombs were

raining down all over the nearby wharfside. Within seconds, new fires were burning out of control throughout the entire dock.

Rose joined the dozens of rescue workers in their attempts to calm people who had been blown off their feet by the full bomb blast. Other residents were hurriedly emerging from their houses and back yard shelters, and rushing around in total bewilderment. One woman came running out of a damaged house, shouting out hysterically, and with blood streaming down her face. Rose tried to comfort the woman and treat her head wound, but she had a hard time attempting to calm her again when another enemy plane machine-gunned a barrage balloon in the sky just above them, causing it to burst into a great ball of flame.

With residents from all the surrounding streets running around in total chaos and confusion, Rose stopped to pick up a young woman who had tripped whilst carrying a small baby. As she did so, the voice of a fire station officer boomed out through a megaphone: 'All residents please evacuate this area as quickly as possible. Take only essential personal belongings. Make your way calmly to the Church Hall in Smithfield. Women and small children will be given priority. Please evacuate this area! Please evacuate this area!'

Within moments, a long stream of local residents were heading off towards Smithfield by whatever route they could safely take. As they went, the air was filled by the constant firing of ack-ack anti-aircraft guns, naval pom-poms, and explosive incendiary bombs. Children were crying, families were doing their best to keep together, and helpers from the Civil Defence were trying to keep the whole evacuation as orderly as possible.

Rose watched Bill rush to join the scores of other firemen, struggling with the fires now breaking out all over the dockland area. She hated to see him go. She didn't know why.

Suddenly the Fire Chief in charge of the incident was yelling out at the top of his voice, 'We've lost the water mains! We'll 'ave ter pump up from the river!' As he spoke, an incendiary bomb dropped within a few yards of Rose, and burst into a blinding white flare.

'Out of the way, miss!'

The order came from a young teenage boy, an AFS bike messenger, who was quick-thinking enough to grab hold of the bomb's fin, and smash it on to the ground. The lethal weapon broke up into two pieces, immediately reducing its effectiveness.

Rose was shaking from head to foot, and remembered how she had once tried to tackle a similar bomb by covering it with a blanket! She was astonished by the boy's courage, and as she watched him disappear it made her think of her young brother George, who was also a bike messenger in the AFS. Her blood was chilled by the thought of young Georgie, no longer a schoolboy, and at only sixteen years old subjected each night to the risks and horrors of war just like any soldier on the battlefield.

By now, firemen were rushing past her, carrying lengths of hose to fire pumps along the edge of the river. 'Wot's goin' on?' Rose asked, rubbing smoke out of her eyes.

'All the water mains are fractured!' called one of them.

'We've got ter pump some water up from the river! We need all the 'elp we can get!'

Rose didn't know what had hit her. She was supposed to be an ambulance driver not a ruddy fire fighter. But when she saw hordes of local residents rushing forward to help carry the hoses, she didn't think twice about joining in.

Soon, a human chain had been formed, and the lengths of hose were being held secure all the way from the river's edge to the wharfside warehouses, where nearly all the fires were now raging out of control.

'Down with the pumps!' came the order from some unseen fire officer, and as the pumps were turned on, water started to snake its way towards the nozzles, like a giant python digesting its prey.

Then a most extraordinary sound was added to the mayhem around the blazing docks. Rose, holding on to her length of hose as though her life depended on it, turned around to see two Salvation Army women, known with affection locally as Dolly and Ethel, as they started to beat their tambourines. Rose thought they were an incredible sight, two old dears standing side by side on the river's edge, great warehouses burning fiercely behind them, whilst they sang together the praises of their Lord: 'Onward, Christian Soldiers'! As they sang, everyone joined in – Civil Defence workers, fire fighters, the girls from the AFS, men, women, and youngsters from the dockland streets – one massed voice rising up to the heavens, completely overwhelming the drone of enemy planes flying overhead, and the constant barrage of ack-ack gunfire. It was the most beautiful sound Rose had ever heard, and she would never forget it.

As soon as the hymn singing came to an end, Rose left her place in the human chain holding on to the fire hoses, and, together with some of the other ambulance girls, went to help with the rescue work. She could hardly believe her eyes when she came across an elderly man, who had dragged his favourite armchair out into the middle of the street, sat on it, and, despite the bitterly cold weather, refused to budge. It took a lot of persuasion to get him to move, and he only did so when Rose told him they were serving free beer up at the Church Hall. Before going, however, he insisted on locking the front door of his house.

It took several hours for the infernos to be brought under control, during which time Rose had ferried countless casualties to both the London Hospital and Bart's Hospital in Bishopsgate. But, thanks to the army of volunteers, enough water had been pumped out of the river to stop the fires from spreading any further into the entire London Docks.

The all clear sounded at about five o'clock in the morning. By that time, the cobbled streets and pavements in the tiny dockland streets were covered in a layer of ice, the frozen spray and fall-out of water from the dozens of fire hoses.

Tired, weary, and filthy dirty, Rose collected together five of Bill's mates who were not seriously injured but needed some medical attention in hospital. To Rose's relief, Bill himself was there to help her get them into the back of the ambulance, where they sat on the benches, their knees covered with blankets.

'Look after 'em,' said Bill, as he watched Rose close the

back doors of the ambulance. 'We'll need 'em again ternight – poor sods!'

Rose smiled with him. 'Not this lot, yer don't!' she called, as she opened the driver's door and climbed in. 'Go on – sling yer 'ook! Yer smell like yer need a barf!'

Bill laughed. 'It's a drink I need!'

'Push off, mate!' growled Rose, trying to close the driver's door. 'I've got casualties in the back!'

'Nah – not now! Ternight.' Bill held on to the door. 'Wot about joinin' me?'

Rose took off her tin helmet, medical shoulder bag, and respirator, and put them on the empty passenger seat beside her. 'Some people 'ave ter go ter work, yer know,' she quipped tantalisingly.

Bill persisted. 'Wot time're yer on duty?'

'Push off!' Rose wrestled the door with him.

'Wot time?' Bill insisted.

Rose pretended to be bored. 'I don't know! Depends on "Minnie".'

'Meet yer 'alf-past six. D'yer know that pub round the corner from yer station?'

'The George? Yeah, I know it.' Rose started up the ignition. 'But I can't make it.'

'Why not?' Bill grinned. 'I'd like ter get ter know yer – Rose 'Umble.'

Rose did a double take. ''Ang on! 'Ow d'yer know me name?'

Bill was holding on to the driver's open door. 'Oh, I know a lot about *you*, don't yer worry! I do me 'omework, yer know. 'Alf-past six – The George – okay?'

Rose slammed the door. 'Go an' get a barf!'

As she drove the ambulance slowly out amongst the smouldering remains of the docks, Rose caught a glimpse of Bill in her wing mirror. He was still grinning, and waving madly to her.

She smiled to herself. It had been a hard and gruelling night. But, thanks to that dope of a fireman back there, it had also been a very interesting one.

The George was tucked away in one of those robust self-contained side streets, where everybody knew everybody, and it was something of a dare to venture beyond the Whitechapel Road which crossed one end of the street by the United Dairy yard. The pub itself was well supported, mainly by the locals, but also by volunteer workers from the Civil Defence and St John Ambulance depot nearby. Like everything in the area, The George had had its full share of bomb blast, and the windows had been blown in so many times that Eric, the Guv'nor, had finally replaced them with timber boards on which he had painted in large letters, 'BOOZING AS USUAL'. But despite all the bombs, the pub never closed. Even on a tough night, with the sound of mobile ack-ack guns firing up at enemy planes from the street itself, The George stood ready and waiting for all those hardy souls who couldn't care a monkey's brass for 'Itler.

Rose hadn't been into the pub since Amanda was killed. The two of them sometimes popped in for a quick fortifier before stepping out into the front line, Rose with her shandy, and Amanda on any short she could lay her hands on, when it was available. Everyone who used the place agreed that although it was small, The George was one of the most friendly pubs in the East End.

Rose got to the pub dead on the dot of half-past six. She had not intended to go at all, but there was definitely something about Bill that made her curious. It wasn't that she was attracted to him – at least, that's what she kept telling herself. After all, he wasn't particularly good-looking, with his short curly blond hair, nose that was too small and ears that were too big. But he was well-built, must be over six foot tall, she reckoned, though a bit on the skinny side. And in any case, she just wasn't interested in getting mixed up with any bloke. That was only too obvious after the night her instinct had told her to ditch Michael Devereaux. When Rose talked to Michael, she felt as though he were looking right through her, although Bill whatever-his-name-was – well, he seemed to like talking *with* her not *at* her. What's more, she approved of what he had said to his mates about women *not* being the weaker sex. Yes, this bloke was worth having a drink with, even if it was just a quick one – and absolutely nothing more.

The moment she entered the Public Bar, Rose knew the Woodbine crowd were in – not that that was surprising, for The George was a working men's pub, and Woodbines were a cheap fag. At first, Rose didn't see Bill, because a battle-to-the-death darts match was in progress and the place was jammed tight, but by the time she had squeezed her way to the bar, Bill came up behind her, and put his hand on her shoulder.

'I'm 'ere, Rose!' he called above the darts match cheers. 'Glad yer could make it. Wot can I get yer?'

Rose had to shout back over her shoulder to be heard. 'Can we find somewhere quiet?'

They had better luck in the Private Bar. Although there

were no tables free and nowhere to sit, there was at least room at the bar counter to park themselves. Rose had her usual shandy, and Bill a draught Guinness. He also bought Eric, the Guv'nor, a pint of mild and bitter, but after they'd exchanged a few friendly words with him, they were left alone.

'So wot's all this about doin' yer 'omework on me?' Rose asked, studying Bill closely over the top of her glass.

'Did that a long time ago, when I was in 'ospital. Got one of me mates to check up on yer. Good Angel gel, right?'

Rose couldn't take her eyes off him. This was the first time she'd seen him looking so clean and tidy! 'Since yer know so much about me, wot about you? I don't even know yer name. Is it still "just Bill"?'

Bill chuckled as he lit up a Weights. 'Layton. Bill Layton. I come from over Befnal Green. I was born up near Bow Green, though. Yer know – Bow bells an' all that.'

'Fancy!' Rose quipped. 'So I'm talkin' ter a *real* cockney!'

They laughed together.

'D'yer live alone?' Rose asked, rather coyly.

'Nah – wiv me mum. She's a widow. I lost me dad six years ago. 'E was a brickie. Scaffold fell on 'im – tons of it. 'E was a good dad ter me. I miss 'im.'

Rose felt a bit awkward, so she quickly changed the subject. 'So – 'ow long yer bin in the fire service?' she asked.

''Bout seven or eight months, somefin' like that. I'll keep at it 'til the war ends – if I make it that long!'

'Don't be stupid! Course yer will!' Then she added enquiringly, 'They 'aven't nabbed yer fer call-up then?'

Bill's reply was a bit evasive. 'Nobody wants me,' he said, shrugging his shoulders and gulping down some more Guinness.

Rose was curious. 'Really? Why's that?'

'Psychologically unsuitable.'

'Huh?' Rose nearly choked into her shandy. 'Wot the 'ell does *that* mean?'

'Oh, I dunno.' He was looking uncomfortable. 'Somefin' ter do wiv bad eyesight, I reckon.' Then he made a wry, throwaway remark that appeared to mean something to him. 'Apparently I don't 'ave very good vision – so they tell me.'

Rose didn't understand what he was talking about. 'My bruvver's in the Army,' she said. 'Royal Artillery. 'E was at Dunkirk.'

'Oh – right.'

Rose was a bit surprised by Bill's bland response. And she was a bit curious to notice that when two young Army conscripts came up to the bar to order some drinks, he very pointedly turned his back on them.

Just then, 'Moaning Minnie' wailed her nightly tune. Everyone groaned in the Private Bar and jeered in the adjacent Public Bar.

'Ladies and gents!' called Eric, the Guv'nor. 'The downstairs shelter is now open – for anyone 'oo needs it! Uvverwise – booze up!'

A great cheer arose and everyone carried on drinking.

'Better not be too long,' said Rose, drinking up a little faster. 'Looks like anuvver night of it.'

'Don't yer ever get scared out there?' Bill asked.

'Wot of?' replied Rose, puzzled.

'All on yer own, drivin' that ambulance in the fick of it. It's bloody risky.'

'So's yer work.'

'Yeah – but we're an 'ole lot of fellers. We're used ter roughin' it.'

Rose put her empty glass down on the counter. ''Ere we go again. So wot's all this about gels not bein' the weaker sex no more?

'Yer not,' Bill answered quickly. 'I meant wot I said. We couldn't win this war wivout the likes of you – anyone can see that. But yer can't get away from the fact that there *are* some fings that gels just can't do.'

'An' vice versa,' Rose replied cheekily.

Bill grinned back. 'An' vice versa.'

They said goodnight to Eric as they left the pub. Things were beginning to hot up outside, for the first barrage of ack-ack could be heard in the distance. They strolled together to the end of the road, during which time Rose felt a strong urge to say something to Bill. The trouble was, she didn't know what.

'It turns me up ter see gels an' women like you caught up in all this,' Bill said, looking up at the ominous sky. 'Yer'll take care of yerself ternight, Rose, won't yer?'

Rose was taken aback. It felt so good to have someone show concern for her – especially a feller. 'I bet yer say that ter all the gels,' she said in a very sweet feminine way.

Bill stopped walking, and turned to look at her. 'I don't, yer know.'

They were now facing each other in the dark. Behind them came the faint rumble of gunfire and gradual approach of enemy planes droning in the sky above them.

Although they couldn't actually see each other, the silence between them suggested a great deal. For some reason, Rose expected Bill to take hold of her hand, or even be daring enough to kiss her. But he didn't. For Rose, that feeling was not at all what she had anticipated.

'Fanks for the drink,' Rose eventually said.

'Fanks for comin',' Bill replied. 'Same time termorrer.'

Rose was taken off guard. 'Termorrer? I don't know, Bill. I'm not sure – not just yet.'

'Well, if yer do decide, yer know where ter find me.'

'I'd better be goin',' she said, not really wanting to do anything of the sort.

There was another moment of silence. Then Bill spoke. 'See yer then.'

'See yer,' Rose replied.

Then, without saying another word, they each walked off in opposite directions.

The same time the following evening, Rose went back to The George. She was not entirely surprised to find Bill there too. After all, he had told her where she could find him. Rose went back every evening from then on, and always Bill just happened to be there.

It wasn't too long before they got to know each other rather well.

Chapter 20

North London didn't really notice the first signs of spring until well into April. By then the daffodils were beginning to make a strong showing in the garden beds of Islington Green and the little window boxes of the bomb-blasted terraced houses. Chapel Market was a riot of yellow, and the penny bunches of spring flowers on sale were soon snapped up to brighten many a war-torn front parlour.

Nellie Humble was absolutely thrilled when she saw her first daffodils of the year. There were only two of them, poking up between a gap in two broken flagstones in the back yard, but as far as she was concerned, they were the closest she would ever get to growing her own flowers. The funny thing was, she had no idea how they got there, for they had just suddenly appeared some years before. It was well into May before they died down, to miss some of the worst times of what was now becoming known as 'The London Blitz'.

Since that eventful night at the docks in March, Rose had been spending very little time at home. In the early hours of every morning, tired and exhausted, she crept into her bed, just as Queenie and the twins were about to get up and go to work. On most days she fell into a deep sleep and didn't wake up until around two o'clock in the afternoon. But of late, her routine was beginning to change, for, apart from meeting Bill in The George for a drink most evenings, she had taken to spending more time with him, mostly on their days off.

Nellie, of course, was the first to notice the change in Rose. Every time she came home from work she found her eldest daughter making herself up in a tiny hand mirror on the kitchen table, or combing her newly grown long hair, which she tucked so meticulously under a hairnet before putting on her uniform cap. But it was more than that: Rose was becoming a different person, more gentle and feminine. Nellie was curious, and just a little jealous. It felt strange for once not to be the centre of her daughter's attention.

'Did yer 'ear young Badger's bin made a signaller out on some ship?' It was a Friday afternoon and Nellie was finishing off her ironing whilst listening to *Music While You Work* on the wireless, before the family came home for tea. ''Is grandad says 'e's doin' really well,' she said spikily. ''E's worf 'is weight in gold, that boy.' She flicked a sly glance up at Rose, who was getting ready to go out. 'Badger's very fond of *you*, yer know.'

Rose sighed. 'Yes, Mum, I know,' she replied, aware that Nellie had brought up the subject time and time again. 'Badge writes ter me at least free times a week – remember?'

'Yes, and 'ow many times do yer write back, I wonder?'

'I write whenever I can, Mum. An' that's not very often when yer fink 'ow much time I 'ave ter meself!'

Nellie was pretending to hum to a song on the wireless,

but she was in fact watching her daughter carefully as she ran her hand up and down one of the stockings she was wearing to make sure that there was no ladder in it. 'Rosie,' her mum asked casually, 'd'yer reckon 'e's good-lookin?'

'Wot? 'oo?'

'Young Badger. The girls down the market never stop goin' on about 'im.'

This was too much for Rose, and she snapped, 'An' neiver do you!' She stopped what she was doing, went to the wireless set, and turned it off. 'Look, Mum,' she said firmly. 'Badge's a really nice boy, an' I'm very fond of 'im. But 'e ain't my boyfriend. Now I've told yer that before, an' I'm tellin' yer again! So please don't keep goin' on about it, okay?'

Nellie stopped ironing for a moment, and looked quite offended. 'I don't know wot yer're talkin' about, Rose 'Umble!'

'Oh yes yer do!' Rose took the iron from her, and put it back on to the folded newspaper Nellie used as an iron rest on the kitchen table. 'Yer've bin tryin' ter match me off wiv Badge practically since the day 'e was born!'

'That's not true!'

'Oh yes it is, an' yer know it. Honest, sometimes yer treat me like a lump of lard,' she said jokily. 'Always tryin' ter knock me inter the shape *you* want! When yer're down that tube each night, all comfy cosy, don't yer ever fink of yer poor daughter dodgin' in an' out of them bombs?'

'Never!'

'Liar!'

'Don't speak ter yer muvver like that!'

Her mum's indignation only made Rose laugh. 'Come over 'ere, you!'

She led Nellie over to a comfortable wooden armchair on one side of the range, and plonked her down there. 'Now yer listen ter me, Mrs 'Umble.' Rose crouched down in front of her and took hold of both her hands. 'If I tell yer somefin', will yer promise not ter tell the uvvers?'

Nellie refused to meet her eye, and looked all haughty. 'I won't promise nuffin'.'

'Then I won't tell yer.'

'I promise.'

Rose had to smile. She knew as well as anyone that her mum could no more be angry with her than the man in the moon. 'I'm courtin'.'

'Ah!' Nellie said, immediately. 'I fought as much! That's the reason for all the makeup, is it?'

Now it was Rose's turn to be indignant. 'Makeup! A bit of powder an' some lipstick? Wot d'yer take me for, Mum – a tart?'

At that moment, there was a thumping sound from the other side of the room. It was coming from the main waterpipe, which had been behaving rather badly since a bomb in Upper Street a few weeks before had caused the whole building to vibrate badly. Nellie had found her own remedy for the problem, so she got up, collected a scrubbing brush from the washing-up bucket, and gave the offending pipe a sharp whack. Then, without further ado, she returned to her chair, where Rose was still crouched on her heels.

'So, 'oo is 'e?' she asked, as if she wasn't really at all interested.

''Is name's Bill.'

'Is 'e the fireman?'

Rose's mouth dropped open. 'Yer know! Yer old witch!'

'I don't know nuffin',' Nellie insisted. 'Nuffin' at all.'

'Then 'ow d'yer know 'e's a fireman?'

Nellie shrugged her shoulders non-committally.

'Honest, Mum!' chortled Rose, in mock outrage. 'Old Churchill'd be proud of us 'Umbles. 'E could drop the 'ole family in France an' use us as secret agents!'

This made Nellie laugh, and so Rose inevitably did, too. As she watched her mum shake up and down with laughter, Rose had a brief chance to recapture some of those rare idyllic moments when she was a kid, when Nellie had the most infectious laugh of anyone she knew. Her eyes would close, her face would crumple up, and as she leant her head back her nose would twitch until she just had to rub it with the back of her hand. Even now, Rose loved her mum's nose. To her it was the most beautiful part of her face, so well-proportioned that it just demanded to be looked at. And her hair was just as lovely as ever, that same rich red that she had passed on to her four daughters, and which she now wore with such dignity in a matronly bun behind her head. True, there were a few strands of grey just appearing above the ears, but when she laughed they made her look younger not older. Rose thought that by the time her mum reached old age, the mixture of red and grey was going to make her one of the most beautiful old ladies in the whole world.

'When're we goin' ter meet 'im?' Nellie asked, once she had stopped laughing.

'Oh, come off it, Mum!' Rose said, feeling just a slight colour coming to her cheeks. 'I 'ardly know the bloke.'

'An wot about poor old Badger?' Nellie asked. ''E's really set on yer, yer know.'

'I know 'e is. But when 'e comes 'ome, I'll talk ter 'im. Don't worry, Mum. I'll try not ter break 'is 'eart . . .'

Rose had no time to finish what she was saying because Nellie suddenly let out a piercing scream and leapt up from her chair. 'Get it away from me! Get it away from me!' she shrieked.

Rose wondered what the hell had happened until she noticed a small house spider silently making its way along the arm of Nellie's chair, clearly heading in the direction of the minute web it had spun at the side of the range. She wanted to laugh, but when she saw her poor mum cowering by her bed in the back part of the room, she thought better of it. She carefully allowed the tiny insect to crawl on to her finger, then, going to the open window, blew the spider away.

'Good fing yer got an 'ead for 'eights,' she said to herself.

This time Rose had no intention of killing a spider. The last thing she wanted was any more bad luck.

When Rose came out of the house, Uncle Popov was in the shop downstairs playing a second-hand C. E. Little & Sons upright to a prospective buyer. Rose knew the piano well. It was made of a beautiful timber that had been stained very dark and so highly polished that she could see her face reflected in the lid. Since the timber was rosewood, Rose felt she had a special interest in it. Apart from a small chip in the front of the keyboard cover, the piano was well worth the twenty pounds the old man was asking for it.

Making quite sure that she couldn't be seen, Rose lingered outside the shop window and listened to the sweet sounds that were coming from her favourite piano. Until now, she had forgotten how well Uncle Popov could play, and that he had been a piano tuner in his native Ukraine. Rose herself didn't know anything at all about 'posh' music, but, for a few heavenly minutes, the sounds that the old man was coaxing out of that lovely piece of furniture were helping her to forget the horrific noises of war.

Rose was already beginning to enjoy her day off, and as she turned into the market and saw one side of the street bathed in the warm bright sunshine of the first day of May, she felt as free as the air itself, as though she had just been released from prison. There were quite a few wolf whistles as she made her way between the busy stalls, for the barrow boys were so used to seeing her in her St John uniform, that it came as a shock to see her in a bright cotton summer dress. As she walked, the flimsy material fluttered around her knees, and the sun seemed to be urging her to keep her head up so that it could flood her face with natural warmth. Rose looked good all right, and she knew it. She couldn't wait to see what Bill thought of her.

Rose's feeling of elation was even greater when she caught a glimpse of two young people sitting side by side on what used to be Peanut's old stall. One of them was a pretty girl of about eighteen, but the other, in Army uniform, with the familiar cheeky grin, was someone she could recognise a mile off.

'Peanut!'

As Rose ran to him, Peanut jumped down from the stall and opened his arms wide. 'Ginge!' he yelled, greeting her with a warm hug. ''Ow are yer, mate?'

'All the better for seein' yer, yer old git!' Her old sharp tongue was a sure sign that Rose was thrilled to see him. 'Why don't yer never write no letters? Everyone fought yer was six foot under or somefin'!'

Peanut laughed. 'Wishful finkin!' he quipped. Then he turned to the girl he had been sitting with, and helped her down from the stall. 'Ginge, I want yer ter meet a new mate of mine. Mabel – this is Ginge. Ginge – Mabel.'

'Wotcha, Mabe!' Rose said, immediately offering Peanut's girlfriend a handshake and a huge smile.

''Allo, Ginge,' replied the girl shyly, shaking Rose's hand. 'Pete's told me a lot about yer.'

''Oo?' asked Rose, puzzled.

'See!' said Peanut. 'All these years we've known each uvver an' yer've never even bovvered ter find out me proper name. Charmin!'

Rose grinned. 'Well, yer still Peanut ter me, mate! An' yer always will be!' Then she turned to Mabel, and added, 'Don't tell me yer're really goin' out wiv this big streak?'

''Fraid so,' said Mabel demurely. 'Wot's more 'e's asked me ter marry 'im.'

'Wot?'

Rose suddenly felt a hundred years old. Like most of her barrow boy mates in the market, she had known Peanut all her life.

'Don't look so shocked,' joked Peanut. 'Even an ol' bloke like me can sweep a gel off 'er feet if I try 'ard enough.'

302

All three laughed, and Rose hugged them both. 'I'm really 'appy for yer,' she said, with great affection. And turning to Mabel, she said, 'As much as I 'ate ter admit it, Mabe, yer've got quite a bargain 'ere!'

Their laughter was suddenly cut short, when Fred Oakes shouted out from his second-hand bookstall.

'Quiet everyone!'

There was so much jokey banter and trading going on up and down the market that hardly anyone heard him. So he yelled out again, this time cupping both his hands as a loud-hailer.

'Shut up, all of yer! Down! Down! Down!'

The entire market was silenced. It started at one end of the street. Then, as the sound of people's voices began to fade, it spread from one corner to the next. Even the budgies in Sid Levitt's 'Pets' Emporium' stopped chirping.

'Wot is it?' Rose called to Fred, hardly daring to use her voice.

'Ssh!' Fred called back, with finger on mouth. 'Listen!'

Rose was puzzled to see that Fred was looking up at the sky, so she did the same. Then Peanut and Mabel did likewise.

In the eerie silence, all they could hear at first was the distant rumble of traffic coming from nearby Upper Street, but after a moment or so, the drone of planes could be heard drifting in high above, from the direction of King's Cross. It was a faint sound to start with, but an all-too-familiar one, and as Rose's eyes scanned the almost cloudless blue sky, there were many more doing the same throughout the market, a sea of faces turned upwards.

Then a woman yelled out, 'Jerry!'

Automatically, everyone took cover beneath the flimsy protection of the market stalls.

'It can't be Jerry,' Rose said to Peanut. 'We 'aven't 'eard "Minnie".'

Despite the fact that no air-raid warning had been sounded, no one was taking any chances. As the droning sound drew closer and closer, the afternoon shoppers and traders held their breath. Some of them even crossed themselves. Soon the air was filled with the noise of what sounded like heavy bombers flying low over the rooftops, but it was not until the first of them came into view that a true picture began to emerge.

'It's not Jerry!' someone yelled. 'It's *our* boys!'

Gradually, everyone got to their feet. They could see a great mass of blue sky shimmering with the wonderful sight of British bombers roaring away above the barrage balloons, and closely guarded by their Spitfire and Hurricane fighter-plane escorts. They were so low that their shadows passed over the complete length of the market, casting strange patterns on to every hopeful face watching them.

'Free cheers for our boys!' yelled one of the traders. 'Hip, hip!'

The whole market vibrated to the sound of people cheering their heads off, whilst the great air armada thundered past and headed off south towards the English Channel. As they went there were shouts of, 'Give 'em 'ell, lads!' and, to gales of laughter, 'Right up Adolf's 'ooter!'

For several minutes, Rose, Peanut and Mabel watched the spectacle and joined in the cheers, applause, and mad waving that had quite suddenly and unexpectedly brought so much joy to those who were starved of such a boost to their morale.

As she left the market, Rose turned briefly to wave to Peanut and Mabel. She had never seen her old mate Peanut look so happy. There was no doubt in her mind that the stupid git had actually fallen in love.

As usual, Bill was right on time. Rose had soon found him to be a meticulous time-keeper who got quite agitated if she arrived late, which she often did. In some ways, Rose thought the two of them had very little in common. In contrast to Bill, she was completely casual and flexible in her daily routine, whereas he was very set in his ways, and liked to plan out his day with carefully timed precision. But the more they got to know each other, the more Rose grew to like him. In fact, she was growing to like Bill an awful lot, for he had a gentle way of dealing with her, of making her feel that she was somebody special. She particularly loved the way he got up and gave her his seat in pubs, and helped her off a bus or tram if they were going anywhere. She knew she was pandering to his old-fashioned charm, but, coming from a family of three sisters and two brothers, for just once in her life it felt good to be getting all the attention.

'Yer look t'rrific,' said Bill, the moment Rose joined him outside the grand Gaumont Cinema in Holloway Road. Although he was a bit tongue-tied, he couldn't take his eyes off her.

Rose would have liked him to greet her with a kiss, just a peck on the cheek or something, but as a boyfriend, he was turning out to be pretty laid-back.

'Yer don't look so bad yerself,' she answered, admiring

his white shirt, grey flannels, and sports jacket, but she was puzzled to see him wearing a tie in such warm weather. 'Seems a shame ter be goin' ter the pictures on a day like this,' she added, not really meaning what she said, for she had been looking forward to her one and ninepence of dark with Bill.

'We don't 'ave ter if yer don't want,' he said rather glumly. 'Go for a walk if yer like.'

'Nah,' said Rose coyly. 'Now we're 'ere, we might as well go.' But her nose turned up when she looked up at the posters in the glass case outside the picture house. 'Not mad about George Formby, though. They've got a good war picture on at that new place – the Savoy – down the road . . .'

Rose could not have said anything worse, for Bill's immediate reaction was to reach into his pocket for a fag. 'I can't see wot's wrong wiv George Formby. At least 'e's good for a laugh.'

Rose suddenly felt awful, as though she had ruined her date with Bill in one fell swoop. 'I don't mind wot I see, Bill – honest I don't . . .'

'Course yer do,' Bill answered sourly. 'Uvverwise yer wouldn't've said it, would yer? I don't know wot yer see in war films. We get enough of all that muck in real life.'

'I've told yer, Bill,' Rose said, doing her best to reassure him. 'I don't mind George Formby. If yer want ter see it, let's go in.'

Bill had the fag in his mouth, but hadn't lit it. 'Yer mean it?' he said, feeling a bit guilty. 'Yer really do?'

Rose said nothing. She just took him by the hand, and led him through the front doors of the cinema.

When they took their seats in the back of the circle, *Let*

George Do It was on its final reel, but as it was a continuous performance, they tried not to look at the screen as they settled down. As soon as the lights went up, Bill went off to the Gents, which gave Rose an opportunity to look around at the splendid auditorium with its beautiful gold and blue proscenium arch, tasselled stage curtains, and rose-pink seats. Despite the fact that there was bound to be an air raid during the programme, the cinema was nearly full, especially in the back row of the circle, which seemed to be reserved exclusively for snoggers. Rose couldn't wait for Bill to get back and for the lights to go down again.

By the time he got back to his seat, the mighty Wurlitzer organ had swivelled out on to the left-hand side of the stage, and Edward O'Henry, the Gaumont's popular organist, was already working the audience up into a rousing sing-song. Bill immediately joined in, and to Rose's amusement, his voice could be heard booming out well above everyone else's as the place echoed to the sound of 'Bless 'Em All'.

Rose had quickly forgotten the awkward little exchange she'd had with Bill, and was now having a wonderful time. Edward O'Henry, waving with one hand and frantically playing with the other hand *and* his feet simultaneously, finally disappeared with his Wurlitzer back into the bowels of the orchestra pit. As the house lights faded with him, Rose sat back in her seat in anticipation of her own snogging session. She didn't have to wait long, for the moment the double stage curtains started to part, Bill very quietly slipped his arm around her shoulders. But as the first flicker of film started to project on to the screen, and the bell-ringing title music of *Gaumont-British News* boomed out into the auditorium, Rose immediately felt Bill's whole body go tense.

'British Quit Greece!'

The audience watched in gloomy silence as the first news item showed British troops under fierce aerial attack by Nazi dive-bombers off the southern coast of Greece. The newsreel scenes were harrowing, with shots of battle-weary soldiers desperately trying to evacuate in small boats that would take them out to the safety of British vessels at sea.

During all this, Rose noticed that Bill was keeping his eyes fixed firmly down to his lap. Then, quite unexpectedly, he got up. 'Goin' ter the Gents,' he whispered.

'Wot again?'

But people were already having to get up to let Bill pass along the row.

For the first time, Rose became anxious as she watched Bill's silhouette disappear through the side doors. Why had he suddenly become so agitated? Was it just that he had a weak bladder or something, or had the newsreel shots upset him? This made her think back to that awkward moment in the street before they came in. Why was he so tetchy about not wanting to see a war film? Rose continued to watch the newsreel, but couldn't really concentrate on it. All she could think about was how oddly Bill had behaved, and what a moody person he was.

When Bill got back, the newsreel had come to an end, and once George Formby had started to sing and twang away on his ukelele, Bill's arm was soon back around Rose's shoulders. At one time he even turned to give her a peck on the cheek, which she immediately returned by kissing him full on the lips. Whilst this was going on, they failed to notice the proverbial warning that was being flashed on to the screen over one of the usual frantic chase sequences that was the hallmark of nearly every George Formby comedy.

> The air-raid warning has just sounded. Those patrons who wish to leave are requested to do so as quietly as possible. For those patrons who wish to remain, the programme will continue as normal.

Hardly anyone left the cinema. Rose and Bill were far too occupied with more important matters, and when the picture came to an end and the lights went up, Bill's arm was still around Rose's shoulders. Despite the thundering of ack-ack gunfire outside, they were still staring close into each other's eyes, totally oblivious to the rest of the audience who were slowly filing out.

It was still quite light outside, although a little chilly. For ever the gent, Bill took off his sports coat and made Rose put it on. It was far too big for her, of course, but she liked the feel of it around her back and shoulders, especially the warmth it still carried from Bill's own body.

Despite the cacophony of gunfire and enemy planes droning overhead, Bill decided to walk Rose back to the piano shop. On the way they felt relieved that for just one night, they were not in any of the fire engines and ambulances they could hear racing off to the next incident.

Dodging in and out of falling shrapnel, Rose and Bill made their way slowly along Holloway Road, he with his arm around her waist, and she leaning her head against his shoulder. Above them the gradually darkening sky was

streaked with the usual nightly searchlight beams and
barrage balloons that were so high up they looked like
small silver blobs bouncing up and down in a gentle breeze.

All the way to the Angel, Rose never once mentioned
Bill's strange reaction to the cinema newsreel they had seen
earlier that evening, nor had she any intention of doing so.
Not for the time being, anyway.

Chapter 21

During the first week of May, Rose saw very little of Bill. This was not out of choice, but because her ambulance duties were keeping her busy in what was generally regarded as a gathering momentum of the air raids on London. It was not a good time for the Humble family, for on one night alone Albert, on Home Guard patrol with Charlie Spindle outside an Air Training Corps Drill Hall, narrowly escaped being killed when an enemy plane dropped a land mine by parachute. Luckily, the two men, who were standing in a shop doorway at the time, were far enough away to escape serious injury, but they were quite literally blown off their feet to land in a pile of muck that had seeped up from the fractured underground sewers. But at least it caused a laugh, for when some of their mates arrived to help, the two men were assured that they had never smelt so clean in all their lives!

Queenie also had a frightening experience. One morning, when she was looking after Mrs Wu's kids up in Sedgwick Street during a rare daytime air raid, a bomb was dropped on the other side of Jarman Square, shattering every window in the house, and sending the poor Chinese kids into hysterics. Millie also had a nasty scare when the trolley-bus on which she was travelling to work was suddenly rocked by a bomb and nearly toppled over. From that time on, Millie vowed to travel only by tube.

One particular night turned out to be the busiest Rose had ever known. Yet again the London Docks had come under fierce air attack from a determined wave of enemy bombers, and Rose was called out in her ambulance to a bomb-blasted dockside street which was burning fiercely. There she found not only firemen trying to contain the blaze, but also the locals, frantically using their government-provided stirrup pumps in a pathetic last-ditch effort to save what was left of their modest little homes. Many people had been seriously injured, and in the course of an hour or so, Rose had ferried dozens of casualties to hospitals in Smithfield and Mile End. It turned out to be a really hazardous operation, for the enemy were using the glare from the burning warehouses to target freight ships tied up alongside the docks.

During the night there was a lull in between the waves of enemy bombers, so Rose was finally persuaded to take a break. As she made her weary way towards the three mobile canteens, there were still dog-fights going on overhead, and down by the riverside embankment she could see a great commotion going on amongst a crowd of local people, police, and Civil Defence workers. All were pointing up excitedly towards the sky, where one of the enemy planes, hit by ack-ack fire, had burst into flames, and was disintegrating before their very eyes.

'Up there! See 'im!'

A docker was working the crowd up into a frenzy, getting

them to cheer and shout as the pilot of the plane, picked out in the glare of a searchlight, floated down by parachute directly above the river itself.

A moment or so later, the remains of the stricken enemy plane tumbled out of the sky, and landed on top of some warehouse buildings on the Bermondsey side of the river. Fires sprang up immediately, transforming the crowd's cheers into anger.

'Get the bastard!' someone in the crowd yelled.

'String 'im up!' yelled another.

The shadowy figure finally dropped into the water, closely followed by his parachute, which having fluttered down, for several moments threatened to drag the pilot along in the fast-flowing tide.

The crowd on the embankment had now become very hostile, shouting, jeering, and shaking their fists in rage out towards the river.

Meanwhile, two special constables were hurrying down the steps on to the sand and shingle riverbank. There was no police launch available, so they quickly made their way to one of a group of rowing boats tied to hooks on the stone river wall. It seemed an impossible task they were attempting, for, apart from the surrounding glow of burning fires, it was a pitch-black night, with the moon only occasionally popping in and out from behind slow-moving clouds.

With Rose looking on in near disbelief, events suddenly became more sinister. By the light of the riverside fires, the crowds were just able to pick out the helpless figure of the German pilot, who had managed to break loose from his parachute and was now desperately trying to swim against the tide.

'Leave 'im out there!' yelled an angry, full-throated docker. 'Let the bastard sink!'

The crowd roared their approval, and some of them then rushed down the steps to the riverbank, and became involved in an angry scuffle with the two special constables, who were trying to cast off in the rowing boat.

Rose had mixed feelings as she watched the angry struggle just below where she was standing. She knew exactly how these people felt. They had every right to feel hate towards someone who had shown such disdain for innocent human life. After all it was *their* homes and *their* lives that were being destroyed so ruthlessly. But in her heart of hearts, she couldn't help feeling that just standing aside and watching a man drown without mercy was just as barbaric as dropping a bomb on to innocent people.

As the struggle between dockers and special constables continued, out in the middle of the river the German pilot was gradually losing his battle against the unyielding fast-flowing tide. Several times Rose thought she could hear him calling out for help, but his voice was completely overwhelmed by the background sounds of police, fire, and ambulance bells, distant ack-ack gunfire, and the jeers and whistling of the small hostile crowd.

And then came a sudden, dramatic intervention, as someone suddenly came rushing through the embankment crowds, shouting, 'Wot the bloody 'ell're yer all doin?'

Rose turned with a start and was totally shocked to see Bill Layton tearing his way through the crowds. 'Bill!' she called, as loud as she could.

Bill appeared not to have seen her, for he immediately

314

became embroiled in an angry exchange with the hostile dockers on the riverbank below. 'Are yer all bloody mad or somefin'?' he growled above the pandemonium. 'There's a bloke fightin' for 'is life out there!'

'You keep outer this – you!' snapped one of the more aggressive dockers, who was struggling to hold back one of the two constables.

'Wot about our lot?' a local woman screeched at Bill, her face blackened from the fires. 'We're all fightin' for *our* bleedin' lives, too, mate!'

Bill immediately came back at both of them. 'Yer can't fink in that way!' he insisted, with great passion. 'That bloke out there ain't 'Itler. 'Itler's back 'ome safe an' sound in Berlin. To 'Itler an' all the rest of 'is gang, that bloke in the river out there's just a number. As a human bein' 'e don't mean a bloody fing ter none of 'em!'

'The only good German's a dead one!' yelled an enraged woman, to another roar of approval from the crowd.

'There're plenty of good British dead, too, missus!' Bill growled back, defiantly. 'So wot's the point of it all – tell me? It's war that's brought us all ter this. We go ter war wivout usin' our 'eads, wivout usin' our 'earts. We go ter war 'cos we fink we're right!'

'We *are* right!' a man roared, from the back of the crowd.

'Jerry started it!' called an elderly woman's voice from somewhere.

'We *all* started it!' shouted Bill, his voice dry and hoarse from the choking flames he had been fighting all night. 'Okay! So yer all want that bloke's blood out there. Why? Is it 'cos yer fink that by lettin' 'im die yer'll all feel better again? Or is it 'cos yer 'ave ter get yer own back on someone

315

– no matter 'oo! Well – go on then! Do it! Let 'im die! But I tell yer this much, if yer do it, then yer're just as guilty as 'im out there!'

For a moment the crowd listened to Bill in silence, until a rough-and-ready woman shouted out, 'Why don't yer get back an' fight some fires, mate? That's wot yer paid for!'

Once again the crowd roared out their agreement, and even Rose couldn't keep quiet any longer.

''Ow can yer talk like this, Bill?' she called. 'That bloke out there's our enemy – 'e's bin bombin' the 'ell out of these streets. Why should we save someone 'oo just wants ter wipe us off the face of the earth?'

Everyone around wildly applauded her.

''Cos it's wrong ter kill *anybody*!' Bill answered, without considering who he was talking to. 'Wot's the sense in an eye for an eye? It's not that poor sod out there yer should be blamin'. It's the criminals who put 'im up there in the skies, in the streets of every bombed city, in ships on every ocean, on the battlefields of every country. Them at the top!' he yelled, sounding more and more as though he were giving a speech. 'For Chrissake – stop the killin' before it's too late!'

'Get back ter the bloody fires!' screeched another woman. 'While yer're blowin' yer 'ot air out 'ere, our 'omes're goin' up in smoke!'

Again the crowd roared their anger at Bill, and for one terrifying moment Rose was convinced that Bill was about to be lynched. So she quickly stepped forward and tried to diffuse the tension. 'Come on, Bill – this is war. We're all in it tergevver, i'n't we?'

Staring right through her as though she were a stranger, he replied tersely, 'That's yer opinion, miss – not mine.'

''E's goin' under!' yelled one of the dockers, still struggling with the two special constables on the riverbank below.

As they looked out towards the river, everyone cheered. The German pilot, heavily weighed down by his boots and flying gear, appeared to be losing his battle for survival, for his head was consistently disappearing beneath the surface of the water, and it was obvious that he was being dragged along by the outgoing tide down river, through the lower Pool of London, and out towards the distant Thames Estuary. After all the bravado that had gone before, the crowd fell silent, as they watched the helpless figure in the water beginning to lose his battle.

While this life-and-death drama was going on, Rose suddenly noticed that Bill was sprinting off along the embankment, throwing off his helmet, tunic, and boots as he went. 'Bill!' she yelled. 'Don't be a bloody fool!'

Bill ignored her calls, and as soon as he had reached more steps further along the embankment, he hurried down them on to the riverbank.

'Bill . . . !'

Rose's shouts immediately drew the crowd's attention.

All eyes strained to watch as the impassioned fireman started to wade into the murky waters of the River Thames. He was an incongruous sight, still dressed in his uniform shirt, braces, and trousers. Then, quite suddenly, there was a splash and they all saw him plunge into the deeper part of the water, where he began a hazardous swim out to the German pilot, now flapping about helplessly in the choppy waters. Even though Bill was obviously a good swimmer, Rose feared that he would need all his strength to make progress against the outgoing tide. Her mind was fraught with anxiety and self-questioning. Why was Bill risking his life like this? What was he trying to prove?

''E's nearly there!' shouted an AFS woman driver.

'Stupid sod!' yelled one of the dockers down on the shore. 'Bloody go down wiv 'im!' he spat angrily.

Rose was on tenterhooks as she watched Bill finally reach the German pilot, who was now in great difficulty and too weak to co-operate with his rescuer. He had already drifted at least a hundred yards down river, and the task of getting him safely back to the bank was going to take a gargantuan effort. As soon as Bill had managed to get his arms around the pilot, he moved off, swimming backstroke all the way.

It took Bill nearly a quarter of an hour to get back to the riverbank with the pilot. Waiting for them were several police regulars, a Red Cross medical orderly, and a police van.

The crowd, who had rushed along the embankment to protest, were kept well back by the regulars, so they jeered, whistled, and yelled abuse, but Bill ignored them.

'That's a right charlie, that one!' said one of two AFS firewomen standing just behind Rose. 'Is 'e one of ours?'

'Yeah,' said the other. 'That's Bill Layton up B Division.'

'Must be bonkers,' sniffed the first woman. 'Fancy riskin' yer own life for a ruddy Jerry. An' did yer 'ear all that rubbish 'e said about the war?'

'I know,' replied the second woman indignantly. 'Still,

let's face it. 'E's only practisin' wot 'e preaches, i'n't 'e? Bleedin' conchy!'

Rose's heart missed a beat. She didn't even turn round to look or say anything to the two women.

After a moment or so, the police regulars came up the steps from the shore, practically carrying the weak and helpless German pilot. Rose didn't see his face, for he was far too exhausted to lift his head, but she saw enough to discover he was not a young man.

Whilst the prisoner was put into the back of the police van and given medical attention by the Red Cross orderly, Bill appeared at the top of the steps, where he found himself face to face with Rose. He tried a weak smile on her. It didn't work.

Rose lowered her eyes, paused a moment, then, without saying a word, walked off.

It was about four o'clock that morning when 'Moaning Minnie' finally sounded the all clear. By that time Rose had ferried her last casualties of the night to hospital and had taken her ambulance back to the St John depot in Whitechapel. After a good soak in a hot tub, she got dressed and went to the roof to watch the dawn rise over the London skyline.

There was no one there, for old Mr McKay, the St John official fire-watcher, had long since gone back home to bed. Rose took the opportunity to sit down on Mr McKay's look-out chair. The sky was already a pale shade of blue-grey, and when the first glimmer of sunlight began to sneak up the dome of St Paul's Cathedral in the distance, every rooftop over the whole of London was tinged with a dazzling golden hue. Although so much of the city was still smouldering from the night's aerial firebomb attack, this was Rose's favourite view of her dear old London. Up here she could see all the familiar sights – Big Ben and Westminster Abbey, St Paul's in the heart of the ancient City of London, and just a short distance away, the Tower of London with its indomitable twin drawbridges across the Thames. Rose also loved the view of the river, but today she couldn't bring herself to look at it.

As the sun became stronger, she closed her eyes and allowed the warm glow to caress her face, but instead of feeling revived, she felt nothing but utter despair. Bill a conchy, a conscientious objector, rescuing a Jerry from the river, and refusing to fight for his own country! How could he have deceived her in such a way? Why couldn't he have told her that he was a pacifist, a prickly little coward who had no right even to walk on the same pavement as his own countrymen? Rose felt bitter – terribly bitter, yet all the signs had been there, right from the first time she had met him in that bombed-out church in Shoreditch. What was it he had said? 'This is wot 'appens when people start fightin' each uvver. Nuffin's sacred.' And then she remembered what had happened during their first drink together in The George, and how he had turned his back on those two soldier boys who had come up to order drinks at the bar. Over and over she kept thinking how stupid she had been not to have caught on to the reason for his odd behaviour, such as not wanting to see a war film, or to sit through a newsreel in the cinema. Oh God, she thought – how could she have fallen in love with such a traitor?

When Rose opened her eyes again, the sun was so

dazzling it was showing the city in a whole new light. Everywhere she looked she could see burnt and gutted buildings that were nothing more than skeletons of their former glory. It was yet another illusion shattered.

Rose got back to the Angel soon after eight o'clock. It had clearly been a tough night there, too, for a local power station had taken a direct hit and there had been no electricity supply in the area since the previous evening. And the moment she turned into the market, Rose knew that something else was wrong.

A small group had gathered around Mr Cabbage at his vegetable stall, and when Rose saw that Nellie was amongst them, she feared the worst.

'It's Badger,' Nellie said, choking back tears. 'There's bin a telegram from the Admiralty. 'E's missin' in action.'

'Sounds like 'is boat's gone down,' said Charlie Spindle, who was with Rose's mum. 'There's no way of knowin' if the poor lad's dead or alive.'

'Oh God,' Rose said, half to herself. For one brief moment, all she could think about was Bill's self-righteous speech on the embankment just a few hours before: 'For Chrissake – stop the killin' before it's too late!' Stop killing who? she asked herself with so much pent-up anger. 'I suppose it's not possible they've made a mistake?' she asked hopefully.

Mr Cabbage himself answered her. 'They wouldn't've sent no telegram unless somefin' 'ad 'appened,' he said glumly. 'It's 'ard, ain't it, Rosie gel – real 'ard? Don't fink I don't know 'ow much young Badge meant ter yer. 'E fought the world of yer, too, yer know.'

It was the first time Rose had seen the old man without his straw boater. She had always thought that he wore it to disguise a bald pate, so it was a surprise to discover that his head was covered in a rich crop of neatly combed white hair. 'Yer mustn't talk about 'im as though – well, as though 'e's not comin' 'ome no more. They didn't say 'e was dead or nuffin', did they? Surely, "Missin' in Action" just means – well, 'e's just not turned up – not yet, anyway.'

Mr Cabbage tried to take some comfort from what Rose was saying, but his eyes were strained and red from crying.

'We must all say a little prayer for Badge before we go ter bed ternight,' said Elsie Dumper, who was so upset she had abandoned her bottled preserves stall.

'Yeah, that's right,' came the comforting voice of Sid Levitt, who hadn't even bothered to unload his 'Pets' Emporium' from the van. 'All keep our fingers crossed, eh, Alf?'

Then Ned Morris called across from his 'Genuine China' stall, 'You mark my words, Alf. Yer can't kill off a good lad like young Badge. I'm tellin' yer, one of these days yer goin' ter be seein' 'im walk right back down these stalls.'

Although Ned's confident assurance was well meant, it upset several of the traders, and, for fear of showing their distress in front of Mr Cabbage, they had to turn away.

'There's only one fing yer can all do,' Rose proclaimed quite suddenly. 'Keep the market goin'. Don't let 'Itler get us down. This is *our* market, *our* street – it belongs ter us, an' no bleedin' Jerry's goin' ter take it away from us! Let me tell yer somefin'.' She was now raising her voice to talk to all those gathered around. 'Badge went off ter fight so that people like you an' me could come an' go in this market whenever we like. We mustn't let 'im down, mates, 'cos the day the likes of you an' me go under, this 'ole ruddy country goes down wiv us. So – just do wot Badge would want yer all ter do. Keep the market goin! Business as usual!'

'Business as usual!'

The whole market echoed Rose's call to action. No sooner had she spoken than everyone was back at their stalls uncovering them for the start of the day's business.

'Yer a good gel, Rosie – *our* gel!' said Mr Cabbage, taking hold of her hand and kissing it. 'Badge knew wot 'e was doin' when 'e fell for you.'

A few minutes later, back in her own bedroom, Rose quickly undressed, drew the curtains, and got into bed, which, as usual, hadn't been made up by either Queenie or the twins before they left for work.

For several minutes, she just lay there, staring up at the ornate stucco mouldings around the electric light rose on the ceiling. Badger's face was before her. She could see him as clearly as if he were in the room with her right now. That bright, eager face with the cheeky barrow boy grin, always rushing over to see her whenever she set foot inside the market, always ready to accept anything she said whether it was good, bad, or indifferent. And then she thought how different he was from Bill, how different he was from *all* men. Just thinking about poor old Badger made her feel miserable and guilty. If only she could have loved him in the same way that she had begun to love Bill! Badger was such a kind, loving, funny, honest, and just plain good young bloke. As Rose anguished over the thought that she might never see him again, she felt that she could never forgive herself for not returning his love. However, one thing was now absolutely certain in her mind: never, never, never did she ever want to see Bill Layton again.

But when her eyes did eventually close, the first person who stood before her in her dream was, sadly, not Badger.

It was a conchy named Bill.

Chapter 22

A few days later, Rose was invited to meet her future sister-in-law, Sylvie, for a swim. They chose the Cally Baths in Caledonian Road, mainly because in the early afternoons there weren't too many kids around and they could splash about in comfort. The only drawback was that it was an indoor pool, and during the current hot weather, the water was warm and not very refreshing. Furthermore, the roof of the poor old baths had taken quite a pounding from firebombs over the past few months, so there was always the sound of repair work going on.

In her present depressed state of mind, Rose didn't really want to go out anywhere when she was off duty, but when she saw Sylvie again and joined her in a few clumsy lengths up and down the old pool, she felt a bit more cheered than of late.

'I 'ad a letter from Gus the uvver day,' said Sylvie, as she and Rose paddled water together in the shallow end, their backs leaning against the safety rail. 'I reckon meself 'e's somewhere out in Norf Africa.'

'Wot?' answered Rose, surprised. ''Ow can yer tell? I fought all soldiers' letters're censored.'

'They are, but before 'e went, me an' Gus worked out our own code. It's all ter do wiv numbers an' fings. Like – say 'e writes, "'Ow's old muvver so-an'-so in number seven?' – well, I only 'ave ter look it up in our exercise book an' see that seven equals whatever country we worked out. I've got an 'ole list of 'em.'

'That's clever,' said Rose. 'Wot's the number for Soufend?'

They both roared with laughter, which echoed right across the pool.

When Sylvie's laugh faded, however, she showed a moment of anxiety. 'I couldn't bear it if anyfin' 'appened ter Gus, yer know.'

'Don't be silly, Sylve. 'E's far safer out there than we are back 'ere!'

'Yeah, but yer know wot Gus's like: always first in line whenever there's anyfin' dangerous ter do. 'E's such a bleedin' 'ot 'ead.'

As they stood there, a couple of twelve-year-old boys were engaged in a rowdy game close by, splashing each other and Rose and Sylvie at the same time.

'You two splash me once more,' Sylvie yelled, 'an' I'll separate yer from yer breaf!'

The kids thought better about rubbing Sylvie up the wrong way, and swam off to the far end of the pool.

Rose loved Sylvie's sense of humour. She was always good for a laugh, and Rose didn't get many laughs these days.

'Look, Rose,' Sylvie said, as soon as the kids were far enough away, 'I fink I'd better come clean wiv yer. I 'ad a reason for wantin' ter see yer.'

'Wot's up?'

Sylvie hesitated just long enough to summon up the courage she needed to continue. 'I saw that feller of yers – yer know – that fireman? 'E come ter see me up the 'ospital.'

Rose tensed immediately. 'I don't know wot yer talkin' about, Sylve,' she said sharply. 'I ain't got no feller.' She quickly eased herself up out of the water, and sat on the edge of the pool.

Sylvie followed her, and they sat side by side. For a moment neither said anything. The pool had been very heavily chlorinated, and the sharp tang was irritating Sylvie's eyes. She rubbed them with the back of her hand, then pinched her nose to try to sniff out the pungent smell. ''E told me about wot 'appened the uvver night – yer know, down by the docks.'

'I don't wanna talk about it, please, Sylve.'

Again, Sylvie thought twice before going on. She took a moment to tuck back a few straggles of hair that had popped out from beneath her green bathing cap. 'I know 'ow yer feel,' she said eventually. 'If I was told someone I knew was a conchy, I'd 'it the roof. I bet Gus would, too!'

Rose didn't answer, or even look up at Sylvie. She just stared down into the pool and wiggled her toes aimlessly in the churned up water.

'The trouble is,' Sylvie continued, 'it ain't easy when yer're stuck on someone.'

Rose answered without looking up. 'I'm not stuck on 'im.'

''E is on you.'

'That's 'is problem,' Rose replied unyieldingly.

'Look, Rose,' Sylvie said, turning to her, 'I know it's none of me business, but I fink yer're makin' a mistake. Of course 'e's wrong – we all know that. When conchies get on their 'igh 'orse, all they can ever fink about is their own point of view. But then I 'ave the same trouble wiv Gus, yer know.'

At last Rose looked up at her. 'Wot d'yer mean?'

'Well, 'e's always goin' on about politics. An' if I ever dare ter disagree wiv 'im, 'e just tells me ter shut up 'cos I'm only a gel, an' gels don't know nuffin' about politics. One of these days, I'll give 'im a nasty shock. When the war's over I'll put up for MP an' take over from Churchill!'

As usual, Sylvie knew how to relieve the tension, for this made Rose laugh.

'Wot I'm tryin' ter say, Rose, is that yer can love someone wivout 'avin' ter agree wiv 'im all the time. I love Gus. I don't care 'ow many times 'e tells me 'ow 'e's going' ter put the world ter rights, I just love 'im wiv all me 'eart.'

Rose's face crumpled up, and she turned her gaze down to the pool again. 'Sylve, yer don't know 'ow Bill treated me the uvver night. It was as though I di'n't exist. 'E di'n't even acknowledge my presence.'

'Maybe 'e was too ashamed,' suggested Sylvie.

''E 'as every right ter be,' said Rose sourly. ''E's a coward, a traitor.'

'A coward?' asked Sylvie. 'Workin' in the Fire Service?'

It was a question that stuck in Rose's mind.

Later that afternoon, Rose made her way to work at the

St John Ambulance depot in Whitechapel Road. She was on split-turn that week, so it meant that she had to be on duty from four until midnight. It was a lovely mild spring Saturday afternoon, and when she got off the bus at her usual stop just outside Toynbee Hall in Commercial Street, there were plenty of people around, either shopping in the little back streets or just taking a quiet weekend stroll in the sun. During the nice weather, Rose always liked the walk from the bus stop, for it gave her plenty of time to relax her mind before coping with all the horrors of the nightly air raids. Needless to say, it was impossible for her to escape the sights of war, for on her journey, she noticed many a bomb-damaged terraced house or shop from which a Union Jack was draped defiantly over a boarded-up window.

Rose's route to the St John Ambulance depot nearly always took a short cut, which gave her the chance to avoid the busy main roads, but it also meant that she would have to pass The George, which she had carefully avoided for the past few days, fearing that Bill might try to make contact with her there again. However, it was not yet opening time, and so once she had passed the BOOZING AS USUAL sign on the boarded-up window outside, she felt perfectly safe to continue on to the main Whitechapel Road at the end of the street.

She had just turned into the ambulance yard itself when she saw Bill walking towards her from the drivers' rest rooms. Her first inclination was to turn away and enter the building by the Whitechapel Road entrance, but she decided otherwise, came to a halt, and allowed Bill to approach her.

''Allo, Rose,' he said rather sheepishly. He was already in uniform for the coming night's duties. 'They told me yer was on split-turn.'

'Are yer sure yer can bring yerself ter talk ter me?' she asked coldly. 'I'm surprised yer even remember me name.'

'Please, Rose,' he said, stretching out his hands in the hope that she would let him hold hers.

Rose stepped back out of reach.

Bill looked depressed. 'I made a mistake,' he said, clearly in anguish. 'I should 'ave told yer.'

They were unaware that some of the other ambulance girls were watching them through the window of the drivers' rest rooms.

'Why *di'n't* yer tell me?' Rose asked, staring him straight in the eyes.

It was painful for him to reply. 'I couldn't bring meself . . . I . . . fought I'd lose yer.'

Rose's answer was ice-cold. 'Yer were right.'

Once again Bill tried to approach her. 'Look, Rose, I can't 'elp wot I am. That's part of me, 'ow I feel, 'ow I live an' breeve! Ever since I was a kid, I've 'ated any form of violence. I never got into any scraps at school, never liked toy guns or anyfin' that could shoot ter kill. I couldn't kill – *anyfin*'!' He stopped, took off his cap and ran his fingers through his well-greased hair. 'When the call-up papers come, I never even opened them. I knew wot they were, of course, but I just couldn't bring meself ter tear open that envelope.' He sighed, and looked at her. His face was crumpled with pain. 'I could never kill a man, Rose. I could never actually look through a rifle-sight and – press that trigger. I'd sooner kill meself first.'

They had to stand back to allow an ambulance to leave the yard. The St John girl who was driving waved to Rose as she passed. Once she had gone, Bill continued, but without turning to look at Rose.

'I don't want ter lose yer, Rose,' he said, twisting his cap around in his hands. 'Yer're too special.'

Rose waited a moment before answering. Her back was pressed against the wall of the narrow yard lane in which they were standing, and she could smell the remains of the exhaust fumes left behind by the ambulance. 'Yer've got every right ter wot yer fink,' she said slowly and carefully. 'But I've got principles, too, Bill. My dad fought in the last war. 'E never wanted ter go eivver. But if 'e 'adn't 'ave gone, if all the uvvers like 'im 'adn't 'ave gone, wot d'yer fink this country'd be like now?'

Bill tried to interrupt her, but she wouldn't let him.

'Yer know somefin'? I never even knew wot the word "conchy" meant 'til the war started. I first 'eard it down the market. The boys was goin' on about these fellers 'oo 'adn't got the guts ter fight, who 'adn't got the guts ter own up why they wouldn't pick up a gun ter defend their own families. They said it was because they was nuffin' more than cowards.'

'Is that wot *you* fink, Rose? *D'you* fink I'm a coward?'

Rose took a deep breath. 'Look, Bill, I come from a pretty ordinary family. We ain't 'ad much of an education, but we do know the difference between wot's right an' wrong. If I was ter carry on walkin' out wiv yer, wot d'yer fink I could say ter me dad, or me bruvver, or all those boys in the market 'oo've bin dragged off ter 'elp keep this country free? I could never look 'em in the face again – never.'

Bill listened to her carefully, then said quietly, 'Yer still 'aven't answered me question. Do *you* fink I'm a coward, Rose?'

Rose looked at her feet, and didn't answer.

Bill waited a moment. Then he put on his cap again, straightened himself up, turned, and walked off.

Uncle Popov had taken an unusually long time to finish his meal. It wasn't that he was being deliberately slow, but in the last few weeks he was beginning to feel his age, and becoming decidedly more frail. Nellie didn't mind how long he took over his food. Some weeks before, she had noticed how slowly he had been getting around, so, just like any concerned mum, she had decided that, as the old chap was clearly not feeding himself properly, once he had closed up shop every day, he should take his evening meal with the family.

The only problem this evening, however, was that 'Moaning Minnie' had wailed earlier than usual, and they could already hear ack-ack gunfire getting nearer and nearer, and poor Uncle Popov was taking ages to chew on a piece of toad-in-the-hole.

'Get yerself down the tube as soon as yer can, gel,' said Albert, who was already putting on his tin helmet ready for Home Guard duty. 'I don't like yer 'angin' round wiv all this goin' on.'

'We shan't be long, don't worry, Bert,' Nellie called from the washbasin in the back part of the room. 'I'll just wait for Uncle Popov ter finish, an' we'll be on our way.'

'Please!' The old man put his knife and fork down quickly, and tried to get up. 'I finish my food. You must go – all!'

Nellie came rushing back. 'No!' she said bossily. 'Yer stay right where yer are an' finish yer tea. There's no need ter rush. We got all the time in the world.' Then she turned to Queenie and the twins, who were getting their things ready for another night down the tube. 'Come on, you free! Get a move on now!'

'Mum,' said Millie. 'You won't ever serve us whale meat, will you?'

Nellie was used to Millie's out-of-the-blue questions. 'Now wot're yer talkin' about?'

'This boy in the library says there's a butcher's shop in the Cally that sells whale *and* horse meat. You won't ever serve it to me, will you?'

'Don't be silly, Mill,' said her mum. 'As if I'd ever do such a thing.'

'She might try yer on some fried worms though!' chirped in her dad, roaring with laughter at his own joke.

Polly laughed at her dad's teasing, but not Millie. It was a sign that, although in some ways they were both quite unworldly for their seventeen years, the' twins were beginning to develop very different personalities. Polly was the one who had wanted to do things for herself. Over the past year she had started dressing in completely different clothes to her sister, and to do her hair differently. She even tried to convince herself, and others, that she and Millie didn't really look like twins. The war had turned Millie into a sensitive young

333

thing, for she was terrified of the air-raids, and hated to think of people being killed in the streets so close to her own home. Despite all this, however, the twins remained the best of friends, and, because they were the only members of the family who had always spoken posh, the boys in the market still referred to them as '*The Toffs*'.

Suddenly a bomb was heard whistling down not too far away. Everyone froze where they stood, all staring at each other with fear in their eyes, just waiting for the explosion. When it came, the whole place rocked from side to side, and the electric lightbulb and shade swung madly to and fro in the middle of the ceiling.

Nellie and Albert exchanged anxious looks.

'Come on, gels,' Albert called urgently to his three daughters. 'Let's get goin' now. I'll take yer up the tube meself.'

'Don't forget the eiderdown, Queen,' said Nellie, bustling around now with some urgency. 'Poll, Mill – the sandwiches are in that bag on the boot box. Don't worry 'bout the tea. I'll bring it wiv me when I come.' She turned to Albert, knowing that he was about to protest. 'I'll be quite all right,' she said quietly. And nodding towards Uncle Popov, added, 'I'll just let 'im finish, then we'll boaf come along.'

Albert clearly didn't care for the arrangement, but he knew his Nellie. She had a good head on her. 'Okay then,' he called to the girls. 'Let's go!'

Laden down with cushions, magazines, a library book each, and, amongst sundry other things, the sandwiches, the twins made their way out of the room.

'Bring me slippers, please, Mum!' Polly demanded, as she went out.

'And don't forget some cups for the lemonade!' demanded Millie.

'Yes! Yes! Yes!' scowled Nellie, holding the door open and just waiting to get them out as quickly as possible. 'Out!'

Polly and Millie rushed down the stairs yelling. 'See you later, Uncle Popov!' and 'Bye, Uncle Popov!' as they went.

Uncle Popov's mouth was too full of sausage toad to answer them, so, although they had already left the room, he waved his hand.

Queenie was next to go. She was lumbered with the eiderdown, two more cushions, a folding chair for her mum, and a string bag with some fruit and broken digestive biscuits. 'Don't be long, Mum,' she called from behind the huge eiderdown thrown across her shoulders. 'Those two're goin' ter drive me bonkers!'

Nellie laughed. 'I won't be long, dear.' And before Queenie left, she gave her a quick peck on the forehead. Then she called down the stairs to all three of them: 'Try an' get that place by the scales!'

'We'll try, Mum!' called Polly.

'Don't 'ang around too long, gel,' said Albert, adjusting the strap of his gas mask box over his shoulder. 'I don't like the sniff of ternight. They're over too early.'

'It's all right, dear,' she said, putting her arm around his waist and walking him to the door. 'It's nuffin' different ter any uvver night. We're gettin' used ter all this.'

'Well – just be careful, mate,' he said, giving her a peck

335

on the cheek. 'Keep a watch out for fallin' shrapnel. There's a lot of ack-ack out there.' He started to go out, but then had second thoughts. Turning around, he took Nellie in his arms, and kissed her full on the mouth. 'I wish we was sleepin' in our own bed ternight,' he whispered in her ear. 'I could do wiv a bit of a cuddle.'

Nellie grinned, and pushed him out. Then, as she heard him thumping down the stairs in his Home Guard boots, she called out to him: 'If yer see young Georgie, tell 'im ter keep under cover! An' tell Rose I've made 'er some Spam sandwiches. I've left 'em under a plate in the pantry!'

'Okey-doke!' came Albert's return call.

Nellie waited for the front door to slam, then she went back to Uncle Popov. The handkerchief the old man had tucked into his collar as a makeshift table napkin was covered in sausage gravy.

Nellie smiled. She could see just how much he had enjoyed his meal.

It was about half-past seven when Rose got her first call-out of the evening. Prior to that, she had spent almost an hour sitting with Mr McKay on the roof of the St John's depot. He had been too busy to chat to her, for wave after wave of enemy bombers had been passing overhead, high above the city skyline, all frantically disgorging their deadly cargo as they went. It seemed that this was going to be a night in which no corner of London would be left unscathed.

As Rose drove her ambulance out of the St John yard, the sun was still so strong that she had to use the driver's visor to protect her eyes. Every street she passed was bathed in a slowly deepening scarlet, with endless figures silhouetted against the light as they rushed around with stirrup-pumps, buckets of water and sand, shovels, pitch-forks, and anything they could lay their hands on to combat the firebombs raining down on them. For her entire journey, small pieces of red-hot shrapnel were constantly dropping on to the road and pavements around her, and she even heard tiny fragments tinkle down on to the roof of the ambulance itself.

The incident she had been called to was a chemist's shop in the heavily populated Commercial Road, which had been hit by a high explosive bomb. The air was stinking with foul smells from the drugs that had been destroyed in the blast, and anyone who had to work any-where near the debris was ordered to wear a respirator. Rose's one fear was that she would meet up with Bill again, and while she was collecting her first casualties from the shop and surrounding houses, she kept an occasional lookout for him amongst the hordes of fire-fighters tackling the blaze.

By sheer coincidence, she did catch sight of young Georgie, who was in the process of collecting an impor-tant message from the Senior Fire Officer to his station back in Aldgate, but the moment he saw his big sister coming towards him, he pretended that he hadn't seen her, and pulling his outsize tin helmet down over his ears, he remounted his bike, and pedalled off as fast as he could. Even so, Rose couldn't help feeling proud of 'that little sod'.

Then suddenly she felt scared, more scared than she had ever felt before. High above her, the skies were being savaged by the largest armada of enemy bombers that she had ever seen.

There was no doubt about it, tonight *was* different. All Rose could think about was her own family.

For some reason, Nellie Humble had always insisted on doing the washing-up before she went down the tube. God knows, Rose and Albert had told her about it enough times, saying that if there was no one there to see it, it didn't matter if the washing-up was done or not! But Nellie always answered that it mattered to her, because *she* knew if it had been done or not, and she certainly didn't relish the thought of coming home to a whole pile of dirty crocks after a night sleeping rough on a cold tube platform. Anyway, she didn't care what Rose and Albert thought. They were always scolding her, and she always ignored them.

So, despite the fact that all hell was breaking loose outside – ack-ack fire, bombs exploding, police, fire engines, and ambulances rushing about all over the place – Nellie was determined to finish her washing-up and leave the place tidy. It was just as well, for dear old Uncle Popov had taken so long to finish his sausage toad that if she hadn't done something to pass the time while she was waiting for him, she would have started to worry about the family.

It was after eight o'clock in the evening when Nellie and Uncle Popov finally got their things together. Because the old man was now very shaky on his feet, Nellie wouldn't allow him to carry anything. It would take her long enough to get him to the tube as it was, without lumbering him with Polly's slippers or Millie's cups for her lemonade, and that was without the added problem of how to dodge the shrapnel on the street in the middle of an air raid.

'There is something I wish for to tell you, Missus Nellie,' Uncle Popov said, as he was tucking his woollen scarf snugly around his neck. 'One day, I would like for you to teach me how to cook.'

Nellie, who was fixing her hatpin, turned with a start. 'You? You learn 'ow ter cook? Don't be daft, Uncle Popov. I've 'eard yer talkin' about the fings yer cook lots of times. I bet yer're a *real* chef!'

'No!' insisted the old man, shaking his head emphatically. 'No Russian cook – English cook! Toad round the hole, mutton pie, treacle pudding, fish and chips!'

Nellie roared with laughter. 'Yer know wot yer like all right, don't yer, yer old devil! All right, mate – yer're on! Cookin' lessons it shall be!'

Uncle Popov laughed and clapped his chubby hands together excitedly. '*English* cook lessons!'

Nellie laughed with him, but their laughter came to a sudden halt when an enormous thud on the roof of the building knocked them off their feet, and sent them sprawling on to the floor. Plaster collapsed down on to them from a huge gap in the ceiling.

'God in 'Eaven – wot is it?' Nellie spluttered, crunched up on the floor, and trying to protect herself from all the plaster and dust.

'Bomb!' Uncle Popov called, practically choking with dust, and doing his best to retrieve his spectacles, which were buried somewhere under the plaster debris on the floor. 'We have bomb?'

'It can't be!' Nellie's hat had been knocked off, and her neat and tidy hair was flaked with white plaster dust. 'There ain't bin no explosion.' Then she attempted to move, and was only too relieved to be alive. 'Stay where yer are,' she said. 'I'm goin' ter draw the blackout.'

Using the edge of the kitchen table, she managed to pull herself up. Making her way to the window at the front of the house, she gently drew back the blackout curtains, and peered out. In the street below, one or two people had gathered. She didn't know who they were, but they were anxiously pointing up to the roof of the building, so she unlatched the window, opened it, peered down, and called out, 'Wot's goin' on?'

A man immediately called back: 'Stay where yer are, Mrs 'Umble. There's somefin' on yer roof!'

'Wot? Wot is it? Can yer see?'

'No! It's too dark.'

Eventually, Nellie recognised the other figure below. It was Mrs Jigley from number nineteen just across the road. 'Wotever yer do, don't move around, dear! Not 'til we get someone!'

This immediately scared the life out of Nellie, and her first reaction was to go back to help poor Uncle Popov, who was still struggling to get up from the floor.

'We've got ter get out of 'ere,' she said urgently. 'Fink yer can make it?'

'Yes!' The old man was coughing and spluttering, and shaking all over. 'Come. We go!'

Nellie took hold of Uncle Popov's hand, and gently led him to the door. 'Let's take it nice an' slow,' she said, carefully turning the door handle. Gradually, she opened the door, which creaked so loudly it made her squirm. Then they inched their way out on to the first-floor landing. 'We've only got twelve stairs,' she said, her voice low, but echoing down the well of the building. 'I know, 'cos I count 'em every time I scrub 'em!'

As she spoke, there was a screeching of car brakes in the street outside. Then a whole lot of jumbled up voices were calling out orders and directions, none of which Nellie could hear too clearly.

As she and Uncle Popov reached the second stair down, she heard a man's voice calling out through a megaphone: 'This is the police! All unauthorised persons should evacuate this area immediately! I repeat: please . . . evacuate . . . this . . . area!'

For a moment, Nellie and Uncle Popov remained rigid and still on the stair where they were perched. It seemed to them that they had already been stuck there for hours. But just as they made the effort down one more stair, the same megaphone voice outside began calling out again: 'Mrs Nellie Humble. This is the police. If you can hear me, please listen carefully. There is an unexploded parachute mine on the roof of this building . . .'

Nellie gasped. 'Oh God!' she said to herself.

The police warning continued: 'Any movement you make will be highly dangerous. Remain where you are – I repeat – remain where you are! A naval bomb disposal unit is on the way. I repeat – a naval bomb disposal unit is on the way!'

Nellie had her eyes closed as she listened to the megaphone warning. In the dark, she could hear Uncle Popov wheezing hard, so she squeezed his chubby old hand as tightly as she could. 'It's goin' ter be all right, mate, yer'll see,' she whispered reassuringly. 'Only ten more stairs ter go.'

Her gaze was fixed firmly on the front door at the bottom of the stairs. She could see torch beams shining on the glass panels of the door from the street outside. 'Wot d'yer say?' she asked. 'Shall we 'ave a go?'

In the dark, Uncle Popov's voice was quiet, but determined. 'We go!'

'That's my boy!'

Slowly, ever so slowly, they stretched first one foot, then another, down on to the next stair. Nellie could feel her heart thumping faster and faster, but she could still see those torch beams shining on the glass panels of the front door. To her that meant life, it meant seeing Albert and Rose and Queenie again, and the twins and young Georgie.

'Nearly there,' she said, her voice cracking with nerves, and barely audible.

'Nearly there,' whispered Uncle Popov.

They moved down another stair, and Nellie began to feel more and more confident. She knew that if they could just reach the next stair, they would get out of the place in one piece. The next stair was five from the top, and she'd always thought of that stair as her lucky one because it still had an old beer stain on it from the time Albert got drunk and sat down on the stair, and spilt some on it.

''Ow we doin' then?' she asked the old man, that very dear old man who had adopted them, and given them not only his shop, his house, but also a great part of his affection.

'We go!'

'That's my boy – Gawd bless yer!'

Their next movement was their last. As they stretched a foot each down on to the lower stair, there was an enormous explosion, and a blinding blue flash.

Nellie's beautiful front door with the two glass panels was just too far beyond their reach.

Chapter 23

Rose got back to Islington shortly after midnight. She had been given the news about the parachute mine explosion on her home by her divisional superintendent, who provided transport to get her there. On the way back through the city, there was carnage and flames in every street, for the air raid was proving to be the most intense and ferocious of the entire Blitz.

As soon as she saw the surrounding streets, Rose knew the worst had come. In Chapel Market, windows had been blown out, the remains of chimneypots were lying on the pavement, and many of the traders' deserted stalls were turned on their sides. Fires had broken out in several of the side streets, and the whole area was teeming with firemen, ambulances, and Civil Defence volunteers from all parts of the community. But the real horror for Rose was when she turned the corner and saw for the first time what had once been her home.

The piano shop and the rooms above it were now no more than a smouldering heap of ruins. In fact, half the terraced block had been wiped out, including Mr Isaac's tailor shop on one side and a cluster of little houses on the other. The street opposite had also taken the full force of the blast, and window-frames had been blown out, their curtains now fluttering uncontrollably in the cool night breeze.

Rose noticed the lifeless corpses laid out side by side on the pavement, each covered with a blanket or sheet. Deep in shock and despair, she approached the still figures with great trepidation.

''Oo're yer lookin' for, miss?' asked a special constable, who, with a nurse and the vicar from the local church, was keeping guard on the gruesome human remains.

'I'm lookin' for me mum,' Rose said after taking a deep breath.

'Wot's 'er name, dear?' asked the nurse.

''Umble. Mrs 'Umble. We live over the piano shop.'

The nurse and the constable exchanged an anguished look.

'Sorry, miss,' said the constable gravely. 'No survivors. We got one man out. An old chap. 'E's over there.'

Rose reluctantly turned to look at where the constable was nodding. She recognised Uncle Popov's baggy striped trousers and black buckled shoes protruding from beneath a Red Cross blanket that was covering the rest of his body.

'Wot 'appened?' Rose asked the constable.

'Bloody parachute mine! Come down on the roof, didn't explode. Went off before the bomb disposal boys could get 'ere. Some of the neighbours went up wiv it. A few of our own boys, too.'

All three ducked as another bomb came whistling down in the distance. In the background, there was the constant sound of fire engines and ambulances rushing off to more incidents.

The nurse tried to comfort Rose by putting her arm around her waist. 'What can I do ter 'elp, dear?'

'Me mum,' Rose said, feeling as though all the blood had been drained from her body. 'Where's me mum?'

The nurse looked to the constable for guidance. 'Unaccounted for,' he said, checking a clipboard by the light of his torch.

'Yer mean – she's still there?'

'We don't know, miss. They're tearin' the place apart lookin' for any sign of life . . .'

Rose didn't wait another moment. She rushed off to the bombed ruins of the piano shop, where, with the help of police tracker dogs and torchlights, groups of volunteers were frantically scrabbling all over the heap of rubble trying their best to remove debris. Everything was clearly a desperate race against time.

'Oh Christ, Rose!' said Charlie Spindle, fighting back tears. 'I can't believe this 'as 'appened! That bloody 'Itler!' he snarled through clenched teeth.

'Charlie,' Rose said urgently, ''ave they found Mum yet? Is she still under there?'

'I just don't know, gel,' he spluttered, wiping the dirt from his face, having helped in the rescue work for the past couple of hours. 'Yer dad's over there searchin' for 'er. Poor sod's goin' 'alf bonkers!'

Rose turned to see Albert crouched down on the top of a pile of debris, tearing at the wreckage with his bare hands. 'Dad!' she shouted. 'I'm 'ere, Dad! It's Rose!'

Albert was too crazed with what he was doing to hear her, so Rose quickly clambered up on to the debris, and picked her way across the hazardous surface of the rubble.

For her, it was a heart-breaking experience to see so many familiar things littered amongst the remains of her own home, personal possessions such as clothes and partly burnt magazines, household pots and pans, bits of broken china, a light shade, and the remains of her mum's favourite armchair.

'Dad!' Rose was now yelling at the top of her voice, but still Albert didn't turn round.

When she was within a few yards of him, she was given a hand up by Sid Levitt from the market. 'Thank Gawd yer're 'ere, Rosie,' he croaked, his throat sore from the smoke. 'Yer dad won't listen ter anyone. 'E's convinced yer mum's still alive down there.'

Albert was frantically removing chunks of bricks and pieces of masonry. It was an incredible sight, for he was caught in the glare of dozens of torch beams, coming from all those people who were desperate to find some hope of life beneath the ruins of this quiet Islington backstreet.

'Dad.' To get some response, Rose had to grab hold of his hands and make him look at her. 'It's me, Dad. It's Rose. I'm 'ere now. We're tergevver.'

For a brief moment, Albert stared at her. His eyes were glazed over in shock. 'Can't stop now, gel,' he said, hardly seeming to recognise her. 'Yer mum's waitin' for me.'

Rose stared, appalled at the lost look in her dad's eyes.

Just then, a massive barrage of naval pom-pom guns opened up from Highbury Fields, just down Upper Street, and that was followed immediately by a concentration of ack-ack gunfire, probably coming from Finsbury Park further on. Above them, the endless drone of enemy planes was filling the sky, and every so often there was the sound of machine-gun fire as a barrage balloon was targeted, and suddenly burst into a great ball of flame.

'Keep yer lights down as much as yer can!' called a policeman through a megaphone. 'An' no smoking. We've got a fractured gas main just at the end of the road!'

Rose suddenly found herself tearing away at every piece of rubble she could lay her hands on. She didn't know why. Inside, everything was telling her that she and her dad were wasting their time. How could her mum, how could *anyone*, survive such pitiable destruction as this?

Nellie Humble couldn't see very well. She had spent the last few hours pinned down by what looked to her like huge pieces of wood, and since there was no way she could move her hands or her legs, her instinct told her to stay where she was, not even to try to move her head. At the back of her mind, she could hear voices, voices that she might or might not have known. They sounded as though they were a hundred miles away, just like all those other strange sounds – noisy bees humming, footsteps on the roof. It was all like a great jigsaw puzzle to her, pieces here and pieces there, and no knowing where they had to fit.

And then, for the umpteenth time, dust came trickling down on to her face. Nellie closed her eyes and just let it happen, but it did make her cough.

'Over here!' yelled Rose. 'I heard someone!'

Several volunteers came scrambling up the debris to her. 'Wot is it?'

'I don't know!' she called. 'But I definitely 'eard it. It sounded like coughin'. There's someone down there!'

'Nellie!' Albert started shouting out at the top of his voice. 'We're comin', gel! 'Old on!' He was on his knees, yelling down into any hole or space he could find.

'Get some torches over 'ere!' called an ARP warden, who was already digging into the debris with a shovel.

Rose tried to get a better overall view of what part of the building they were working on by climbing on something heavy. As she did so, it made a weird metallic sound. When she looked closer, she could just make out a name ingrained on the highly polished piece of wood she was standing on: 'G. E. Little & Sons Ltd'. It was all that was left of Uncle Popov's unsold rosewood piano. Just close by, however, there was at least one survivor. It was *Baby*, the patchwork doll with button eyes that her mum had made for her on her tenth birthday.

Nellie's eyes were dazzled by the thin streaks of light piercing the tiny crevices in the wreckage. So she closed them, and imagined that she was back at school. It was Guy Fawkes' Day, and there were lots of lights there – sparkling, crackling, leaping up into the sky to burst into a spectacular array of minute coloured stars. The image brought a smile to her face, and if only she had been able to free her hands, she would have clapped them together and cheered and shouted out for more.

'Nellie . . . !'

What she was hearing now was the strangest sound of all, echoing out in the night, far and distant, clear and precise. She felt it had to mean something, yet she didn't know what, only that it was a good sound, and she would just like to stretch out her hand – and touch it.

'Nellie ...! Where are yer, gel? It's Bert ... I'm 'ere ...!'

Nellie's eyes sprang open with a start, but this time she was confronted with a very different image. Holding quite firm to a piece of wood just a few inches from her face, was a tiny creature. Nellie tried to focus on it, but all was blurred. Then, the moment she managed to concentrate hard enough, everything became clear again. Gradually, a smile came to her face. It was a spider, an ordinary common house spider, no bigger than a farthing coin.

For several minutes, Nellie and the spider stared at one another, but unlike so many times before, Nellie was not afraid. As more thin streaks of light filtered through the rubble, the constant movement on the surface above brought down more dust, which went straight on to Nellie's chest, and made her cough.

'Nellie! Where ... are ... yer?'

Despite the heavy sounds of the air raid, Albert's voice boomed out across the debris of his former home. This time, he and everyone else had heard someone coughing under the wreckage, but he could not locate the precise direction the coughing sounds were coming from. 'Nellie ...!' he yelled, over and over again.

People were lying flat on their stomachs all over the wreckage, stretching their hands into any gap they could find, desperately trying to find some traces of life. The two police tracker dogs were now barking their heads off and tearing at the rubble with their paws, showing they had picked up a human scent.

After another ten minutes, Rose, who was frantically

pulling at the rubble, also flopped down on to her stomach. She was now in despair that they had run out of time.

'It's no good!' yelled one of the CD workers. 'We're wastin' our time!'

Utterly exhausted by their strenuous efforts to find someone still alive, one by one the team of volunteers stopped what they were doing and perched themselves down on top of the rubble. Then the police removed their tracker dogs, who were still barking and yelping excitedly, determined not to admit defeat. The only person left now was the pathetic figure of Albert, his fingers bleeding from the jagged pieces of masonry he had been trying to move. For him, the search for his missus would never end.

Rose, lying flat on her stomach, her face pressed down against a chunk of familiar brick wall, gradually felt tears coming to her eyes. She had never been a crybaby, but now her tears were dropping straight on to the familiar old bricks beneath her.

Above, the sky, Rose's 'largest ceiling in the world' was still being torn apart, and every sound she heard was like a knife being plunged into her side – bombs whistling down, ack-ack and pom-pom guns firing non-stop, people shouting out in desperation from every street, fire engine bells, ambulance bells, police car bells – and all the time, that relentless mind-shattering drone of wave after wave of enemy planes swarming in their hundreds across the bright full moon.

Rose allowed the tears to tumble out, but when her blurred vision gradually cleared, she found herself looking at a strange image directly in front of her. Although it was minute, it had two tiny eyes of its own – a small house spider, perched defiantly on a broken piece of timber just inches from Rose's face. For several moments the two of them kept perfectly still, just weighing each other up. There was a strange, inexplicable contact between them, nothing to do with sound or movement, just a summing up of thoughts. Then, with remarkable precision and purpose, the tiny creature reversed fearlessly along the piece of wood, straight into a small gap in the rubble. Sensing that she ought to be doing something, Rose raised herself up on to her elbows, pulled her body towards the gap where the small spider was heading, and watched it disappear altogether into the rubble.

'Over here! Bring some light! For Chrissake – 'urry!' Rose didn't know why she was yelling but, as she stared at that small gap in the rubble, it was as though a voice was calling to her loud and clear that this is where she had to look, this was where there was hope.

When somebody offered her a torch, she grabbed it and beamed the light straight down the small chink through which the spider had just disappeared. It took only a few seconds for her to catch sight of her mum, who was completely covered with debris, her head only just visible.

'She's 'ere!' yelled Rose at the top of her voice. 'Oh Christ, she's 'ere!' She was crying and laughing at the same time. ''Old on, Mum!' she called, through the small gap. ''Old on! We're comin!' Then she thrust the torch back at the man who had given it to her, shouting, 'Get 'er out of 'ere! Get 'er out!'

Rose got to her feet as her dad came across to meet her. For a moment, they just stood there, balanced on top of the rubble, staring into each other's tormented eyes. Then Rose threw herself into his arms, and they sobbed together.

* * *

It took the rescue workers over an hour to dig Nellie Humble out of the wreckage of the old piano shop. When they finally brought her to the surface, her eyes were closed, and a doctor estimated that she had probably been unconscious since the explosion.

Rose and Albert went in the ambulance with Nellie to the hospital. Before she left, Rose took a quick glance back at the pile of rubble that was once her home.

She just hoped that no harm would come to a certain small spider, who by now would be trying to make a new home for itself.

Chapter 24

The night of Saturday, 10 May 1941 turned out to be the most devastating air raid London had ever known. From dusk to dawn, hundreds of bombers flew two, and sometimes three, missions across the English Channel, to pulverise anything and everything from east to west of the capital city. In the space of just a few hours, thousands of large and small homes and shops had been reduced to dust. The Luftwaffe did not discriminate between rich and poor. By the time 'Moaning Minnie' had wailed out her long-awaited all clear, some of London's most cherished landmarks had either been extinguished or severely damaged. The Chamber of the House of Commons was one casualty, completely gutted by fire, and part of the roof of Westminster Abbey had come crashing down on to the ancient floor, scattering debris everywhere. On that fateful night, the people of London everywhere had sacrificed at least something, either the lives or health of their loved ones, or their homes and belongings. But if the aim of this massive onslaught was to undermine the morale of the population, then the Nazis had seriously miscalculated.

At the first light of dawn, the traders of Chapel Market

had started the tremendous task of clearing up the carnage of the night before. Barrow boys, young and old alike, took to the street with brooms and shovels and buckets of carbolic. Their girls and women were with them, carefully picking up every piece of broken glass and placing them all in wheelbarrows, to be recycled for the war effort. And just round the corner, an army of market helpers were busily sifting through the smouldering rubble of the old piano shop, like a regiment of ants hard at work, recovering with great care every conceivable item of the Humble family's personal and household belongings they could find. It was a sight to inspire, but for the market traders, it was a labour of love.

By nine o'clock in the morning, every market stall was in action again, with bunting and Union Jacks draped everywhere. Hastily scrawled notices had been pinned up declaring, 'BUSINESS AS USUAL', 'PULL THE OTHER ONE, ADOLF!' and 'NEVER SAY DIE!' For the rest of the day the mild spring air echoed to the sounds of 'Get yer luvely taters 'ere, gels!' and 'Wot will yer give me for this fine pair of genuine brand new knickers?' and 'Broken biscuits for the Blitz! Speshul reduced! Pennuff a pound!'

The costermongers of Chapel Market had regained their humour – and their pride.

A few miles away, in the Royal Northern Hospital in Holloway Road, Rose and Albert were at Nellie's bedside. Queenie, the twins, and George were waiting in the corridor outside, comforted by Sylvie, who had heard about the piano shop bomb whilst on night duty at her own hospital in Whitechapel Road. The twins in particular were very tearful, for not only was their mum in a deep coma and fighting for her life, but they had also lost their home and everything that had always been such a part of their own lives.

Rose sat bolt upright on a hard hospital chair. Her face was totally expressionless, and despite the rigours of the night's drama, she was determined to remain as strong as her mind and body would allow. Albert, still in a state of shock himself, was on the other side of the bed. Neither he nor his eldest daughter exchanged a word with one another. It was as though they couldn't bear to hear the sound of their own voices. The bed curtains were drawn all round, and from time to time they could hear the heavy breathing and groaning of the other patients in the ward, who were all elderly. Rose did not take her eyes off her mum for one single minute. To her, Nellie looked absolutely beautiful, for the dirt and grime of her horrific night beneath the rubble had been washed off, and her hair tied neatly behind her neck. Although she seemed to be breathing normally, Nellie was still in a coma. From time to time, she moved one of her hands, and it seemed to Rose as though she was trying to say something, but no words passed Nellie's lips, not even a mumble of recognition.

Eventually a nurse popped her head around the curtain. 'I'll have to ask you to leave now,' she said softly. 'Doctor's waiting to have a word with you in Sister's office.'

Rose's stomach turned. This was it. She was expecting the worst. She and her dad walked through the ward, where most of the night's casualties had been brought. It was a pathetic sight. Small clusters of relatives and friends were gathered around the bedsides, trying to be bright and cheery, trying to show that the patient would survive all that had happened. To Rose, it was only too obvious that many of them wouldn't be there when she came back to visit. She prayed inside that her mum wouldn't be one of them.

'Is she going to die?' asked a tearful Millie, who was so distraught she had to be constantly hugged by Sylvie.

'Don't be daft, Mill!' Rose said confidently. ''Umbles don't give in that easy!'

Rose exchanged a brief glance with Sylvie. There was despair from both of them.

'I want yer all ter go 'ome wiv Dad an' Sylvie,' Rose said, trying to stretch her arms around the entire despondent group. 'I just want ter 'ave a few words wiv the doctor.'

''Ome?' asked George indignantly. 'We ain't got no 'ome.'

Rose could have kicked herself for being so careless. 'We're spendin' the night at the Church 'All,' she replied quickly. 'The Council are goin' ter let us know termorrer where we can put up.' Her eyes were on Sister's office, where she could see the doctor waiting to see her. 'Come on now,' she said, edging them towards the lift along the corridor. 'Go wiv Dad and Sylve. I'll be along as quick as I can.'

'I want ter see the doctor, too,' said Albert, who was still in a state of shock, and clearly uncoordinated in his thoughts.

'Leave it ter Rose, Dad,' said Sylvie, helping her future sister-in-law out of a difficult moment. 'Let's go back an' try an' get some shuteye.' She turned to Rose and asked quietly, 'Sure yer'll be all right?'

Rose nodded. Then she watched her small family group disappear down the corridor, and into the lift. Her whole body tingled with apprehension as she turned, and made her way briskly into Sister's office.

By the time she came out, Rose had been told how seriously injured her mum really was. Nellie's spinal cord had been fractured, and her legs crushed beneath the fallen debris. Although it was clearly too early to determine whether she would be able to get around again, it had to be a distinct possibility that she would not. However, the worst news was yet to come. An early X-ray had shown that Nellie had received serious injuries to her head, and there were early suspicions that she had suffered some form of brain damage.

Rose left the hospital in a daze. In her mind, she couldn't quite piece together all the horror that had taken place during the past few hours. She found it hard to believe that at this same time the previous morning, the sun was shining in a cloudless blue sky just as it was now, and she was still lying in that great double bed that she had shared with Queenie and the twins. More important, her mum was full of life, making the tea and preparing the bread and marge for the family before they all went off to do their different jobs for the day. And Uncle Popov – dear, wonderful old Uncle Popov, playing his rosewood upright for prospective customers, and just waiting for closing time so that he could sit down to another meal with his family, the family he had adopted, and who had embraced him with all their heart. But not any more. Never again. That part of Rose's life had gone forever, and nothing could ever be the same again.

Rose left the Royal Northern by the Manor Gardens exit. The aftermath of the previous night's air raid had brought a flurry of ambulances speeding to and from the emergency entrance, and, as she crossed the road, she hardly noticed the thick curls of dense black smoke still billowing up behind her from amongst the quiet working-class terraced streets of Holloway. But she did stop just once. It was as she reached the corner outside the old 'bug-hutch' picture house, the Holloway Empire. From here she could take a last glimpse at the wards on the upper floors of the grey-bricked hospital. She could almost imagine her mum was peering and waving down at her from the ward window, calling out that she wasn't to worry because everything was going to be all right.

For a moment, she just stood there, her back leaning against a faded poster advertising Will Hay in *Oh, Mr Porter!* one of the last pictures that had played at the old 'bug-hutch' before it had closed. Her body was numb, and she suddenly felt so helpless and alone. Her mum had always been at the very heart of the Humble family – never once had any of them even considered the possibility that anything could happen to her. But if that heart should ever stop beating, how would they cope? How could she, Rose, face up to the responsibility of taking her mum's place? A wave of despair came over her, and she wanted to shout out at the top of her voice: 'For Chrissake – why our family? Why me?' All she wanted was for someone to take her in their arms and say, 'Don't worry, Rose, gel. We'll get yer fru this, yer'll see. Don't ever forget – yer're an 'Umble!'

'Rose.'

At first, the voice calling her name seemed part of her muddled state of mind. But when she turned, it was hard to believe that Bill was just stepping out of a boarded-up doorway of the old picture house.

'I've bin waitin' for yer.' He paused awkwardly, to draw on his fag. 'I went lookin' for yer round Chapel Market.' Then he exhaled quickly. 'Some of yer mates told me they'd taken yer mum to the Royal Northern. I – I 'ad ter see yer. I – I 'eard wot 'appened last night.' He was fumbling for words. 'I – I don't know wot ter say ter yer. It's – terrible.'

Rose finally spoke. 'Wot do yer want, Bill?'

'I want *you*, Rose. I don't care what yer fink of me principles. I just want yer ter love me for wot I am. 'Cos I love you, Rose – God knows I do. I love yer more than anyfin' else in the 'ole wide world.'

Rose lowered her eyes, and looked aimlessly at the pavement.

'Let's get fru this bloody war tergevver, Rose,' he continued, drawing on his fag to keep his nerve. 'I'll do anyfin' I can ter support yer fru all this. Try not ter fink of me as a conchy. Don't fink of me as a coward. Just fink of me as a feller – a feller who's fallen in love wiv the only gel that's ever meant anyfin' to 'im. Give me a chance, Rose. That's all I ask.'

Rose's head was still lowered, and she made no attempt to respond.

Bill watched her closely, and didn't know what to do. Finally, he stubbed out his half-finished fag on the pavement, then plucked up enough courage to step closer to

her. 'Rose,' he said softly. Then with one hand he slowly
raised her head.

Tears were rolling down Rose's cheeks, but as Bill held
her chin up with his hand, she smiled. He leant forward,
and gently kissed her on the lips.

From that moment, there was no more talk of conchies
or cowards or traitors. And for Rose, it was time to heal, to
start building the Humble family life all over again.

But for them, and everyone else who had suffered such
pain and anguish on that formidable night in May, starting
again was not going to be such an easy task.

For the first few nights after the destruction of the old
piano shop, Rose, Albert, Queenie, the twins, and George
had no choice but to stay in St Mary's Church Hall in Upper
Street. They were not the only bombed-out families
billeted there, but thanks to the WVS, the Salvation Army,
and other voluntary workers, their short stay there was
made as comfortable as possible. In the meantime, the
traders had not only scoured every brick and stone for the
Humble family's personal and household possessions, but
they also organised a whip-round which raised nearly a
hundred pounds to see their old mates through the initial
stages of their ordeal without a home.

Almost a week later, the Islington Council were able to
offer the family accommodation in one of their new prefab-
ricated houses, which had been specially built to cope
with the homelessness of bombed-out victims. Although
Rose, Queenie, and George liked the new place, Albert
and the twins thought it an unfriendly sort of a dump, with
machine-made walls that made them feel they were living

in an air-raid shelter. What they really pined for, of course, was the cosiness of their rooms above the old piano shop, and the company of dear Uncle Popov, with his baby grand and favourite uprights. But the great advantage of living in such a place was having the first real space they had ever known. There was a fair-sized parlour, square in shape and with two nice modern windows, a kitchen, and three bedrooms. The big treat, however, was the bathroom, which was the eighth wonder of the world to a family who, all their lives, had been forced to take their weekly bath at the rather seedy Caledonian Road baths.

The great disadvantage was that the 'toy house', as the twins called it, was situated in a completely different part of Islington, on a blitzed site in a Holloway backstreet just off the main Upper Hornsey Road. All the family missed their mates in the market, and vowed that when the war was over they would return and pick up the threads of their life with the people they knew and loved.

As expected, Rose took charge of the running of the house, and made sure that the family got back to a normal routine as soon as possible. Rose herself was given as much time off as she needed from the St John Ambulance Brigade, and thanks to the money donated by their Chapel Market mates, she used her time to buy second-hand furniture and other necessities for the new house.

The one problem was Albert. Since the night of the explosion, he had spent every available moment he was allowed, visiting Nellie. When he wasn't at the hospital, he was often seen wandering round the streets, gazing aim-lessly into shop windows, always appearing to be searching for something.

Rose was very concerned about him, but was assured by her mum's doctor that there was very little anyone could do for him, and that he should be allowed to work out of his system the terrible trauma he had gone through. Despite this, Albert never gave up hope that Nellie would recover, and he set about decorating the 'toy house' for when she came home.

To everyone's surprise and delight, Albert's optimism proved to be well-founded, for after a few days, Rose received the momentous news that Nellie had come out of the deep coma she was in. At her doctor's suggestion, the entire family gathered around their mum's bedside, and waited for her to show any sign of recognition. Eventually, life seemed to return to Nellie's eyes, and she gradually started to recognise every member of the family. It was a highly emotional experience for them all, and when Nellie began to speak a few words to them, they wept and hugged each other, and thanked God for giving them back their mum again. Sadly, however, their elation was to be short-lived, for Nellie's doctors were eventually to confirm their first suspicions that the injury to her spinal cord was inoperable, and, combined with the damage to one part of her brain, the chances of her ever leaving hospital were very remote.

The night of 10 May had turned out to be the last of the Blitz. No one knew this immediately, of course, but the newspapers were already talking about 'Hitler's last fling' and how the people of London had defied the might of the world's greatest aerial armada. The lull in the air raids brought a great deal of welcome relief, not least for Rose and the family, and all their friends in Chapel Market. For the first time since the Blitz began, people were beginning to feel new hope, especially after hearing the sensational news on the wireless that Rudolf Hess, Hitler's third-in-command, had mysteriously parachuted into Scotland and was now being held as a prisoner in the Tower of London.

During the following weeks, Rose spent each afternoon visiting her mum in hospital, but after she had finished cooking tea for the family, whenever Bill was free from fire duties, she spent the evening with him. It was a glorious feeling to know that they could walk the streets without fear of bombs or falling shrapnel. Throughout those vulnerable weeks, Bill kept his word and gave Rose tremendous support. Once the family had got over their initial resentment at having a conchy around the place, they actually discovered that they really quite liked him. He was particularly good with Albert, and occasionally accompanied him to the hospital to visit Nellie, although he always waited outside in the corridor until visiting hours were over. By this time, Rose had deliberately erased Bill's pacifist convictions from her mind, and although she had begun to feel less antipathetic towards them, the love that was growing inside her was for the man, not his principles.

However, at the end of the third week, the calm that Bill was bringing into Rose's life, received its first setback.

'Gus!'

The whole family seemed to rush into Gus's arms when he suddenly thumped through the door of the 'toy house'. For several moments, they all stood there, hugging each other to and fro, the twins and Queenie crying on to their big brother's uniform, Rose and Albert fighting back tears as they hugged him from behind. The only one who showed very little emotion was George, who had been far more upset about his mum's injuries than he ever dared show.

'Three days' compassionate leave,' said Gus, trying to embrace all the family at the same time. 'They couldn't let me go any sooner. Too much ter do.'

'Is it Norf Africa?' asked Rose, as soon as the family group had given him room to breathe. 'Is that where yer've come from?'

''Oo told yer that?' Gus replied, a bit aggravated.

'Sylve,' said Rose. 'She told me about the code yer've worked out between yer.'

'Well, she should keep 'er mouff shut!' Gus snapped, tearing off his cap, and flipping it on to the parlour table. 'The Army go to a lot of trouble ter keep our movements secret. Sylvie 'ad no right ter go around blabbin! I'll 'ave it out wiv 'er when I get back 'ome!'

Gus's outburst took Rose by surprise. It was the first time she had seen her brother as aggressive as this since their younger days. 'She di'n't mean no 'arm, Gus,' Rose said almost apologetically.

For the next hour or so, Gus sat and talked with the family, each one taking their turn in telling him what had happened on that devastating Saturday night three weeks earlier. Everyone had their own graphic account of the night's events, and by the time he had heard how his mum had been dug out of the ruins of the old piano shop, Gus was so upset he just couldn't take any more.

To Rose's surprise, Gus went on to give their young brother and sisters a lecture.

'From now on,' he said a bit pompously, 'yer take orders

from yer sister – right? 'Til Mum comes back, Rose's in charge. If this family's goin' ter stick tergevver, yer've got ter be'ave like grown-up people. I know what war's like. If yer don't 'ave a purpose, yer get yer 'ead knocked off!'

For one brief moment, Rose resented this. 'If ever a family knows about war, Gus, the 'Umbles do.'

'Nellie's told Rose 'ow ter take care of fings,' said Albert, puffing his pipe from a used match he had just re-lit on the gas stove. 'She an' Bill take care of us fine.'

Gus swung a quick look at Rose. 'Bill? 'Oo's that?'

'Just a friend of mine.'

Although Rose had tried to avoid Bill's name being mentioned, Gus pursued his curiosity. 'Is this the bloke Sylvie's bin talkin' about? A fireman or somefin'?'

'Yes. 'E's in the AFS.'

'Yer goin' steady then?'

'Don't be stupid, Gus!' she said cagily. 'I 'ardly know the bloke.' And with that, she made off towards the kitchen. 'D'yer want a cup of tea or anyfin'?'

'Rose!' Gus snapped. 'I asked yer if yer're goin' steady wiv this whoever-'e-is? It's important for this family ter know.'

Rose stopped in the kitchen doorway, and turned. 'Now just 'old yer 'orses, Gus!' she said resentfully. 'I do 'appen ter know wot's important for this family. In case yer didn't know, I 'aven't exactly bin away on me 'olidays!'

Gus was in the most petulant, provocative mood, and Rose didn't like it.

'Wot sort of a person, is 'e – this Bill?' Gus asked, lighting up a Woodbine. 'Swept yer off yer feet, did 'e?'

Rose didn't care for this exchange with her brother. She

came back into the room, drew the blackout curtains, and switched on the light. 'Wot's it to yer, Gus?' she said, her back turned to him.

At this point Queenie intervened. 'Bill's a nice feller, Gus. 'E's bin really good ter us. In fact I don't know wot we'd 'ave done wivout 'im.'

'That's right!' said Millie, sitting on the arm of her dad's utility chair. 'He does lots of jobs round the house for us.'

'And he often goes with Dad to see Mum at the hospital,' added Polly.

Gus looked up with a start. He had surrounded himself with a haze of fag smoke. ''E goes to see Mum in 'ospital?' he asked curiously. 'Sounds like 'e's really got 'imself in wiv the 'Umbles.'

'D'yer 'ave any objections ter that?' asked Rose indignantly.

'No objections, Rose,' Gus said sarcastically. Then leaning back in the armchair he was using, he blew smoke rings in the air above him. 'When's 'e get 'is call-up papers then?' he asked casually.

'Bill doesn't need call-up papers,' explained Millie. ''E's a pacifist.'

Rose could have murdered her young sister there and then, but it was too late to retract. Her innocent remark caused Gus to sit up with a start.

'A – wot?'

'A pacifist. You know – he refuses to go to war.'

Gus immediately stood up, and went across to Rose. ''E's a conchy? This bloke of yers – a bloody conchy!'

Her brother's remark infuriated Rose. 'It's none er yer business, Gus!'

'None of my business? Yer've 'ad a bloody coward in this 'ouse, an' yer tell me it's none of me business?'

'Bill is *not* a coward!' Rose said angrily. ''E's a decent, hard-workin' man, 'oo's bin the most marvellous support ter me and everyone in this family.'

'A marvellous support – but 'e won't fight. Is that it?'

Rose would listen no more. She turned her back and stormed off to the kitchen, slamming the door behind her. She knew he would follow her in eventually, but didn't expect him right away.

'Are yer out of yer bloody mind or somefin'?' Gus yelled, also slamming the door behind him. 'D'yer want ter make this family a laughin' stock?'

Rose swung round on him. She had a dishcloth in her hand, and for a farthing she would have thrown it right into his face. 'I'm tellin' yer for the last time, Gus! This is none of yer business! I'm old enough to go out wiv 'ooever I please. Yer're not me keeper, an' yer're not the boss of this family!'

''Ave yer told any of the boys in the market about this?'

'I don't 'ave ter tell anyone anyfin' about me own private life!' Rose snapped. 'An' if I did, ten ter one they'd be more understandin' than you'd ever know 'ow!'

Gus suddenly started to wag his finger at her. As she looked at his face, she couldn't believe how much he'd changed. His eyes were blazing with anger, and for someone who had only been inside the front door for little more than an hour, his behaviour was totally mad.

'In case it's slipped yer mind, yer own farver fought for this country. 'E was one of fousands who kept the likes of that conchy of yers free ter walk the streets. Now I'm doin' the same, an' I want yer ter know that I resent it, Rose. I resent the idea of yer bringin' a smell like that into contact wiv *my* family!'

'An' in case it's slipped *your* mind, Gus – this is *my* family, too! I 'appen ter love this "coward", as yer call 'im, an' no one in the 'ole world is goin' ter turn me against 'im!'

For a moment, the two of them stared each other out, eyeball to eyeball. Then Gus turned, and stormed out of the room, slamming the door so hard, he nearly brought down the flimsy 'toy house' ceilings and walls on top of her.

Gus's homecoming had been unexpected and ugly. It was the first rift in the Humble family that anyone had ever known. By the time Gus had come to the end of his compassionate leave, he had been to see his mum at least four times. He also took his dad to the pub, and gave his young brother and sisters some cash to buy themselves presents.

It was, however, quite some time before he spoke to Rose again.

Chapter 25

Somewhere in Europe
Date?

Dear Ginge,

Bet your surprised to hear from me! Bet you thawt I
was dead or somethin. Well I am alive, but only just
becos wen my boat went down I had a sort of acident to
my foot. They (Jerry) say it turned to gangreen which
ment big trouble. But I'm O.K. now. Lucky to be alive
really! I cant tell you what the date is becos they
(Jerry) dont tell us anyfin. But I think it was Xmas
about a couple of munths ago becos some of the lads in
the camp here made a Xmas tree out of paper and old
socks! I tell you – it was a real larf. I can't rite much
becos the Red Cross say we're only alowed to send 2
letters and my other won is for granma and grandad.
Have to go now. Hope your well. See you won day.

Lots of love – Badge.

Badger's letter brought a real smile to Nellie's face. As
Rose read it out to her, she frequently nodded with

approval, and every so often she would mumble to herself, 'Good boy, Badger!' and, 'Trust Jerry!' And when Rose had finished reading it, she took the scrap of exercise book paper it was written on, kissed it, and gave it back to Rose again.

It was almost nine months since Nellie had first been brought into hospital, and everyone thought she had coped with her disability really well. She had very quickly accepted the fact that she would never be able to walk again, so she made a virtue of living her life out in a wheelchair by allowing everybody to wait on her hand and foot. When Nellie finally left the Royal Northern Hospital, the authorities there wanted her to go into a convalescence home out in the country somewhere, but she strongly resisted that, saying that she wanted to be near her own kind. She was given a place in one of the Borough Council's homes for the elderly, which suited her much better because it was situated in a quiet square behind Pentonville Road. From there she could practically smell the air of her beloved Chapel Market, and all her barrow boy pals could pop over every so often and ''ave a little chat wiv our old mate.'

'Good ol' Badge,' said Rose elatedly, sitting up tall in her chair. 'I knew all the time they couldn't kill *'im* off!' Rose tucked the letter back into her uniform coat pocket. 'But I bet 'e 'ates bein' locked up in a stinkin' prisoner-of-war camp!'

'Don't yer worry 'bout Badge,' Nellie said, with a twinkle in her eye. 'That boy knows 'ow ter take care of 'imself.'

Rose stood up, and retied the bow at the back of her

mum's hair, which had become a little straggly. Rose never got tired of visiting Nellie in the afternoons, because, contrary to what she had been warned of by the doctors, Nellie had regained quite a lot of her old sparkle. She had also put on a lot of weight, the result of the bars of black market chocolate she was always being brought by her barrow-boy pals! Many a time Rose had thought back to those dark days soon after the Humbles were bombed out, when everyone had been so convinced that Nellie was at death's door. How wrong they had been!

Rose's only real concern was the place where Nellie was living. To her, it somehow didn't seem right that her mum should be confined to a home for old people when she was still only in her late forties. The room itself was comfortable enough, except that she had to share it with three other people, all of them aged over eighty. Luckily, Nellie's fellow 'guests' spent most afternoons in the day room, listening to Geraldo and his Savoy Orchestra on the BBC Home Service.

'I 'ad a word wiv yer doctor yesterday, Mum,' Rose said cautiously, knowing that what she was about to say could be tricky. ''E said there's no reason why we shouldn't bring yer 'ome for a visit one day, if yer feel up ter it.'

'No!'

Nellie's quick stinging reply and her glazed suspicious look immediately unsettled Rose. 'Yer – don't want ter come 'ome?'

'This is me 'ome now,' Nellie replied, turning a vacant look out of the window.

'But we've got a luvely 'ouse waitin' for yer. Dad's done it all up. 'E can't wait ter show it off ter yer.'

Nellie continued to stare out of the window. Outside, long thick icicles were hanging down from the window ledge above, which made her feel like she was peering out through the iron bars of a prison cell. 'Home,' she said inwardly, only just audible.

This was one of those moments which Rose had come to dread. She could be having a quite ordinary conversation with her mum, when suddenly Nellie would sink into a kind of conscious delirium. Rose sat on the bed at the side of Nellie's wheelchair, put her arm around her shoulders, and spoke gently to her. 'Wot is it, dear? Tell me.'

Nellie, still staring out of the window, shivered.

'Cold?' Rose asked with concern. 'Are yer cold, Mum?'

Nellie shook her head. ''Ot!'

Rose was disturbed by her mum's sudden strange behaviour. Although the room had an open fire burning in the grate, it was a cold winter's day outside, and not particularly warm inside. 'Come on then,' she said. 'Let's take yer woolly off.'

Nellie held out her arms, and let Rose pull off her cardigan, her eyes still fixed on the frosty window.

Rose was beginning to run out of conversation. 'Hey, Mum,' she said in desperation, 'guess 'oo was on the wireless last night. Vera Lynn. Yer know – "We'll Meet Again"?'

This seemed to do the trick, for when Nellie swung around, she had broken into a broad smile.

'Wot's that favourite song of yers she sings?' Rose started to sing the first line of the song, '. . . The white cliffs of Dover . . .'

Rose was delighted when her mum carried on singing. She was absolutely amazed that Nellie could remember every single word, which is more than Rose herself had ever been able to do with any song. Then the two of them were singing in perfect harmony at the tops of their voices, and it was only as they reached the final words that the door opened and in walked the matron, Mrs Williams.

'Come on now, Mrs Humble,' she said in a really sickly nanny-type voice. 'It's time for our bath.'

Rose hated the way Matron spoke to her mum as though she were a five-year-old kid. Nevertheless, she got up from the bed, and allowed Mrs Williams to manoeuvre Nellie's wheelchair towards the door.

'Isn't it lovely to have your daughter here to sing with you?' she called to Nellie loudly, as though she were deaf. 'We shall have to get you both in a nice sing-song with all the other ladies, won't we?'

Rose could have hit the woman. Her mum wasn't a kid, she wasn't an old woman. She was Nellie Humble, her own mum, and she still had a whole life before her.

'See yer same time termorrer, dear,' Rose called.

'See yer termorrer,' Nellie answered, raising her hand in a little farewell wave. Then, with her eyes still fixed on her eldest daughter, she mumbled quietly, 'Rose . . .'

'Wot's that dear?' asked the shrill-voiced matron.

'Our Rose,' Nellie said again, this time her voice much stronger, and with just the slight suggestion of a knowing smile.

'That's right, dear,' said Matron, shamelessly condescending. 'We'll pick you a nice one when the summer comes.'

With that, Nellie was wheeled out of the room.

Rose stayed behind for a few moments, to tidy up Nellie's things before her mum's elderly roommates returned from their afternoon's session with Geraldo. As always when she left Nellie at the end of a visit, Rose had a sinking feeling inside. It was painful not to see her mum as she had always known her – busy, alert, and such a good caring mum. But Rose was grateful for one thing: the way her mum had remembered all the words of that song showed that, despite the occasional mental blockages, she was just as keen and alert as ever. Every time she left her behind, Rose felt guilty. Nellie was such a part of the Humble family, and it was tragic that she had forgotten so much about their past life together during those wonderful years living above the piano shop.

Rose picked up her shopping bag, thrust her mum's dirty clothes into it, and made for the door. It was only then that she noticed what her mother had been looking at on the frost-covered bedroom window. In between the crisscross of bomb-blast tape, Nellie had scrawled something. Rose had found her doing it when she came into the room earlier in the afternoon. Melting the ice on the inside of the windowpane with one finger, Nellie had spelt out just one simple word: 'HOME'.

'Moaning Minnie' wailed out soon after Rose had got onto the 653 trolley-bus at Highbury Corner. These days nobody took too much notice of the siren, because since the end of the Blitz in May of the previous year, most of the air raids had been hit-and-run affairs, and the scale of damage and civilian casualties had been reduced considerably. The reason for the Luftwaffe's scaling down its aerial onslaught on Britain appeared to be because in June 1941, Hitler had invaded Russia, which, in the words of Mr Churchill, was one of the most outstanding blunders in history. But whatever it was, as Rose travelled home on the top deck of the 653, she could see only too well how grateful Londoners were to Russia, for the Red hammer and sickle flag was flying from dozens of bombed-out shops, houses, and offices all along the Holloway Road from Highbury Corner to the Nag's Head.

When she got back home to the 'toy house', Rose found Bill had arrived with a quart bottle of brown ale, and was systematically consuming every mouthful of it with Albert. The two of them were in a boisterous mood, for she could hear them belting out 'Bless 'Em All!' the moment she entered the street.

Rose was relieved to know that Bill was gradually being accepted by the family. It hadn't been easy, especially after what had happened to Nellie, for the bitterness the family felt towards the Nazi pilots who had practically ruined their lives was deep and unforgiving. To Albert, Bill was a conchy, a coward who didn't have the guts to fight for his own country, and the idea that his own daughter was mixed up with such a man filled him with disgust. Bill knew it was an uphill task to win over the family's confidence, but during all the months since that disastrous last night of the Blitz, he had worked hard to give them all as much practical help as he could. He did it mainly by encouraging them not to bottle up their feelings of how they felt about the horrors they had been subjected to. He encouraged them to talk about the night they lost their home, of dear Uncle Popov, and of their mum's terrible ordeal beneath the debris. The only way to go forward, he told them, was to face up to the past. It was the twins, Polly and Millie, who were the first to treat Bill as a friend, and when Rose told them about the number of times he had been injured whilst fighting fires during the air raids, they both told their dad that he could hardly be considered a coward. Because of her own antipathy towards men, Queenie took a little longer to change her mind about Bill. It finally happened when she found herself talking to him quite naturally about her own work, with Mrs Wu and the kids. He seemed to talk to her as an equal, and never once referred to the accident she had had at the Small Arms factory, or the head-scarf she wore in public at all times. Albert's conversion came much later. It happened one Sunday dinnertime when Rose deliberately left him alone with Bill in the pub, and the two of them talked together about the war, and how Bill thought all the men and women who fought on a battlefield were heroes. Albert was feeling a bit low about not having Nellie home with the family, but it was Bill who had tried to explain to him that he had to keep strong and happy for Nellie's sake. The one big problem had been Gus. When he was home on compassionate leave, he had adamantly refused to meet Bill, and during another forty-eight hours pass before being posted to active service overseas, he had done everything in his power to poison the family's minds against Rose's conchy boyfriend. This came to a head after George had been telling how Bill had once saved him from serious injury during an air raid, in which George had been blown off his messenger's bike by the blast from a high explosive bomb just near the fire station where he worked. Only

Bill's quick thinking had saved the boy from being crushed by falling masonry, and from that moment on, in George's eyes, Bill Layton was no conchy, he was a hero. When Gus heard about this, he had a flaming row with his young brother, and by the time his leave had come to an end, the family were left in no doubt that, in his opinion, Rose's boyfriend was still a conchy, and wasn't fit to be in the same house as a Humble. Luckily, the family did not share Gus's jealous, prejudiced feelings.

'Come on, Dad, drink up!' spluttered Bill, as Rose walked in. 'I'm on duty at seven. We've got ter finish this before I go.' He jovially topped up Albert's pint pewter tankard the twins had bought their dad for his birthday.

'Yer don't 'ave ter do anyfin' of the sort,' snapped Rose. 'I wouldn't want ter be 'oldin' an 'osepipe wiv you ternight!' She marched straight across to them, confiscated the almost empty bottle of brown, and took it off to the kitchen.

Bill and Albert frowned in sympathy with each other.

After a moment, Bill followed Rose into the kitchen. 'Well?' he said, sounding quite sober. ''Ow'd yer get on?'

Rose shook her head. 'She won't do it.'

Bill sighed deeply. 'I fought as much.'

'Me own feelin' is she feels secure in there. The only 'ome she's ever known are those two rooms above the piano shop. She spent practically 'alf 'er life there.'

Bill pulled out a chair from under the kitchen table, and sat down. 'Wot're goin' ter tell yer dad?'

'I dunno,' said Rose, sitting opposite him. 'The trufe, I suppose.'

'Yer'll 'ave ter be careful. When I got 'ere earlier, 'e was dustin' an' polishin' the sideboard. Says 'e wants it nice an' clean for when Nellie gets 'ome.'

'Look, Bill,' Rose said anxiously. 'There's somefin' I 'aven't told 'im – or any of the uvvers.' She drew her chair close to the table so that she didn't have to raise her voice. 'Mum's never goin' ter be allowed 'ome. She's not right. There's somefin' about 'er . . . she gets these – moods.'

Bill was puzzled. 'Moods? Wot d'yer mean?'

'I don't really know wot I mean,' Rose replied in anguish. 'But every so often, she seems ter lose 'er memory, an' can't make 'ead nor tail of a conversation. Sometimes I don't fink she even recognises me no more. It 'appened again this afternoon.' She sighed deeply. 'We've got ter face up ter it, Bill. Mum just i'n't fit enough ter come 'ome. We wouldn't know 'ow ter cope.'

'Oh yes we would!'

Rose and Bill turned with a start. Albert was standing in the parlour doorway.

'I fought that's wot yer was up ter,' he growled, striding across angrily to them. 'Yer don't want yer mum 'ome, do yer, Rose? Yer just want 'er ter spend the rest of 'er days rottin' away in that bloody 'ell 'ole!'

Both Rose and Bill leapt up from the table.

'That's not true, Dad,' Rose said nervously. 'I'd give my right arm ter get 'er 'ome wiv 'er own family where she belongs, but she's just not well enough. Anyone can see that!'

'I won't listen ter yer!' snapped Albert. 'I won't listen ter none of it!' He briskly recovered the quart bottle of brown, and drained the remains of it into his empty glass. 'There's no reason why we can't look after Mum 'ere. This is a good 'ome. One of the best!' Then he turned his angry glare on Rose again. 'Yer mum's always looked after this family. Now it's our turn ter look after 'er!'

Rose exchanged a quick, anxious glance with Bill, who could only respond by shrugging his shoulders.

Albert saw this and addressed his next remark to Bill. 'I s'ppose this was all *your* doin'?'

Bill was taken aback. 'Come off it, Dad!'

'Don't yer call me Dad!' ranted Albert. 'I'm not yer bleedin' farver!'

Rose snapped back at him angrily. 'Dad!'

'Well, it's true!' Albert replied. 'It's not in yer boy-friend's interest ter 'ave my Nellie 'ome – is it? 'E don't know wot it's like to lose someone yer've loved all yer life! Gus was right. Yer got no right in this 'ouse!'

Rose went quite numb and was quite sure that her dad had gone stark raving mad. Suddenly Bill's hard-won relationship with the family had taken a step backwards. 'Don't listen to 'im, Bill!' she pleaded. ''E don't know wot 'e's sayin!'

'Oh yes, I do!' growled Albert, who had clearly been drinking before Bill had arrived. 'Gus was right. Yer know wot 'e said ter me? 'E said, "Dad," he said, "once a conchy, always a bloody conchy. They're a menace ter this country!"'

Bill deliberately made no response. 'I'd better go,' he said calmly, backing towards the door.

Rose called after him, 'No, Bill – wait!'

Bill stopped.

'Now listen ter me, Dad!' said Rose forcefully. 'I love Mum. I've always worshipped the ground she walks on.

But a part of 'er just ain't wiv us no more. Can yer understand that, Dad – can yer?'

Albert walked to the kitchen window, turned his back on her, and stared straight at the blackout curtain.

'Okay,' Rose continued, 'we can 'ave Mum back all right. She ain't no prisoner. We can go ter that nursin' 'ome any time we like to bring 'er back 'ere, an' look after 'er, an' give 'er all the love an' care that she deserves. But wot then?' She moved up close behind Albert, who kept his back turned to her. 'She's not the same person, Dad. Oh yes, she's got the same beautiful face, same beautiful eyes, same beautiful smile . . .' Her voice started to crack. 'But Mum's not the same person that she was. Don't yer understand, Dad? There's only a small part of her left.'

After a moment's pause, Albert slowly turned around, and, with a glazed expression, replied calmly, 'I'd sooner 'ave a small part, than no part at all.'

To most people's surprise, the air raid that night was no hit-and-run affair. Before they went on duty, Rose had arranged to meet Bill at their usual rendezvous, The George, and on her way, ack-ack shells were once again bouncing across the dark, ice-cold sky.

When she got to the Private Bar, Bill was already waiting for her. Ignoring the usual customers who were sitting around drinking hard, Rose immediately threw her arms around him, and hugged him. 'I'm sorry, Bill! I'm really, really sorry! I just don't know wot's come over Dad, honest I don't. 'E's talkin' like a lunatic.'

Bill eased her away, put his hand under her chin, and raised it. 'Yer don't 'ave ter apologise ter me, Rose,' he said softly, his eyes smiling at hers. 'An' yer mustn't blame yer dad. Wot that man 'as 'ad ter go fru is nuffin' more than a nightmare.'

Rose looked up at him. She was astonished by his laid-back reaction.

'Of course 'e wants 'is ol' woman back. That's the least the poor sod's entitled to. I tell yer, Rose, this war's full of people like yer dad. Over this last year or so, you an' me 'ave seen it dozens of times, every day we go out on duty. Only last week, we dug this old boy out of the debris from some pokey little 'ouse down Roman Road. Lost 'is missus, 'is 'ome, an' everyfin' 'e ad in the world. 'E couldn't cope wiv it, Rose. Wivin a few minutes, everyfin' 'e 'ad ever known was taken away from 'im – gone forever.' He paused. 'If I was ter lose yer, Rose,' he said quietly, 'I don't know wot I'd do. You an' me 'ave only known each uvver for a few monffs, but 'ow many years 'ave yer mum an' dad bin tergevver – twenty-odd? Livin' durin' a war, Rose – that's a lifetime. No, don't blame 'im, 'cos *I* don't.'

Suddenly all hell broke loose outside – guns cracking, a naval pom-pom moving on its specially adapted carriage up and down the street, and the sound of an aerial dogfight high above the rooftops.

Minutes later, an ARP warden came bursting into the bar. 'Out!' he yelled in panic. 'Everyone out – quick as yer can! 'Urry!'

Rose, Bill, and all the other customers automatically did as they were told. Nobody knew why until they got outside and saw that the whole street was lit up by a dazzling, flickering glow: a barrage balloon had burst into a great ball of flame and was drifting straight down on to the roof of The George.

'Christ!' yelled Bill, grabbing Rose's shoulders and rushing her off to the end of the street.

Behind them, customers were running out of every door of the pub. Eric, the Guv'nor, was shouting every obscenity he could think of as the remains of the flaming balloon fluttered relentlessly towards the roof of his pub.

'It's comin' down!' yelled one of the terrified customers.

'Keep right back!' yelled a police special constable.

From one end of the street to the other, people were yelling their heads off.

Finally, the remains of the silk material fluttered down on to the roof of The George, immediately setting fire to the wooden timbers beneath its tiled roof.

'Get some water up there!' called Eric, the Guv'nor. 'Come on, you bloody lot! Move it!'

'Leave it, Eric!' Bill shouted. 'Wait 'til the lads get 'ere!'

But Eric had already grabbed a stirrup-pump and bucket of water from one of his neighbours, and was frantically trying to put out the flames that had so quickly set alight the wooden shutters over the pub windows.

From the distance came the sound of fire engine bells, but before the fire brigade had even reached the corner of Whitechapel Road, a firebomb had dropped out of the sky and landed right in the middle of the road outside the pub itself.

Eric immediately turned around, saw what was behind him, and threw the stirrup-pump hose to the ground. Then, without a moment of fear, he picked up the firebomb by its fin, and, in an effort to put it out, started banging it on the ground.

'No, Eric!' yelled Bill, sprinting towards where the

amiable pub guv'nor was grappling with the deadly weapon. 'No! Keep away from it . . . !'

Before Bill could get anywhere near, there was a loud explosion, a blinding flash, and whilst everyone threw themselves flat on their stomachs, Eric was catapulted straight up into the air, to land in a mutilated heap in an adjacent front garden.

Women screamed, and people came rushing from all ends of the street, but it was too late.

Seconds later, two fire engines and their pumps arrived to tackle the pub blaze. By then it was burning fiercely, and despite their strenuous efforts, The George was beyond help.

Bill and Rose walked slowly to the end of the street, and as they reached the corner of Whitechapel Road, they paused only briefly to glance back at the final moments of the pub that they would always associate with their own coming together.

It was a painful reminder of how fragile their bond was: this hell of a war was far from over.

Chapter 26

Rose had heard a lot about Agnes Layton. Many a time when she and Bill were out together, he would refer to something 'the old gel' had said, or done, or should have done. Bill was clearly very fond of his mum. Now Rose was getting to meet her for the first time.

'When 'e was little 'e'd kick anyfin' that just 'appened ter be lyin' in the gutter as he passed. Tin cans, cardboard boxes, apple cores – anyfin'! Football mad, 'e was. Just like 'is dad.'

There was no holding Agnes when she got talking about her son, and she was obviously excited beyond belief at having Bill's young lady over to Sunday tea.

Bill and his mum lived in a two-storey terraced house in one of the more 'select' backstreets of Bethnal Green. It was more or less a two up two down setup, with a small scullery tacked on at the back in which to do the cooking and the other household chores, and, as in many similar houses, the scullery was the only space available for the regular Saturday evening bath in a very basic aluminium tub. Agnes was very popular with her neighbours because she was a patriotic 'Dig For Victory!' fanatic, and was always the one to go to for tips on how best to grow

potatoes in your own back yard. She had turned her own
small plot into an allotment in which she grew all kinds of
vegetables around and on top of her corrugated-iron
Anderson shelter.

'Still, yer'll find 'im a good boy round the 'ouse,'
continued Agnes, embarrassing her son with every word
she spoke. 'When 'e gets back after night shift, 'e always
brings me a nice cup of tea in bed.'

Rose laughed to see Bill cringing with embarrassment.
Now she could see why Bill had been so reluctant to
introduce her to his mum before now. It was perfectly
obvious that Agnes was determined to sell her son as a
prospective husband.

'More tea, dearie?' Agnes asked Rose, without waiting
for a reply. 'An' yer must try one of Bill's rock cakes.
Makes 'em wiv dried egg, dried milk and saccharins. Yer
take it from me – they're luvely!'

Rose nearly choked on the custard cream she was
eating. 'Bill!' she spluttered. 'Yer never told me yer can
cook.'

Bill was about to answer, but his mum was there before
him. 'Cook? Bill?' she asked with amazement. 'Yer should
just taste 'is roast 'taters!'

Rose turned to Bill. 'Fancy!' she smirked wickedly.

Bill could take no more, and got up from the tea-table to
light a Weights. Then he went to the mantelpiece over the
tiled-surround fireplace, and picked up a framed snapshot.
'This is me dad,' he said, taking the photo across to Rose.

Rose wiped her fingers on her hanky, and took the
photo. It was of a handsome young man in some kind of
uniform.

'Wot d'yer fink?' Bill asked, whilst Rose was looking at the photo. 'See any resemblance?'

'None at all!' Agnes chipped in. 'Most people told me Bill looks more like the milkman!'

Agnes roared with laughter at her own joke, but Rose knew it was only an attempt to disguise her true feelings, for, despite the fact that his mum had become fiercely independent, Bill had told Rose that Agnes greatly missed her long-departed 'old man'.

''E's very good-lookin',' said Rose, still studying the snapshot. 'Wot's this uniform?' And looking up pointedly at Bill, added, 'Was 'e in the Army?'

'Civil War in Spain.' Once again it was Agnes who answered. ''E was always gettin' mixed up wiv causes an' fings. Yer should just 'ear some of the tales 'e come 'ome wiv. Massacres an' killin' an' executions – 'orrible! 'E used ter tell us all about it, di'n't 'e, son?'

Rose was watching Bill carefully. He didn't answer; he simply took the framed snapshot from Rose and put it back on the mantelpiece again.

'Well, I must go an' do the washin'-up!' Agnes said, getting up and busily collecting crocks from the table. Rose tried to help, but Agnes immediately eased her back into her chair. 'No, no dearie. You two stay 'ere an' 'ave a nice chat tergevver.' Then she turned to scold Bill. 'An' for goodness' sake put some coal on that fire! It's freezin' in 'ere!'

Agnes picked up as many cups, saucers, and plates as she could, then turned to look directly at Rose. 'Look, dearie, Bill's told me all about the terrible times you an' yer family 'ave bin fru. 'E asked me not ter talk about it, but – well, I just wanted ter say that – I know yer can never replace yer own kin, but if yer ever feel at the bottom of yer wits, I've always got a friendly shoulder yer can lean on.'

Rose got up from the table, and smiled. 'Fanks, Mrs Layton.' And she kissed Agnes on the cheek.

'Everyone calls me Mum,' insisted Agnes. 'Gawd knows why. Yer'd fink I was an 'undred years old or somefin'!'

Rose laughed, and hurried to open the scullery door for her.

Bill put some coal on the fire. Then Rose stretched her arms around his waist, leant one cheek against the flat of his back, and said, 'She's a luvely woman, Bill. I really like 'er.'

'She's okay,' he replied, 'when she lets yer get a word in edgeways!'

Rose smiled, pulled him around to face her, then kissed him firmly on the lips. It wasn't very often that they had a chance to be alone together like this, and she relished every moment. Over the last few weeks, Bill had opened out considerably. For a long time he had been quite shy to display any intimate affection for her, but of late, things had changed. She was glad, because he had wonderful lips, and as she pressed her own against his, she could feel his warm breath mingling with her own.

For several minutes they just stood there, hugging each other close. Rose smiled as she heard Agnes singing merrily to herself in the scullery. In some ways, she reminded her of her own mum, or at least, as Nellie used to be when Rose was young. Oh, she thought, wouldn't it be nice if the two mums could meet. What would they talk about? she wondered. But she knew it could never happen now. The thought prompted her to hug Bill even harder. Over his shoulder she looked around Agnes's cosy front parlour, at the sofa with its cushion covers with sayings such as 'Tomorrow is another day' embroidered by Agnes herself. And the framed photograph of the King and Queen hanging on the wall alongside a newspaper picture of Mr Churchill, all three of them draped with Union Jack bunting. And the neat gate-legged table, with its bright yellow tablecloth and Sunday-best china, the white lamb's wool rug in front of the fire, the tasselled lampshade on the standard lamp, and the frilled laced curtains covering the crisscross tape on the bay windows. This was Bethnal Green. This was the East End. Everything about the room spelt 'home'. How Nellie would love it.

Finally, Rose's eyes picked out the framed snapshot of Bill's dad on the mantelpiece. 'Did yer love 'im very much?' she asked tenderly.

Bill seemed to know at once who she was referring to. 'Yes,' he replied.

'Of course yer did,' said Rose. 'I don't blame yer.'

It was a week or so before Rose and Bill were able to get together again, for their shift work was constantly clashing. However, at least Rose was able to get to see her mum more or less every day, and as the harsh grey cold of winter gradually made way for the first signs of spring, life at the 'toy house' became more relaxed. It helped, of course, that the air raids on London had greatly subsided, and it was a wonderful feeling to be able to walk out in the street at night without the constant fear of an aerial onslaught. However, no one took this period of calm for granted, especially as 'Moaning Minnie' had a nasty habit of wailing out unexpectedly, sometimes in the middle of the day, when a stray enemy bomber would sneak through the flotilla of low-drifting barrage balloons, to make a quick, surprise attack on an innocent civilian target.

Since the explosion at the old piano shop, Albert Humble had practically withdrawn from all thought of a regular job. Charlie Spindle and his other mates in the Home Guard had often tried to get him to rejoin them, but his only interest was to sit with Nellie for as long as he could each day. Luckily, he had the family, and as long as they were around to support him, he could just about cope with a fairly sedentary life. But when Queenie came home from work one evening, and announced that she had something important to tell the family, Albert felt as though his life was again about to collapse around him.

'Yer want ter leave 'ome?' asked Rose incredulously. 'Wot're yer talkin' about, Queen?'

Queenie had deliberately waited until all the family were gathered around the tea-table. It was a difficult enough decision to make, and she wanted to get it over as quickly as possible. 'The fing is, Mrs Wu's decided ter take the children and leave London. She's got some friends 'oo 'ave an 'ouse in a place called 'Igh Wycombe. She wants me ter go wiv 'em.'

'What do yer want ter do that for?' asked Polly. 'There must be plenty of other children yer could look after in London?'

'It wouldn't be the same, Poll,' said Queenie, with some difficulty. 'I've grown fond of the kids. I don't want ter be parted from 'em. Not just now, anyway.'

Rose thought hard for a moment. 'Queenie,' she said finally. 'Are yer sure yer'll be safe an' sound wiv Mrs Wu? Will yer get accommodation an' all that?'

'Of course I will!' Queenie answered confidently. 'I shall 'ave me own room. That's more than I've ever 'ad in my 'ole life.'

Queenie's remark prompted Rose to flick an anxious glance at their dad. For the moment, he was busily eating his tea and not saying a word.

'It's a big step ter take, Queen,' warned Rose.

'I know it is. But I want ter go. I 'ave to.'

Rose watched her sister closely. It was hard for Rose to believe that Queenie was now twenty years old. She thought back to their childhood. They weren't easy days, for she and Queenie had never really got on well together. But they *were* sisters, part of the same family and the same blood, and they shared the same hopes and disappointments. Despite their differences, they had come through a period of the most appalling despair. Queenie's accident at the small arms factory had left an indelible mental scar. It had caused her virtually to shrivel up inside, to keep her distance from all the close friends she had made over the years, and, most distressing of all, it was now clear it had thwarted her desire to marry and have kids of her own. As Rose watched her sister toying miserably with her meal, she saw how very beautiful Queenie had become. Even the cotton turban she consistently tied around her head to cover the few remaining tufts of red hair, gave her an elegance that many a girl of her age would cherish. No, whatever happened, Rose was determined to give her younger sister all the support she was entitled to.

'Yer're too young.' Albert was apparently concentrating on his Spam fritters, so his first comment came out of the blue. 'I shall tell yer mum. She won't like it.'

Queenie's face crunched up in anguish, but Rose quickly gave her a reassuring look.

'We mustn't interfere, Dad,' Rose said. 'Queenie's old enough to go 'er own way now.'

'She ain't twenty-one 'til next year.'

Rose answered firmly. 'A few monffs make very little difference.'

'It does ter me,' replied Albert, chewing food, and holding his knife and fork up vertically as though he wanted some more. 'I'm still the 'ead of this family, yer know.'

'Even birds 'ave ter leave their nests sooner or later, Dad,' Rose said. 'Anyone knows that.'

She could see her father was trying to put a brave face on the anguish he was feeling inside. He stopped eating, put down his knife and fork, then pushed his plate to one side. He had left at least half his meal. 'Yer do wot yer want – I can't stop yer.' Then he looked up at Queenie, and seemed to be staring right into her very soul. 'But I'm warnin' yer. Yer mum's not goin' ter like this. Oh no. She's not goin' ter like it at all.'

It was so hot in the Holloway Road that Rose had to take off her uniform jacket. She hadn't expected the weather to be like this so early in the year, but April could sometimes be a bit like that – sneaky, and unpredictable. On a nice day, she always preferred to walk to the nursing home rather than queue for a trolley-bus or a tram. If she hadn't been on duty the night before, it usually took her about forty-five minutes, but today she was making a short detour, so that she could pop in to say hallo to the boys in Chapel Market.

The moment she turned the corner from Upper Street, Rose got her first whiff of all those wonderful smells she had loved since she was a kid – the smell of fruit and veg, fried onions, second-hand clothes, and horse manure. Nothing had changed. Then, as she caught her first sight of the market, and saw all the traders milling around their stalls, she realised something *had* changed. Where were the *sounds* of the market, the clanging of spoons against saucepans to draw attention, the ice-cream bell and Mr Pinetti's barrel-organ? Where were the sounds of the barrow boys, yelling themselves silly with their usual pitch, such as, 'Apple-a-pound, pears!' and *'Just for you, lady – a very speshul price!'* The sounds just weren't there.

In the distance, she caught her first glimpse of her dear old mate, Mr Cabbage. She immediately noticed how much older he was looking these days, but put it down to all the worries he and his missus had gone through with Badger, first hearing he was 'missing in action', and then getting a letter from a Jerry prisoner-of-war camp to say that he was alive, but suffering from a foot injury. It came as quite a shock when Mr Cabbage told her the reason why the market was being drowned in such an unnatural silence.

'It's young Peanut. Trod on a land mine somewhere out in Norf Africa.' Mr Cabbage wiped his eyes on his black and white striped apron, took off his straw boater, and fanned himself with it. 'We only 'eard this mornin'. 'Is mum come over an' told us. It's 'ard ter believe. I've known that boy since the day 'e was born.'

Rose listened impassively. She was too stunned to react or say anything. Peanut – a costermonger to his fingertips, a friend to everyone in the market. As Mr Cabbage wiped the tears from his eyes, Rose turned around to look at Peanut's old stall, still as colourful as ever – green, black and gold – but now empty, for ever. All she could think of were all those happy days when he had given her handfuls of free nuts to take home, so many in fact that her mum was able to store them and keep them for Christmas. And all those rides he used to give her on Guv'nor, his old carthorse. And then she remembered the last time she had seen him, so proud in his Army uniform, perched on the edge of his own stall over there, he and his little Mabel, all set to become his wife, swinging their legs to and fro, as though life had so many exciting things waiting just ahead for them. Dear, wonderful Peanut. She had known him all her life and now he was gone.

Mr Cabbage was sobbing quite a lot, so Rose put her arms around him. ''E's still 'ere, Mr Cabbage,' she said affectionately. 'Yer'll never get rid of ol' Peanut.' And with her eyes still fixed directly on the empty green, black and gold stall, she added, ''E's too much a part of the place.'

By the time she reached the nursing home, Rose wasn't in the best of moods, but she cheered up to find her mum bright and alert, and sitting in her wheelchair in the glass conservatory at the back of the building. Rose thought Nellie looked so pretty, her eyes almost a perfect match for the blue cardigan Charlie Spindle's missus had knitted for her.

'I've bin waitin' ter see yer, dear,' Nellie said. She seemed more lucid than she'd been for a long time. 'Yer dad left a little while ago. 'E was tellin' me about Queenie –

yer know, wantin' ter leave 'ome ter go an' live wiv those Chinese kids.' She casually tidied the tartan blanket over her knees. 'I told 'im 'e mustn't stop 'er. Young Queenie's got ter find 'er own way in life.'

Nellie was always the practical one in the family, able to see beyond reason, and take risks. Here she was, Rose thought to herself, paralysed from the waist down, half her brain missing, and talking more sense than all the rest of the Humble family put together.

'Yer know, I fink she'll make a good nanny,' Nellie said, nodding her head up and down as she talked. 'Anyone our Queenie works for'll be bloomin' lucky ter get 'er!'

A few minutes later, Nellie said it was too hot in the conservatory, and asked her daughter to take her out into the garden.

It was April, and buds were beginning to appear on the cherry trees. The air was clear and fresh, and as soon as Rose stopped the wheelchair alongside a small ornamental fish pond, her mum blissfully breathed in the fresh spring air, a smile on her happy face.

'Yer know somefin', Rose?' Nellie said. 'Sometimes yer dad gets a little muddled. It's my fault really. I shouldn't've let 'im 'ave 'is say so often. Mind you, a man 'as a right ter say wot 'e finks.' She looked up at Rose, who was standing behind her, and with a twinkle in her eye, added, 'Even if 'e is talkin' a lot of ol' rubbish!'

Rose laughed with her, and was delighted to find her mum in such a sharp state of mind. It was the first real sign of improvement, the first real sign that perhaps, after all, her mum could eventually be rehabilitated in the outside world.

For a few moments, there was silence. Rose and Nellie, each with a gentle smile on her face, gazed out at the modest landscaped gardens. Nearby they could see what looked like a greenhouse, with its glass panels, like the conservatory they had just come from, covered in a crisscross of blast-proof tape. Although there was a gardener, no one had yet cut the lawn, for it was still too wet from the early spring rains. But there were plenty of daffodils in the different-shaped garden beds, and a few cheeky white-faced daisies were pushing up through the green damp grass.

'Yer're a good gel, Rose,' Nellie said suddenly. 'I always told yer dad yer'd be the one ter turn up trumps.'

'Yer never told *me* that!' joked Rose.

Rose laughed, but not her mum. Nellie turned round to look up at her daughter, and with a faint smile on her face, said, 'Well, I'm tellin' yer now.'

Rose, standing behind her, stooped down and wrapped her arms around her mum's shoulders. For a moment or so, they remained just like that, gazing out into the garden, and watching a busy blackbird whilst it poked its beak in and out of the lawn, determined to find a few grubs.

'Let's sing somefin', Rose,' Nellie said. 'We ain't sung nuffin' tergevver for a long time.'

'Wot would yer like?'

'You choose.'

Rose thought for a moment, started to hum, then quietly sing, 'Lily of Laguna'. After she had got to the second line or so, Nellie joined in, and they swayed to and fro in time to the melody. Right in the middle of the song, however,

Nellie suddenly stopped singing. ''Allo, 'allo!' quipped Rose. 'Forgotten the words, 'ave yer?'

Nellie didn't answer.

Rose, puzzled, asked again. 'Mum?'

When Nellie still didn't answer, Rose moved around in front of her.

'Mum?'

Nellie's eyes were wide open. They had no expression.

For one terrifying moment Rose thought her mum had died. Panicking, she put one hand on Nellie's shoulder, and waved the other one up and down frantically in front of her.

Nellie blinked, glanced away briefly, then looked back again, this time straight at Rose. Her eyes showed suspicion, even anger.

'Mum?' Rose asked, stooping down to take a closer look at her. 'Wot is it, dear? Wot's wrong?'

Nellie simply stared at her. There was no recognition, no attempt to make contact. Her eyes were cold and still, like stone. She said nothing.

Without warning, Nellie Humble had entered her own private twilight world.

Chapter 27

During the summer of 1942, the Luftwaffe concentrated
their aerial attacks on the coastal areas of Britain, and so,
apart from the occasional hit-and-run raids, the skies over
London remained relatively calm. Elsewhere on the battle
front, however, the picture continued to be gloomy. British
troops were retreating from Field Marshal Rommel's
powerful Panzer divisions along a wide front in North
Africa, several British warships were sunk on active duty
off the coasts of Malta, Crete, and in the Arctic, and the
Russians were fighting for survival on their own land.

Nellie's sudden mental failure sent the Humble family
into a deep state of depression. During every visit they
were reduced to sitting in silence at her side, waiting for her
to say one word – just one word – to show that she was
aware of their presence, but after half an hour of a gruelling
wait for recognition, the strain always proved too much,
and they had to leave her behind in that strange inner world
which she had inhabited with such sudden and unexpected
haste. It was particularly hard for Rose, for, with the
exception of Albert, she had been closer to her mum than
any member of the family. There were times when Nellie
had seemed more like a sister to Rose, for they often used

to sip tea together in that first-floor room above the old piano shop, gossiping about each day's events in the market, and trying to sort out the endless family problems. The doctors had no real explanation for Nellie's sudden mental deterioration. They thought that it was most probably the result of a stroke.

With the continuing lack of intensity in the air raids, some of the St John Ambulance girls took turns to fire-watch on the roof of the depot in Whitechapel. No one had ever really got over the loss of the Brigade's regular fire-watcher, old Mr McKay, who had been killed by an unexploded ack-ack shell which had crashed down on top of him on the roof during that fatal last night of the Blitz. Whenever it was Rose's turn to do fire-watch duty, she always thought of the little chats she used to have with Mr McKay, and his earnest belief that 'freedom's something you have to fight for'. Today, sitting on the St John roof, she couldn't help but think how sad it was that he had never lived long enough to see the lights come on again across his regular view of the London skyline.

'Penny for yer thoughts.'

The last person Rose expected to see up here in the middle of the day was Gus's fiancée, Sylvie Parsons. 'Wotcha, Sylve,' Rose said brightly. 'Yer ears must be burnin'. Me an' Dad was talkin' about yer last night. Wot yer doin' up 'ere?'

'Come ter see yer, of course,' replied Sylvie, perching herself on the stone parapet along the edge of the roof. 'Long time no see.'

Rose was immediately suspicious. Despite the fact that

Gus had virtually estranged himself from her and the rest of the family, he had never been able to prevent Sylvie from keeping in contact.

'Is anyfin' up, Sylve?' Rose asked directly.

'Oh no,' said Sylvie, sounding just a touch unconvincing. 'Well – not really.' She peered at the street below, which was quite a long way down. ''Ow's Mum?'

'Just the same,' sighed Rose.

'Still don't recognise yer?'

'Nah. I don't fink she ever will.'

'It's so sad,' Sylvie said. 'That luvely woman, wiv so much ter live for. It's just not fair.' Then she turned back to Rose. ''Ow's Dad takin' it?'

'It don't bear finkin' of.' Rose leant forward in Mr McKay's fire-watching chair, rested her elbows on her knees, her face on her knuckles, and stared down at the stone roof slabs. 'Most days 'e just wanders round as if 'e ain't quite 'ere. 'E spends 'ours wiv Mum each day, just sittin' on a chair at the side of 'er, 'oldin' on to 'er. I reckon somefin's just curled up an' died inside 'im.'

For several minutes they sat together in the hot summer sunshine, talking about how terrible it was for the twins, having to live at home in such a distressing atmosphere. And it was upsetting too for Georgie, who was unable to express how he felt, and spent as much time as he could knocking around with his mates up the market. Every so often Sylvie pulled up her uniform skirt to fan her legs, for the air was very muggy, and behind her a shimmering blue heat haze was draped over the entire city skyline.

It was some time before Sylvie mentioned Gus, but that was clearly the real reason she had come to see Rose. 'I 'aven't 'eard from 'im for quite a time,' she said almost casually. 'I was just wonderin' if 'e's written ter you at all?'

Rose straightened up in her chair. 'Written ter *me*? Yer've got ter be jokin', Sylve! Gus ain't made contact wiv me since 'e come 'ome on leave. 'E'll never forgive me for 'avin' a conchy boyfriend.'

'I know. I 'ad a go at 'im for that,' sniffed Sylvie indignantly. 'The trouble wiv yer bruvver is 'e's so convinced 'e's right all the bleedin' time! I could murder 'im sometimes!'

Sylvie then went quiet again, and turned to look back over the city. Rose began to sense that something was troubling her future sister-in-law.

'The last time yer 'eard from Gus,' asked Rose, 'where was 'e?'

'No idea,' Sylvie said despondently. 'We don't do that code fing no more. Gus says I 'ad no right ter go tellin' people about it. 'E was still goin' on about it the last time 'e was 'ome.' She suddenly sat up straight, and became very practical. 'The trufe is, Rose – I'm not sure yer bruvver wants ter see me no more.'

Rose was horrified. 'Wot?'

'Oh, I don't care, really – it's up ter 'im. But the last time 'e wrote ter me, 'e was sayin' peculiar fings like, "I know yer must be lonely back there all on yer own, so I'll quite understand if yer don't want ter wait for me."'

Rose sighed in exasperation. 'That bleedin' bruvver of mine! Sometimes I fink 'e's quite bonkers!'

Behind them, a flock of crows swarmed over the rooftop, heading for the nearest pigswill bin in the streets below.

They made an awful noise, and the two girls had to wait before continuing their conversation.

'I wouldn't mind,' said Sylvie, 'but I wrote back ter 'im weeks ago, an' 'e still 'asn't replied.'

Both girls turned when they heard the thump of ack-ack gunfire coming from far distant Essex. Although no air-raid siren had sounded, Rose immediately got up from Mr McKay's fire-watcher's chair, and put on her tin helmet. Sylvie got up at the same time, and once Rose had collected her binoculars, they stood side by side gazing out across the bomb-scarred London skyline, just waiting for the first sign of enemy planes. But the ack-ack sounds ceased as suddenly as they had come. The raiders were clearly being given no chance to reach the outskirts of the city.

'Yer know wot I fink yer should do, Sylve?' said Rose, her eyes still focusing through the binoculars. 'I fink yer should take me stupid bruvver at 'is word, an' go an' 'ave a good time.'

'Oh, I couldn't Rose,' Sylvie said quickly. 'I luv 'im too much for that.' Then she crossed her arms and, gazing out at the skyline before her, added, 'An' in any case, I'm goin' ter 'ave 'is baby.'

Rose had a few hours off before she was back on duty again, so she grabbed a quick cheese sandwich in the St John staff canteen, and made her way back to Islington to spend half an hour or so with her mum in the nursing home. She didn't really like going there in her navy-blue serge uniform tunic and trousers, but as there wouldn't be any time to get back to the 'toy house' before her evening shift, she had no alternative.

405

On the way she stopped at Chapel Market and bought Nellie a half-pound of broken digestive biscuits, and a tub of Italian water ice from Mr Ginetti's rainbow-coloured stall. The nursing home was about five minutes' walk away from the market, but, despite the afternoon heat, the water ice survived the journey remarkably well wrapped in newspaper.

When Rose arrived, Nellie was, as usual, sitting in the gardens. Her wheelchair had been placed in a secluded position next to the ornamental pool, but because of the war-time restrictions on water and fuel consumption, the fountain statue of the Greek god Apollo was not working. As it was such a lovely hot day, some of the other patients and their visitors were also taking in the afternoon sunshine, but they kept their voices low, so all that could be heard was a soft murmur.

''Allo, Mum! 'Ow are we terday, dear?'

Rose always hated herself when she found she was shouting at her mum, for Nellie wasn't deaf, but because so many of the elderly patients in the home were, it seemed the right thing to do. But Nellie wasn't old, and seeing her amongst so many decrepit people was a hard thing to take.

'Look wot I've got for a really pretty gel.' Rose was appalled to find herself talking to her mum just like the matron. She quickly took the tub of water ice out of its newspaper wrapping.

Nellie hadn't acknowledged Rose's presence. It was difficult to tell if she even knew she was there. She just sat upright in her wheelchair, staring dead ahead of her, tapping one finger slowly and methodically on the tartan blanket covering her lap.

Rose removed the lid from the tub, found the small wooden spoon Mr Ginetti had given her, and started to feed the water ice to her mum. As each spoonful was offered to her, Nellie opened her mouth wide, so wide in fact that she could have devoured a whole apple. It was a sad and bizarre sight, for Nellie was being fed like a small child, occasionally retaining a spoonful of water ice in her mouth until it had melted, and then swallowing it. Sometimes, it dribbled down her chin, and Rose had to dab it with her hanky. The only consolation was that Nellie was clearly enjoying her treat, for once she had taken one mouthful, she quickly expected another.

As soon as Nellie had finished, Rose wiped her mum's mouth with her hanky, then sat alongside her on a functional wooden bench. As always, she gently took hold of one of Nellie's hands, and spent the next few minutes stroking it tenderly, hoping that it might just prompt some kind of recognition.

After a moment or so, Rose leant towards Nellie, and spoke directly into her ear. 'Hey, Mum, d'yer remember that Bank 'Oliday we went down the canal tergevver. D'yer remember who was wiv us? Do yer?'

There was not even a flicker of contact from Nellie. She merely stared ahead impassively at some goldfish, whose brightly coloured scales were shimmering in the dazzling sunlight in the ornamental pool.

'Come on, now,' Rose continued. 'You can remember – course yer can! There was . . . Dad . . . yer Albert. Yes . . . and 'oo else? Queenie! Yes, she was there. Yer know Queen, don't yer? An' wot about – the twins? Polly? Millie? They was there, too. So was young Georgie! 'E's a bad boy that Georgie, ain't 'e, Mum – eh? Always teasin' yer wiv those spiders?' To try to create an image, Rose shuddered. 'Aargh! Nasty, 'orrible fings – ain't they?'

Nellie remained impassive, but Rose did think she felt some movement in the hand she was holding.

And so it went on. Rose tried every little device she could think of. Dates, times, birthdays, people, places, events – every memory she tried to recall was received in abject silence. For Rose, it was a frustrating, painful experience, and a hurtful one. As she crouched in front of Nellie and tried to make contact by staring directly into those deep blue eyes, she felt hurt, rejected, as though her mum was somehow doing this terrible thing deliberately. Why, why, why was she cutting herself off like this? What had she, Rose, done so wrong that her mum could distance herself from her in such a cruel way? It was like looking at a woman who was already dead. In fact, more than once Rose had told herself that she would much rather her mum were dead than for her to live such a pointless existence as this.

'Box!'

Rose looked up, shocked. Nellie had said something! She quickly dried the tears that had gradually been forming in her eyes, and crouched in front of her mum again. 'Yes, Mum! Tell me! Wot is it, dear? Tell me!'

'Box!' Nellie's voice was firm and precise, but her eyes remained fixed dead ahead of her.

'Yes, dear – box! Wot about it, Mum? Tell me! Tell yer Rose. Wot box?'

'Here we are again!' Matron's voice cut into Rose like a knife through butter. 'And isn't it nice to have our lovely daughter with us on such a lovely day, Mrs Humble?'

'Please, Matron!' Rose snapped. 'My mum's just spoken ter me!'

'My goodness!' replied Matron, suddenly crouching alongside Rose in front of Nellie. 'You mean she's said something? She's actually spoken?'

'She said a word, just one word! But she said it clear as daylight. I was tryin' ter get 'er ter tell me wot she meant.' Rose drew as close as she could to Nellie, and asked her again. 'Come on now, Mum – tell me. Tell yer Rose. Box. Tell me about box.'

Matron suddenly sat up straight. 'Is that what she said? Box?'

'Yes!' snapped Rose through clenched teeth. 'Box!'

'Box!' Nellie's voice, loud and strong, suddenly interrupted them.

'Yes, dear – box!' said Matron, patting Nellie on her knee. 'We know all about that, don't we?'

'Wot d'yer mean?' asked Rose, turning to watch Matron as she got to her feet again. ''As she said it before?'

'Oh yes. Lots of times,' answered Matron. 'In fact, some of the staff said they've heard her saying it over and over again when they've gone in to see her first thing in the morning.'

Rose stood up and glared at the woman. 'Yer're tellin' me me mum's bin sayin' this word all along, an' yer've never told me?'

'Come now, young lady,' replied Matron, who was determined not to be offended, 'one word is not a recovery.' Before Rose had a chance to answer, she moved round the back of Nellie, and took hold of the wheelchair. 'Now, if you'll excuse us, I think we're in need of the potty!'

She leant over Nellie's shoulder and called to her in a high-pitched child's voice, 'Here we go, Mrs Humble!'

Rose watched Matron push Nellie's wheelchair back into the house, aghast at the insensitivity of the woman in charge of the place. Her mum had spoken!

As Matron reached the conservatory door, she paused to smile and pass a few words with one of the other visitors. Whilst she was doing so, Rose watched her mum quietly waiting in her wheelchair. She seemed quite impassive, totally unaware of anything going on around her. Or was she? What *was* going on in that tired, demented mind? Did she know how Rose felt about her? 'Our Rose' Nellie had called her when she was in hospital. Rose refused to believe that there was not a part of this wonderful woman that was still back home in those rooms above the old piano shop, home with the family that found it so difficult to exist without her.

Eventually, Matron finished her socialising, and started to push Nellie's wheelchair again. Before they disappeared back into the house, Rose tried a half-hearted wave, but when she saw that Nellie didn't even turn her head, she thought better of it. Anyway, what did it matter? At least Nellie Humble had given her eldest daughter something to think about.

From that moment, Rose could hear just one word churning over and over again in her mind: *Box!*

That night, Rose finished work at about half-past ten. It had been an eventful day. What with Sylvie's news that she was two months' gone with Gus's baby, and then hearing her mum's voice again after so long, she had plenty to think about. The evening itself had been quite eventful, too, for at about seven-thirty, 'Moaning Minnie' had decided to remind everyone that there was still a war on. However, the air raid only lasted forty minutes, and during that time, dozens of people crowded the streets to cheer their heads off, as they watched two enemy bombers being shot down by a solitary RAF Spitfire in a fierce dogfight high over the rooftops. Even so, Rose received many emergency calls, and had to speed her ambulance off to the aid of people who had been badly injured by chunks of falling shrapnel.

Bill was waiting for her when she left the St John Depot. This had become a habit over recent weeks for, despite the lateness of the hour, it gave them both a chance to unwind, and just be together.

There was still one fish and chip shop open in Whitechapel Road, so Bill bought two penny portions of chips, then sprinkled Rose's with salt and his own with salt and vinegar. Rose and Bill felt really good as they walked along the main road, a huge harvest moon shining their way, munching some good crunchy chips out of an old copy of the *Daily Herald*.

Rose told Bill all her news. As always, he was a sympathetic listener, and let her talk it all out of her system.

'Wot box?' he asked, after Rose had described her extraordinary visit to her mum that afternoon. ''Aven't yer got any idea wot she meant?'

'It's bin on me mind all night,' she said, blowing on a very hot chip before she leant her head back and popped it into her mouth. 'But I just don't know.'

'The mind's a funny fing,' suggested Bill. 'It always 'as a few tricks up its sleeve.'

It was such a beautiful night that they decided to sit down for a bit on a coping stone outside a terraced house. They had to keep their voices fairly low in case they woke up any of the residents sleeping inside. It seemed as though the whole of London was bathed in a glowing mantle of white, with shadows so deep and sinister, they could have been painted by an artist. Bill remarked that it was a good thing Jerry wasn't over tonight, for, with all this light around, the place would be a sitting duck.

They sat for nearly an hour, nattering about people they liked and didn't like, lamenting the days before the war when they could buy any food at all, provided they had the lolly. Rose told every bit of scandal she could remember about one or two of the girls back at the St John Depot, and Bill spent at least ten minutes going on about his station fire officer, who didn't know the difference between a turntable ladder and a centrifugal pump!

When they got to Rose's bus stop, it came as no real surprise to discover that the last bus back to King's Cross had already gone. However, there was still the night service, so Rose decided that the only thing she could do was to hang around for another hour until it came. She was not expecting the suggestion that Bill then made.

'Look, Rose,' he said tentatively. He had her pinned up against the bus stop pole itself, with his arms around her waist as he spoke. 'Yer can tell me if I'm out of bounds, but—' He stopped in mid-sentence, as though his courage had suddenly given out. Then he tried again, leaning his forehead against hers. 'The fing is,' he whispered in her

ear, 'Mum's gone off ter see 'er sister in Edmonton. She
won't be back 'til the day after termorrer. If yer want, yer
could stay at 'ome for the night.'

Rose remained silent. Bill's offer had taken her by
surprise.

'I won't do nuffin' – I promise,' Bill said awkwardly.
'That is, not unless yer want me ter.'

Just over half an hour later, Rose was taking her uniform
off in Bill's bedroom. He insisted on letting her go first, and
waited downstairs until she called him up. It was a pokey
little room, with newspaper cuttings of football players
plastered all over the walls. Rose had no idea how the two
of them were going to squeeze into Bill's single bed, but as
she had come this far she didn't care. Once she had discarded
her uniform tunic, shirt, tie, and trousers, she removed the
heavy hairnet that had kept her hair so tidy whilst on duty.
She took a quick look at herself in Bill's shaving mirror,
which he kept on top of his chest of drawers; her gingery red
hair had grown long again after that painful experience with
Michael Devereaux. Then, she took off her bra, relieved, as
always, to escape its constraint.

She was about to get out of her knickers, but suddenly
lost her courage. So she went to the door, opened it
slightly, and called out down the stairs, 'Okay, Bill. Yer
turn!' After switching off the light, she hurried over to the
bed, pulled back the eiderdown, single blanket and sheet,
and slipped in. Her heart was thumping faster and faster as
she heard Bill's feet coming up the stairs.

The first she saw of him was when he opened the door,
his figure silhouetted against the electric light flooding the

413

landing outside. Then he switched off that light, came in, and closed the door behind him.

The room was now in total darkness, for although there was a full harvest moon outside, the blackout curtains had been drawn, and not even a chink of light filtered in.

'Rose?' Bill called softly in the dark. 'Are yer sure?'

Rose paused only a brief moment. 'Yes.'

For the next few minutes, she could hear him getting out of his uniform, first one boot cast off lazily, then another. He had already removed his uniform jacket when they first came into the house, so she knew that the next garment to come off had to be his trousers.

It took several minutes for Bill to strip right down, and whilst she was lying there, Rose tried to imagine what he looked like. Of course, she would know precisely when they got up first thing in the morning, but, although this was not her first time, it was certainly already more civilised than Michael Devereaux's quick bash behind the trees in Hertfordshire. For a start, whatever she was about to do, she was doing it with someone she loved. She just hoped Bill felt the same way about her.

Eventually, she felt the eiderdown, blanket, and sheet being pulled back. When he got in, the first thing she noticed was that, like her, he was still wearing his underpants. Despite her nervousness, it made her smile; he was as shy as she was.

His first move was to slide his arm around her shoulders. She could hear him breathing, and it sounded wonderful. For one moment, Rose wondered why it had taken so long for them to reach this point in their relationship. But then, she knew Bill was a very special kind of bloke. He had to be certain.

She felt the movement of his head as he turned towards her on the pillow. His lips found her ear, and he kissed it.

'Are yer *quite* sure, Rose?' he said, his voice a soft whisper.

Rose didn't answer. She just turned over on her side to face him. Bill did likewise.

Their bodies clamped together, and they kissed more passionately than they had ever done before. Rose always knew that Bill had plenty of hair on his chest, for she had often noticed them through his shirt, but when she actually felt their roughness pressed tightly against her breasts, she knew that she just had to give herself to him.

They made love throughout the night. When morning came, Rose was still locked in his arms. In these dark days of tragedy and unhappiness, he was the one ray of light giving her a sense of purpose, a sense of joy. And she loved him.

Rose got back to the 'toy house' soon after nine in the morning. On the way home on the top of a number 14 bus, she looked out at the world through fresh eyes. Whatever she did, wherever she went, she had someone who loved her, loved her for herself, loved her because she was just Rose Humble. A sense of freedom and joy swelled up inside her. She was now able to face up to anything life had to throw at her.

When Rose got home, she was surprised to find George standing at the front door. 'Georgie,' she said, a bit taken aback. 'Wot yer doin' up so early?'

'Where yer bin?' he asked aggressively, his eyes red and raw.

Rose took umbrage at such a question from her own kid brother. 'In case yer din't know, Georgie, I'm a big gel now. I don't 'ave ter tell *you* where I'm goin'!' She swept past him, and straight into the house.

Polly and Millie were in the front room with their dad. To Rose's dismay, they were all huddled together, sobbing profusely, united in grief. Only then was Rose told what had happened.

Nellie Humble had died at four o'clock that morning.

Chapter 28

The first spots of rain came soon after eleven thirty that morning. It had, of course, been promised by the weather man on the wireless, but as no one ever believed a word the poor man said, it came as a bit of a shock when it actually arrived.

Rose and Albert never used an umbrella, and so they got quite wet during their ten-minute walk from the 'toy house' to the Royal Northern Hospital. Albert didn't even bother to wear his cap, for despite the rain, it was still quite warm, and he couldn't care less if his thinning grey hair got wet. The twins and George stayed at home. They hadn't stopped crying since they heard the news about their mum, and none of them wanted to eat any breakfast. Rose told them there was no point in their going to the hospital with her and Dad, because identifying the body of someone you love is a painful business, and it was far better that they just remembered their mum as she used to be when they were all kids together.

Even as they made their way down Manor Gardens from Axminster Gardens, Rose could smell the hospital. It was a smell she had come to know so well over the past year or so, as she ferried air-raid casualties to the emergency units of hospitals all over the East End. It was a smell of death, other people's death, and now it had reached her own family.

Albert had not talked to Rose all the way from home. She knew that he blamed her for not being around when he needed her the most. It made her feel sick in her stomach when she thought of how he, George, and the twins must have felt when those two police constables from Hornsey Road Police Station had called at the 'toy house' in the early hours of the morning. The shock, the pain, the disbelief of being told that the very heart of the family had simply stopped beating – it was too unbearable even to think of. Oh God, why couldn't I have been there? thought Rose, as she and her dad moved slowly down that rain-swept road towards the hospital entrance. Why did it have to happen on the one night that she had at last found a new beginning with the man she loved? A few hours later – just a few hours – and she would have been there to take the brunt of this soul-destroying news. It wasn't just grief that Rose felt as she and her dad walked through the hospital entrance. It was guilt.

Nellie's face looked as beautiful in death as it had done in life. She had such a calm and serene expression on her face. Her lips were as fine and delicate as ever, and reminded Rose of all the times they had kissed her, Albert and the kids. There was no anger on this lovely face now, no bewilderment, no suspicion, no resentment. Nellie Humble had just decided that enough was enough. As Rose stooped down to kiss her mum gently on her forehead, she could almost hear her saying, 'Right, gel! I've done *my* bit. Now it's up ter you lot!'

Like Rose herself, Albert was crying for the first time since they left home. He was inconsolable, and with her arm around his waist, she had to lead him out of the bleak mortuary as quickly as possible.

'I'm afraid by the time our people got there, she was already gone,' said a softly spoken young hospital doctor, who didn't look much older than George. 'The matron of the nursing home did all she could, but when something happens as suddenly as this, there really is very little hope.' He lowered his voice. 'It was a massive stroke. Over very quickly.'

After collecting Nellie's death certificate from the almoner's office, Rose and Albert left the hospital. It had stopped raining, so Rose decided that before they made their way back home, she would take her dad for a quick cup of tea at Lyons Tea Shop near the Nag's Head along Holloway Road. The place was packed with morning shoppers, most of whom had come in to shelter from the rain, so they had to queue a bit before they got their two cups of tea. After Rose had found them a table, they sat down opposite each other, and for a few minutes sipped their tea in grieved silence.

Rose was first to speak. 'We've got ter be sensible, Dad,' she said, her hand covering his. 'Yer know, when yer fink about it, Mum really left us some time ago. I reckon that fer the past few monffs she's bin preparin' us for all this.'

Albert looked up at her with a stony expression. '*You* may be prepared for it, but *I* ain't. I'm the one that's lost 'er. She's gone! I'm never goin' ter see 'er again.'

To Rose, her dad looked just like a small, helpless child. 'We've *all* lost 'er, Dad,' she said. 'Fink wot it's like for all the rest of us – Queenie, the twins, young Georgie. And 'ow d'yer fink Gus's goin' ter take it when 'e 'ears the news? 'E idolised Mum, yer know 'e did.'

'It's all right for you lot,' said Albert, choking with pent-up grief. 'Yer've all got yer lives ahead of yer.' He suddenly pulled his hand away to pick up his cup. 'Mine's all be'ind me now. Me an' Nell.'

'Stop it, Dad!' Rose snapped sharply. 'Mum'd be really upset if she 'eard yer talk like that! Just remember, the 'Umbles're a family. We've got ter go on livin'.'

At the next table, a youngish woman had just walloped her small child, who was bawling the place down. Rose turned and glared, so the woman glared back, yelled at the child, 'Stop yer bleedin' row!' then picked him up and carried him out.

'Listen ter me, Dad.' Rose leant across the table to him, and lowered her voice. 'There's somefin' I've got ter ask yer – about Mum.'

Albert was listening, but continued to stare down at his cup of tea.

'The last time I saw 'er – yesterday afternoon in that nursin' 'ome – she suddenly said somefin'. It was the only time I'd 'eard 'er speak fer monffs, but that bleedin' matron said it wasn't the first time. Dad,' she leant as close to him as she could, 'wot did she mean by the word "box"?'

Albert, no help at all, just shook his head.

'Fink 'ard, Dad! She was tryin' ter tell us somefin'. Somefin' important to 'er. "Box!" Wot did she mean?'

Albert shook his head again.

'Come on now!' Rose was doing her best to be gentle with him. 'I can't cope wiv this all on me own.'

Albert slammed down his cup into the saucer. 'Yer should've fought about that last night, when yer muvver was dyin!'

Although Rose had been expecting an outburst like this, his stinging response still hurt her. 'That's not fair, Dad,' she replied, sitting back in her chair again. 'I 'ave ter go ter work, yer know. There's no way I could've known.'

Albert suddenly felt ashamed of himself, and he broke down. How could he tell Rose how he really felt? How could he tell her that with the strain of these past few months he was at breaking point? Without Nellie at his side, life was meaningless. He was in total despair.

Rose, aware that people at the other tables were watching them, quickly leant forward and covered his hand again. She knew how he felt. She knew that he would never hurt her intentionally. 'It's all right, Dad,' she said softly, tenderly. 'It's all right. Go on now, drink yer tea.'

Albert picked up his cup and put it to his lips. His hand was shaking. 'She 'ad so much ter live for,' he sobbed, 'so much left she wanted ter do. Nell was such a stickler for tidyin' fings up. Always 'ad ter be prepared.' Without sipping any of his tea, he put the cup down again. 'She knew wot I was like. She knew I couldn't cope. She knew I'd never be able ter look after the family if she went first. Bleedin' useless, that's me. No good ter man nor beast!' He leant towards Rose across the table. 'I never wanted to be left be'ind, Rose. Yer've got ter believe me. I *always* wanted ter be the first ter go!' His eyes were full of tears, and his nose was bright red from constantly pinching it. 'I don't want ter go on wivout 'er – I just don't!' Unable to control himself, Albert put his elbows on the table, covered his face with his hands, and sobbed into them.

'Is 'e all right, mate?' asked one of two very concerned elderly women sitting at a table nearby.

Rose smiled back. Her own eyes were also brimming with tears. ''E's all right, fank yer,' she answered, gently stroking Albert's hair. 'There's nuffin' ter worry about. 'E's me dad.'

As she watched Albert trying to cope with the sudden anguish that had been thrust upon him, she was relieved that he had at last opened up his heart to her.

She was also grateful that, in his moment of grief, her dad had quite innocently provided her with the key of that elusive *Box*.

After taking her father home, Rose quickly took a bus to the Angel, where she made straight for Chapel Market. She had something important to do, and there was no time to lose.

Rose knew that over the course of the next few days she was going to be extremely busy. Nellie was already being moved to an undertakers in Upper Street, her funeral had to be arranged, and relatives informed. But before she launched into any of that, one task was absolutely vital.

The market, as usual, was brimming with customers. Most of Rose's barrow-boy mates were there, including Mr Cabbage and his missus, Sid Levitt, Elsie Dumper, Ned Morris and Mr Ginetti, but the person Rose needed to talk to urgently was Charlie Spindle.

She eventually found him in Rita's caff, having a quick fag and a cup of tea, and his eyes lit up when he saw her.

The news of Nellie's death completely devastated him and it took him some time to compose himself again.

'Charlie,' said Rose, with some urgency, 'there's somefin' I'm lookin' for, an' I need yer 'elp.'

Charlie moved along the bench seat so that Rose could sit beside him.

'I need ter look fru all that stuff of ours that you an' the boys dug out the piano shop. Are yer still storin' it for us in yer garage?'

A few minutes later, Charlie took Rose to his garage in a small mews just behind the market. His old fruit and veg cart was there, and the place stunk of rotten cabbages and axle grease. Tucked away by the back wall, just behind the cart itself, were three large tea-chests, all containing what was left from the Humble family's household belongings recovered from the wreckage of their home.

'I'm afraid it's all a bit of a jumble, Rosie,' said Charlie, apologetically. 'Nuffin's bin touched since we brought it 'ere.' He watched her make an immediate start on sorting through the tea-chests. 'Need any 'elp?'

'No fanks, Charlie, I can manage,' Rose replied, pulling out old pots and pans and throwing them to the floor.

Charlie called out as he went, 'Well, yer know where ter find me.' After he had gone, Rose knew that it would only be a matter of minutes before the whole market knew about Nellie's passing.

For nearly half an hour, Rose pulled out practically the entire contents of the three chests. Most of the stuff was junk, for everything had been either burnt or badly damaged. She didn't really know what she was looking for, but when her dad had talked about Nellie's 'always wanting to prepare for things', her mind had drifted back to the chat she'd had with her mum on Islington Green, right at the beginning of the war. Nellie had been very depressed about the start of the war, and she'd talked about having left Rose a note, with instructions for if she, Nellie, should die before Albert. But where would Rose find this note, even if it had survived the explosion?

By the time she had completely cleared out the third tea-chest, Rose had almost given up hope. But just as she was pulling out a final layer of heavily chipped enamel tea plates – there it was!

'It's in that tin box where I keep me bits an' pieces.'

Rose could hear her mum's words in her mind. The box! This was it, nothing more than a small black metal cashbox, now dented right down the middle, and just lying on the bottom of the warped old tea-chest.

Rose stared at the box for a moment, then almost timidly, she reached into the tea-chest, and lifted it out. To her consternation, it was locked, and as she had no idea if it even still had a key, she looked around for something to prise it open. Eventually, she found a screwdriver, but when she tried to wriggle it around inside the keyhole, the lock proved too obstinate to move. Then, after a little more force, the box lid suddenly sprung open.

Inside, Rose found several of Nellie's 'bits and pieces': a pearl dress button someone had given her in the market years ago, some hair ribbons, a small copper-coated broach in the shape of a cupid's heart, three or four lucky three-penny bit pieces she had kept from successive Christmas puddings, and two snapshot photos – one of Albert, and the other of all the family, taken when Georgie was still a baby. But, tucked away underneath all that, was the note, which Rose could only retrieve after she had emptied out all the 'bits and pieces' into her hanky, spread out on the floor. With great trepidation, she eased the paper out of the box, and sat down cross-legged on the stone floor to read it.

It was written on paper taken from one of the twins' school exercise books, and as she unfolded it, out dropped a five-pound note. Rose retrieved it from her lap, then started to read what Nellie had written. The handwriting and spelling was, as her mum had warned, a bit hard to decipher, but, even though the words were written two and a half years before, Rose was convinced she could still smell the carbolic soap on her mum's hard-worked hands.

My deer Rosie,

By the time you reed this, I'll be pushing up daysies and youl be left carrying the can. I must say, I don't like the idea of not seeing your dad and all my family again. You lot have always been all that matters to me I hope when I'm gone yorl feel the same about me (joke!) Anyway here are a few things I'd like you to tak care of once I'm tucked up nice and cosy down below.

1. Please look after your dad. He worries far too much about me so I hope that when I'm not around any more you'll get him too think about himself for a change. See that he don't smoke his pipe too much, cos it gives him a nasty coff. Don't forget to give him lamb scrag-end every so offen cos its his favrit. I told you how to cook it Rose – remember?

2. Be kind to Queenie. She aint so bad really and just gets mixed up if she thinks everywon's against her. Tell her to find a nice rich man and make her life easy.

3. Watch Gus's temper! Sometimes he takes after his dad and is a real pain. When the war's over (please God!) I hope he finds a nice girl and settles down. He's got a good mind on him and as long as he keeps away from politics I bet he'll do well. I hate politics! Its' a fools' game!

4. Tell Poll and Mill to keep up with there piano playing and to stop kworraling with each other. O yes, and tell them to find new boyfrends. I cant bear those O'Brien boys or whatever there name is!

5. Please look after Georgie and tell him I forgive him for teasing me with all them spiders (I hate them!) He's a good boy and if everyone pays attenshun to him he'll turn up trumps.

6. Last (but not least!). Thank you Rose deer for being so good to me. I don't know what I'd have done without you all these yeers. I always knew you was the one with the brains and I know you'll put them to good use. Take care of our family wont you. You have all made my life such a good one and I dont know why I deserve it. I'm the luckiest woman in the werld! God in heaven bless you deer Rose. Dont worry. I'll always be around to keep me eye on you.

O yes, I almost fergot. I'm enclosing £5 with this

letter. Please put it toward my funeral and if there is any left over please buy your-self a new pair of shoes cos you need some. And please keep my geranium watered on the kitchen table.

God bless

Your everloving mum.

x x x x x x x (won for each of you!)

P.S. Please tell Albert I've always loved him ver much and I wouldnt have marrid anywon else in the hole wide werld.

Rose found it difficult to finish reading her mum's letter because tears were rolling down her cheeks and on to her lap.

She folded it up and put it back into the small metal box together with the five-pound note. Then she collected Nellie's 'bits and pieces' from the floor and put them back into the box. Last of all she picked up the two snapshots. For a brief moment, she just sat there looking first at her dad, who had been snapped looking very smart in his army uniform. Then she looked at the happy family group, stiff and self-conscious, but all with huge smiles on their faces. After giving both snapshots a long, lingering kiss, she also returned them to the box.

As there was no one around, she let herself go with a few moments of private, uncontrollable grief. Then she looked up at the ceiling of the musky old garage, and with tears streaming down her cheeks, and a voice that was croaking with emotion, she called out, 'Yer silly cow, Mum! Five pounds ain't nearly enough for yer bleedin' funeral!'

* * *

The following morning, Albert Humble got up early, and once the twins and George had left for work, and Rose had gone off for the morning to organise the various arrangements for Nellie's funeral, he popped across to the chemist's shop in Hornsey Road, where he bought a tin of Zubes cough sweets for Millie, and a bottle of aspirins for himself. At the paper shop next door, he bought his usual copy of the *Daily Sketch*, asked the shopkeeper if he had some bob pieces for a ten-bob note, then went straight back home again.

It was still only nine o'clock as he started his preparations.

First he took the tin of Zubes to Millie and Polly's room, where he put them down carefully on the small cabinet at the side of their bed. After that, he went out to the kitchen, and poured himself a cup of water. He sat down, and whilst taking a casual glance at the morning's newspaper headlines, he unscrewed the top of the aspirin bottle, and poured two or three tablets into his hand. He threw the tablets into his mouth, washed them down with the cold water – then repeated the process several times, until the bottle was empty. He folded up the newspaper neatly, left it on the kitchen table, and went to a cabinet just above the sink. There were two more bottles of aspirins there. He took them out, refilled his cup with water, and repeated the same process as before until both bottles were empty.

Albert returned to the back parlour. Although the sun was trying its best to sneak through dark humid clouds, as yesterday, rain was clearly on its way. So after a brief, last look out, he quickly drew the blackout curtains and locked the front door. He had to pull the small, two-person sofa away from the front of the gas fire because there just wasn't enough room to stretch out there, but he was very careful as he moved it, for Rose had bought it out of the money collected by the boys in the market when the Humbles had been bombed out of their home.

Going back to the kitchen, he just had enough time to put the ten shillings' worth of bob pieces into the gas meter. He had a lot more of the same coins in his trouser pocket, so he put them in too.

Back in the parlour, he found himself a comfortable cushion from one of the two utility chairs, and plonked it down in front of the hearth. Then he simply eased himself down on to the fire rug, stretched out, and laid his head on the cushion. When he was quite certain that he was comfortable, he lay back, and closed his eyes. He was now feeling really quite drowsy, so slowly he moved his hand across the rug towards the gas tap. When he finally reached it and turned it on, he could only just hear the hissing sound.

When Rose got home, it was almost two o'clock in the afternoon. By then, her dad was fast asleep.

Chapter 29

There was no doubt that the Islington Cemetery looked its best in June. At that time of year roses were in full bloom in the more formal memorial gardens, and the yellow buttercups, white-faced daisies, lushly green sheaves of grass and white-laced meadowsweet, settled snugly in between the gravestones, surrounded by a magnificent sea of scarlet poppies. But this was late August, when the vibrant freshness of spring and the long humid days of summer were beginning to give way to the oncoming pastel shades of autumn. Nonetheless, it must have been clear to anyone who visited this tranquil place in the leafy suburbs of North London, that at any time of the year all who rested there were in good company.

The costermongers of Chapel Market were out in force that day. Two of their most valued mates were being put to rest, and they had come to say farewell. The black cortège stretched back for almost fifty yards, keeping a slow, steady pace behind the two hearses. At the rear of the procession came three more funeral cars. These contained the more elderly mourners, who couldn't really cope with the half-mile or so walk to the graveside.

The afternoon had started with a short funeral service in

St Mary's Church in Upper Street. As a mark of love and respect for their dear old mates, the barrow boys of Chapel Market had ceased trading at midday. This was reflected in the address by the Vicar, who referred to Nellie and Albert Humble as 'a bright beacon of light in this closely knit community'. Gus, Queenie, and the twins listened attentively to every word the Vicar said. So did Gran and Grandad Wilson, Nellie's own mum and dad, who'd come over specially from Tottenham for the sad occasion. But Rose, George, and Albert's dad from Walthamstow, Grandad Percy, sat quite impassively at the end of the front pew all through the entire service, and only came to life when everyone sung hymns like 'Praise my Soul the King of Heaven'.

After the service, the family got into two big black funeral cars for the journey to the cemetery, and everyone else followed on in a specially hired charabanc. All the vehicles were covered in flowers and other floral tributes, but the most amazing wreath came from the market traders, who had sent one in the shape of a costermonger's stall, made out of dozens of summer flowers such as roses, sweetpeas, gladioli, dahlias, and summer stocks. The sombre procession made a special point of passing by the market, where hundreds of tearful people with bowed and bare heads waited to say their own farewell. 'Not a bad turnout for a couple of ol'-timers like us, eh, Bert?' Rose could almost hear her mum saying it.

The procession took nearly an hour to reach the gates of the cemetery. When it finally arrived, everyone piled out of the funeral cars and charabanc, where they were met by even more mourners, including a small group of pearly kings and queens from the East End, some of whom were also trader commuters to Chapel Market. Resplendent in multi-coloured pearl button outfits and black armbands, they represented the ultimate tribute to two mates who may not have been Cockneys in the true sense of the word, but who were, by the very nature of their long-term friendship, honorary members of the pearlies' most noble club.

The costermongers' procession wound its way to the graveside where Nellie and Albert were to share their last resting place together.

The family were already there, waiting for the Vicar to say his few words before the coffins were lowered into the bleak dark hole. Polly and Millie, who were the most tearful, hugged, and tried to comfort each other. Queenie, who had been given a few days off from Mrs Wu's kiddie-minding in High Wycombe, never for one moment took her eyes off the two coffins. Unlike Rose, she wore nothing but black. Even that constant turban was a perfect match for her black cotton, full-sleeved dress and flat-heeled shoes. George, who had remained grim-faced throughout, had only one suit in the world, which was grey, but he wore it with a black armband, and his grandparents told him later that they were very proud of him.

For the third time in just a few months, Gus had been given compassionate leave, and had just flown home from active duty in North Africa. For the funeral he wore his Army uniform, with a tie and black armband. To Rose's immense relief, Sylvie was at his side. Whatever complicated reason he may have had for his strange letter to

Sylvie, everything seemed to have been resolved. With a baby on the way, it was just as well. But, not at any moment did Gus glance at his eldest sister. Before the funeral, he had even chosen to go straight to the church rather than join the family at the 'toy house'. The reason was obvious: the conchy was at her side.

Once the graveside address was over, each member of the family threw a handful of dry soil down on to the top of each coffin, and before Nellie's coffin was covered over, Rose cast a few blooms of her mum's favourite geraniums down as well.

Suddenly, all eyes turned upwards. A frantic dogfight was taking place in the cloudless blue sky above the cemetery. On the journey from Islington, none of the mourners had really taken in 'Moaning Minnie's' wailing across the rooftops, so it came as a shock to see the crisscross patterns of vapour trails, as the Spitfires and Hurricanes battled it out with a posse of intruders who had managed to penetrate the outer ring of London's defences.

'Fanks for comin', Sylve,' said Rose, turning towards her. 'Mum an' Dad would've wanted yer 'ere.'

Sylvie, whose eyes were still red from crying, hugged and kissed Rose. 'It's so sad, Rose,' she sniffed. 'They were like havin' me own parents.'

Rose smiled at her affectionately. Then she turned to her eldest brother. ''Allo, Gus,' she said warmly. 'Fank God yer're 'ome safe.'

She moved forward to greet him with a kiss, but he backed away from her.

Rose was embarrassed. There were many people from

the market milling around, and her brother's odd behaviour caused some raised eyebrows. Then she noticed that Gus was glaring at Bill, who was standing by her side, so she deliberately took hold of Bill's arm, and clung on to it. 'Bill,' she said defiantly, 'I'd like yer ter meet me bruvver Gus. Gus, this is Bill.'

Bill wearing his NFS uniform, offered his hand to Gus. ''Allo, Gus,' he said boldly. 'Sorry we 'ave ter meet in such circumstances.'

'We're not meetin' at all, mate!' said Gus, his eyes set in anger. 'I don't shake 'ands wiv no bloody conchy!'

'Gus!' gasped Sylvie, trying to pull him away.

Bill, refusing to be intimidated, calmly withdrew his hand.

Rose stepped forward and angrily confronted her brother. 'Just wot's got inter yer, mate? Wot's this all about?'

'I'll tell yer wot it's all about – *mate*!' He pointed a menacing finger at Bill. ''*E's* wot it's all about! That man's got no right – no right at all – ter be 'angin' around *my* muvver an' farver's grave!'

''E's got as much right as you an' me!' Rose snapped.

Gus spat back immediately, 'Rose, yer disgust me! 'Ow can yer let a man like that lay 'is 'ands on yer? Yer should see wot I've just come from. Me own mates bein' shot down every day – right in front of me very eyes! They weren't cowards. They didn't run away the moment they fought their precious arses was goin' ter get shot up!'

'Gus, yer shouldn't talk like that, son,' interrupted Mr Cabbage timidly. 'We're only a few feet from yer own mum and dad's grave. It isn't right ter quarrel before they've even bin covered up.'

'Let me tell yer somefin',' growled Gus, who then turned to address everyone standing around watching. 'Let me tell yer all somefin'! *These* people,' he said, his finger pointing straight at Bill and his voice so raised that it echoed around the gravestones, 'these people would 'ave yer believe that it's wrong ter fight for yer country. They'd 'ave yer believe that the only reason they won't pick up a rifle is not 'cos they're afraid or anyfin' – oh no. They'll tell yer it's 'cos it's better ter make peace than war. Well, try tellin' that ter the people in France! Try tellin' that ter the people in Belgium! Try tellin' that ter the people in Holland, or Poland, or Russia! Try tellin' that ter the Jews!'

He turned back to Bill again. He was now so worked up, a vein was protruding in the side of his neck. 'There's no such fing as peace by discussion! If people want somefin', they'll kill for it!'

'Don't Gus – *please*!' Sylvie tried to pull him away, but he shrugged her off.

'I'm tellin' yer again, mate,' Gus said, once again pointing his finger at Bill. 'Yer're afraid of war 'cos of yer own skin. Yer're afraid of war 'cos yer 'aven't got the guts ter fight like a man!'

There were gasps from some of the market traders, but others, used to Gus shouting his mouth off, started to move away.

'Just 'oo the bleedin' 'ell d'yer fink you are?' yelled Rose directly at her brother.

'It's all right, Rose,' said Bill calmly. 'I'll go.'

He started to move off, but Rose grabbed his arm. 'No, Bill!' she roared. 'You stay right where yer are!'

During the split second before she tackled Gus, a thought had flashed through Rose's mind. This was the brother who had contributed absolutely nothing to the welfare of the Humble family. Throughout his life he had thought of one person and one person only – himself! If ever she had come to him with a problem, he would brush it to one side and accuse her of making a mountain out of a molehill. And now here he was, talking about *his* mum and dad this, and *his* mum and dad that. But it was all rubbish, because most of the time he was always so interested in his own opinions that to him his own mum and dad might never have existed.

'Now yer listen ter me!' she said angrily. 'Yer call this bloke a coward. Yer tell 'im that the reason 'e won't go ter war is 'cos 'e wants ter save 'is own skin . . .'

Gus turned his back on her and tried to walk off, but Rose rushed after him and confronted him face to face. 'All I'm askin' yer ter do is come up the East End one night. Just come an' see 'ow 'e tries ter save 'is skin by climbin' up ladders inter burnin' buildin's. See 'ow 'e tries ter save 'is skin by chokin' 'is bleedin' lungs out to reach people trapped in blazin' rooms. An' see 'ow 'e tries ter save 'is skin by goin' inside bombed factories that are just about ter cave in on 'im. That's got nuffin' ter do wiv war, Gus! It's ter do wiv savin' 'uman life!'

Gus broke loose from her, and marched off. But after a few yards, he stopped, and turned back on her. 'I'm givin' yer one last chance, Rose,' he yelled, now pointing his finger at her. 'Get rid of 'im an' come back ter the car wiv us – or keep away from me for good!'

He stood there waiting for her reply.

Rose couldn't believe how unreasonable her so-called big brother had become. He had always been so full of himself, always so sure that his opinions were right, that it was impossible for anyone else to have even a view about anything. But he'd never been like this before. Oh God, she thought, her mum and dad must be turning in their grave as they listened to their kids scrapping like this.

'Come on,' she said firmly to Bill. 'Let's go.' And without even a glance at Gus, added: 'We'll make our own way 'ome.'

The crowd of mourners parted to let Rose and Bill through. As they disappeared along the narrow gravel path, the dogfight above their heads came to a climax when one of the enemy bomber planes came spiralling down in a twirl of vapour, to crash in a burst of flame in the far distance.

By the time everyone was getting back in their funeral cars and charabanc, 'Moaning Minnie' was wailing out yet again. This time, however, it was sounding the all clear.

Bethnal Green Fire Station was on full alert. The night before, several enemy Heinkel and Dornier bombers had broken through the strong defence cordon around London, and attacked targets which included the West India Docks at Poplar, the commercial heart of the City, and various other locations in North and Central London. Although the extent of the damage had been limited, and nothing like as severe as during the Blitz, nobody was taking any chances.

Bill Layton hadn't had much sleep over the past twenty-four hours, so even though it was after seven o'clock in the evening, he was glad to catch up on a bit of shuteye.

However, he wasn't given the chance to sleep for long, for at about a quarter past eight, one of his NFS mates came up to the crew dormitory to tell him that someone was waiting to see him downstairs at the main station doors. Like all the firemen, Bill was fully dressed in his fire-fighting gear for a quick callout, so all he had to do was to collect his helmet and axe. Then he slid down the fast exit pole, and made his way to the main doors.

'Wotcha. Remember me?'

Bill couldn't believe his eyes. Waiting for him just outside was Rose's eldest brother. He was so taken aback, he was lost for words.

'They told me I'd probably find yer 'ere,' said Gus. 'I asked some of the blokes over at Whitechapel. Thirty-six Fire Force Area, Number Five Fire Region – right?'

'Wot's this all about, Gus?' asked Bill suspiciously.

'Well yer may ask,' Gus replied. 'I wish I knew.' He reached into his Army uniform jacket and brought out a packet of Woodbines. 'Fag?'

Bill hesitated for a moment, then took a cigarette from Gus's packet. Gus pulled one out with his teeth, took a box of matches from the same pocket and lit up for both of them.

'I suppose I've come ter say sorry,' Gus said, inhaling deeply, and holding on to the smoke for as long as possible, 'for wot 'appened yesterday – up the cemetery.'

Again, Bill couldn't bring himself to say anything.

Gus finally released the residue of the smoke from his lungs. 'I 'ave ter say that after you and Rose walked out on me, I 'ad no intention of ever doin' anyfin' like this – that I can assure yer!'

'So why *'ave* yer?'

''Cos Rose was right. I've bin a bloody mug. Fing is – I didn't realise it 'til last night.' He leant his head back, and with the fag stuck in his mouth, he looked up at the sky. It was beginning to get dark, and the blackout curtains had already been pulled across the windows of all the terraced houses in the street. 'Me an' Sylve was 'avin a drink down the boozer near the Nag's 'Ead. Then this air raid come on.' He swung a brief glance at Bill. 'Scared the piss out of me, I tell yer!'

Bill grinned and smoked his fag.

Gus, his hands tucked in his trouser pockets, looked up at the sky again. 'Jerry dropped a bomb a couple of streets away. The 'ole pub nearly come in on us. Yer should've seen it – booze all over the floor. Wot a bleedin' waste!' He drew on his fag. 'Anyway, Sylve took me round ter see the damage, yer know – where this bomb come down. Phor! I've seen some fings in me time, but that—!'

'Did Rose send yer 'ere, Gus?' Bill said suddenly.

Gus looked back at him with a start. 'No way.'

'Then wot're yer doin' 'ere?'

'Tellin' yer that if anyone calls *you* a coward, then they're just as bonkers as I am.' Without finishing his fag, Gus dropped it to the pavement and stubbed his foot on it. 'Look, mate. I saw a load of you blokes in that street last night. Young blokes, old. There was this block of flats – direct 'it, burnin' like Guy Fawkes' Night, people runnin' all over the place, firemen liftin' 'em out of windows, off the roof, any place they could get to. It went on like that for hours. At one time I fought the 'ole street was goin' up. But it di'n't. Yer blokes took care of that. But when it was over, I tell yer – they looked bloody whacked!'

Bill, leaning his back against the wall at the side of the doors, continued smoking his fag.

'Rose tried ter tell me,' said Gus. 'So did Sylve. They both told me that workin' in the Fire Service in any big city durin' the war is just as bad as fightin' wiv a gun on any battlefield.' He turned to look at Bill again. 'I tell yer this much – it's worse. I can't wait ter get back to a peaceful life!'

This made Bill chuckle, but then Gus's expression changed.

'Look. 'Cos I've said wot I've said don't mean that I agree wiv wot yer've done – about yer call-up an' all that. But I do agree that yer 'aven't done it 'cos yer yeller.'

Bill grinned. 'I'm pleased ter 'ear it,' he replied.

As both turned to look up at the sky again, there was a moment of silence between them.

Gus was first to speak. 'So, yer're keen on me sister then?' he said knowingly.

'No,' replied Bill, 'I'm in luv wiv 'er.'

'No kiddin'?'

'No kiddin'.'

Again they leant their heads back and looked up at the sky. The evening light was now fading fast, and searchlights were already automatically practising for any enemy breakthrough.

'We've 'ad an 'ell of a time of it, us 'Umbles,' said Gus, his voice uncharacteristically soft and low. 'We deserve a break.'

'Yer'll get it.'

''Ope so.' Gus paused a moment. 'D'yer want ter marry our Rose?'

'Yer bet yer life I do,' he replied. And he meant it.

Chapter 30

Three days after Nellie and Albert's funeral, Bill asked Rose to marry him. All the family were there at the toy house at the time, and thoroughly enjoyed watching Bill, resting on one knee on the floor and proposing to Rose as though he was a comic in a Music Hall sketch. It may not have been the most romantic proposal, but it helped to raise the family's spirits after a very traumatic period of grief. For Rose, the prospect of having Bill as her husband was a dream come true. She was particularly overjoyed that her eldest brother was in on it, for until that moment, Bill hadn't told her about how Gus had come along to see him at the Fire Station. When Sylvie had suddenly turned up on the doorstep with Gus on one arm and Bill on the other, she just felt like bursting into tears.

'I think you should have a white wedding,' said Millie. 'When I marry Dixon, *I'm* going to have a white wedding.'

'Dixon!' exclaimed George. 'Wot the 'ell's that?'

'Corporal Dixon P. Snelling,' Millie answered proudly. 'United States First Infantry Division.'

'Dixon P. Snelling!' snorted Gus. 'Yer're goin' out wiv a Yank?'

Millie turned her head away snootily. As far as she was concerned there was nothing wrong with having a Yank for a boyfriend. After all, they had been in the war ever since the Japs bombed their ships at Pearl Harbor over a year ago. And now that the Americans were over here to fight against the Germans as well, Millie thought that there was no reason why they shouldn't make them feel at home.

'Stop gettin' at 'er, you two!' scolded Rose. 'She's only fraternisin' wiv one of our Allies!'

Millie swung a glare at her eldest sister. Rose was just as bad as her two brothers.

Then it was Queenie's turn to do some teasing. 'So, Mill, 'as this Dixon P. Snellin' asked yer ter marry 'im?'

'Don't be silly!' sneered Polly. 'She's only known 'im a couple of weeks. She met 'im when we went to an American Servicemen's Dance in Piccadilly.'

''Ere – 'ang on!' said Rose. 'You two bin 'angin' round dance 'alls down the Dilly?'

'Oh don't be so silly, Rose!' said Millie.

'There's nothing wrong with going to dances,' said Polly.

'And anyway, we're old enough to take care of ourselves now, thank you very much!' Millie had the last word, and a very haughty last word it was, too.

Rose wasn't convinced. Even though her twin sisters had outgrown their lisp, as she watched them sitting side by side on the sofa, it still amazed her how difficult it was to tell them apart. It also reminded her of wonderful times when they sat side by side on the piano stool, playing a Viennese waltz for dear old Uncle Popov.

'So, where're you two goin' ter live?' asked Queenie, who was sitting next to Rose at the kitchen table.

'Ask the guv'ner,' Rose replied, nodding towards Bill, who was standing with his back to the window, where he and Gus were each downing a celebratory pint glass of bitter.

'It depends 'ow yer sister feels,' Bill said, addressing Queenie. 'Though I'd prefer ter stay up my way if we can.'

'Wot – Befnal Green?' sneered George. 'That dump!'

'George!' snapped Rose.

Bill and Gus laughed.

'Well, it's true! Wot d'yer want ter go an' live in the East End for? It's much better round 'ere.'

There followed a full family debate on the virtues and merits of living in North or East London. There was talk of who had the best pubs, who was genuine Cockney and who wasn't, and which of these two areas of London would be the best place to live in once the war was over. For about the first time in their lives, George and Millie actually agreed with one another, saying rather snootily that going from Islington to places like Stepney and Bow and Whitechapel and Bethnal Green, was like crossing the border into a foreign country.

In the end, it was Polly who brought the conversation back to a more practical level, when she asked, 'What happens to me and Millie if you go off to live in Bethnal Green?'

There was an immediate silence, in which Rose exchanged a quick, anxious glance with both Bill and Gus.

'Yer can come an' live wiv me an' Sylve, if yer like,' said Gus.

'No thanks!' replied Millie indignantly. 'If you think *I'm* going to look after your baby while you and Sylvie go out on the town each night, you're mistaken!'

Everyone laughed, but the twins were taking it all quite seriously.

'Why don't yer come an' find a job up my way?' suggested Queenie. 'Mrs Wu was tellin' me the uvver day they're lookin' fer people ter run their new mobile library.'

'No thank you!' snapped Millie. 'I hate the country!'

'Me, too!' agreed her twin. 'It's so threatening.'

'Threatenin?' asked Queenie, puzzled.

'All them birds and things,' grumbled Millie, 'watching you from trees all day.'

'And poisonous snakes in your bed at night,' added Polly.

'Poisonous snakes!' spluttered Queenie incredulously. 'In 'Igh Wycombe!'

By this time, Rose was becoming quite anxious about what was going to happen to the twins once she was married. And what about Georgie, who, like his dad, couldn't even boil an egg?

'Anyway, I don't see what everyone's getting so worked up about,' said Millie, sitting demurely straight-backed with her arms crossed. 'We're perfectly capable of living here on our own!'

'That's right,' agreed twin Polly. 'And Millie can have Corporal Dixon P. Snelling here to cocoa and biscuits every night!'

Millie walloped her with a cushion.

'Well, at least yer don't 'ave ter worry about me!' announced George proudly. 'Once I've got me papers.'

Rose turned with a start. 'Papers? Wot papers?'

'Me call-up.'

'Wot?' Rose was thunderstruck. 'George, wot're yer talkin' about?' She got up immediately from the table. 'Yer're too young ter be called up.'

'Where've yer bin these last few monffs, Rose?' he asked. 'Are yer forgettin' I was eighteen six weeks ago?'

Rose suddenly felt sick in her stomach. Yes, of course it was Georgie's eighteenth birthday in July, so why hadn't she realised that he was eligible for call-up? Georgie! It couldn't be! In Rose's mind he was still her kid brother, a babe-in-arms! 'Yer – 'aven't 'eard yet then?' she asked nervously.

'Not yet,' replied George perkily. 'Any minute now though! It's the Royal Engineers for me! Blimey, wot a relief it'll be from ridin' round on a Fire Service bike!'

Rose exchanged a quick, pointed look with Bill. A few minutes later, she went into the kitchen to make some Spam and pickle sandwiches. The Spam wasn't all that fresh, because it had been left over from her mum and dad's funeral tea a couple of days before. But it had to be used up, she told herself, for in this hot weather, it would soon go off, and that would be a waste of a week's ration. But as she stood there, separating each slice of the tasteless substitute for real ham, she wondered why she was even thinking about the stuff. What was really on her mind was young Georgie being old enough to go into the Army, and how this stinking war had taken its toll on the poor old Humble family.

'Yer mustn't worry about 'im, Rose.'

Rose turned from the kitchen table to find Gus standing behind her.

'Georgie's got a good 'ead on 'is shoulders. Bill's bin tellin' me 'ow well 'e stood up to a pretty rough time durin' the Blitz.'

''E's too young, Gus,' said Rose, slicing the bread. 'Takin' boys of that age – it just don't seem right, that's all. I keep finkin' about wot 'appened ter poor ol' Peanut, and Badger locked up in that POW camp.'

'Yer've just got to trust 'im, Rose. In war, boys grow inter men much quicker.'

Rose had never heard Gus talk in such a gentle, sympathetic way. She found it a great help. 'Everyfin's 'appened so fast, Gus,' she said, relaxing a moment from the bread slicing to look up at him. 'I blame meself for wot 'appened ter Dad, yer know. I should've seen wot a state 'e was in. Every time I look at that gas fire in there, I keep tellin' meself I could've prevented it.'

'No, Rose.' He came around the table, took the bread knife from her, and put it on to the table. 'Over the last couple of days I've spoken ter a lot of people 'oo knew wot 'e was like after Mum was pulled out of that wreckage. Yer know, Dad gave up a long time ago. 'E di'n't want anyfin' unless Mum could be around ter share it wiv 'im. The same fing must've 'appened to a lot of people. The war's torn all sorts of families apart.'

Rose sighed. 'But wot 'appens now, Gus?'

'Wot 'appens is that yer get on wiv yer own life. Yer've got a good bloke in Bill. 'E'll take care of yer. One of these days, yer'll 'ave kids of yer own. I'll be a dad ter me own kids, and an' uncle ter yers!'

This brought a much-needed smile to Rose's face. 'An' wot about Aunty Polly and Aunty Millie?'

'Yeah! An' Aunty Sylve, Aunty Queenie and – Gawd 'elp us – *Uncle* Georgie!'

They laughed together, and he put his arm around her shoulders. 'The 'Umbles're goin' their own ways now, Rose. It's all part of life. But I tell yer somefin'.' He gently turned her round to face him. 'When I go back ter me unit termorrer, I'll be finkin' a lot about you. These past few years, yer've 'ad a pretty rough deal from me. I don't know why, but – well, I s'ppose I've just bin a bit jealous of yer. Jealous that yer've bin the one with the level 'ead on yer, jealous 'cos yer've bin the one that kept the family tergevver. Mum an' Dad used ter talk ter me about yer, yer know. They used ter say that wivout our Rose, the 'Umbles'd go ter pieces.' He took both her hands and held them. 'I fink they was right, yer know. I'm proud of me sister. We all are. I don't fink I'll ever be able ter repay yer. I wouldn't know 'ow.'

The following morning, Gus left to return to his unit. Sylvie went to Kings Cross Station to see him off, but not Rose. Ever since she was a kid she had hated railway stations. They seemed to have an air of foreboding about them, and even if she was just seeing someone off for a day trip, the feeling in her stomach was that she would never see them again.

As the weeks passed, Rose gradually plucked up enough courage to go back to her St John Ambulance Brigade job. Luckily, the air raids continued to be scarce, with only limited day or evening attacks on the London area. This meant that her call-outs were few and far between, and when their different shifts allowed it, she and Bill were able to see each other regularly. But during this period they spent no nights together, mainly because Rose was still haunted by the memory of that fateful night when her mum died. However, with the eager participation of Polly and Millie, Rose and Bill did eventually get down to planning an October wedding – a *white* wedding, as Millie had requested. However, Rose's clothing ration allowance being somewhat limited, she had to make do with a knee-length white cotton dress from Selby's Department Store in the Holloway Road.

September turned out to be unexpectedly mild. When she was on a split-turn shift at St John, Rose enjoyed walking home from the bus stop in Holloway Road, for it gave her the chance to do a little shopping for tea in busy Seven Sisters Road. Sometimes, Liptons had some fresh brawn on sale, but then there was usually a queue, and it meant a delay in getting home. After another queue for some vegetables at Hicks, the greengrocers, she would cross the road to have a quick browse around the North London Drapery Stores, where she could keep an eye open for any bargain offers on bed linen for when she got married.

On one particular afternoon, Rose stopped off at the Gas, Light, and Coke Company, where she paid the gas bill. She was fairly weighed down with two heavy shopping bags, so it took her a little time to walk along Hornsey Road. As she reached the corner of her own street, she was taken aback to find someone leaning on the gate in her small front garden. Despite the heavy load, she quickened her pace, and as she drew closer she could see that the visitor, who was in some kind of sailor's uniform, was waving at her. Only when she was a few yards away did she finally identify who her visitor was.

'Oh my Gawd!' she gasped, yelling as she ran. 'Badge!' As soon as she reached the gate, she dropped her shopping bags, and threw her arms round her old barrow-boy mate. 'Oh, Badge, Badge, Badge!' was all she could say over and over again.

'Can't get rid of me that easy, Ginge!' he said, just as bright-faced and cheeky as ever.

'Badger, yer ol' sod!' said Rose excitedly. 'Wot's this all about? Yer're s'pposed ter be a prisoner of war.'

'Red Cross exchange,' he replied. 'Some of us for some of them! Just the injured, that's all. Jerry don't do somefin' for nuffin', I can tell yer.'

'Injured?' Rose said, standing back to look at him.

'Nah – nuffin' much. Just a scratch, that's all.'

However, when he stood back and let her open the gate, Rose discovered that he was on crutches. 'Badge!'

'It's nuffin', I tell yer! Lost a foot, that's all. They're makin' me a new one. Solid gold, I 'ope! Still, got the uvver one!'

Rose suddenly felt a sense of deep despair. Badge – of all people, so full of fun and mischief, always keen to avoid taking buses and trams when he could be walking instead. Badge, a cripple for the rest of his life. It left her numb and shattered.

Rose took him inside the 'toy house' and made him some tea. To her amusement, he topped it up with a drop of rum from a quarter-bottle he kept in a pouch tied around the waist of his bell-bottoms.

As they sat face to face across the kitchen table, Rose noticed how pale and gaunt he had become. He had lost quite a bit of weight, which was not surprising considering his period of meagre rations as a prisoner of war.

Rose found it a tonic talking to Badge. It was just like old times to hear him gossiping again about their mates in the market. He also had a few near-the-knuckle stories to tell about life in the Navy, but, typical of him, he made light of the circumstances in which the corvette he had been serving on had been sunk by a German U-boat out in the Atlantic. The only time he showed any sign of distress was when he talked about the bombing of the old piano shop, and the tragedy of losing Nellie and Albert. And he had one other important matter to talk over with Rose.

'So did yer get my letters?' Badger asked, lighting up a Players Number 1 and sipping his rum tea.

Rose lowered her eyes guiltily. 'Yer was marvellous ter keep writin', Badge,' she said awkwardly. 'It was so – foughtful of yer.'

Badger bit his lip nervously for a moment, then drew on his fag. 'Look, Rose, the reason I come over ter see yer, is – well, I want ter put me cards on the table.'

Rose was suddenly intrigued. 'Wot d'yer mean?'

'About – you an' me.'

Rose felt panic, and lowered her eyes.

'Wot I'm tryin' ter ask is – do yer still love me?'

Rose just didn't know how to cope with this. Over the past few weeks she had wanted to take Bill up to the market with her, to introduce him to all her mates up there as the man she was going to marry. But, time and time again she had put it off, and now Badger was going to be hurt deeply.

'Yes, Badge,' she said with great anguish. 'But there's somefin' I 'ave ter tell yer.'

'Me, too,' replied Badger. 'Promise not ter frow a wobbly at me?'

Rose did a double take. What was this all about? 'Course not, Badge.'

Badger perched his fag on the edge of the ashtray Rose had given to him, and stretched across the table to hold her hands. 'Fact is, Ginge,' he said uneasily, 'I've got someone else.'

Rose's eyes widened.

'Yes, I know it's come as a shock ter yer,' he said earnestly. 'But I just couldn't 'elp meself. It's this gel – this Red Cross nurse 'oo looked after me when I got back. I can't tell yer 'ow it 'appened, Ginge – honest ter God, I can't. All I know is, well – the moment I saw 'er, I felt somethin' inside – right *'ere!*' He punched his fist against his chest.

Rose listened in disbelief – and relief! But she had no intention of revealing her true reaction.

'Are yer upset, Ginge?' he asked anxiously. 'Tell me – are yer?'

Rose crunched up her face and lowered her eyes. Then she nodded her head up and down as if her whole world had fallen apart.

'I'm sorry, Ginge,' Badger said guiltily. 'Believe me – I really am sorry. I wouldn't 'ave done this ter yer for the 'ole wide world. But I just couldn't 'elp meself.'

Rose looked up and tried to assure him with her expression that she would do her best not to cry. 'I understand, Badge,' she replied with great sincerity.

'These fings 'appen, an' we just 'ave ter live wiv 'em.'

Badger gave a sigh of tremendous relief. 'Aw – fanks a lot, Ginge,' he said, staring at her with gratitude. 'Yer're a gel in a million!'

A little later, Rose walked with Badger to the bus stop in Hornsey Road. She was amazed at how well he was coping with the very basic Navy issue crutches he was hobbling along on.

Just as they caught sight of the number 14 bus coming down Hornsey Road, Badger remembered something he had forgotten to mention. 'Oh by the way,' he said almost casually, 'd'yer ever remember that geezer – wot's 'is name – Mike Deverow, or somefin'? Fink 'e was a pal of yer Queenie, wasn't 'e?'

Rose was surprised to hear Michael Devereaux's name mentioned again after such a long time. 'Yes. I do remember 'im – I fink. Why?'

'Got the chop on combat, out in Burma. Bloody Japs executed 'im wiv a sword. Poor sod. Wot a way ter go!'

The bus drew to a halt at the stop. Rose and the conductor helped Badger up on to the platform, and then to a seat on the lower deck. Then the bus pulled away, with Badge leaning round, waving madly as it went.

As Rose watched the bus chunter down Hornsey Road, and then turn right to disappear along Seven Sisters Road, she felt disloyal not to be thinking about her dear old mate Badger. But her mind was far away, back in time, to some remote woods out in Hertfordshire, where the lives of two vastly different young people were brought together for the first and only time.

* * *

The night before they were married, Rose and Bill returned to the site of Uncle Popov's old piano shop. There was nothing left there, of course, only a stark bare gap where years ago a young couple brought up a family of four girls and two boys.

It was a very dark night, and quite cold, but, as they stood in the eerie silence, Rose told Bill that there was no need to use his hand torch. She could see every sight, and hear every sound that she had ever known in this dear and wonderful place. And, for as long as she lived, she would never forget them.

Chapter 31

The war in Europe was entering a decisive phase. By the winter of 1942, British and American airplanes were carrying out day and night raids on targets in Germany, the Russians were finally forcing the Nazis to retreat in Leningrad and Stalingrad, and in Britain the ban on the ringing of church bells was lifted for three hours on Christmas morning.

In late October, Rose and Bill were married in St Mary's Church in Upper Street. Rose's white cotton dress with frills around the wrists and hemline was admired by everyone, particularly Millie, one of the bridesmaids, who included Polly, Queenie, and Sylvie, now four months' gone. A fifth bridesmaid was Charlie Spindle's five-year-old granddaughter, Mavis, but she proved to be a bit of a problem because she kept crying during the marriage ceremony, mainly because her mum had yelled at her for whacking her best friend on the head with her posy.

Bill's best man was Arthur Dickson, who was one of his NFS mates from the Bethnal Green Fire Station, and after the service, six other fire-fighters had formed a guard of honour outside the church.

During the service, pews were filled by rarely seen

relatives from both bride and groom's side. In front of them all was Bill's mum, the inimitable 'Dig for Victory' fanatic, Agnes Layton. Many of the seats had been taken up by Chapel Market traders, who had deserted their stalls for the day, and turned up in a veritable black market fashion show, ranging from navy-blue suits and brown shoes for the men, to home-made cotton and taffeta dresses and feathered hats and wobbly high-heeled shoes for the women. One of the principal guests was, of course, Badger, there with his Red Cross girlfriend, Susie, and every time Rose looked across at him, his cheeky face beamed. Of course, he must have realised Rose had been Bill's girl since before his return, but Badger never mentioned it.

The only person who couldn't be there was Gus, whose unit was still on active duty somewhere in North Africa. But he did get home at Christmas, when he made 'an honest woman' of Sylvie by marrying her in a somewhat low-key registry office wedding in Islington Town Hall.

Rose and Bill eventually moved into a couple of rented furnished rooms on the ground floor of a terraced house in Bethnal Green. It wasn't much of a place, but at least it was clean and dry, and had a scullery for cooking and the weekly dip in a tub. It also had a tiny back garden, which Rose treated like an estate, and planned to use for growing flowers and vegetables as soon as it was warm enough to get out there.

With the Luftwaffe's occasional hit-and-run daytime attacks continuing on London, Rose and Bill had very little time together. However, whatever time there was brought Rose the most joyous love she had ever known. She loved Bill more than she had ever thought possible. Everything he said or did made her feel special, and even if they quarrelled because she thought him too staid about certain things, he knew exactly how to deal with her, and that usually meant compromise on both sides.

'Come off it, Rose,' he would say, with a huge grin on his face. 'There're two of us in this blinkin' family, yer know. Yer want your way, an' I want mine. What say we talk it over?' In fact, during those first few months of marriage, Rose had soon discovered that Bill wasn't nearly as staid as she had first thought, and he had a strong mind of his own. Whenever Rose was being too bossy, Bill would call her 'Rose 'Umble', which always quickly brought her down to earth again, for she had come to feel proud of being known as Mrs Bill Layton.

And so Rose Layton had a man who was everything she had ever wanted, and when they made love together, she knew that that love was mutual.

She thanked God that at last her luck had changed.

The sky above Bethnal Green was dark and ominous. It was a cold, wet March evening, with a persistent icy drizzle, which settled on the shining grey paving slabs. A helpless moon constantly struggled to break free from the dark rain clouds. The winter had been dreary so far – rain, snow, fog, subzero temperatures, and endless heavy skies – not the kind of weather to cheer people up in the middle of a war. But at least the first three months of 1943 had been reasonably quiet. Since those horrific nights during the Blitz, the people of London's East End had been tensely awaiting any sign of a renewal of an aerial bombardment by the Luftwaffe. Although in the last two years the bombing had eased, and they were beginning to hope that they would never again hear the dreaded wail of an air-raid siren, they remained wary and nervous.

In the busy Roman Road, which had already had more than its share of bomb damage, there was a much friendlier sound echoing in the dark than that of old 'Moaning Minnie'. Rose and Bill had just had a family celebration in The Bricklayers Arms, and, together with Gus, Georgie, the twins, and Queenie, they had linked arms to bellow out at the top of their voices, 'Side by Side'. The odd passer-by did glare at them from time to time, but then how could anyone possibly know that Sylvie Humble had just presented her husband, Gus, with a seven-pound, two-ounce baby boy, and that both 'muvver an' kid were doin' very nicely, fank yer,' in the London Hospital down Whitechapel Road.

'Which way?' called George, now in an RE Army uniform.

'Cross over Cambridge 'Eaff Road,' Gus called back. Like George, he was togged up well in a heavy Army greatcoat. 'Bus stop's just over there on the left.'

The party gradually caught up with George as he reached the junction with the main Cambridge Heath Road.

Bill, following on behind with Gus, was in his fireman's uniform, all ready for night duty. 'I still fink yer'd be better off takin' the tube down Stepney Green,' he called, puffing on his fag. 'Yer'll get so perishin' cold waitin' at that bus stop, yer nackers'll fall off!'

Everyone laughed except Rose. 'Don't be so coarse, Bill!' she growled, but was quite amused herself.

'Well make up yer mind!' snapped George, who was

rumoured to be a bit of a heart-throb amongst the girls around the camp where he was based. 'Which way? Bus or tube?'

By the time the others had followed him to the opposite side of the road, the decision had been dramatically made for them. The quiet night air was suddenly pierced by 'Moaning Minnie's' wail, which had rarely been heard lately.

'It's a bloody air raid!' called Bill incredulously. 'I don't believe it!'

Taken completely by surprise, everyone turned their eyes towards the dark night sky, which was already streaked with the thin white beams of searchlights. The party just stood exactly where they were, not knowing what to do. Their first inclination was to run, but their experience during the Blitz had warned them not to panic.

'Let's get back 'ome!' yelled Rose, trying to compete with 'Minnie'. 'Quick as we can . . . 'urry!'

By the time she and the others had rushed back across Cambridge Heath Road, the chilling siren had given way to the menacing drone of enemy bombers drifting in high above them from the direction of the Mile End Road and the Essex coastline beyond, like a deadly swarm of giant wasps, moving in for the kill.

With Rose and Bill leading, none of the group showed any panic as they calmly hurried back along the Roman Road. As they did so, the streets were suddenly filled with people emerging from houses, pubs, and the nearby cinemas. What had only a few moments before been a quiet Bethnal Green evening, was now transformed into a scene of frenzied activity. Women were carrying small children, their menfolk following on behind loaded down with blankets, holdalls – anything they might need for a long night's stay in the public shelter. ARP and Home Guard volunteers seemed to appear from nowhere, wearing their tin helmets and carrying hand torches, their eyes turned ominously towards the sky.

The first salvo of ack-ack shells streaked up from their units just as Rose, Bill and the family had reached the corner of Globe Road.

'Keep goin'!' yelled Rose. 'We can all get inter the Morrison back 'ome!'

No sooner had she spoken than a new, more terrifying sound filled the air. It was a screeching sound, like nothing anyone had ever heard before. The explosion that followed caused buildings to shake and shudder, and the ground vibrated as though the East End were experiencing its first earthquake. Someone screamed, and as Rose and the family huddled together for protection, people everywhere were throwing themselves to the ground.

'Christ Almighty!' yelled Bill, wrapping his arms as tightly as he could around Rose. 'Wot the 'ell's *that*?'

As soon as everyone in the street had recovered sufficiently from the ear-shattering blasts from the unidentified explosions, there was a mad rush towards the public shelter in the new Bethnal Green tube station at the junction of Cambridge Heath and Roman Roads.

'What're we goin' ter do?' yelled George, just as a double-decker bus stopped alongside, and disgorged its passengers and crew, who immediately joined the frightened crowds heading off towards safety. The moment George spoke, another salvo of deafening rocket shells shot up into the sky and burst into a terrifying series of explosions high above the rooftops. Some of the women in the crowd shrieked out in panic. From that moment, everyone bolted towards the tube entrance.

'It's too late! We'll never make 'ome!' yelled Bill. 'Down the tube! Everyone – fast as yer can!'

Rose, Queenie, and the twins quickly merged with the crowds. Gus, George and Bill tried to keep up with them.

Although the new Central Line tube station was still being built and not yet open for passengers, it already had the reputation for being one of the safest public shelters in the district. By the time Rose and her sisters had reached the narrow unfinished entrance, they found it absolutely jammed with a surging mass of frightened people, all desperate to reach safety before the next salvo of mysterious explosions.

When those explosions finally came, there was pandemonium. Hundreds of terrified people were trying to shove and squeeze their way through the narrow wooden entrance. Rose and her sisters found themselves caught up with them, and, amongst the voices calling out from behind, was Bill, 'Rose! Where are yer, gel?' If there was a reply, he couldn't hear it, for the names of so many people were being yelled out in the dark, as the crowd surged down the unfinished concrete and wooden steps. There was hardly any light at all in the station concourse, and all Bill could see was a sudden flash of familiar red hair, from Rose, and Polly and Millie. But the few steps leading down to the booking hall were so densely jammed that Bill's vain efforts to stretch his hand over the top of the crowds to touch Rose proved an impossible task.

From the booking hall, Rose and her sisters were swept

along with the rest of the crowd towards the top of the stair-case which led to the platforms below. As they got there, another deafening salvo of explosions suddenly rocked the entire foundations of the station. Convinced that a new type of bomb was being used against them, the crowd just entering the station panicked, jostled and pushed, and in a chorus of shrieks and screams, surged forward, leaning hard against all those who were already packed tight into the totally inadequate booking hall below.

People at the foot of the steep staircase were screaming out as they first of all stumbled, and then started to collapse on top of each other.

'Help . . . !' 'Can't move . . . !' 'Can't breathe . . . !' 'God 'elp me . . . !'

The desperate cries of anguish rose up from the staircase.

Millie was the first of the family to stumble. She screamed out, and tried desperately to cling on to the shakey hand rail, but a large fat man fell against her, and she collapsed on to the steps. Queenie was next. She used all her strength to push her shoulders back against the tide of stumbling people behind her. 'Poll!' she yelled, as she and her young sister tried to stretch out their hands in an effort to clasp on to each other.

Rose went down almost simultaneously. Her long, flowing red hair got caught under someone's arm, and she squealed out in pain as she tried to pull it loose. 'Bill . . . !' she yelled, over and over again, until her voice was eventually muffled beneath the people piling down on top of her from behind.

Further up the stairs behind Rose, Gus was supporting the weight of several people being swept off their feet.

464

After several desperate moments, he, too, was forced to succumb to the pressure, and he literally crumpled down on to an elderly couple who had already collapsed into a heap on the step below him.

'Somebody 'elp...! Stop pushin' back there...! Give me some air...! I can't breeve! Mum! I want me mum...! Alf...! Rita...! My baby...! Lily...! Where are yer, Gran...?' The horrifying shouts and screams for help filled this dark, cavernous hell.

'Bill! I can see yer!' called George, as he suddenly caught a glimpse of his brother-in-law.

Bill, struggling to hold on near the top of the stairs, turned, and yelled back. 'Where's... Rose...?'

'Here...' Rose was calling, but her voice was too weak to be heard by anyone. She was crunched up on a stair, with two women piled on top of her, fighting for air, and feeling totally isolated in the cruel, bleak darkness. 'Dear God – 'elp me!' she whispered to herself in the stifling atmosphere. 'Mum... Dad... if yer can 'ear, please... please 'elp me...'

Further down the steps, Queenie, pinned down by a woman and two screaming young children, was struggling to find a space big enough for her to breathe some air. On the step below, she could hear Polly sobbing in pain: 'Queenie... Where are you, Queenie? My leg... I've broken my leg!' Queenie managed to ease her head out through a perilous gap between the bodies lying across her. Her turban had been ripped off, leaving her few remaining tufts of ginger hair completely exposed. ''Old on, Poll!' she called. 'Just 'old on...!'

Behind them, Bill was using every bit of energy he had to

ease himself down the steps over the pile of terrified people trapped there, but it was an impossible task.

At the top of the staircase, George and a whole lot of other men had finally succeeded in halting the lunatic surge down the few steps from the station entrance.

Halfway down the lethal staircase, Rose felt the life ebbing away from her. As she lay there helplessly, she felt as though she was drowning beneath a sea of human flesh, with all the faces she had ever known flashing before her in these bewildering moments of darkness. Mum . . . Dad . . . Queenie, the twins, Georgie, Gus . . . Uncle Popov . . . Sylvie . . . all those kind and loyal faces in her beloved market . . . Mr Cabbage, Charlie Spindle, Elsie Dumper, Mr Pinetti, Sid Levitt, Ned Morris . . . and the three men who had helped to shape her life . . . Michael Devereaux – poor, misguided Michael, who had no idea what love really meant . . . and Badger – the heart of gold, the face that cheered the start of any day, the believer in all that was true and honest . . . and Bill – her own dear, wonderful, solid Bill, who had taught her the meaning of life, and loved her, and cherished her . . . Gradually, the images before Rose began to fade.

It was several minutes before the shrieks and screams finally stopped. It had seemed like hours. All that was left now were the groans and sobs, the exhausted cries of the elderly, and the frightened whimpering of small children.

It was all over.

After

It wasn't such a bad day. Quite chilly, but no more than you would expect from an early March day. Mind you, the weather was far better than it had been on that same day fifty years before – grey and chilly, an icy cold drizzle that made the pavement slippery to walk on. But at least they were able to hold the memorial service over at the Anglican church without being interrupted by old 'Moaning Minnie' – and there weren't any barrage balloons bobbing up and down over the Bethnal Green rooftops, or bombers droning overhead, or ack-ack fire to scare the people down the tube. Best of all – there was no war. This was 1993.

Rose never ceased to be amazed how different it all looked from her day. As she and her two small great-grandchildren strolled down Roman Road together, they passed new council flats put up where some of the old shops and houses used to be, blitzed sites that had been turned into communal gardens, shops with television sets flickering out in the windows, and flashy new cars and motor-bikes that to her looked a bit out of place in a working-class area. Even the telephone boxes, now all made of glass, weren't painted red any more.

Spring was still a few weeks off, so the trees were looking

a bit bare in St John's Church gardens. But when she came this way, Rose always liked to stop outside the church gates for a few minutes, because it gave her pleasure to see a patch of green right in the middle of a busy thoroughfare. It also gave her the chance to stand for a few moments of reflection just outside the entrance to Bethnal Green tube station.

'Where shall we put the flowers, Gran?' asked little Tim, who was the grandchild of her eldest daughter, Amanda.

'Why don't we just put 'em against that wall over there,' answered Rose, pointing. 'Just by the tube gate.'

Tim let go of his gran's hand for a moment, and laid his bunch of six early daffodils where she had told him.

'That's the idea, darlin'!' said Rose, with great encouragement. 'Now it's yer turn, Chrissie.'

Tim's sister was even younger than he, but she had her own bunch of primroses and snowdrops, which she'd pulled up from her mum and dad's back garden in Stepney, so she quickly propped them up alongside her brother's offering.

'Wot 'appen's now, Gran?' asked a very curious Tim.

'Wot 'appens?' replied Rose. 'Well, we wait while yer Great Auntie Millie 'as a good look at 'em.'

Both kids turned around to see who she was talking about.

'Where is she?' asked Chrissie, very puzzled. 'I don't see 'er.'

'Well now,' said Rose, with a slight grin, 'yer may not be able ter see 'er, but from where she is – she can see you.'

Tim still wasn't satisfied. 'Yes, but—'

'Ssh!' Rose had her finger against her lips. 'Remember wot I told yer before we come? Mustn't make a noise for one 'ole minute.'

She held on to their hands, and they stood facing the two small bunches of spring flowers, propped up so proudly against the insignificant tube station wall.

Oh yes, thought Rose. Millie's looking at the flowers, all right. She'll be looking at them and saying to herself, *'They're very nice, Rose, but I much prefer summer flowers.'*

As she stood there, with her great-grandchildren on either side, Rose had a gentle smile on her face. Although she was now in her seventies, she still had a very appealing smile. She had also retained her striking features, and there were even a few strands of gingery red surviving in her perfect head of pure white hair. But when she started thinking, as she always did at this time of year, about the 173 people who had lost their lives just a few feet below from where they were now standing, the smile became very wistful. How could it have happened? she had never stopped asking herself. How could so many people have died just because they had never heard the Army's new ack-ack rocket shells before, and lost their nerve because they thought the weapons were a new type of enemy bomb? It was all such a cruel waste of life, especially of her dear young sister, Millie's life.

Every year at this time, Rose had come to this same spot, and stood there, replaying in her own mind the horrific events of that terrible evening. She could hear the shouts, the screams, the crying, and the calls to God for help. And if she closed her eyes as she was doing now, she could feel herself being lifted up from that death-laden staircase, more dead than alive. And she could remember the tears trickling down her cheeks when she saw the faces of Bill, Gus, George, Queenie, and Polly waiting at her bedside. She had survived to start a new beginning, and, with the exception of her dear Millie, so had all her family. They had survived to create their own families, Gus with Sylvie, and herself with Bill. Polly had also survived, later to marry her bass-playing boyfriend, Pete. But she had never really got over losing Millie, the twin sister with whom she had shared so much of her young life. Rose also felt a twinge of sadness when she remembered that Queenie had never regained the urge to marry. And young George had had his problems too, for it had taken him two marriages before he finally settled down. Yes. Rose was grateful to be given the chance to live her life with Bill and the family they had brought into this troubled world. But to whom was she grateful? she pondered. Why did she only ever talk to God when she needed His help?

'Is the minute over, Gran?' asked a tiny voice from her side.

Rose opened her eyes again, and turned to look at little Chrissie. 'Yes, darlin',' she answered, with a huge, affectionate smile. 'It's all over. Time ter go now. Mustn't be late ter get yer grandad's tea.'

She held their hands tightly, and was about to walk on when a stream of warmth suddenly gushed up from the tube platforms below, to escape into the ice-cold air of a grey March day. And as she and her two young companions strolled off, back along the way they had come, Rose could still feel that gentle warm air from the tube station staircase on her cheeks.

It would still be there with her until she returned at the same time next year.

More Enchanting Fiction from Headline:

VICTOR PEMBERTON

OUR STREET

From the bestselling Cockney author of
OUR FAMILY

The war is five years old and, in bomb-torn North London,
fifteen-year-old Frankie Lewis sometimes thinks it will go on
for ever. But one foggy night his life takes an extraordinary
turn. Inveigled by his mates, 'the Merton Street gang', into
playing yet another vindictive prank on the old German-
Jewish widow who lives just off the Seven Sisters Road,
Frankie finds himself hauled unceremoniously across her
doorstep and pulled into a world of books and culture he
never knew existed.

Fascinated by Elsa's tales of life before the war, and with her
now-dead British officer husband, young Frankie, who,
although close to his elder sister Helen, has an unhappy
relationship with his own apparently uncaring parents, soon
becomes good friends with Elsa, helping out in her chaotic
bric-à-brac shop and confiding his troubles to her – from his
own crush on the pretty Highbury schoolgirl Margaret to his
sister's unwanted pregnancy.

But Elsa, determined to give Frankie a start in the world, has
plans for his future which he would never have dreamt of,
plans that her scheming brother-in-law, local property owner
Jack Barclay, is equally determined to thwart...

Don't miss Victor Pemberton's first Cockney saga,
OUR FAMILY, 'A wonderful story' Nerys Hughes

FICTION/SAGA   0 7472 4144 9

A Selection of bestsellers from Headline

THE CHANGING ROOM	Margaret Bond	£5.99	☐
BACKSTREET CHILD	Harry Bowling	£5.99	☐
A HIDDEN BEAUTY	Tessa Barclay	£5.99	☐
A HANDFUL OF HAPPINESS	Evelyn Hood	£5.99	☐
THE SCENT OF MAY	Sue Sully	£5.99	☐
HEARTSEASE	T R Wilson	£5.99	☐
NOBODY'S DARLING	Josephine Cox	£5.99	☐
A CHILD OF SECRETS	Mary Mackie	£5.99	☐
WHITECHAPEL GIRL	Gilda O'Neill	£5.99	☐
BID TIME RETURN	Donna Baker	£5.99	☐
THE LADIES OF BEVERLEY HILLS	Sharleen Cooper Cohen	£5.99	☐
THE OLD GIRL NETWORK	Catherine Alliott	£4.99	☐

All Headline books are available at your local bookshop or newsagent, or can be ordered direct from the publisher. Just tick the titles you want and fill in the form below. Prices and availability subject to change without notice.

Headline Book Publishing, Cash Sales Department, Bookpoint, 39 Milton Park, Abingdon, OXON, OX14 4TD, UK. If you have a credit card you may order by telephone – 01235 400400.

Please enclose a cheque or postal order made payable to Bookpoint Ltd to the value of the cover price and allow the following for postage and packing:

UK & BFPO: £1.00 for the first book, 50p for the second book and 30p for each additional book ordered up to a maximum charge of £3.00.
OVERSEAS & EIRE: £2.00 for the first book, £1.00 for the second book and 50p for each additional book.

Name ....

Address ....

....

....

If you would prefer to pay by credit card, please complete:
Please debit my Visa/Access/Diner's Card/American Express (delete as applicable) card no:

Signature .... Expiry Date ....